HUNTING
SEASON

BY

CARON HARRISON

Published by

Caron Harrison
Ballabunt Croft
Cooil Road
Braddan
IM4 2AQ

ISBN 0 9531155 3 4

Printed by
Premier Print
Unit 1, Snugborough Trading Estate
Braddan
Isle of Man IM4 4LH

Acknowledgements

Firstly I would like to thank my loyal readers who have repeatedly demanded when this fourth book would appear, prompting me to get on with it. I would also like to express my thanks to Captain (Retd) Peter Starling, curator to the Army Medical Services Museum, Aldershot for providing me with the necessary background information to BMH Iserlohn, also to Bill Shepherd, Estate Manager to RAF Hospital, Wegberg in the 1980's for his input as to the nature of the job. Any inaccuracies in the novel are a result of my taking liberties with the facts. Finally my thanks must go, as ever, to my husband, Nigel, for his unstinting support.

ONE

"There's a letter for you," Anna told her brother, nodding over her shoulder to the hall as she laid the table for lunch.

Her sparkling grey eyes told Karl she knew who had sent it, and that she seemed to think it would be good news. For once, Karl thought as he sauntered out to see what had excited her so. Since Katherine's death eight months ago, he had received many letters of condolence. Why should Anna think this one was any different?

It was dark in the hall after the bright September sunshine. Blindly he reached for the stack of mail propped against the stuffed pheasant, and was about to take it to the kitchen to see better when he paused, his eye caught by a foreign stamp. It was not a British one, which appeared every so often on letters from his two sons or sister-in-law in Herefordshire. He peered closer and read the words 'Republica Oriental del Uruguay'. It was from Ilse!

His eyes were used to the gloom now and he turned away from the kitchen, needing privacy to deal with this unexpected turn of events. His heart had begun to beat faster, though whether from excitement or anger he was unsure. Ilse had been a huge part of his life, good and bad, since the Second World War when they had become engaged and had a son, Siegfried. The war had changed everything and after two years spent as a prisoner of war in England, he had ended up marrying Katherine, bringing up his family in England and trying to forget about Ilse. Now someone had told her at last about Katherine's death and that he was back here in West Germany.

He sorted through the rest of the letters, delaying having to open Ilse's. There were two for his father, Dieter Driesler, one for Anna's husband, Stefan Lipinski, two for their elder son, Uwe, and a French postcard for younger son, Lothar, from one of his numerous girlfriends. Nothing else for himself. He propped the other letters back against the pheasant and stared at Ilse's in his hand. He knew Anna was holding her breath in the kitchen to hear what it said. She and Ilse had always been good friends and Anna would encourage contact between Karl and his old flame. Karl was not so sure he was ready for it.

Still avoiding the kitchen, he opened the front door of the half-timbered house and stepped outside into the lane. He sat down on the bench facing golden meadows, clumps of woodland and the distant small town of Medebach, and opened the envelope.

Inside was a sympathy card in Spanish depicting an arrangement of white lilies. The picture jolted his memory back to the funeral and all the other cards he had received, and his eyes instantly moistened. He gave them a cursory wipe then opened the card and began to read.

31st August 1969

Dearest Karl,

I have only just heard the terrible news from Sophie. All she said was that you were back in Germany without Katherine, as though I should already know what had happened. I assume everyone thought someone else had already told me, or else nobody wanted me to be in touch at such a sensitive time. I had to telegram Sophie to ask her to confirm that Katherine had died, which she did.

I want you to know how truly sorry I am, as I know how much you loved her. Please don't think this note is any more than it is. I just didn't want you to think I was a heartless and self-centred creature for not having been in touch earlier. I am just happy for Sophie and the twins' sakes that you are near enough now for Friedrich and Freia to enjoy their Opa's company at last. I think, despite everything that happened, that Siegfried would have been pleased you're there to help keep an eye on his children. He seemed to have warmed to you so much at last just before his death.

Fate has now struck you a double blow, but I know you are strong, Karl.

Take care of yourself,

Ilse

It was a definite foot in the door, Karl decided. Very carefully written not to sound too keen, but a reminder of their mutual interest in their grandchildren and that Ilse was still on the scene. He smiled and cast his gaze towards the tall white spire of Medebach's church of St Peter and Paul where once he had envisioned himself marrying Ilse. Any kind of wedding was impossible now unless she divorced Paul, but she was surely too loyal to him to do that. She had fled from the law with him to Uruguay, abandoning her children and prospective grandchildren to be with Paul. So why did he have the feeling she wanted him back?

He read through her words again, grunting in disbelief at her comment that he was strong. I used to be when you first knew me, he thought ruefully, but the war put paid to that.

"All right?"

Karl looked up to see his father standing at the front door.

"Yes. Why?"

"Anna said you had a letter from Ilse. We were wondering if you were ..."

Karl laughed. "No, I'm not crying or anything, though I confess these cards do tend to have that effect." He showed his father the picture of the lilies. "I'm beginning to handle it better ... most of the time."

Dieter sat down next to him and laid a soothing hand on his arm. "I know. It takes time. It's only two years since your mother died and it still hits me hard on occasions. Don't be afraid to show your grief. We all understand."

Karl nodded. "And it's almost a year since Siegfried died," he pointed out. "Three close deaths in such a short space of time. Hopefully that's the end of it all for a long time now."

"Then I'll be the next, " Dieter said with a smile. "Well, I'll have had a good run, but Katherine and Siegfried... That was cruel fate. You've suffered enough. It's time you had some happiness again." He paused for a significant moment. "So how is Ilse?"

"She's married to Paul, Papa."

"She wants you back. I saw it at Siegfried's funeral." His furrowed brow creased even more in concern. "Be careful, Karl. Paul's not a person to trifle with. I suspect Ilse's first husband found that out."

"Don't worry. I'm not ready yet to look elsewhere and certainly not at a married woman. Besides, I've got all Medebach's widows, spinsters and the odd divorcée giving me interested looks already.

I'm only forty-eight. I've got time."

Dieter grunted in amusement. "It's nearly as bad for me and I'm seventy-three! We Drieslers have never had problems attracting the ladies, have we now?"

"No, we certainly haven't!" Karl laughed, affectionately slapping his father's thigh. "Well, we'd better go in for lunch or else Anna will get cross. I expect she's dying to hear what Ilse had to say."

Once all four, Stefan included, were seated at the table eating their pork cutlets, Karl obliged. "Ilse had only just heard the news," he told them casually. "She wanted to send her condolences."

"Was that all?" Stefan asked astutely. "I'm surprised she's not jumped on the first plane over here, the way she was clinging to you at Siegfried's funeral."

So he had spotted it too, Karl thought. He noticed his father's raised eyebrows at Anna in a covert glance of agreement. She nodded gently and Karl sensed their conviction, like his, that Ilse would be seeking him out.

"Katherine would hate me going back to Ilse," he muttered.

"Katherine's not here to mind," Anna said gently.

Karl ate the rest of his meal in silence, his thoughts ensnared by the card in his jacket pocket. When he and Stefan returned to the sawmill for the afternoon stint, he set about feeding beech trunks through the bark stripper as a suitably mindless task for himself, leaving Stefan to the office work. When he had left Katherine's farm in England to their two sons' management, his German family had willingly made room for him. His brother Rudi and brother-in-law Stefan were used to running the sawmill, however, and Karl did not feel he had the right to interfere now, despite being the elder son. His stay here would have to be temporary. He could not expect to impose on Anna and Stefan for the rest of his life. Besides, he would need privacy some day: a home of his own to entertain in.

The last thought caught him unawares and he switched off the machine for a few moments' peace while he tackled this revelation.

Ilse's done this, he realised. She's put ideas into my head, despite denying that intention. It's progress anyway, the fact that I'm considering the future at last.

His hand rested on the silvery-grey bark of the next beech log awaiting stripping. It was a peculiarity of beech trees that their smooth trunks attracted graffiti like a blank wall in a city. Someone had carved the letters BL and the year 1956 as a memento of his passing through the forest, and it reminded Karl of the tree that still stood there with his and Ilse's initials on it, carved by himself in 1941. Their love had been given a permanence that had defied both their efforts to destroy it. Katherine had recognised that permanence but had never completely forgiven him for that one night of indiscretion with Ilse. Nevertheless, she would have understood the inevitability of their love reuniting them, given the possibility. He must think of his own feelings now, not Katherine's.

That night he woke up at four then could not get back to sleep. After tossing and turning for an hour he got out of bed and stood at the open window, where the scent of pine trees wafted in on a gentle breeze. Above the treetops the moon shone brightly, unsullied by its recent visitation by Apollo 11. Along with the rest of the world, he had watched Neil Armstrong and Buzz Aldrin land on the moon, but he could not connect to the wonder of it all when his mind was dwelling on a piece of earth in a Herefordshire graveyard.

He allowed the tears he had been holding back for the last hour to fall. The still, quiet beauty of the night sky brought him closer to her. Her presence was still in this room they had shared together on visits. Wherever they had once been together, he could feel her with him. Not her spirit. He had dispensed with religious beliefs before the war. Death meant an end, not a beginning. But memories lived on, and she was forever a part of his. He had hated visiting her grave as it screamed out the fact of her non-existence to him. He had only gone occasionally because Sarah and the boys seemed to expect it of him, but he would be glad not to go again. There was something to be said for a cremation then dispersing the ashes to the wind or in the forest. That was where he wanted to go: back to the forest.

The voices of the trees were murmuring to him on the breeze. 'Forwards', they were saying, 'forwards'. He nodded to himself. The black void of the future had shrunk a little today, was lightening through shades of grey. The sun was rising and colour was returning to his life.

Down in the yard the cockerel crowed and the household's two brown cows lowed gently in the nearby meadow, wanting milking. One of the house cats slunk across the dewy grass back to the barn after a night's hunting, leaving a trail of dark footprints behind her. As she reached the path, she sat down in the weak sunshine and began to wash her face, delicately licking a front paw and wiping it over her ears and bloody mouth.

Karl realised he needed to wash his own tear-streaked face and went out to the bathroom before Anna got there first. Today he would think about finding himself a new job and a new life.

TWO

Sabina put down the phone and turned to her husband, Wolf. "Daddy was remarkably upbeat today. I haven't heard him sound so cheery since last Christmas, when he was beginning to get over Siegfried's death. He must be on the mend."

"I heard you talking about him getting a job. Has he anything in mind?" Wolf asked, putting down the newspaper he was scanning for cinema listings. It was a Friday night and they both needed some entertainment after the week's work. Sabina had to work alternate Saturday mornings in the travel agent's but tomorrow she was off and they could stay out late.

"Not at the moment, but obviously something where his fluency in English would be useful."

"Has your firm got an opening for him?"

"Much as I love my dad, I don't think I'd want to work with him all day. Besides, I'd be the gooseberry, wouldn't I?"

Wolf's jaw dropped. "Ah. I see. You don't mind?"

"Of course not. As I said, I love my dad. I don't want him to be lonely for the rest of his life. Mummy wouldn't have either."

Wolf turned to the employment section of the *Dortmunder Rundschau* and began reading out some likely prospects while Sabina got on with preparing supper. "How about this one? The university wants a library assistant."

"Wolf! Don't be daft. Can you see Daddy stuck in a library all day? He'd go nuts. He needs to be outdoors."

"I just thought his English might be useful there."

"Maybe, but look again."

Wolf scoured the pages, but all the jobs seemed to require qualifications his father-in-law did not have, or were just too mundane for an intelligent and practical man who had successfully run and expanded a family farm for the last twenty odd years. "Nothing," he finally declared as Sabina set a plate of scrambled egg and sausage down on the kitchenette table beside him. "Perhaps you ought to ask amongst your English friends here if they know of anything appropriate."

"That's a good idea," she said, sitting down next to him. She tucked in to her food, gazing in thought out of their fourth floor apartment window over the rooftops of Dortmund's suburbs. What kind of a job would he want? Nothing too physically strenuous now, but perhaps supervising some kind of outdoor work with a bit of office work thrown in. He was very methodical and had liked to keep the farm accounts up to date. She would certainly ask around.

"What about his prison record?" Wolf suddenly asked.

"Oh bugger! I'd forgotten about that. That won't help."

"It depends on whether potential employers recognise him or not. Popular opinion seemed to be on his side during his trial."

"Yes, but that was for a murder that wasn't proved in the end. His prison sentence was for attacking Siegfried. The full story of that never got out, so they mightn't look so favourably on someone who broke his own son's nose. They wouldn't know how much Siegfried baited him."

"Except that Siegfried was named as one of the neo-Nazis involved in the murder case," Wolf pointed out. "That makes a difference."

"Well, this is all useless speculation, anyway. He's got to find a job to apply for, before he can be rejected because of his criminal record."

Wolf saw that Sabina had got herself upset over the issue. "Come on, eat up. Then we can go out on the town," he urged her, stroking her chestnut curls. "Or do you want to take your mind off things first?" His hand slipped down her neck to her blouse, opening the first button to reveal the top of her bra. His fingers worked their way inside and soon he had achieved the desired effect as Sabina smiled, pushed away her almost empty plate and brought her mouth to his.

They spent the whole evening in, Wolf being determined to take his wife's mind off her father's job prospects. They were just resting on the pillows after their second bout of lovemaking when the telephone rang.

"It'll be for you," Wolf said, lazily stretching out beside her.

"I know," she said, reaching for her dressing gown. She padded out into the hall and picked up the receiver. "Hello, Sabina Garisch."

"Bina, it's Margit. I'm surprised I caught you in on a Friday night, or are you working tomorrow?"

"No, it's my Saturday off. How are you, anyway?"

"Fine, fine. The job's shit, but it pays well enough. I'm going to be taking some leave soon, thank heavens as, guess what, Mutti's coming back for a visit! Short notice or what, but she suddenly decided she needed to be here to put flowers on Siegfried's grave, as it's the first anniversary at the end of the month. She missed her grandchildren's first birthday, but couldn't miss her son's first deathday."

"I see. It's a long way to come just to lay some flowers."

"You know what she was like about Siegfried. Favourite son, and all that. How's your dad doing now, by the way?" Margit asked out of genuine interest. She had had a teenage crush on Sabina and Siegfried's father and still carried a flame for him.

"Much better, actually. He's thinking about finding a proper job now. I was going to ask some of my English friends over here if they knew of anything suitable."

"There are plenty of English here in Iserlohn," she said, referring to the British Military Hospital personnel.

"Now that's a thought!" Sabina cried. "And very few of them speak even a word of German. There must be quite a demand for bilinguals in a place like that."

"Yes, but I believe they tend to employ British citizens where they can."

"My father has a British passport."

"Does he now?" Margit's mind began to race along the lines of having Karl living nearby, not that she would dream of ever going after him herself. He was far too old. He would be more like the father she had never really had. Her natural father, Erich Röbel, she could only vaguely remember as a bit of a drunkard, while her mother's second husband, Paul Zopf, had always been rather aloof. Sabina's father, on the other hand, had always seemed such fun and prepared to muck in with the children's activities.

"I tell you what," she went on, "I know someone, actually a German girl, who works there. I'll ask her if she knows of anything suitable. I know what your dad's like, more or less."

"Would you? It would be fantastic if he did get a job there. He'd be a lot closer to Wolf and me as well as to Sophie and the twins."

"Sure. I'll ask her tomorrow. I'll be seeing her at the swimming pool." Margit remembered the reason she had called. "By the way, I was wondering if we could borrow your folding bed while Mutti's here? Heinrich has managed to get a long weekend away from the barracks specially to see her, and since she'll be having his room, he'll have to sleep in the lounge and the sofa's not really long enough."

"Of course. Do you want us to bring it over?"

"If you wouldn't mind. Wolf's car's big enough whereas mine isn't. You must come for Sunday lunch – make a day of it. Perhaps we could go out riding together. I haven't been for ages."

"Sounds fun. What time do you want us on Sunday?"

"Whenever. As soon as you like, really. Ten, eleven then we can ride before lunch if I can arrange it."

"I'd better just check with Wolf, but I'm sure he didn't have any plans. Hold on." Sabina hurried back into the bedroom, cleared the plans with Wolf then returned to the phone. "That's fine. We'll see you on Sunday with the bed. Don't forget to ask your friend about jobs."

Margit laughed. "I won't," she promised. "See you then."

As Sabina got back into bed, Wolf noticed how thoughtful she had become. "What's up?"

"Ilse's coming back for Siegfried's anniversary, staying with Margit. That's why we're going over, to take the folding bed."

"So? We won't be seeing her, will we?"

"No, but she's bound to want to see Daddy."

"Oh." He paused. "Would that be so bad?"

"You bet it would! For one thing she's married to Paul, and even if she weren't, there's no way I'd want *her* as my new stepmother."

"Your father has every right to choose whoever he wants, Liebling," he said reasonably.

"I know, but I would never feel comfortable with her, never. Not after the pain she caused Mummy."

Wolf knew about Karl's indiscretion with Ilse the summer he had brought Sabina over to live in Germany with the Zopfs. Paul Zopf had been away on business and Ilse had taken the opportunity to satisfy her lust for Karl. Indiscretion was the right word as Siegfried had found out, bragging later to Karl that Katherine had been told of his adultery. It was this incident that had resulted in Siegfried's broken nose. Wolf sighed.

"Your father might not want her anymore."

"Pigs might fly!"

"You're jumping to conclusions, Bina. Ilse's married to Paul. She's made her home with him in Uruguay."

"Yes, but wouldn't it be convenient for her to find yet another reason to want to stay here in Germany."

"You're not being fair on her."

"Perhaps I know her better than you do, Schatz."

Wolf shrugged. Sabina was fiercely loyal to both her parents, but her father's fling with Ilse was the one transgression in his very chequered history that she was not prepared to make allowances for. "So what are we going to do tomorrow?" he asked, snuggling against her stiff body, feeling it gradually relax as he massaged her lower back.

"The housework," she moaned as his hands moved lower, before she giggled. "Wolf, you're insatiable!"

*

The rain deluged down on Sunday, preventing any riding or other outings. Wolf opened the first of the bottles of Sekt they had brought along with the folding bed, and resigned himself to listening to female chatter all day. Margit and her two younger sisters, Edeltraud and Roslinde, had shared the apartment in Iserlohn along with their brother, Heinrich, ever since Paul and Ilse fled to Uruguay when Paul's continuing Nazi connections came to light. Heinrich was now away doing his national service, leaving the girls in charge of the apartment. They always managed to find some little repair job for Wolf whenever he and Sabina visited, especially electrical repairs. Sure enough, this time their television set was playing up and he sat patiently tweaking the vertical frame hold while the females finished the lunch preparations. He kept one ear cocked for the conversation he knew Sabina was interested in, but Roslinde was too full of her mother's impending visit to allow any other topic to crop up. It was only once they were all seated around the table, glasses and plates filled, that she kept quiet long enough for Margit to break her news.

"I spoke to my friend, Silke, yesterday about a job for your dad, and she said she thought something might be coming up in her office. Apparently the chap they've got at the moment can't cope and everything's in a terrible mess. He has to organise the workmen who do all the repairs to the buildings and married quarters but his German just isn't up to scratch. They're in the process of transferring him to some job elsewhere in the Civil Service. Silke's only an assistant there but she's virtually running the office. Unfortunately she's not eligible to apply for that grade of job."

"It sounds ideal if Daddy can get it," Sabina said excitedly, "although he might not be eligible either." Her voice trailed off as she remembered his conviction for assault. But that had been in Germany. If he was applying to the UK Civil Service, would it count? She had no idea. "It sounds like they're desperate for someone. Perhaps they'd bend the rules slightly for the ideal candidate." Or ignore his conviction. That seemed too much to hope for, but it was worth a try. "Perhaps you could ask this Silke to send him an application form. He doesn't have to fill it in, but he may be interested."

Margit nodded. "I'll give her a ring later. She sounded quite keen to get somebody competent in there with her. Perhaps she'll be able to swing it for your dad. She's quite good at that sort of thing!" Margit said with a suggestive smile.

Sabina wondered what else Margit had told this Silke about her father, but Margit was already moving the conversation on. "So how are the evening classes going, Wolf? Have you got any exams this year?"

"Yes, loads. The big one's a design project, which has to be presented with a working model in January. I've come up with a new visual display system for schools or conferences. Should be a good market for it if I can get a manufacturer."

"Good luck with it. I'm sure you'll do well for yourself one day. It's just getting started is the problem, isn't it."

"Yes, before somebody else steals your idea," he said darkly. "Until it's patented any of the lecturers could pinch the idea, saying it was his and that I had just developed the concept into a practicality. You have to be so careful with that lot. Crooks, half of them!"

"Well, that's business for you," Margit laughed. "And you'll be joining them one day."

"I'll be as honest as the day is long," Wolf promised. "I've had enough scheming and treachery to last me a whole lifetime."

Like his friend, Siegfried, Wolf had been heavily involved with the neo-Nazis, but it was his father who turned out not to be his father, who had been the most treacherous. His death at Karl's hands had revealed the extent of his treachery, and Wolf had turned his back on National Socialism for ever.

Sabina saw his continuing anger with his so-called father and held up her glass. "Here's to honesty!"

"To honesty!" they all echoed.

And the glossing over of prison records, Sabina thought a moment later.

*

His sons were hopeless at writing about anything other than farm matters, so Karl relied on his sister-in law Sarah's monthly letters to keep him up to date with events back at Lane Head Farm. His elder son Richard's relationship with Vanessa Turner was proving as stable and enduring as Karl had hoped for, while younger son Paul, named after his old friend Paul Zopf before he became Ilse's second husband, was slowly getting over his mother's death. Karl was increasingly grateful to Sarah for having stepped in and taken over guardianship of the two boys. After Katherine's death he had needed to escape and not burden Richard and Paul with his problems. He had needed wrapping up in a cotton wool cocoon while he slowly metamorphosed into a new being who could exist without Katherine. Now he was just about ready to emerge from that cocoon, to cast off his sorrows and fly off on his own wings for the first time in twenty-three years. Katherine had held him aloft all that time. He owed it to her not to come crashing down once he started flying solo.

Sabina's telephone call on Sunday evening was his first pre-flight test. After telling him where she and Wolf had spent the day, she felt duty-bound to tell him why, much as it pained her to do so.

"Ilse's coming back to be here for the twenty-second," she phrased her announcement delicately, knowing how much Siegfried's death had hurt her father. "She'll be staying with Margit." She waited expectantly for some comment from him.

Karl was momentarily taken aback, the information coming so soon after Ilse's letter, which had mentioned nothing about it. "I see."

"You won't be seeing her, will you, Daddy?"

"Any reason why I shouldn't?" he asked boldly. Her antagonism towards Ilse had provoked an unexpectedly determined reaction from himself to do that very thing – see Ilse.

"Well, I just thought …" Sabina had the sense not to continue but Karl still needed to chastise her.

"It's my life, Bina. I'll do what I want."

Sabina felt shocked by his atypical curtness. She tried to restart the conversation by telling him about the job at the British Military Hospital in Iserlohn. As she was telling him she realised it only compounded matters. Iserlohn was where Margit and her sisters lived and where Ilse would be staying. Now she was suggesting her father applied for a job in the town.

Karl made the connection too, but not only that, the job sounded genuinely right up his street. "And she's sending me an application form?"

"Her friend is." Sabina found herself suddenly reticent. If only Ilse had not said she was coming back. How long would she stay for? With any luck she wouldn't be there more than a week or two. "Have you any plans for the twenty-second?" she asked tentatively.

Until a few moments ago Karl had none, feeling the same about Siegfried's grave as he did about Katherine's, but now he was not so sure. "I might go to the cemetery, then visit the twins. I haven't seen them for a few weeks. Sophie might not feel like being alone on that day."

"She won't be. She'll have her parents, sister and Ilse fussing over her."

"All the more reason for me to be there to make it a whole family gathering."

Sabina could not argue with that. "I suppose."

18

"When's Ilse arriving?" he asked.

"This Thursday. The eighteenth."

"And leaving?"

"I don't know. Margit didn't say." Sabina knew the answer already to her next question. "You're going to see her, aren't you?"

"Yes."

THREE

The application form duly arrived on the Tuesday morning with a hand-written note from the girl Sabina had mentioned, wishing Karl luck with it. It was a basic Civil Service application form but with an additional sheet relevant locally. He had thought about it ever since Sabina's call on the Sunday and he had no hesitation about sitting down straight away and filling it in. His school examinations seemed irrelevant and inappropriate now, so he dwelt instead on his wealth of practical experience and fluency in technical English in his covering letter. For references he could only suggest his good friend, Robert Murdoch, a suitably eminent Edinburgh psychiatrist, and his bank manager in Hereford. He hoped they would do, as being self-employed there was nobody else he could have asked.

When it was all filled in, he put it in an envelope then asked Anna if there was anything she needed as he was going into town to post it.

"My, you are keen!" she said. "Is it really so terrible living here?"

He grinned, knowing she understood full well his reasons for wanting to be more independent. "Stefan and Rudi are ogres, while you starve me and give me too many chores," he said, giving her a big hug. "But I want to go to the Ball now, Anna. I'm ready, I think."

She laughed at his fantasy. "I'm so glad, Karl. But just make sure you pick the one who fits the shoe, and not the first to come along."

"By that do you mean Ilse?" he asked anxiously. He had thought Anna liked Ilse.

"Not specifically. I just feel you can afford to …" She paused, embarrassed.

"Play the field a bit first?"

"Maybe. Anyway," she hurried on, "I could do with some bread, apples and ham and a packet of tea. I keep forgetting you like the stuff."

"And I keep forgetting to ask Sarah to send over some decent tea. It's just not the same over here." He reached past her to the dresser and grabbed his father's car keys. "That's something I'll need. A car of my own," he remarked thoughtfully. And some means of paying for it, he realised.

In Medebach he parked near the post office and dispatched his application form. As he dropped it into the post box, he could not help but wish himself luck with it. Katherine would have called it a prayer, but Karl had deserted her God long ago. Having set his new future in motion, he headed for the grocer's shop and made his purchases with the help of a bored assistant who was too young to bother herself with an ageing widower like himself. It was another story outside, however, when he was confronted by a woman who had been in the year below him at school, who had always fancied him, as had most of the girls in the school, then had lost her husband in the war. She had never managed to find a replacement and now saw it as her task to ensnare him for herself. She assumed that their old association would help matters, but forgot that he had never fancied her.

"Karl! How are you? Doing a bit of shopping for Anna, I see."

"I'm fine, thank you, Maria. And you?" he asked politely.

"Not too bad. Looking forward to the pig-roast on Saturday. Will you be there?"

"Yes, we're all coming."

"That's good. It's nice to see you getting out and about a bit now."

He only managed to get away from Maria after promising her a dance on Saturday. That's the trouble with Medebach, he thought as he headed back to the car. Everybody knows me and my business here. I really need to get away. He glanced at the post box on passing by, and thought about his application form lying inside it. I want that job, he decided. I really do.

Having dealt with one part of his life, Karl turned his thoughts to another on the drive back to Haus Fichtenblick. He had not yet contacted Sophie about paying a visit on the twenty-second. Despite his brave words to Sabina, he was unsure about facing Ilse again. The attraction between them was certainly still strong, but she was, after all, married. He had no right to tempt her away from Paul. But it would not seem right to be absent from Siegfried's grave when Ilse had taken the trouble to come all that way herself. She was due to arrive in West Germany on Thursday. He would leave it up to her whether she contacted him, but he was already committed to the pig roast and Maria on Saturday. He pictured the expression on Maria's face if Ilse turned up. The whole town knew their history, and Maria would have to back off. It might be worth inviting Ilse just for that very reason. Then he remembered Heinrich was home for the weekend especially to see his mother. Ilse would not want to miss him. It would have to be Monday the twenty-second and he must phone Sophie.

Sophie did not seem surprised to get his call. "I thought you would want to be here on Monday," she said above little Friedrich's shrieks in the background. "What time will you arrive?"

"It depends on your plans totally. Are we all going together to the cemetery or would you rather be alone, if we look after the twins?"

"I was going to walk down there with them. That stops me getting too upset. We'll take some flowers. It's up to you whether you want to come with us, go alone, or go with Ilse."

Karl remembered Ilse's grief at the funeral and how she had relied on his support. Perhaps she would need it again. Perhaps he should not be alone with her. "We could all go together, if you don't mind?" he decided.

"Fine. That's probably a good idea."

"How long is Ilse staying, do you know?"

"With me or with Margit?"

"Here in Germany."

Sophie stopped to think. "I don't think Margit said. Why, are you wanting to snatch her back from Paul, now that you're free?"

Her attitude was typically blunt so he decided to take advantage of her brutal honesty. "Do you think she would have me?"

Sophie laughed. "Like a shot! And wouldn't it be perfect for the twins if their grandparents got together at last."

Her enthusiasm astounded him. "You'd approve?"

"Why not? Paul doesn't really need Ilse any more, especially since she's so miserable out in Uruguay. He's got loads of girlfriends, as ever. She's much better off back here."

"I see." The last was a revelation. He had not realised Ilse was quite so unhappy in her exile. It also put pressure on him to decide whether he should take up with her again, but then Anna's words came to him - play the field first. Perhaps he shouldn't be in too much of a hurry. "Well, I'll certainly go with her to Siegfried's grave, but we mustn't get ahead of things, must we?"

*

Maria had been pleasant enough company on the Saturday night. Karl had ended up having several dances with her, but had also danced with other hopefuls to spread the load. The whole experience made him more determined than ever to escape Medebach's stranglehold, but it also helped pass the time before Monday had to be faced.

Instead of his usual sawmill work clothes, once again he donned the dark suit that had seen him all through his trial, then both Siegfried's and Katherine's funerals. As he straightened his tie in the mirror, Karl wondered what developments the day would bring. Everyone seemed convinced Ilse was after him and most felt that he should have her, despite her marriage to Paul. Only his father warned again against such a path, mainly on the grounds that divorce should not be an option in marriage. Anna, the romantic, saw it as their destiny to be reunited. Rudi was encouraging it, whereas Sabina was definitely against it. "And what about you, Karl?" he asked his reflection. "Should I encourage or dissuade her? Should I string her along until I've sorted out my own feelings?"

With a shrug to himself he glanced at the photo of Katherine on the dressing table. She would not have approved. Even Katherine's forgiving nature would not have stretched that far. Would he even be happy with Ilse? He had never lived with her, after all. Their romance had been based on a few short periods of leave during the war. They had not had enough time to tire of each other. He picked up the silver-framed photo, taken by himself at the twins' christenings only a year ago and stroked the glass over Katherine's face. She had understood him so well. Could anyone else ever do the same?

Carefully he returned the frame to its place on the dresser and left his room. After a quick bite to eat he started his drive north through the hills of the Sauerland towards Soest, where Siegfried and Sophie had bought a house together. He chose not to take his normal route via Brilon and Rüthen, but took instead the Arnsberg road before turning up to the Möhnesee. It was on this road that Siegfried had chosen to end his life by driving through the barrier on a sharp bend and down a ravine. He had taken his old neo-Nazi colleague, Gustav Halstrup, with him, committing suicide and murder in order to get the neo-Nazis off his and Karl's backs. Gustav's presence in the car seemed to have convinced the neo-Nazis that Siegfried's loyalty to them was never in doubt, although Sophie's suspicions had been aroused by Gustav. She still did not know the truth, unlike Karl.

He was unable to stop at the exact spot where it happened as he would have dangerously blocked the road, but a bit further on was a lay-by and he pulled in for a moment's reflection. Their time as father and son together had been so short. A few months of friendship then it was gone. He had vowed to keep an eye on Siegfried's children and try to shield them from the continuing neo-Nazi influence of Sophie and her parents. To this end he had to stay friendly with Sophie, which was not difficult as she was a nice girl when she kept off the subject of politics. At least she respected his right to see his grandchildren.

He set off again then stopped at a flower shop where he bought a suitable arrangement to lay on Siegfried's grave, arriving at Sophie's in time for morning coffee. Ilse arrived shortly after, accompanied by Margit, and Karl realised it would not be an easy meeting, today of all days. He went out to the hall with Sophie to greet them.

Ilse had clearly been prepared to see him. No sooner had she kissed Sophie then she turned towards him, both hands reaching for his.

"Karl, it's so lovely to see you again." She reached up and gave him a peck on the cheek.

Karl noticed her perfume was the same and that she was as perfectly turned out as ever, her blonde hair tied up in a neat chignon, her make-up concealing the gentle creases of maturity. Her regular games of tennis in Uruguay kept her shape in trim, and he found himself thinking how attractive she was still.

"You too, Ilse," he readily replied.

"How are you faring?" she asked, still holding on to his hands.

"All right. Better, actually."

"Good. I was so shocked when I heard from Sophie. It was so unexpected, like Siegfried, really."

"Yes, it was."

There was an awkward pause before Sophie intervened. "We were just about to have coffee. Would you both like one?"

"Please," Ilse and Margit chorused.

"Why don't you go into the lounge, Ilse, and meet the twins without me there to distract them," Sophie suggested, beckoning to Margit to assist her with the coffee-making.

"What a good idea!" Ilse trilled. "Come on, Karl. They know you. You can tell them who I am!"

Karl followed her into the lounge where the twins had been left playing with some toy bricks. Ilse swooped on them in delight, kneeling down to hug them both to her. Freia was happy to oblige, but Friedrich was not so impressed by the stranger in the house and backed away, turning instead to his grandfather for reassurance.

"It's all right, Friedrich," Karl soothed him, picking him up and sitting him on his lap. "This is Oma Ilse." She had sat down beside him with Freia on her lap.

Friedrich was familiar with Sophie's mother as an Oma and readily accepted the concept that he had another Oma. He looked at her, sizing her up with his big grey eyes then clearly said: "Oma!"

Ilse was thrilled. It was the first time she had been called that. Not to be outdone, Freia joined in with a slobbery kiss for her new Oma. Ilse wiped a tear from her eyes and beamed at Karl.

"Aren't they gorgeous! And so like Siegfried at that age, although he was a half-starved little mite then. But you never saw him, of course," she remembered.

"No, but I mean to see as much of these two as I possibly can."

"So do I."

"Before you go back, you mean?"

"I'm not going back, Karl." She looked him boldly in the eye. "I've left Paul."

Her words came as no surprise after what everyone had been saying but he needed to hear her reasons for himself. "Why?" Friedrich had suddenly grown bored of sitting still and threw himself towards the floor where the toy bricks had resumed their fascination.

Fortunately Karl had a firm grip on him and eased him gently down before returning his astonished gaze to Ilse.

She smiled. "He didn't need me and I was bored. Simple really."

"Don't you love him still?"

"Yes, but I felt I was needed more back here."

"And he was happy with that?"

"He'd seen it coming for a long time. Maybe not happy, but he accepted it very gracefully. He's a good man." She had been staring into Karl's eyes, but her sudden sense of guilt at leaving her husband made her look down to her lap where their granddaughter lay kicking the arm of the sofa. Glancing back up she saw the wariness in his eyes and realised she must not rush him. He was still grieving for Katherine. "Margit tells me you're applying for a job in Iserlohn."

"Yes, but I don't expect I'll get it with my prison record."

"You never know." She studied his face further. Looking at him had always given her, and many other women she had to admit, such pleasure. His classically handsome features had mellowed with age but he had lost none of his sex appeal. His tall, muscular frame had not gone to flab as Paul's had, but since the war he had acquired a very noticeable vulnerability, accentuated now by his loss of Katherine.

Ilse realised she had little time alone with him and suddenly reached for his hand. "I just want you to know, I'm here for you, Karl." His fingers curled hesitantly around hers before withdrawing.

"Thank you, Ilse," he said simply, unwilling to encourage her further. He felt awkward with the situation and hoped Sophie and Margit would not be much longer. He leant forward and pushed a wooden train in Friedrich's direction, letting the toddler take over as driver. Freia promptly jumped down from Ilse's lap to join in and Ilse had to hurriedly divert her with a rubber crocodile, snapping its jaws in her face, before a fight erupted over the train.

Once peace had resumed, Karl continued his conversation with Ilse. "What do you intend doing with your time? I don't suppose Paul will support you?"

"No, of course not!" she replied light-heartedly. "For the moment I'm staying with the girls, but I'll find myself a job and an apartment somewhere."

"In Iserlohn?"

"Who knows?"

Margit and Sophie finally entered with the tray of coffee and cakes, satisfied they had given Karl and Ilse enough time together. The remainder of the morning passed in entertaining the twins and catching up on news until Sophie's parents and sister arrived at midday. The Wendts greeted Ilse warmly, Karl only slightly less so. It was from neo-Nazis Peter and Lisl Wendt that Karl still felt most at risk of revenge for his part in the death of their colleague, Josef Garisch. He had been acquitted of the murder but he never let his guard slip when in their company. Their new roles as co-grandparents seemed to have ameliorated the situation, and for that he was grateful.

The weather had cooled considerably and leaves were beginning to turn brown and fall in the brisk breeze as they all set off for the cemetery. Their pace was dictated by Sophie's persisting limp, the relic of her car accident two years previously. They all clutched their floral tributes, processing up the high street towards the village cemetery where Siegfried lay. As they approached they grew quiet, apart from the twins, whose babbling and chatter helped maintain their spirits.

Sophie stood for a minute in silent tribute after laying her flowers before moving aside for the others. As Karl laid his flowers down on his son's grave, his throat tightened and all the grief of the last year for both Siegfried and Katherine rose near the surface again. This was why he hated graves. He sensed Ilse draw near, saw her lay her flowers down, heard her blow her nose, felt her clutch his arm for comfort rather than her daughter's. He turned to her and held her as he had before. Try as he might, he could not deny the bond between them. He felt her respond and he looked down into her tear-streaked eyes. Instead of Ilse's blue ones he saw Katherine's, flashing green with accusation and reproach. A blast of guilt shot through him and he moved away, turning his back on Ilse so she would not see his confusion.

Ilse, thinking he had wanted simply to hide his tears from her, put her arm round him. She felt his muscles tense, as though wanting to shrug her off, but he soon relaxed again and turned to face her.

27

"I'm sorry. I suppose I'm not quite ready to move on," he muttered.

"That's all right. I understand." She smiled up at him through her tears. She could wait until he was ready.

FOUR

Sarah Carter sat astride her favourite horse, ambling through the Herefordshire country lanes beside her old friend Audrey Kellett. The two had met at school, had learnt to ride together, shared their first cigarette together and their most secret desires. Now their destinies had come full circle after years apart. Sarah had divorced her husband seventeen years previously, when he became the lover of Gustav Halstrup, who later died in the same car crash as Karl's son, Siegfried. Audrey was now estranged from her husband, Andrew, whose relentless pursuit of Sarah's sister, Katherine, had caused her death.

As they rode along a muddy cart track through a meadow now empty of cattle, Sarah told Audrey about her niece Sabina's latest letter. "Bina's got a bee in her bonnet about Ilse again."

Audrey loved hearing the latest gossip on Sarah's dead sister's family. She had always fancied Sarah's brother-in-law, Karl, from the moment she had first seen him at the Penchurch Christmas Bazaar in 1946. She could clearly remember that hers had not been the only head turning that afternoon. He was nearly everything a man should be, in her opinion: tall and handsome with his blond hair and steel-grey eyes. Sarah had told her they were blue, but Audrey had instantly set her straight on the matter. As a prisoner of war, however, he hadn't a penny in his pocket, and he was neither free nor available; fraternisation with POWs to that extent had still been forbidden. That had not stopped her seducing him when the opportunity arose, however, and the experience had been extremely pleasurable, its illegality giving the act extra spice. After Katherine married him, he had been out of bounds, but that had never stopped her daydreaming about him. Now he was free again and Ilse's name was already cropping up.

"What's Bina been saying about her?"

"Well, as you know, it was the first anniversary of Siegfried's death on the twenty-second and Ilse decided to come over from Uruguay to be there. Karl went up to Sophie's too, for the day, so they were bound to get together, and Bina fears that'll be it."

"But Ilse's still married. Karl would never steal another man's wife. Fiancée, certainly," she added, remembering she had been second best for her husband, Andrew. He had really wanted Katherine as his wife but Karl had taken her from him.

Sarah reached down from her horse to open the field gate then held it open for Audrey to pass through. "I agree, but Bina thinks otherwise. But then she knows Ilse and we don't. Maybe Ilse has always wanted him back."

"Quite probably," Audrey said, holding back her horse to wait while Sarah secured the gate again.

"And I think Katherine was always rather wary of Ilse's feelings towards Karl," Sarah went on. She glanced up at the tumbling clouds, which were threatening rain, and her discourse on Ilse was cut short. "Come on, before we get soaked!"

She urged her horse into a trot up the lane towards the distant buildings of the riding school, their regular Saturday afternoon hack almost over. She and Audrey spent most weekends together as two single, middle-aged women intent on enjoying life while they could. During the week they both worked as secretaries in Hereford. It was a huge come-down from Sarah's previous job in the planning department of the Greater London Council, but it enabled her to keep an occasional eye on her nephews, Richard and Paul, at Lane Head Farm, cleaning, cooking and shopping for them. At the weekends Richard's girlfriend, Vanessa, took over those duties, as well as sharing Richard's bed she suspected, but that was the way things were these days and Sarah had never been prudish. Far from it, she thought, remembering her and Audrey's meeting last weekend with a couple of schoolteachers from Birmingham who were discovering the delights of the countryside. She smiled, anticipating the reunion with them in a pub in Worcester tonight.

"Shall I drive this evening?" she offered as they dismounted in the stable yard.

"Thanks. It's just a shame we have to go so far to avoid gossip."

"I don't know why we bother, really," Sarah replied. "If we were young hippies, nobody would think anything of it. We were born into the wrong generation."

"I've often thought that," Audrey said. "This lot have got it made, what with the Pill and all. It's a godsend."

The rain was just starting to fall and they hurried their horses into their stalls to untack them. When they reached the dark and secluded confines of the tack room, Sarah reverted to their earlier conversation. "I still don't see why Bina hates Ilse so much now. She was quite willing to live in Ilse's house until all that business when Karl shot Wolf's fake father – accidentally or otherwise!" she hastily added, seeing Audrey's frown at her slip. Both she and Audrey believed Karl had actually shot the politician who was hiding his Nazi background, but Karl's case had been judged 'not-proven' and he had got off. "I suppose it's Ilse's neo-Nazi connections," she went on, hanging up her horse's bridle. "Bina probably doesn't want Karl having anything to do with that lot." She winced at the thought. "She's got a point, really."

"Was Karl really once a Nazi?" Audrey asked tentatively. It was a forbidden subject, but she had always been curious. "I know he was in the SS, but is that the same thing?"

Sarah saw a young girl of twelve entering the tack room and put her hand on Audrey to warn her. It was not until they were safely in Sarah's red Mini, speedily driving back into Hereford that she was able to answer. "You asked about Karl being a Nazi, but I really don't know. It was such a tricky subject that I never really broached it. I know he got into some kind of trouble with the Nazis, and Ilse left him because of it. Both Karl and Katherine were very cagey on the subject. I've no doubt he was anti-Nazi at the end of the war, but before that ..." She paused. "I think the children know all about it."

"But not you."

"No. It was all tied up with his mental breakdown, and he didn't want the whole world to know. I respected his wishes and never really asked, although I was always dying to know. The one person who does know everything is Robert, of course, but he would *never* tell!"

"Medical 'in confidence' or just because he's Karl's best mate?"

"Both. I know Karl had to visit him in Edinburgh after Siegfried died. Robert seemed to sort him out OK, but it does leave you thinking that Karl is still very vulnerable to mental problems. How he'll cope without Katherine, I don't know."

"Is that why you were so keen he went home to Germany? You didn't want to be the one to cope with another breakdown?"

"No, it wasn't selfish reasons! Richard and Paul are too young to deal with his sort of problems, and I could see he needed his own people around him. They've done a good job too, from what Bina says. Apparently he's thinking about getting a job now, wanting a bit more independence."

"Not enough to return here, though," Audrey commented wistfully.

Sarah laughed. "I know you'd have him!"

"Wouldn't I just," she sighed. Her friend's equally wistful expression caught her by surprise. "You want him too, Sarah! Go on admit it!"

Sarah tried to conceal her lust. "He's my brother-in-law. It wouldn't be right."

"Why ever not?"

"Because …" It was territory she had always avoided thinking about. She avoided it now. "I hope you haven't got any designs on young Paul, now that he's starting to broaden out and resemble Karl more as every day goes by."

"Don't talk daft. I'm no baby snatcher."

"No? I seem to remember a certain young man called Daniel, who had just turned sixteen when -"

"All right!" Audrey conceded. "Guilty as charged. I was doing him a favour, though."

"I'm sure," Sarah laughed at her incorrigible friend's exploits. "But I'd think twice about doing the same for Paul. Karl might not appreciate your intentions, if he ever got to hear about it."

Audrey heeded the warning. "I wouldn't want to fall out with him."

"Nor would I, especially since Paul's supposedly in my care."

They arrived at Audrey's terraced house on the outskirts of Hereford, near the Bulmer's cider works, just as the skies were clearing again. Audrey stepped out of the car into a puddle and cursed.

"I'll pick you up at seven," Sarah called across to her.

"Fine. I'll be ready."

"That's a likely story," Sarah riposted with a wave goodbye, before turning the Mini around in the street to head back towards her own rented house on an estate to the east of the city. The rent she received for her own flat in London easily covered her modest house here, leaving enough over for her pension and holiday funds. Financially secure, she had no need to find a man, unlike Audrey, but she had always enjoyed their company, despite her early disappointment with her ex-husband, Perry. She had soon discovered life was more fun without him.

Once inside her house, she hurried upstairs to have a bath and wash her hair in preparation for the evening in Worcester. The two teachers, both divorced, had beaten the two women at darts, necessitating tonight's return match. Everyone's behaviour had been delightfully flirtatious, and Sarah knew Audrey was itching to get to know Patrick, the more exuberant of the two, much better. From what she had seen, Patrick felt likewise. She had found Ron interesting, if not as charming as Patrick, who would have been her choice had not Audrey batted her eyelashes quicker. "Gentlemen prefer blondes," she sighed to herself as she rinsed her chestnut locks in the sink, "even if Audrey's blonde does come out of a bottle these days."

She stared at her reflection in the mirror as she dried her hair. Not too bad, she mused. A few lines here and there, a smattering of grey hairs. She had held onto her looks reasonably well for a woman of forty-four, better than Katherine had with so much to worry about in the past two years. Sarah brushed her hair back into the style Katherine had favoured throughout her marriage, off the face and under control. It made her resemble her sister slightly more than usual, and she suddenly wondered why she had done it. So Karl would want her? Despite herself, she imagined him coming up behind her, touching her neck, embracing her, herself responding to his caress. She shivered with the sudden rush of desire, then the guilt hit her and she hurriedly released her tresses before her imaginings went too far. Brushing her hair into its sideways sweep again, she prepared herself for a lusty evening with Patrick and Ron.

*

"How are you feeling? Nervous?" Dieter asked his son as they met at the top of the stairs.

It was the morning of Karl's interview in Iserlohn. The call for an interview had arrived within a week of his sending off the application form, indicating either super-efficiency or desperation. Margit's friend had told them it was desperation. It had to be for them to consider him as a likely candidate.

"Not too bad," he replied, "even though I've never been for a job interview. I've always been the one doing the hiring."

"Just be yourself and don't say anything that's not true," Dieter advised him, following him downstairs. "I know I always looked for honesty in a worker when I took him on. You're just what they want, so tell them that."

Karl grinned. "A bilingual, practical jailbird. Well, we'll see what they think. I wonder how many others they're interviewing."

"Not many, I shouldn't think."

Karl set off shortly after breakfast to drive the one hundred and twenty kilometres to Iserlohn. He knew the route well and he let his mind wander until he arrived at the outskirts of Iserlohn with a good half hour to spare. Not wanting the distraction of facing Ilse before the interview, he had arranged to lunch with her afterwards. To kill time he drove down to the ornamental lake, the Seilersee, where he could wander round for a few minutes. He briefly watched the swans and ducks cavorting in its shallow waters and under the fountain then turned his gaze on his surroundings. Behind him was a thickly wooded hillside, the trees beginning to show their autumn colours. Ahead of him lay the town, growing bigger with each visit, but still surrounded by plenty of woodland with the occasional grey slate roof showing through the trees. He knew the town reasonably well from his visits to Ilse and Paul's impressive house in the adjacent wooded hills, but he could not imagine himself living here. Iserlohn spelt Ilse in his mind, but was that such a bad thing now?

He looked at his watch. Time to go.

The hospital was situated nearby. Karl noticed with some surprise a German eagle atop a stone pillar at the entrance. Clearly the hospital had been some kind of German Army barracks during the war. Now there seemed to be a lot of activity going on about the place, with green military ambulances plying back and forth as though some major disaster had occurred. Amidst all the hubbub a corporal directed him to the administration department, where it was much quieter. His interview was for eleven-thirty and he presented himself to the secretary of the senior administrator at twenty-five past eleven. She told him to take a seat nearby and just as he sat down, a man walked out of an office up the corridor, the sweat on his brow betraying him as another interviewee. Their eyes met, but they did not smile, rivals as they were. Karl thought he looked younger than himself, but was not sure whether that was a good or bad thing. He had to wait the full five minutes before promptly at eleven-thirty the secretary showed him into Major Pascoe's office.

Two men occupied the office, one of them clearly Major Pascoe. Robust with dark brown if greying hair, he reminded Karl rather disconcertingly of Katherine's former fiancé, Andrew Kellett, who had been an army captain at the end of the war. Beside him sat a civilian, who was probably the Area Works Officer from the military hospital at Bielefeld who had sent Karl his interview letter.

"Mr Driesler. Sit down, please." Major Pascoe smiled warmly, instantly dispelling any impression of Andrew Kellett. He checked his notepad as Karl made himself comfortable on the upright chair in front of the desk. "Firstly, my apologies for the chaos here at the moment. A Taceval was dumped on us this morning and half the people who should be here have had to disappear and organise bandage counting or something equally time wasting." He saw Karl's blank look and explained. "Taceval – tactical evaluation – an exercise. The powers that be regularly hurl them at us out of the blue. Never mind, it all adds to the excitement!"

Karl smiled, warming to Major Pascoe immediately. "I hadn't noticed any chaos," he said politely.

"No? Perhaps it's no worse than usual then. Anyway, to business. Mr Whitworth here will have most to ask you. Mr Whitworth?"

The Area Works Officer folded his arms across his belly and leant back in his chair. "Tell me, Mr Driesler, why do you think you're qualified for the position? Your credentials are somewhat unusual, shall we say?"

This was the one question Karl was well prepared for. "I'm fluent in technical as well as colloquial English and German, I have experience in managing people and resources, can work to budgets and have military experience. Perhaps most importantly, I understand both the British and German mentalities and can hopefully avoid misunderstandings."

Mr Whitworth's expression remained impassive but Major Pascoe nodded gently. It was the answer he had hoped for and expected having read the application form in front of him, and it confirmed fluency in English at least.

"And what would you say to an irate Glaswegian housewife who finds a German decorator, who speaks no English, has turned up at her married quarter unannounced to paint her entire house?" the stony-faced Mr Whitworth asked next.

"Such an event shouldn't happen, but I doubt even you could understand a really irate Glaswegian." Karl thought he detected a twitch of Whitworth's lips but he clearly saw the major grin.

"Possibly," Mr Whitworth conceded politely," but what would you say, assuming you had understood her?"

It could have been a tough question considering Karl knew little about the workings of the system, except that Margit's friend had sent him a very full briefing of the work and the situations that cropped up. "I would apologise and check that the workman was at the right house. If he was, it could be the case that the husband was informed and forgot to tell his wife. If she accepts that, she might be angry with her husband but not with the decorator, and let him in."

"That's a fair scenario. But what if, let's say, her child was ill in bed and she refused to let him in?"

"The decorator would have to be given other work to do until the situation was resolved."

Mr Whitworth made a note on his pad, leaving Karl guessing as to whether he had given the correct response or not. Next he produced a circuit diagram of the electrical supply to the hospital, which he passed to Karl. "Show me where the circuit breakers are, please."

Karl studied the diagram and quickly pointed to the correct marking. He was then presented with a variety of similar tasks, each testing some area of skill, either technical or linguistic. Finally came the hardest question of all.

"And what else, if anything, do you think we need to know about you?"

It was an open question but Karl knew immediately what the man was after. "My prison record," he volunteered.

For the first time Mr Whitworth stayed silent and Major Pascoe took over the proceedings. Although Karl had mentioned it briefly in his application letter, Pascoe pretended ignorance. "In a British prison?"

"No, if you don't count POW camps."

"Then we have no record of it. We don't need to know about it."

Karl stared at both men in amazement and saw their look of complicity. Were they going to sweep it under the carpet? They really did want him if they were prepared to overlook such a detail. He was beginning to feel a lot of strings had been pulled to get him there, but by whom and why?

Mr Whitworth folded up his notepad and put it aside on the desk. "Well, I think that's covered just about everything. You said you're available to start immediately?"

"That's right."

"Good. Now, do you have any questions you want to ask?"

"Yes, the job description states that I would be entitled to medical treatment here, but what if I was elsewhere in West Germany? I would still need German health insurance, surely?"

"No, as an attached civilian worker here any medical costs would be borne by the UK government."

"And accommodation is provided?"

Major Pascoe spoke up. "On site. We need you accessible most of the time, but to compensate for that the position entitles you to honorary membership of the Officers' Mess. It's the Oktoberfest this week!" He grinned broadly in eager anticipation of the event.

Karl allowed himself a smile at the image this conjured up of drunken British officers singing German beer hall songs. "Presumably there'll be a lot of loose tongues there. Surely I'd need security clearance?"

Pascoe waved dismissively. "Done. You'll sign the Official Secrets Act of course."

They were talking as though he already had the job, and when the interview was over and they stood to shake hands, Karl knew he had got it, despite Mr Whitworth merely saying he would hear within a few days. Someone had paved the way very carefully for him, and that someone had to be Margit's friend. Margit desperately wanted him in Iserlohn, near Ilse.

On leaving the hospital he drove straight to Margit and her sisters' apartment near the centre of town. It was twelve-thirty by the time he rang the doorbell labelled Röbel, then climbed the communal stairs to the second floor, where Ilse stood waiting at the apartment's front door.

"Well?" she asked eagerly, beckoning him inside and shutting the door.

He beamed down at her. "I'm fairly sure I got it. I wasn't told outright, but I was given a pretty good idea it was mine. I should hear officially in a few days."

Ilse flung her arms exuberantly round his neck and kissed him on the cheek. "I knew they'd want you! Wasn't Margit clever to think of you working there!"

"She was indeed." Her embrace caught him off guard and he backed off slightly, disentangling himself from Ilse. He glanced around the hall, seeking a distraction from her, and recognised an expensive dresser from Ilse's former Iserlohn home. "I remember that piece," he said. "Did you keep much of your old furniture?"
Unabashed by his rebuff, Ilse chuckled. "As much as we could cram in here. I hope to make furniture my business soon. Roslinde's heard about a job going in a furniture shop owned by the father of a school-friend. If there's one thing I do know about it's furniture, the number of houses and apartments I've had to furnish in my time!" She led him through into the living area of the apartment. "I've made some lunch for us, if you don't mind eating in. Are you hungry yet?"

"Yes, I am, but I hope you've not gone to too much trouble."

Ilse headed towards the kitchen and Karl followed her. "It's given me something to do. My days are a bit empty just at the moment." She picked up an oven glove and removed a casserole dish from the oven, putting it down on a board. She pointed out a loaf of bread to Karl for him to cut a few slices. "At some point," she went on, bringing out plates from the oven, "I've got to buy some winter clothes, but until I start earning, shopping's out. It's quite like the old days again, do you remember, when Erich threw me out and you had to rescue me?"

"I hardly rescued you, Ilse. You saved yourself by getting to Medebach."

She handed him a breadbasket. "Yes, but you gave me the strength to start again. I could never have done it without you and your family." She had moved closer but when Karl looked away towards the casserole dish she realised she was rushing things again. "Right, that's everything. Let's take it all through. Do you want wine or beer?"

"Beer, please." He carried the plates, bread and a bowl of salad over to the elaborate dining table then got the drinks while Ilse served out the beef goulash. It was a recipe she had used many times in her early married life, but had never made it for Karl. Indeed it was the first time she had ever cooked for him. Previously when he had visited her and Paul she had had a cook. Now she lived in more straitened circumstances.

"*Zum Wohl!*" she said, raising her glass. "To our futures."

Karl noted the plural. "Our futures."

During the meal Ilse kept the conversation light, enquiring after his sons, Richard and Paul, and filling him in on the activities of her brood. He was beginning to feel more at ease in Ilse's company now. Indeed, it seemed perfectly natural to be sitting here with her until, for no apparent reason, his thoughts turned to that previous meeting alone with her, which had led to him betraying Katherine. He shuddered at the memory and the harm his adultery had caused. He still felt he was betraying her, even now.

Ilse noticed his distraction. "Everything all right?"

He put down his knife and fork and reached for her hand in a positive attempt to overcome his sense of guilt. "You'll just have to be patient with me I'm afraid, Schatz. My emotions are still all over the place."

His term of endearment thrilled her. It meant he intended resuming his former relationship with her once he felt able to. She smiled, trying to hide her triumph. "I understand. It's only been eight months and now you'll be busy settling in to your new job and me in mine, hopefully. We'll have plenty of other things to think about for a while."

"True enough," he said, relieved that his slip of the tongue in calling her 'Schatz' again had not done more damage. Much as he loved her still, he did not want to rush into a relationship with her. Anna's words of advice on the subject had taken root. It would be the easy thing to take up with Ilse again, but would it be the best? And would he ever get over his fierce sense of guilt at being with her?

FIVE

The house had three bedrooms, a cellar and a small garden. It came fully furnished and equipped. Karl signed the relevant 'march-in' forms, accepting the state of repair and inventory, was handed the keys then left to his own devices.

He had expected a room in the Officers' Mess, but as a widower with a child of school age, he discovered he was entitled to a house. How often Paul or Richard would visit was debatable, but the opportunity was there, and other family members could stay at any time.

He prowled around the house, opening cupboards, finding where everything was. He decided to take the master bedroom as his, simply because he was entitled to it. Having made that decision, he propped open the front door and began to unpack his meagre belongings from the car, a second-hand but reliable VW Beetle, which had been a present from his father.

"I've not been able to give you much in the past," Dieter had said, when handing him the keys. "Let me do this for you now."

So now he had his own house and transport, a new job to look forward to and a new life to begin.

As he came back out to fetch his second box-load of belongings, an imposing looking woman approached him from a larger married quarter across the road. Her shoulder-length hair was swept back by an Alice band and she carried her husband's rank firmly on her broad, tweed-clad shoulders. Karl had seen her type many times at county gymkhanas and was not intimidated by these heiresses of the Empire.

"Good morning," she boomed, holding out her hand in greeting. "I'm Virginia Mitchell, the road representative. Welcome to Iserlohn, Mr Driesler. You're the new DWO, I gather."

"Yes." Karl shook her hand, somewhat taken aback that she had been briefed about him.

Mrs Mitchell smiled. "It's my job to know," she told him. "I'm informed by the CO's wife when new people move into the patch, so I can come and welcome them. Civilians sometimes find it a bit startling, but we're all used to it and like it, especially coming to a foreign country where there's so much to find out about. But I think you're German, aren't you, Mr Driesler?"

He wondered how much else about him she already knew. "Yes. I've only had to drive up from near Winterberg."

"Oh, I've been skiing there. It's lovely. Is your wife coming later?"

He had just discovered the limit of her knowledge. "I'm a widower," he told her, realising it was best the neighbourhood knew straight away.

Mrs Mitchell looked stricken. "Oh, I do apologise! Someone should have told me. I just assumed, since you'd been allocated this quarter, that ..."

"Don't worry about it."

She looked embarrassed now. "Normally I would ask the wives round for coffee so they can get to know everyone, but ... well ... you'll have to come for dinner and meet a few people that way."

Karl felt moved by her welcome. "Thank you. That's very kind of you."

She managed a smile again. "Well, I'd better leave you to settle in. If there's anything you need or want to know, we're just over there. My husband's called Simon. Don't hesitate to call. People do," she told him.

He nodded, and as he watched her cross the road back to her house, he realised it felt good to be back among the British. He had missed them.

It did not take him long to unpack his clothing, put Katherine's photograph on the table by his bed then put away the few grocery items he had brought with him. Mention of coffee just now made him fill the kettle and put it on the gas stove to boil while he found a cup and saucer in one of the cupboards. Despite the bubbling of the water in the kettle, the house felt very quiet suddenly and he plugged in the small radio Rudi had given him. While tuning it in, he came across English voices on the British Forces Broadcasting Service and decided to stay on that station. It was almost like living in England again, but with his family close at hand.

He had the whole of Friday and the weekend to himself before starting work on Monday. First off he would need to make the bed and get more food in. He had seen the Naafi shop nearby, but it would be good to find the nearest German grocery store as well. Major Pascoe had arranged to meet him in the Officers' Mess for a drink at seven, so he had to decide whether to eat before or afterwards. Before might be advisable, he decided, remembering the Major's fondness for the Oktoberfest.

Later that afternoon, while stowing a crate of beer in the cellar, Karl realised one of his first major purchases might have to be a washing machine. There was a sink and plumbing down there, as well as a clothesline strung across the ceiling. He sighed at the amount of domestic work having his own house entailed, but it would be worth it, he thought, to be able to have family to stay.

As seven o' clock drew near, he made himself a meal of frankfurters and potato salad then got changed into a suit and tie and headed off for the Mess. The Officers' Mess boldly proclaimed its former ownership by sporting a weather vane on the roof depicting three German soldiers marching into a sentry box. He found the sight somewhat disconcerting; too much of a reminder of his own time as a soldier. But those days were long gone and he must put them behind him again.

Major Pascoe was already at the bar. On seeing Karl enter the crowded room, he waved his almost empty beer glass to call him over. Karl weaved his way through the throng of uniformed officers, feeling conspicuous in his civilian clothes. It would be different at the weekend, he supposed.

"What would you like?" Pascoe asked him the moment he reached the bar.

Karl noticed the dark beer in Pascoe's glass and opted for the same. "A pint of bitter, please, Major." He could find out later if they had any decent German lager in stock.

"The name's John." He motioned to the bar steward for two pints, signed his chit and handed Karl his beer. "How's the house? All right?"

"Wonderful. Bigger than I was expecting." He moved aside to let a burly senior officer reach the bar.

John Pascoe nudged him and in a stage whisper said: "Lt. Col. Mick O'Reilly, consultant anaesthetist. You'll like him."

Mick O'Reilly turned on hearing his name. "John! Can I get you one?" He noticed Karl and waited expectantly for an introduction.

"Thanks, but I've just got one." John laid a chummy hand on Karl's shoulder. "This is our new DWO, Karl Driesler."

"A Jerry, eh? Should be a lot more efficient than old Arnold." He held out his hand, which Karl noticed was covered in fine scratches. "Welcome to the club. Don't mind this lot. They'll soon get used to you. We foreigners must stick together."

Karl recognised the distinctive Irish accent and knew he had an ally. He shook Mick O'Reilly's hand warmly. "Thank you. I've already been made most welcome."

The lieutenant colonel leaned forward and whispered: "There's some won't like you. Arnold was one of them. Couldn't be doing with Jerries. That's why he made such a mess of his job. Still, hopefully you'll soon sort it all out for us. Darling Silke's nearly had a nervous breakdown trying to fix his many cock-ups. The entire place would have fallen down months ago without her."

Silke was Margit's friend, the one who had been so helpful in getting him the job. Self-preservation, obviously, Karl thought, but she had proved herself very efficient so far.

Mick parked his large rump on a vacant bar stool and soon Karl was part of a growing group as Mess members gathered to inspect the newcomer. There was a hush of sympathy when it transpired he had only comparatively recently lost his wife, followed by numerous offers of dinners and social evenings as well as nights out on the town.

By the time Karl got back to his quarter later that evening he felt overwhelmed by the camaraderie, which had taken him back to his own army days. He guessed it helped that most of the men there were medics first and officers second, as he had experienced none of the stuffiness he associated with the likes of Andrew Kellett and a few other British officers he had come across during and after the war. Nevertheless, he remembered Mick O'Reilly's warning about some not liking him. No doubt he would meet them soon enough.

The house felt cool so he put on the kettle to make tea, despite being awash with beer. The feeling of camaraderie he had experienced in the Mess made him think of his old army comrade Ernst Winter, who had sought him out the previous year after reading all about Karl's trial in the German press. Ernst had been in a sorry state, on his own and longing for the good old days. Karl had kept in touch ever since, less so since Katherine's death. Now he felt the need to write to his old pal in Berlin. He might even pay Ernst a visit.

He knew he had some writing paper in his box full of documents and assorted desk-type rubbish pulled from a drawer in his old room. Now he had a whole bureau to fill. He tipped the box's contents into the flap compartment of the bureau, found the stationery he was seeking and sat back down at the kitchen table with his cup of tea and a packet of biscuits.

He had written two sides before he remembered Ernst's rather extraordinary circumstances in Berlin. He had let slip that he was supposed to be a Soviet spy, convincingly faking an interest in communism in order to survive in his prisoner of war camp there. After the war the Soviets had provided him with documents in his real name so he could take up his old life again, but acting as a sleeper agent. Ernst had confided that he had no intention of spying for the Soviets, and, if called upon to do so, would rather shoot himself.

As long as Ernst kept under cover and did nothing there was no problem, but should he ever fall under suspicion then Karl's friendship with him could compromise his job here. For a moment Karl was tempted to screw up his letter and not write again, but he realised he could not abandon Ernst like that. He had to take the risk but be scrupulously careful about what he wrote, in case it was ever intercepted. He remembered the family's jokes about James Bond during Ernst's visit, but whether he was being paranoid or not, his experience during the war had taught him to be careful.

He read back over what he had written but it was innocuous enough, and if it gave Ernst pleasure to keep in touch with an old comrade, then it was worth the risk.

Signing off, he put the letter in an envelope addressed to Ernst then wrote his own address on the back. He had two addresses available. His family in Britain could use the British Forces Post Office system, in which case his mail would be addressed to the Officers' Mess where he had his own pigeonhole. Ernst and his German-based relatives, however, would be using the *Bundespost*, which would deliver to his door. It felt rather like when he had been a POW billeted at Lane Head Farm, having two addresses again – the camp and the farm.

Inevitably his thoughts turned immediately to his first days there with Katherine and he allowed himself the simple pleasure of recalling the early days of their romance. His eyes still prickled with tears but at least now his throat did not constrict with grief. He smiled, wiped away the tears and took his cup and saucer to the sink. Rinsing them under the tap he pictured Katherine doing the same at the end of the evening before filling a glass of water to take up to bed. Now her chores were his, and he felt very alone. As he switched off the radio he heard a car drive by. The urge to have human contact was overwhelming and he went to the window.

The kitchen looked out over the road and should have had net curtains, but the British were lax about such rules. He drew aside the green gingham curtains and peered into the darkness. A local taxi was delivering a couple to their house a few doors down. He watched the husband and wife walk up the front path together and disappear inside to their conjugal bliss.

Karl picked up his glass of water and went to bed suddenly feeling lonelier than he had in months. As he tossed and turned he felt increasingly constrained by the tucked in, standard-issue blankets. He had to lie diagonally on the double bed so he did not overlap the sides. Tomorrow he would go into town and buy himself a proper German feather quilt.

*

Saturday morning in the Karstadt department store proved an expensive business for Karl. Having bought his quilt and two covers, on his way out he saw a framed print of gentle green meadows full of sheep by a muddy brown river. It was so evocative of his former life that he had to buy it to brighten up the bare walls of his house.

Burdened by his purchases he brushed against a young woman

standing behind him at the till. "Sorry," he said automatically before realising the young woman paying for her purchases was one of Ilse's daughters, Roslinde Röbel.

"Hello, Karl," she greeted him jovially. "Fancy seeing you here!"

It was the first time she had seen him since Katherine's death, and the eighteen-year-old's smile was abruptly replaced by the familiar 'oh-my-God-what-do-I-say-next?' expression. He had learnt to cope with it, just as he had learnt to cope with everything else. "Hello, Roslinde. How are you?"

"Fine, thanks." Surprisingly she managed to move the conversation on herself. "Do you want a hand with any of that? You look as though you're about to drop that bag."

"That would be a great help. If you could take this one? It's not too heavy, just awkward." He handed over the picture. "My car's not too far away."

They left the store and walked down the busy street, Roslinde clutching the glass of the picture protectively to her body. As they stowed Karl's purchases in the front of the blue VW, Karl could not let such a long-standing acquaintance just walk away. "Do you want a lift anywhere?"

"I was just on my way home actually." Her eyes lit up. "Mutti's in. She'd love to see you. She said you'd got a job at the British hospital."

So at least two of Ilse's daughters approved of her mother's actions, he thought. Pleasant as his last meeting with Ilse had been, he had felt she was far too keen to resume their former relationship immediately. He had phoned her to let her know he had got the job, but had avoided contacting her since. But as he drove off with Roslinde next to him, he decided it was as good a time as any to see her again, and at least Roslinde and perhaps the other two girls would be in to prevent Ilse getting too carried away. Most likely he would end up staying for a meal, which would be welcome.

He parked outside their apartment building and Roslinde unlocked the outer door. "We'll surprise Mutti!" she whispered on their way up the stairs.

Opening the door, Roslinde put down her carrier bag then called out: "Mutti! Guess who I've brought home."

An apron-clad Ilse appeared at the kitchen door, cigarette in one hand, wooden spoon in the other. "Karl!" Appalled at the state she was in, she swiftly stubbed out her cigarette on a saucer, snatched off her apron and flung the spoon into the sink.

Roslinde grinned at Karl. "We bumped into each other in Karstadt," she called out to her mother, beckoning Karl through into the lounge.

Ilse reappeared, patting her hair into place, then stepped forwards to give Karl a kiss on the cheek. "It's lovely to see you again. You've moved in now, I take it?"

"Yesterday. I've been buying some things for the house this morning."

Roslinde decided to be helpful and get out of their way. "Shall I make some coffee, Mutti?"

Ilse looked questioningly at Karl. "Or beer?"

"Coffee's fine, thank you."

"I can't believe you're going to be so close now, after all these years!" Ilse said, showing him the sofa to sit down. She sat herself next to him. "It's a shame you've just missed Margit and Silke. It would have been nice for you to meet Silke before you start work."

"Yes. I think she did an awful lot of wangling to get me the job. I really can't understand why they gave it to me."

Ilse nodded. "She certainly did, with our encouragement! We persuaded her you were perfect for the job after all we'd heard about her last boss. She's a bright girl and why she's stuck at working there in that chaos, I don't know. She could do so much more with herself, but then it's her choice, isn't it?"

"I suppose so, but then I don't know her circumstances."

Ilse pursed her lips. "No, you wouldn't." She changed the subject as though protecting Silke's privacy. "Well now! What's your house like and have you a telephone?"

While he was describing everything to her, Roslinde came in with the coffee and some chocolate cake. Karl noticed she had not made herself any and her next announcement worried him.

"I'm just off to see if Thomas is in. Back later! *Tschüs!*"

There was no sign of Ilse's other daughter, Edeltraud, in the house. They were alone. "How's your job-hunting going?" he asked.

"Fine. I start at the furniture shop next month. Like you, it helps having friends to find jobs." She passed him his coffee cup and took the opportunity to move closer to him. "Karl, I know you find this difficult at the moment and I quite understand. I respect Katherine's memory as much as anyone does, but I left Paul to be near you. I'm here for you when you want me, and I'll try not to get too close before you're ready, hard as that is for me." She ventured a caress of his anxious face. He neither withdrew nor responded and she let her hand fall to her lap.

Deciding he needed to be brutally honest he made his feelings clear. "Thank you, Ilse. It's good to know you're here as a friend, but at the moment I can't go any further. I still feel I'm betraying her, being here with you."

She smiled, despite his words. She knew it was only a matter of time.

SIX

On Monday morning Major Pascoe gave Karl a full tour of the hospital. The interior reflected its origins as a field artillery barracks as much as the exterior did, with old rifle racks still in evidence in the corridors and stone carvings of German soldiers over doorways. After introducing him to the various heads of department, they headed for Karl's new office. Before they got there he decided he had more sensitive information to impart and lowered his voice.

"If old Arnold had hung about a bit longer he could have shown you the ropes," Major Pascoe said, sounding peeved as usual whenever he spoke about Karl's predecessor. "I'll tell you this officially before you hear it as gossip, but Arnold had a bit of a breakdown. The job got on top of him, his wife left him and ... well ..." He shrugged expressively. "Thanks to 'darling Silke' as we all call her, we've managed to keep our heads above water, but it leaves you with a lot to sort out. Unfortunately, Arnold never updated his attitude to your compatriots. To him it was still 1945 when he first came over here. Relationships with the local workforce are pretty poor now, which is why we were so keen to employ a German in this position."

"I see."

They had arrived at the office. Major Pascoe smiled and opened the door. "So here we are." His smile broadened as he caught sight of the young woman sitting at the smaller of the two desks in the cramped room, and he extended his arm out theatrically towards her. "And this is our darling Silke, or Fräulein Sommer as I ought to introduce her." He nodded towards Karl. "Your new boss, my dear. Herr Driesler."

Margit's friend stood up and extended her hand with a jaunty attitude and carefree smile. Karl approached and shook her hand warmly. He reckoned she might be a bit older than Margit, twenty-six possibly, and not intimidated by anyone, least of all a new boss. A modern woman, most definitely, he decided, noting her brazen flaunting of standard office-wear. Instead of the usual demure suit she had on a trendy black and yellow striped jacket over a yellow jersey top.

"Welcome to the madhouse, Herr Driesler," she said in English with a noticeable American accent.

Karl wondered briefly whether she was referring to the lately departed Arnold, but decided she was just being flippant. "Thank you, Fräulein Sommer."

Major Pascoe cleared his throat. "Well, I'll leave you two to get stuck in while I head off to do some work of my own. Best of luck, Karl."

Silke took charge as soon as Pascoe had closed the door. "Well, there's a lot to show you, Herr Driesler. Do you want a coffee before we begin, or later?" She had switched to German, and had the local Westphalian accent without a trace of an American twang.

"Later. But first I want to thank you for helping me get the job, sending me all that information and everything."

She grinned. "Margit's probably told you what it's been like here. You sounded ideal for the job so I just did all I could to help you get it. Saved my sanity, if not Mr Arnold's."

"Yes, Major Pascoe told me about that."

"His own fault. Mr Arnold's, I mean. He got on the wrong side of the workforce and that was that. Nothing ever got done right. Talking of which," she said, slapping the side of the adjacent filing cabinet, "we'll start off with the easy stuff. These are all the forms we use, known by letters and numbers which you'll have to quickly get used to." She opened the drawer and flicked through the sections. Karl noticed her hands were scratched just like the anaesthetist, Lt Col O'Reilly's, as though she had been ferreting around in a bramble bush. "Under here are folders for each of the married quarters – officers' and ORs'." She took one out to let him view the contents. Inside it detailed such things as when new carpets and curtains had been issued, and any other maintenance issues. "That's pretty run-of the-mill. I've managed to go through that lot and start making a forward planner of when different quarters are due decorating or whatever. The bigger and better stuff is over here." She led him over to the other side of the room and a larger bank of filing cabinets. "These are all to do with the hospital. Perhaps it's best if I just leave you to look through them in your own time. Here," she said moving on to the adjacent cabinet, "are the building and estate plans, technical and whatever." She next took him over to his desk and opened the diary sitting prominently on top. "You'll see meetings with various departments are scheduled regularly, and I've put in the inspections you're supposed to do this month." She looked up at him suddenly. "Are you ready for that coffee yet?"

"That sounds a good idea."

While she disappeared off up the corridor to fill the electric kettle, Karl turned to the hospital cabinets and glanced inside. An unruly mass of bulging files threatened to spill out and he hurriedly closed it again as Silke came back into the room.

"Needs sorting and archiving, a lot of that," she said, plugging the kettle in to a wall socket by a tray on which stood the coffee-making provisions and two mugs. "I can do that once I've more time when you're up and running." She spooned instant coffee into each of the mugs. "Mr Arnold liked this stuff and I've got used to it." she apologised. "I hope you don't mind. How do you take it?"

"Black, no sugar."

She eyed his lean figure and laughed. "I might have guessed! Me, I take it with milk and two sugars, which is why I'm the shape I am."

If she was fishing for compliments about her curvaceous figure, she was in for a disappointment. Ignoring her comment, he took his coffee from her and settled down at his new desk to browse through the diary. Arnold had kept the diary reasonably well, filling in what he had achieved each day. As he sipped his coffee Karl thought about what Major Pascoe and Fräulein Sommer had said. Labour relations seemed to be the key issue here. The sooner he met the workers the better; after lunch probably.

Engrossed in his reading, he was vaguely aware of Silke dealing with phone calls and a visitor to the office. "I'm off for lunch now, Herr Driesler," she suddenly announced.

He looked up. "Oh, right. See you later."

She hesitated a moment before asking: "Are you going to the staff canteen? I wouldn't recommend it, unless you like overcooked cabbage."

He smiled at her forthrightness. "I'm used to English cooking. But no, I thought I'd walk into town and find somewhere. I'd quite like some fresh air."

She looked relieved. "That's all right then. Mr Arnold used to bring cheese and pickle sandwiches with a hard-boiled egg every day and eat them in the office. Stank the place out." She put on her black woollen overcoat, a large purple velvet hat, picked up her tangerine tapestry shoulder bag and left the room. The whole effect reminded him of Sabina and Margit's visit to Carnaby Street, when the pair had returned to Lane Head Farm with an extraordinary array of vibrant or outlandish clothing. At least Silke's skirt wasn't quite as short as one Margit had bought, but it had been enough to divert Major Pascoe's eyes. Perhaps there was good reason why Silke's name was given the prefix 'darling'.

Her talk of food made him realise how hungry he was and he put down the workforce register he had been studying. It was a blustery day outside but the clouds were not heavy enough for rain and he set off through the parkland surrounding the hospital for the fifteen-minute walk to the town centre. For a moment he considered calling in at the furniture shop where Ilse had started work, but decided against it. Such a move could become a habit and he was still unsure of his commitment to her.

As he walked briskly through the leaf-strewn streets he remembered how close to her he had felt after Siegfried's death. He had needed to maintain the link with her, keep open access to her memories of their son. Katherine's death had changed all that. Rather than opening up the path to Ilse, it had seemed to erect more of a barrier. Perhaps he would feel differently in a year's time.

The pub he found was offering North Sea mussels as its dish of the day. As he soaked up the last of the peppery broth with his bread, he was glad he had heeded Silke's warning about the canteen. Whatever the weather, he decided, he would have a proper walk and meal away from the hospital otherwise he would find himself swamped by the place.

His walk back was brisk, as he was keen to make contact with the maintenance crew before they resumed work. He nipped back into the still empty office, found the list of names then headed for their rest room. From outside he could hear their earthy dialect as they discussed the previous Saturday's Borussia Dortmund game. He opened the door and recoiled as a dense cloud of cigarette smoke enveloped him. The lad nearest the door noticed Karl's presence and, seeing the suit, stood up, if somewhat slowly. The other four men fell silent and looked at him, laying claim to their territory by remaining seated.

"Good afternoon, gentlemen," Karl said formally, risking a step inside their lair. "I'm the new District Works Officer, Karl Driesler. Perhaps you'd like to introduce yourselves."

As each gave his name he respectfully shook Karl's hand. When it came to the turn of the lad by the door, Karl gave him a close look. "I saw you smoking near the oxygen cylinder store this morning, Hussels," he said quietly. "You could blow yourself and the place up. That's why there are 'No Smoking' signs there. Don't do it again or you're out. Understood?"

"Yes, Herr Driesler," Hussels said, sounding suitably chastened.

They already sensed he was a very different proposition from Mr Arnold. Hopefully he would have their co-operation. He cast his eye over the group, addressing them all. "I hope we'll make a good team, and that any problems can be quickly dealt with. Feel free to approach me with anything that you think could be done differently."

"Like getting a shag out of Silke, you mean?" Hussels whispered to the man next to him.

Karl gave him a frosty glare, but decided to let the comment pass. He noticed the blackboard on the wall on which their work assignments for the week were neatly tabulated in Silke's handwriting. So she came into the lions' den. No doubt she gave as good as she got. With a nod to the group he left the room and headed back to his office, thinking over Hussels' whispered comment. Almost the entire male staff seemed to lust after the vivacious Silke. Perhaps that was why Arnold's wife had left him.

She was busy on the telephone when he entered the room, and waved in greeting. "I'll tell him when he gets in," she said in her American English to the person on the other end of the line. "Goodbye."

"Tell me what?" he asked when she had put down the receiver.

"That there's a group from orthopaedics going out bowling tonight and that you're invited too, if you want to go." She smiled. "They're keen to make you welcome."

"Couldn't you have let me speak to whoever it was?" he asked reproachfully, before adding more hesitantly: "Was it a male or female you were speaking to?"

"It's OK, it was a male," she reassured him. "One of the surgeons. Apparently you met him in the Mess." She gave him a sly grin. "You're worried about the nurses, aren't you? You think they'll be after you, once they know you're available."

"I'm not available," he told her shortly.

"I'll make sure they know that," she replied, unruffled. "Margit said her mother and you had a thing going."

"Did she indeed!" Karl frowned but said nothing more. Perhaps it would be best if everyone thought he was committed elsewhere, otherwise it would be like the women of Medebach all over again.

"Are you going bowling then?"

He hesitated. It would seem rude to refuse, especially when the alternative was listening to the radio alone in his house. "I might as well."

"Good," Silke commended him. "Meet them in the Mess at seven-thirty."

*

"He's never in!" Sabina declared, impatiently putting down the telephone receiver.

"How can I make his birthday arrangements if I can't ever speak to him?"

"Try again after ten, otherwise you'll have to try his work number tomorrow," Wolf muttered, not raising his head from his studies.

"If I don't get in first he'll get invited out by Ilse. Probably has already," she moaned. "And I've made sure I'm not working that Saturday."

"What he does is his own business."

"Yes, but everyone's expecting him in Medebach. Opa especially will be disappointed if he doesn't go."

"Well, keep ringing tonight until you get him then." He grinned to himself, deciding to wind Sabina up. "Unless he doesn't come home tonight. You never know! He might get lucky with some pretty nurse!"

"Oh for goodness sake! Don't be daft." She looked at her watch. It was nearly nine o'clock. "I'll try at ten-thirty. Hopefully he'll be in by then."

"You sound as disapproving as any mother, Liebchen! Honestly! Isn't it good that he's getting out and enjoying himself?"

"I suppose so," she admitted, then muttered: "It's more than we're doing."

Wolf put down his electronics manual. "Ah, I see. It's my studying that's the problem."

Sabina said nothing. It was true. Her father's occasional weekend visits were often the only time she and Wolf got out at the moment, but since he started his new job they had hardly seen him. Last weekend it had been a Saturday night dinner engagement at a neighbour's house, followed by Sunday spent with Ilse. This coming weekend he would be at Soest with Sophie and the twins – and no doubt Ilse too.

Wolf noticed her silence. "It's not for much longer, you know that. Once these exams are over it'll make all the difference. I can get a better job – we might even be able to afford a small house, if that's what you'd like. I know you miss the wide open spaces of Lane Head Farm."

"I don't expect that much space," she chuckled, going over to him and plonking herself on his lap on top of his book. "I know, I'm being selfish, but I just seem to work all day, spend my evenings doing housework and watching television or reading a book."

"Go and join a club or something: squash, a choir, flower arranging, indoor tennis, amateur dramatics. There must be something in the city to get you out of the flat and give me some peace and quiet!"

She gave his nose a playful tweak. "Flower arranging? Who do you think I am? My mother?"

"Yes, the way you worry about your father." He tweaked her nose back. "There's a folk group playing live at the pub tonight. Why don't you go along there and I'll join you in an hour. We can have a quick drink then we'll come back and you can give him another ring."

"All right. I'll go and leave you in peace."

"Good." He slapped her bottom gently. "Off you go then."

As Sabina set off down the damp pavements, she thought about what Wolf had said about buying a small house in due course. She had immediately pictured Sophie's chalet-style detached house, but that was way beyond their present means. If Wolf found a new job it could be anywhere, not necessarily in Dortmund. He had set his sights on a career in Research and Development and might want to go to Frankfurt or Düsseldorf, or wherever electrical engineering was big. Her mother had spent her entire life on the farm, but her own future could be excitingly uncertain.

The strains of a Bob Dylan number greeted her as she pushed open the pub door on which was an advert for the folk group playing that night. It was unusually crowded inside, the advert successful in attracting customers. The folk group turned out to be a duo comprising a vocalist and another young man playing an acoustic guitar. Both wore plum coloured, tie-dyed T-shirts and jeans, both had long brown hair parted in the middle. Brothers, possibly. She ordered herself a beer, then forced her way towards the alcove where the performers were and found a seat at a table with a group of fellow regulars. Her foot was soon tapping to the music as she sang along to the English lyrics.

When Wolf arrived at ten, it was to find his wife crooning James Taylor's 'Wonderful World' to the pub audience. He applauded loudly with them when she had finished and waved. She waved back with a huge grin on her face, shook the hands of the guitarist and vocalist who had invited her to sing with them, and joined him at the bar.

"Your new career?" he asked, as she gulped down the beer the barman had given her on the house.

"Could be!" she laughed, stifling a belch.

"You'll be joining the cast of 'Hair' next," he teased.

"Not on your life!"

"You enjoyed that though. I could tell."

She nodded. "Yes, I did."

Wolf looked across at the group. The guitarist was waving at them, trying to attract Sabina's attention. "It looks like they want you back."

She followed his gaze. "Shall I?"

"Why not?"

Wolf watched as Sabina consulted with the two men on the stage. Soon they launched into another ballad, Paul Simon's 'The Sounds of Silence'. Sabina was a big fan of Simon and Garfunkel and knew most of their songs by heart. 'Scarborough Fair' came next, the regular vocalist harmonising with her. By the end of the evening Sabina had been asked to join them for a few sessions at different venues of an evening. Wolf was happy to agree and Sabina was delighted at the prospect.

By the time they got in it was past eleven o'clock. Sabina looked at the telephone, then at her watch again. "Well I can't phone now, it's far too late. I'll just have to try him at work and hope I can get hold of him. What did I do with his work number?" She rummaged in her bag and found her diary. "Ah! Here it is."

"Are you going to invite him to one of your gigs?" Wolf asked, grinning at her.

She spluttered into gales of laughter then fell into his arms.

"Come on, Joni Mitchell. Let's go to bed before they book you for the next Woodstock," Wolf said.

*

Karl had no funds to buy a washing machine and no time now to go to a laundrette. He hunted through his scant wardrobe and found a crumpled white shirt hidden underneath a lumberjack style checked shirt. It would have to do. Pulling it out he took it down to the kitchen to iron it. He was due at Ilse's at eight for a pre-birthday meal, having been reassured by her that she was inviting her new boss and his wife, Hans and Corinna Münzel, too. At least she wasn't inviting any of her and Paul's old friends, he thought with relief.

He gave the shirt the once over with the iron, hung it on a hanger then went up to the bathroom for a wash and shave. Each night that week he had either worked late, digesting and sorting through the files, or had been invited to attend some kind of social function.

Everyone was either taking pity on his widowed status, or else making use of having a handy interpreter at the local restaurants as hardly anybody seemed able to speak any German. If he was to have any clean shirts for work next week he would have to visit the laundrette tomorrow evening. The following day was Saturday, his birthday, and Sabina and Wolf were fetching him on the way to Medebach first thing in the morning. Even so it would mean ironing late on Sunday when he got back, and tomorrow he would have to buy some groceries in his lunch hour.

Clutching a small bouquet for the hostess, he arrived at the flat in Iserlohn at eight precisely. Roslinde opened the door and welcomed him inside as Ilse bustled out of the living room attired in a mauve jersey dress, borrowed from Margit by the look of the short hemline. It clung revealingly to her figure, though whether intentionally or because it was perhaps a size too small, Karl was unsure.

"For you, Ilse," he said, handing over the flowers. "It's very good of you to go to so much trouble."

"Thank you, Karl." She kissed his cheek as she took the flowers from him. "But it's no trouble. I've got my helpers, you see," she said indicating her three daughters in attendance.

He laughed. "I could do with you lot at home."

"Having trouble with the housework, are you, Karl?" Margit asked cheekily.

"You could say that. But it's my fault. I've been out most evenings this week and haven't given myself time to get the chores done. It should be better next week."

There was a ring on the doorbell as the other guests arrived, and soon Karl found himself engaged in conversation with Ilse's new boss, the furniture salesman, while the women chatted to each other on the sofa. Roslinde and Edeltraud kept everyone well supplied with drinks until Margit announced from the kitchen that the meal was ready.

It was an informal dinner party, with Ilse's three joining in to make seven. Karl found himself at the head of the table facing Ilse, with Margit on his right and Corinna Münzel on his left. Frau Münzel proved exceptionally reserved, eating her meal quietly and seeming content to listen in on the conversation going on between Ilse and her husband. Margit took the opportunity to grill Karl on how he was finding his new job.

"Everybody's being wonderful," he told her. "They're all doing their best to explain what's needed, and trying not to be too impatient with me when I don't know how the system works. But I'm getting there. Silke's a great help, of course. She seems to be able to charm most people into waiting a bit longer for whatever it is they're wanting doing." He grinned. "They all call her '*darling Silke*'. I was a bit worried about her reputation at first, but now I see that she's more like a favourite niece to them all."

"Even for you, I think!" Margit laughed.

"Getting that way," he agreed.

"She certainly has a habit of buttering up older men. I think she's in search of a father figure, as she never knew hers. Killed in the war," Margit explained.

"I see." It did explain a lot, Karl decided. He reached for the butter for his roll and noticed Frau Münzel staring at him. She instantly averted her gaze but Karl took the opportunity to drag her into the conversation.

"I gather your daughter is friends with Roslinde, Frau Münzel," he said, topping up her glass of wine.

"Yes."

"Have they known each other long?"

"Yes."

Either she was terrified of strangers or very rude. Perhaps she didn't get out much, Karl thought. He tested his theory. "What do you do in your spare time?"

She looked blank.

"Do you have any hobbies?"

"I sew."

"In a group, like those American quilt makers?" he prodded.

"No."

He noticed Ilse trying to catch his eye from the other end of the table and let her speak.

"I've seen some of your cushion covers in the shop, Corinna," she said brightly. "They're beautiful. They must take hours to make."

"They do, but I can't sell them for much. People aren't willing to pay that much for needlework. If it were a painting or piece of woodcarving ... that would be another matter. These modern artists who just throw paint on and then expect thousands of marks for their work that took ten minutes practically." Once launched she was off, but Karl noticed she only spoke to Ilse and her daughters. He seemed excluded from the conversation. The strange look she had given him suddenly made sense. Perhaps she was aware of his recent history and had difficulty chatting to an acquitted murderer. He decided to leave her be and allowed the conversation to wash over him instead. He watched Ilse cleverly drawing Hans Münzel into the debate on modern art, with Edeltraud proving surprisingly knowledgeable. He took a sip from his glass and let Corinna make her case. When the conversation moved on from art to literature, Karl felt at a loss. Everyone except himself seemed to be well read, so he quietly got on with his meal, listened to the various arguments about the merits or otherwise of adapting books to film, and drank his wine. His mind drifted back to the nineteen fifties when he had been persuaded by Gustav Halstrup to appear in a British war film. It had been quite an experience, not least because of Gustav's attempts to fix him up with one of the wardrobe girls, followed on the same evening by Sarah and her then husband Perry's suggestion he share their bed. Gustav had been the initiator of that too, but it had certainly shocked Karl, and shown him a side to his sister-in-law he had been unaware of previously. How different from Katherine she was in that respect. Sarah seemed game for anything, whereas Katherine's only other partner, as far as he knew, had been her rapist, Andrew Kellett.

"Are you all right, Karl?" Ilse's voice cut through his melancholy.

Karl realised he had completely lost track of the conversation around him. "Sorry, I was ... er ..."

Ilse could tell he had been thinking about Katherine. It would take time, she knew, but sooner or later he would have to let her pass into history. In the meantime, she realised, he had been sidelined by too much talk about the arts. This was his birthday celebration after all, and so, while the girls cleared away the first course and brought out the main course of chicken in white wine and garlic sauce, Ilse brought up a subject close to his heart.

"It would be so nice to go skiing again this winter," she said to the table at large, but her eyes ending up on Karl. "I expect you're keen to get back to it too, aren't you, Karl?"

"Yes. I haven't really done much at all since the war, except for those two bad winters we had in forty-seven and sixty-three. I've got a bit older since then, I fear."

"You're still pretty fit, by the look of you," Ilse said before turning to her other guests. "Do you ski, Hans?"

"Yes, we often go to Winterberg at weekends and we've just booked a trip to the Italian Alps for Christmas."

"That sounds lovely," Ilse said. "Doesn't it, Karl? I did so miss a northern Christmas with all the trimmings. I can't wait for the first bit of snow to fall in Winterberg."

He smiled, caught up by her enthusiasm. "I'll be there like a shot, but I'd have to borrow some skis from Rudi or Stefan. Do you still have yours?"

"Yes, I think the girls have them tucked away in the cellar here with theirs. I nearly got rid of them when we left, but something stopped me."

"They are there," Margit told her, placing a stack of hot plates on the table.

With more talk about skiing holidays and plans for Christmas, the party started to go with a swing at last. Instead of a sweet, a birthday cake was brought out for Karl, and Ilse placed a parcel alongside it. Karl opened it to find a pale blue shirt and a blue and yellow spotted tie.

"Just what I need for tomorrow!" he laughed. "Thank you, Ilse."

By the end of the evening, after several bottles of wine, they were all laughing together. Even Corinna had got over her apparent anxiety about Karl's prison record, and invited Ilse and Karl for a return dinner soon.

As they saw off Hans and Corinna, Ilse saw Karl reach for his coat hanging in the hall. "You're not driving, Karl!"

He could tell from her expression that she was thinking about Siegfried's death. As far as she was concerned it had been caused by drink-driving. But she was right. He wasn't fit to drive.

"I'll get a taxi. Come back for my car at lunch-time."

She put a hand on his arm. "You could stay here." She saw the alarm in his eyes and smoothly amended her offer. "The sofa's quite comfortable to sleep on, if a bit short."

He hesitated, tempted to stay. Suddenly he felt very tired after his busy week. "Thank you. That sounds fine. I'm sorry, I …" He looked around for the girls but they were already clearing up the dishes in the kitchen. "Not yet, Ilse," he said quietly.

She reached up and stroked his face. "It's all right. I understand." She left him in peace, confident the time when he would yield to her was getting closer.

*

It had been a rush getting back in time to shave and get changed before work. He hurried in from the car, hoping no neighbours were looking out, speculating on his nocturnal activities.

When he arrived at his desk there was an envelope with his name written on it. He recognised the handwriting.

"Happy Birthday for tomorrow, Herr Driesler," Silke wished him as she made the coffee. They had established a routine of a mug first thing.

"Thank you. How did you know? Margit?"

"Yes, she said you were going round there for a meal last night, and that her mother was going to make a cake for you."

"She did. It was very nice." He opened the envelope and pulled out the card. He noticed it was simply signed 'Silke'. Perhaps she wanted to be called that rather than Fräulein Sommer. Everyone else did, so there seemed no reason why he shouldn't. He remembered what Margit had said about her father dying in the war. Her early life, especially after the war, must have been very difficult with her mother struggling to make ends meet. Like Ilse and Siegfried in a way.

She handed him his mug of coffee. "New tie?"

"Yes, a present from Margit's mother."

"Ah," she smiled knowingly.

"She gave me this shirt too in the nick of time. All my others need washing. It's an exciting Friday night at the laundrette for me. I expect you've got something much more thrilling lined up, haven't you, Silke?"

She made no reaction to his use of her first name. "Yes. I'm off with Mick to an archery competition near Heidelberg."

"Mick?"

"O'Reilly. The anaesthetist. He and I share a passion for archery, but he can't get away very often with his on-calls. Usually we shoot locally in some private woods nearby."

Karl remembered O'Reilly's scratched hands and Silke's similar injuries. "Do you lose many arrows in the woods?"

"Not many. We try not to miss the targets of course, but once in a while they go into a bramble thicket and it's a devil of a job to find them."

That explained the scratches. He could just picture Silke with her bow and arrows out in the forest, although his imagination dressed her up as Maid Marian with Mick O'Reilly as Robin Hood. Sabina, Richard and Paul had loved watching the television series, and bows and arrows had been popular toys in their make-believe games of cowboys and Indians.

"Well, I hope you both do well in the competition."

"Thank you. I'll be sure to tell you all about it on Monday." As she sat down at her desk a thought suddenly struck her. "November 29th. That makes you a Sagittarian. The Archer. You ought to be good at it!"

"You don't believe all that stuff, do you?"

"No, not really. After all, I'm supposed to be a Virgo!"

There she was, being gently provocative again. Margit was right. He wondered whether Mick O'Reilly's passion for archery was real or had more to do with Silke. Making no comment other than raising his eyebrows at her implied sexual experience, he settled down to work for the morning. He was beginning to feel he was contributing to the place at last. Two telephone callers asked for him specifically, and a blocked drain in the hospital kitchen shortly before eleven was speedily dealt with.

At midday Silke tidied her desk, about to head off for her lunch break. "Herr Driesler," she said, catching his attention, "if you bring your laundry back here after lunch, I'll get it done for you over the weekend."

"That's very kind of you, but I'll need to iron it on Sunday evening."

"No you won't. It'll all be done. Call it my birthday present to you."

"But you're away for the weekend. You won't have time to …"

Silke raised her palm to silence his objections. "It'll be done," she repeated. "Don't worry. Just give your new shirt a rinse and an iron and you'll be all right for Monday."

Karl shrugged in grateful defeat. "I hope it's not your mother who's going to be doing it."

Silke turned to put on her coat. "Just bring it," she said firmly as she walked out of the door.

He had to grin. She seemed to have very little respect for normal office protocol, but she certainly got things done.

He decided to drive into Iserlohn rather than walk to give himself time to get some food supplies in and fetch his shirts for washing. He ate a sandwich while he put the shopping away, cleaned up the kitchen sink and swept the floor in readiness for Sabina and Wolf's visit when they fetched him tomorrow. They might not even come in, but if they did, he didn't want his daughter thinking he lived in a pigsty. Lastly he hand washed some underwear, wrung it out and draped it over the clothesline in the cellar to drip onto the concrete floor. Chores done he headed back to his office.

"Washing?" Silke asked the moment he stepped through the door.

Karl held up a carrier bag then put it down behind the door. "I also brought some of the birthday cake Margit's mother made me." He sat down on his chair with a sigh. "It would go well with a mug of coffee later on."

"You look as though you could do with some now," she remarked. "Late night was it?"

"A bit," he replied reaching for the telephone to forestall any further questions.

*

"Happy Birthday, Karl!" his family chorused, glasses raised.

"It'll be your fiftieth next year," Anna remarked. "I can hardly believe we're all getting so old."

"Thank you, Anna! Just what I didn't want reminding of," Karl protested good-naturedly. "But I must say, I don't feel almost fifty. It must be starting a new job and everything, and all the socialising I've been doing recently. I don't think I've been out so many times in one week in my entire life."

"So they're treating you well, your British friends?" Dieter asked.

"Yes. Too well. I'm getting behind with my housework. My assistant took pity on me yesterday and insisted on doing my laundry for me this weekend."

"I'm surprised Ilse hasn't offered," Sabina remarked. "You seem to be round there often enough."

All eyes turned on her and she realised she had made her dislike of the woman too obvious.

"What's that supposed to mean, Bina?" her father asked.

"Nothing," she mumbled, sounding unconvincing even to her own ears.

Karl gave her a look that clearly meant she should keep her nose out of his life. "Ilse and I were talking about skiing this winter," he said to make his point clear. "But I don't have any skis any more. Could I borrow yours or Rudi's, Stefan?"

"You can have mine," Dieter said. "I don't suppose I'll use them again."

"Of course you will, Papa," Anna rebuked him. "We're all as young as we feel, and you're no exception. We'll have you out on the slopes this year, you'll see. It's just that last year was …well … you know … upsetting and no one felt like it much. Karl can borrow some, or even hire some decent ones. Ours are all so ancient anyway. Have you seen the latest ones they're selling in Winterberg? I'm sure they're much easier to ski on." She turned to Karl. "We'll all have to club together and get you a pair for Christmas."

"You'd need proper boots too," Stefan pointed out.

"Then it's all getting too expensive," Karl objected. "I'll hire some. Just like I'm going to have to hire a dinner jacket for the Mess Christmas do."

"I thought you'd got one," Sabina pointed out.

"Yes, but I didn't think I'd need it and left it at … home in case Richard or even Paul needed it."

"I'll get them to post it out to you," Sabina said, trying to make up for her earlier criticism. "You'll probably need it quite often for Mess functions now. It's strange to think of you in with all those military types. Do they know you were a POW, Daddy?"

"I expect so. Major Pascoe certainly does, so I don't see why the others shouldn't. I think Ilse's the one who's going to find it strangest."

"Are you taking her?" Sabina asked incredulously.

"I was thinking of it. I've got to take someone, so it might as well be her."

"But she hardly speaks any English. She'll be like a fish out of water."

"Who else do you suggest I invite?"

Sabina had to admit she was stumped, but she did not like the idea one little bit and for the remainder of the weekend she could not get her mind off the subject of her father and Ilse.

After they had dropped him off on their way home on Sunday evening, Wolf gave her a piece of his mind. "You mustn't hassle your father about Ilse like that. It's none of your business who he sees."

Sabina kept her head turned, watching the buildings pass by. "I wouldn't mind anybody else, but Ilse's the one person I couldn't bear as my stepmother. My mother hated her, and I do too. She's scheming and shallow, and thinks she can dump her husband as soon as someone more ..." She did not know how to describe her father. What did Ilse see in him exactly?

"More sexy turns up?" Wolf suggested.

"Wolf! Really!" she protested at such a description of her father. But he was right. That was what Ilse saw in him. She shuddered at the thought.

"They've all got it, you know," Wolf said.

"What?"

"Sex appeal. Dieter, Karl, Siegfried too, of course. I think he had it most from what I saw, but perhaps money helped there. You just have to watch women around them, regardless of age. It's not anything they consciously do. They just have it. And your father being newly widowed ... well! Women can't resist him. "

"If my father's so sexy, then he should be able to find someone else. The trouble is, Ilse won't let him."

"You'll have to try to find someone for him then."

"How on earth do I do that?"

He glanced at her and grinned. "I'm sure you'll find a way!"

SEVEN

Several pairs of eyes, both male and female, followed Karl as he walked into the Officers' Mess with Ilse on his arm. Karl was aware that Ilse's married status was a potential problem, but he hoped to avoid the topic cropping up. Steering her towards the ladies' room so she could drop off her coat, he waited along with two other men until she re-emerged, primped and preened, to face the throng. She had bought herself a dark blue velvet evening dress for the occasion, and Karl had to admit she looked stunning. She came up to him, slipped her arm around his and whispered: "I'm going to need a drink to survive this evening."

He nodded. "This way then." He led her through into the bar area where stewards in white jackets moved amongst the guests with trays of cocktails. The room was filling up but he spotted John Pascoe and his wife, Jill, alongside Mick O'Reilly, who had invited Silke as his partner for the evening. Discovering Silke would be going to the Mess had helped Karl decide to invite Ilse, since they knew each other. If Lt. Col. O'Reilly could invite a local woman, then so could he.

The company introduced themselves, and, as he had hoped, Ilse started chatting to Silke in German. At some point during the evening she would have to attempt conversation in English, but hopefully, once she had a drink or two on board, she would worry less about it. For his part, Karl felt remarkably at ease amongst all the mess kits, as he recognised virtually everybody there. It was not even as if he was a total stranger to Officers' Messes, having had a brief experience of them during the war before trouble had come his way. He remembered Ilse being very proud of his battlefield commission up to Leutnant. Now he was proud to bring her here.

Mick O'Reilly was the first to speak to her directly. His Irish accent did not help matters and Karl had to translate for her.

"Lt. Col. O'Reilly asked whether you are a native of Iserlohn," he told her.

Ilse smiled and tried out her English. "No. I am in Hamburg born."

"A fine city," Mick said and began listing its virtues. Poor Ilse struggled to keep up but Silke manfully helped her out and Karl was able to turn his attention to John and Jill Pascoe.

"We're so glad you felt able to come this evening, Karl, and that you found such a charming companion to bring along," John said with a nod at Ilse.

"Well, you all did your best to persuade me and I must say, I think it's going to be worth it," Karl replied. The cost of the evening was crippling, but hopefully things would calm down after Christmas, especially if people thought he had a lady-friend now. "Ilse's an old friend who lives with her three daughters in Iserlohn. We've known each other since the war." He was deliberately painting a picture of her as a single lady, a probable widow, and hoped that would prove sufficient to throw them off the scent.

"She and Silke seem to be acquainted," Jill Pascoe commented.

"Yes, her elder daughter and Silke are friends." The subject of Ilse had gone far enough and he changed tack. "I gather from John you have two children at boarding school. Presumably they are home soon for Christmas?"

Once off there was no holding Jill Pascoe back. She obviously missed her children enormously and was delighted to have such an avid listener in Karl, who was aware that Ilse was patiently standing beside him, trying to understand what was being said. Every so often he would translate something for her, just to give her some idea of what was being said, but he was struck by the fact that he had often had to do the same for Katherine.

A few minutes later they were all directed into the glittering dining hall. The seating plan had Karl and Ilse on the same table as the Pascoes, Mick and Silke, along with another couple. Ilse sat with Mick and Silke to her left, but it was hard work for Karl, nevertheless, to make sure Ilse was not left out of the conversation.

At the first opportunity when the dance band struck up, he asked her out to the dance floor. They had not danced together for five years, since a dutiful waltz at Siegfried's twenty-first birthday party. Circumstances had now drastically changed for them both and mutual silence marked their passage around the floor as they reflected on events and what might lie ahead.

As the evening progressed, he relaxed as he got used to having Ilse as his partner instead of Katherine. After returning from a trip to the gents', he found Ilse on the dance floor with John Pascoe, so he asked Jill if she would like to dance. After that each gent danced with each lady at the table, so it was a while before he and Ilse met up again.

"Enjoying yourself?" he asked her when she rejoined him at the table in a pause while the band refreshed themselves.

"Yes, surprisingly," she replied.

"Why 'surprisingly'?"

"I thought I'd feel very out of things, but they're all so very friendly."

He smiled. "Maybe it's because you're so charming and beautiful yourself."

She flashed him a dazzling smile. "And so are you, Schatz."

Again he felt a sense of discomfort at her use of that name, but he shrugged it off, and during the next dance he held her closer than before. At one point he noticed Mick and Silke close by and grinned as he saw Mick's hand moving lower down her back. He knew Mick's wife was flying over to join him for Christmas, and no doubt Mick was getting his last fling in before her arrival. Mrs O'Reilly, whoever she was, apparently ran a successful recruitment business in London, and seemed to give her husband a long rein. Most of the Mess members had commented that they were surprised she was taking the trouble to come out for Christmas.

When Ilse and Silke headed off to the ladies' together, Mick asked him about his plans for Christmas. "Spending it with Ilse, are you?" he asked with a leer.

"No," Karl replied, taking a sip of port to hide his amusement at Mick's obvious fishing. "I'm going back to England with my daughter and her husband to stay with my sons. I won't have seen them for seven months."

"Ah." Mick realised he had stepped into awkward territory. He did not want to bring up the subject of Karl's dead wife when he seemed to be getting on so well with Ilse. "You're lucky to have children to be proud of. My wife was always too busy with her business to find the time. Still, I've got at least one little Mick running around, that I know

71

of," he winked. "Right little bruiser, he is. His mother says she'll pack him off to the Irish rugby squad as soon as he's old enough."

For a moment Karl was tempted to mention his own illegitimate son by Ilse, but quickly thought better of it. Gossip was rife here, and if they weren't already familiar with his history from all the German news reports of his trial, then it was best kept that way. "Do you get to see him?" he asked instead.

"No. She sends me the occasional photo and request for more money, but that's it."

"Does your wife know?"

"Yes. She's quite happy about it actually. Takes the pressure off her to produce a sprog."

"Really! And what about you and Silke? Is she happy with that too?"

Mick laughed. "What's she been telling you? The little Minx! Wait till I get her on her own."

"She mentioned your archery trip to Heidelberg."

"Us and ten others – or didn't she mention them?" He saw from Karl's expression that she hadn't. "I went along as the token military contact to get them on the US Air Force base. Silke took up field archery when she was in the States and got together a group of archers from here to have a go. She's keen to develop more interest in the sport over here, but at the moment it's mostly an American thing."

"Field archery? What's different from normal archery?"

Mick laughed. "Get her to tell you when you've got a spare hour. Basically it's more like hunting, but not for real. I must say I enjoyed it." He looked across the room and saw Silke and Ilse wending their way back around the tables. "Don't ask her now, though, or you'll never get away with Ilse tonight." Mick leaned closer, chummily drunk. "You are, aren't you?" When Karl made no reply, he confided his alcohol-enhanced observations to him by adding: "She's up for it!"

Mick only had time to wink again before Ilse sat down between them, but Karl already knew full well that Ilse wanted to sleep with him again. He was the one delaying things, but after tonight the prospect did not seem so remote. It was ten months since Katherine had died. Ten long months since he had held a woman close and loved her. Could he do it with Ilse now?

As if she could read his thoughts she looked at him and smiled, then she looked at her watch. He checked his and was astonished to find it was nearly one o'clock in the morning. Around them were already gaps at tables where couples had gone home, most likely to relieve tired babysitters. Karl leaned towards Ilse. "Time to go?"

"I think so."

Karl tried to ignore Mick's knowing look as they said their farewells and headed out for Ilse to fetch her coat. There was a biting frost already as they hurried to Karl's car. He started the engine and began defrosting the windows. He had provisionally arranged with Ilse that he would drive her home after the event, so he had tried not to drink too much. But now the time had come, he was not so sure he wanted her to go. He had felt right about inviting her, right dancing with her and now he felt it would be right to sleep with her. He got back into the car and wiped the inside of the windscreen, which was beginning to clear at last.

He turned in his seat and rested his hand on her coat collar, his fingers brushing her ear lobe in an unmistakably intimate gesture. "Do you want to come back for a drink?" he asked softly.

"I don't think that's what you really mean, Karl, is it?" she replied, leaning up towards his mouth.

"Probably not," he replied, his lips already on hers.

He tasted blood, saw Katherine's dead white face, her throat a cruel gash. Jolting back in alarm he banged his elbow on the steering wheel and swore as the shock of his vision kicked in. Now he could see Ilse's look of bewilderment at his sudden withdrawal from her.

"I'm sorry," he gasped, reaching out to her with a trembling hand. "I can't do this yet."

"Why not? Whatever happened? It was like you had an electric shock or something," she said taking his hand and kissing his fingertips one by one in an effort to stop him shaking. He was shivering now, whether with shock or cold she was not sure. "Let's go back to your place and get you a stiff drink. You look like you've seen a ghost."

It was the worst thing she could have said. His vision had been real, he had been kissing Katherine that last time when she had just died after falling through a windowpane, but he could not tell Ilse that. He was almost shaking too much to drive, but he nodded and put the car into gear. Katherine's face would not leave him, however, and he quickly realised it would be pointless trying to make love to Ilse tonight.

"I'm sorry. I think I'd better just drive you home."

"If that's what you want."

She sounded peeved and had every right to be, he realised, but she had never seen him weak. In her experience he had always been the strong hero, although she was vaguely aware of what had happened to him during the war. But Katherine had seen, right from the start, just how frail he was, had always protected him from his worst nightmares and held onto him when he was teetering on the brink of a breakdown. Ilse had always expected him to comfort her in time of need. Would she give him comfort and understanding now?

"It's still too soon for me," he explained. "I'd thought it would be different tonight but when I tried to kiss you, I knew -"

"Don't worry about it," she said huffily, putting an end to his excuses. She busied herself wiping the mist from the interior of the windows and Karl sensed he had let her down badly, but there was nothing he could do about it now. He concentrated on driving on the icy roads, pulling up a few minutes later outside her apartment. He saw her to the door, but she made no attempt to invite him in, for which he was grateful.

"Thank you for coming, Ilse." He bent down and kissed her cheek.

She returned the kiss stiffly then entered the darkened building. She made the effort to turn round and wave goodbye, but he could see how upset she was by his apparent rejection of her. Shivering still, but definitely with cold now, he returned to the car and drove back the way he had come. There were lights burning in many of the quarters around his, their occupants still revelling at the Mess. Stepping inside his front door, he switched off the outside light and went into the kitchen to get a drink of water, which he took upstairs to bed with him.

He put the tumbler on the table by Katherine's photo, which he picked up and looked at for a long moment. "Oh, Schatz, I can't forget

74

you," he told her, kissing the cold glass. He sat on the bed holding the photograph in its frame. Her eyes looked into his knowingly, as though aware of what he had wanted to do that night. "I'm sorry," he told her. "But you're right. Ilse loves the man I was, not the man I am. I must move on, just like Anna said I should."

He woke late the following morning at a quarter to nine. Scraping the ice off the inside of the window he peered out into the deserted street. Most households would be having a lie-in this morning, except those with small children. He had planned with Ilse to visit Sophie and the twins later in the day so he could deliver their Christmas presents. Now he was unsure whether Ilse would want to come with him, but he needed to find out.

After a leisurely breakfast and a quick tidy of his bedroom and bathroom he went to the telephone. Ilse answered the phone after only three rings, which meant she was up. "Ilse Zopf."

"Ilse, it's Karl. I didn't wake you, did I?"

"No, I was getting some breakfast," she told him. "You're phoning about our visit today, I presume?"

"Yes." He hesitated, wanting her to initiate the decision as to whether she was coming or not.

"I'll be ready by eleven, if you can pick me up then," she told him. Her voice lowered as she continued: "Don't worry about last night, Karl. I really enjoyed the evening. I appreciate you're still grieving for Katherine, and I'm sorry I was a bit … brusque with you. I couldn't sleep after you left, as I realised how rude I'd been. I didn't even thank you for the evening. Do you forgive me?"

"If you forgive me for leading you on," he told her. "I think we'll just have to be simply friends for a while longer."

"That's fine, Karl. Now, I'd better get on with my breakfast or you'll be kept waiting and we'll be late at Sophie's. See you soon."

Karl put down the receiver, relieved at his indefinite reprieve. His vision of Katherine's death last night had come out of the blue, its clarity a worrying reminder of similar visions he had had after Siegfried's death. But those had been in the first few raw weeks afterwards, whereas this one had only occurred when he thought he was starting to get over her death. Would Katherine's bloody lips meet his every time he tried to kiss a woman in future? He shuddered as he had last night. It would be marginally better if it was a vision of her in the throws of passion, but to be reminded of her horrible death like that had knocked the stuffing out of him. He did not want it happening again.

He thought about telephoning Robert Murdoch to see what he thought about the likelihood of it reoccurring, but decided to write it all down in a letter instead to give Robert a clearer understanding of his problem. At least he still had Robert to confide in, but he also had the trip back to Lane Head Farm at Christmas to contend with. He hoped it would not prove a disaster by dragging up the memories too much, but everyone was expecting him now and he had to go.

*

Robert sat back in his leather chair in his study and read Karl's letter with deep concern. It was a real cry for help. His feelings of guilt about Katherine's death had remained dormant for some time, but as soon as he tried to establish a new relationship they had returned with a vengeance, completely blocking his ability to respond to Ilse.

Survivor's guilt was a common enough experience. Ordinarily Robert would have advised a grieving spouse to give it more time, but Karl was wanting a new relationship, had written to him asking for help. Robert could not refuse him. He had to reassure Karl that nobody was blaming him for Katherine's death. Karl also needed to be convinced that he was free to forge new relationships, that nobody expected him to stay faithful to Katherine's memory. But how to say it with sufficient force?

His mind flitted back and forth over what he knew about Karl and his relationships with women. He knew from Karl himself that he had never slept with another woman throughout his married life, with the notable exception of Ilse. That was why he had such a problem with her now, his guilt manifesting itself doubly. But with Ilse now the ultimate goal, perhaps he needed an easier stepping-stone to help him on his way, someone to overcome the first hurdle of permitting himself a relationship with another woman?

Robert snapped his fingers as the perfect answer flashed into his mind. After a long period of celibacy for Karl during and immediately after the war, it had been Audrey who had started the ball rolling again and no doubt she would delight at doing so this time. Even Katherine had countenanced Audrey's help in that way during Karl's mental breakdown. Audrey came with Katherine's approval. Karl had even mentioned to Robert Audrey's offer of comfort last year, indicating the idea was not totally out of the question. Audrey could be the one to help him out of this trough. But how to achieve that? And what if Karl found the link between Audrey and her estranged husband, Andrew Kellett, too close to handle?

Robert decided to ignore the last question. Audrey seemed Karl's best hope at the moment. He looked at his watch, saw it was not too late and dialled Sarah's home number.

*

The North Sea was not the place to be in December. The three weary travellers huddled together on their bench seat feeling each thud as the ferry crashed into the next wave trough. All three had taken travel sickness tablets so no one had yet made a dash for the toilets, unlike plenty of other passengers.

"How much further?" Sabina groaned, glancing at her watch. The overnight crossing from the Hook of Holland to Harwich seemed interminable.

"Another hour and a half," Wolf told her. "Fancy a beer, Karl?" he joked.

"No, just a bed. I'm beginning to wish we'd forked out the extra for a cabin now."

"Beggars can't be choosers, eh? You'll be wishing we'd flown, next."

Karl nodded. He could only afford the trip back to Herefordshire because Bina and Wolf had offered to drive him. Buying everybody's Christmas presents had cleaned him out, despite making the twins' presents. For Friedrich it was a wooden cart, for Freia a pull-along horse. Sophie had allowed them to open their presents early as they were still too young at eighteen months to know when Christmas really was. They had both been delighted with their toys and now, as he sat on the rolling ship, he remembered their excited faces as they tore off the wrapping paper. He wondered what Ilse and Sophie would make of their gifts - photograph frames. It was the best he could do, and at least they would be useful.

"Thank goodness Paul's looking forward to you coming," Sabina said to her father. "Aunty Sarah was quite worried about him before you left for Germany, but he seems to understand your reasons for going well enough now."

"Yes, thank heavens," he replied. "He seemed to sort out his problem with me at the airport, though Sarah probably played a big part in that. She's been so good to those two. I could never have left without her. I did rather desert them in their time of need."

"Richard always understood," Sabina assured him. "It just took Paul a little longer. He writes to you now, doesn't he?"

"Yes, his letters are perfectly friendly. I just feel our relationship has lost something that we'll never recover."

"Maybe it's just that he's growing up, becoming more independent," Sabina suggested.

Karl smiled. "You're right. That's probably it. He's not a boy any more but a young man."

The ship shuddered into an extra deep trough and the threesome grabbed their empty cups as they slid across the table. A fellow passenger groaned and ran for the toilets.

Wolf had worries of his own, which he now voiced. "This man, Andrew Kellett, does he ever show his face these days? Isn't he a danger for you still?"

Karl looked across at Sabina. He did not want to talk about the man.

"Apparently not," she replied. "His name is mud in the county after what he did to Mummy, and he knows it. I gather he spends as much time away now as he can and leaves the estate to his manager to run. He wouldn't dare come anywhere near Lane Head Farm now."

The lights of Harwich docks finally appeared on the horizon. Once disembarked, they headed off on the long and tortuous drive across country to Hereford. There was not one decent stretch of fast road and, compared with their speedy journey on the West German autobahns, progress was painfully slow. They hit the rush hour traffic in Colchester, were stuck behind heavy lorries all the way from Stevenage to Dunstable, and it was only once they were on the A40 past Oxford and travelling through the sheep-spotted Cotswolds that they managed to pick up much speed. By the time they reached Hereford it was mid-afternoon and growing dark again. Nevertheless, Karl could make out the familiar landscape of the Black Mountains silhouetted against the pale red sunset and he felt a lump in his throat.

The lights of Penchurch were like beacons guiding him home. The Walnut Tree pub sported its usual coloured lights around its windows, while other houses displayed their Christmas trees proudly through their windows, curtains not yet drawn against the darkness.

As they drove past the churchyard where Katherine lay next to her father in the cold, dark earth, Karl and Sabina both looked away. Wolf sensed the mood and kept quiet as he drove the last few miles out on the valley road and up the narrow lane to Lane Head Farm, perched halfway up the hillside overlooking the Black Mountains beyond.

The lights of the farm burned brightly, welcoming them back, as they climbed stiffly out of the car. Molly, the Border Collie was already loudly barking her welcome as Richard, Paul and Sarah opened the front door to them. Karl had made three previous homecomings to the farm: once, briefly, when he got married in 1947, again when he was finally released from being a POW in 1948 and the third time after his release from a West German prison in 1968. Each time Katherine had been there.

Sabina took his hand and led him up the front path, shielding him from the window where her mother had met her death. Richard and Sarah too were standing in front of it, while Paul ran towards his father and hugged him hard.

"Welcome home, Dad," Paul said fervently, dispelling all Karl's remaining fears about his youngest son.

"It's good to be here," Karl replied honestly.

It was too cold to stand outside and they hustled each other inside to the warmth of the kitchen, leaving the luggage for later.

Sarah had some mulled wine keeping warm in a big pan on the kitchen range. Tomorrow was Christmas Eve, but the festivities started with the travellers' arrival. She passed round steaming glasses, telling the newcomers: "The fire's lit in the sitting room so we might as well go in there."

Paul led them through into the festively decorated room. Slightly tattered paper streamers hung from the ceiling and central light fitting, and Sarah had perched the traditional holly and ivy fronds over the picture frames and mantelpiece. The boys had cut a good size tree and decorated it with the collection of assorted glass baubles and tinsel. The room looked just as it always had at Christmas, even down to the cotton-wool snowmen each of the children had made at primary school, who stood, as ever, on parade on top of the small bookcase. John Buchan's *The Thirty-nine Steps* still lodged on the middle shelf of the bookcase, just as it had on Karl's first ever night on the farm. His fingers touched it as he passed by, in homage to that event. In those days the English text had defeated him. Now he would have had no trouble reading it.

They all found seats and were soon relaxing and laughing together, while the travellers unwound from the long journey.

"Did you get to see the Apollo 12 Moon landing in the end, Dad?" Paul asked when Sarah eventually left the room to prepare the evening meal.

"Yes. Ilse's lot has a TV and invited me round there. It was amazing how different it all seemed from the Apollo 11 landing. I suppose I got more involved with it all this time."

"But you were watching it on German TV instead of British," Sabina pointed out. "That makes a difference, having translations interrupting the flow all the time. Somehow it makes it less real – more remote rather."

"I didn't notice," Karl said. "Ilse and the others needed to know what was being said of course."

It was the second time he had mentioned Ilse and Sabina felt bitter at hearing that name in this house. She had expected her father to show more tact. With a sigh of vexation she picked up her glass and headed for the kitchen, leaving the men-folk still discussing the Moon landings.

"He seems a lot happier now," Sarah remarked on seeing her niece.

"I seem to remember having a similar conversation with you last

Christmas, only that time he was getting over Siegfried," Sabina commented, noting that her aunt had already prepared most of the meal. "But yes, he is. This job suits him and he likes the environment there."

"Have you been to visit him?"

"Yes. We stayed for a weekend last month, met his neighbours, that sort of thing. They've really taken him under their wing, which is a bit surprising really. I suppose I have a somewhat jaundiced view of army personnel from Mr Kellett and his ex-army friends."

"It's because they were his friends they were all the same." Sarah measured out two heaped cups of rice into the saucepan of boiling water.

"Probably." Sabina turned to the dresser and opened the cutlery drawer. As she began setting the ancient table for six she remembered Wolf voicing his fears about Andrew Kellett on the journey across. "Do you see much of Mr Kellett these days?"

"Not really." Sarah stirred the contents of the large casserole pot simmering on the range. "He's kept himself very much to himself since the police decided not to press charges. Word got round about what happened with your mother and he realises he's lost any respect he ever had."

"Good!" It confirmed what the boys had told her.

"I see quite a bit of Audrey, though. She's as mad as ever when it comes to men. Irrepressible!"

Sabina grinned. "I bet you both have a whale of a time!" Audrey's reputation as a man-eater had been doing the rounds of the village for years. Sabina had first heard about Audrey's history of conquests when she was fifteen, and she had seen for herself at that time how the Kelletts had not got on as a couple. Sabina was following in her mother's footsteps in her devotion to one man, bucking the modern trend towards free love. She suspected her aunt and Audrey were going with the trend, a thought instantly confirmed for her.

"We get around. You'll see her tomorrow, though. I've invited her up, along with Werner and Vera, for a Christmas Eve tea. I hope you don't mind, but since you're here for such a short time we've got to cram people in to see you. I just wish I didn't have to work tomorrow, but Audrey and I are planning on a trip to visit you and your father early in February, so I can't use up my leave."

"February? Around the time Mummy died?"

Sarah nodded. "It'll give everybody something else to think about. Robert phoned and suggested it, actually, just last week. He thought your father might need some distraction around that time."

Sabina pondered the idea. "He's probably right. In fact, I'm sure he is. Let's hope there's some snow and we can get some skiing in!"

"You'll all have a laugh seeing me on skis!" Sarah said. "Right, that's everything cooking," she declared once the rice was simmering nicely. "Let's get back in the sitting room."

As they came back in, Sabina noticed her father was caught unawares by the sight of the two auburn-haired women. It was as though he expected one of them to be her mother, she thought with dismay. It was a fleeting impression only, as he quickly realised his mistake, but it made her appreciate how real her mother was to him still, and how awful the 3rd February 1970 could be for him.

*

Audrey burst in through the back door of Lane Head Farm clutching a huge poinsettia, its bright red bracts mirroring the colour of her face as she struggled to cope with all her packages.

"Lord, it's cold out there!" she commented, discarding her fur coat. Sarah retrieved it and hung it in the hall before someone spilt mulled wine or mince pie on it. "So, where is everyone?" she asked Sarah when she returned from the hall.

"Doing chores. They won't be long. Many hands make light work, and all that." Sarah picked up one of Audrey's carrier bags and peered inside. There was a bottle of whisky and one of port, a huge Stilton cheese, a box of shortbread biscuits and a plastic container with what looked like smoked salmon inside. "You didn't need to bring all this!"

"I couldn't come empty-handed. Besides, I thought they'd like a real taste of Britain again." She helped Sarah stow the provisions away before asking: "How is Karl?"

"Not too bad. Quite good, in fact, most of the time."

"Good. Have you mentioned our plans for February yet?"

"Only to Bina. I was waiting for you to get here and surprise him."

"I only hope it's a pleasant surprise!" Audrey laughed, hearing footsteps then the stamping of muddy boots outside the back door.

Richard, Paul and Karl entered the kitchen, faces flushed from exertion.

"Audrey!" Karl greeted her warmly. "Lovely to see you again." They embraced each other then Audrey stepped back to give him a scrutiny.

"You're looking well, Karl. You've managed to avoid this beastly Asian flu that's doing the rounds?"

"So far. You too?"

"Yes, but someone at work's gone down with it, so no doubt I'll be getting it soon."

Sabina and Wolf came in just then from securing the chickens for the night and feeding Molly her dinner. Just as the greetings started again, Werner and Vera Gimpel arrived and the party began to overflow into the sitting room. Werner was looking less robust than formerly and Karl took him aside to chat to his old friend and employee.

"Have you been in touch with Ernst Winter since you've been over there?" Werner asked him, after the preliminaries had been covered.

"We write every so often, but it's a long way to Berlin." Karl paused then grinned. "Besides, I have to be careful now I'm working for the British government, what with him being in league with the Soviets."

Werner laughed. "Poor Ernst. Still, at least he's survived this long without being bothered by them. But the day they approach him for something he'll use that gun of his on himself for sure."

"Perhaps they've forgotten about him."

"Perhaps they have. I hope so."

Werner continued asking after Karl's new life until Vera came over to tell them food was being served up in the kitchen. As Karl loaded his plate from the array of delicacies on the table he realised Audrey was behind him.

"Sarah and I are planning on a little holiday soon," she told him, reaching for a slice of smoked salmon.

"Oh? That's nice. Where to?"

"Iserlohn," she replied. "We thought we might stay with you, if you didn't mind having us for a week. Bina says you have a spare room."

"Of course you can stay!" he exclaimed. "That would be wonderful."

"We'd try not to get in your way, of course. I know you've got to work, but we could amuse ourselves during the day, try out the buses and trains, and we'd quite like to have a go at skiing, if there's enough snow."

Karl was delighted at the prospect of having visitors. "When were you thinking of coming, exactly?"

"For the first week in February." She looked directly into his eyes so he understood the reasoning behind their plans.

He nodded slowly. "That's a nice idea." Then he smiled. "You won't be seeing the place at its best, unless there's picture postcard snow everywhere."

"Not to worry. It'll be an experience, whatever the weather's like, never having been to Germany before."

"We'll certainly have to visit Medebach and get you on skis if at all possible." His mind began sorting out other details. "And I'm sure I can find some of my neighbours to show you around the place while I'm at work. I might even be able to take a day or two off."

"Wonderful!" Audrey exclaimed. "I'm looking forward to it already."

They had finished filling their plates and made room for Wolf and Richard, who were busy trading Apollo jokes. Karl caught up with Sarah in the lounge and sat with his plate on his knee on the sofa next to her. "Audrey has just been telling me your plans for February."

"I hope you don't mind."

"Not at all. I'm really pleased, but I understand why you're coming then in particular. Do I detect Robert's hand in this?"

She looked stricken. "Did Audrey say?"

"No," he reassured her. "But I wrote to him recently, and this smacks of his influence."

"You're right. It was his suggestion, but we always said we'd visit you some time, didn't we?"

"You did indeed." Karl wondered whether Robert had told them of the contents of his letter, but he doubted it. He had written very frankly about his problem with Ilse, and he could hardly imagine Robert divulging such details to Sarah and Audrey.

It was a mellow crowd who set off later that evening for the Midnight service at the church of St Michael and All Angels. Karl and his sons were not usually churchgoers but it had long been a tradition to start off Christmas this way, and the tradition was not to be broken now simply because Katherine was not with them. Sarah and Audrey were joining them too, before driving back to their homes in Hereford.

Karl knew it would be an ordeal, facing all the villagers again, and he hoped against hope that Andrew Kellett would not be amongst the congregation. It hardly seemed likely, bearing in mind his apparent ostracism since Katherine's death. The last time Karl had been in the church was for her funeral, but it was an altogether different atmosphere in there now, with candles flickering in each window, holly, yew and ivy fronds decorating each pew, and the nativity scene by the door. He had carved the wooden figures himself at the request of the church's previous incumbent, the Rev. John Thornton, and it was one of his legacies to the village, along with a share of the construction of the new Memorial Hall.

He nodded in recognition to each of the villagers, who all smiled warmly, welcoming him back. Sabina sat herself next to him for the service, nestled comfortably close, but he had no need of her comfort. He felt at peace, surrounded by his family and friends. He had promised Katherine's photograph he would cope with his first Christmas without her, and, so far, he was managing to keep his promise.

After the service he stood for a moment in the cold and dark with Sabina by Katherine's grave. He found it a little easier to be there now, trying not to think of her body lying a few feet away. He felt Sabina's arm entwine around his and he hugged her close, aware of her tears. He kissed her forehead lightly and she looked up at him, her eyes glistening in the starlight.

"I miss her so much, Daddy."

"I know, Treasure. So do I." He took her hand and put it where it belonged, in Wolf's. "It's cold. Let's get back home."

*

Richard drove them all in the Land Rover on Christmas morning over to Ledbury, east of Hereford, where his fiancée, Vanessa, lived still with her large family. The Turners had insisted on inviting everyone for Christmas dinner, as a few more guests would not make much difference to such a large gathering. Sarah was making her own way there from Hereford and arrived just before the contingent from Lane Head Farm. They parked in the roadway, greeted Sarah and headed en masse up the front path.

The Turners' house was a rambling, red brick structure surrounded by orchards. Vanessa's uncles all farmed elsewhere in the county, and her three elder brothers still helped on the family farm. Bill, the youngest, had introduced Richard to Vanessa, and often came over to Lane Head Farm to help his friend out at busy times. They now saw themselves as Richard and Paul's safety line when it came to farming matters, and Karl could not have wished for a nicer family for his son to marry into. The smell of roasting turkey wafted across the front garden towards them. Vanessa, her long tresses restrained by a hippie headband of tinsel, greeted Richard at the front door with a kiss under a large sprig of mistletoe, fresh from the orchards.

"Happy Christmas!" she called out to them all, waving the mistletoe gaily. She then kissed everybody under it as they crossed the threshold, but with an extra specially warm one for Karl.

The house was already humming with Turner relatives of all ages, and they were soon swept up into the bosom of the family, stepping over toddlers playing with trains and Dinky cars, shouting their greetings to a very deaf great aunt, and toasting everyone with a large glass of sherry as dinner-time approached.

The small children had a table to themselves in the dining room at one end of the adults' table. To his relief Karl found himself well away from it, as the over-excited and over-hungry youngsters began to squabble about who sat where. Getting the turkey carved and passed around was a marathon session, but eventually everyone had all the trimmings on their plates and could tuck in. Several conversations were taking place around the enormous table, but Karl soon latched on to the one dominated by Vanessa's Uncle John, a battle re-enactment participant. He was telling Sarah about their plans for the forthcoming summer, trying to recruit more musket men for their Civil War battles.

"I keep mentioning it to Richard, and I think I'm wearing him down," he was telling her.

"Did you ever get hold of a supplier for arrow shafts, John?" Karl asked, remembering a conversation from their meeting at the County Show two summers back.

"Yes, I did in the end. Not as good quality as I was hoping for, but then nothing is these days, it seems."

"You don't shoot arrows in battle displays, do you?" Sarah asked incredulously. "That seems a bit dangerous!"

"No," John Turner reassured her, "but we give archery demonstrations. Robin Hood stuff. You know the sort of thing."

"Ah."

"I seem to remember you were keen to have a go at one time, Karl," John mentioned casually.

"Yes. It's less noisy than shooting. I confess my hearing's suffered as a result."

John nodded. "Yes. I've found that too, from using the muskets for so long. Still, things like that come with age to us all. Just look at old Aunt Beatrice over there. Deaf as a post and I bet she never fired a shot in her life." He put a forkful of roast potato in his mouth, chewed briefly then asked Karl: "Do you fancy having a go after dinner?"

"What, at archery?"

"Yes. I keep my longbows in Bob's barn here, since he's got it empty enough to practice in. Mine's full up with all manner of junk," he laughed. "Mostly old tractor parts. No, I'm serious. We'll get the target out before it gets too dark and pot a few shots."

True to his word, John Turner led Karl, Sabina and Wolf outside after they had all enjoyed a coffee after their meal. Inside the barn it was already gloomy but John switched on the solitary light bulb, which emitted just enough light to see by. Against one wall were stacked several longbows, a large straw butt and a quiver full of arrows. He placed the butt on an easel against the far end wall, clear of obstructions. Karl could see from the numerous holes in the timbers there that many people had missed the target in the past.

"Right, " John said stringing up three bows. "You can all have a go." He turned first to Sabina. "This bow will do you. It only has a twenty-six pound draw. It's actually not a longbow but a flatbow, but it makes little difference." He sorted out six shorter arrows and handed them to her along with a finger tab. "Karl and Wolf, you can use these thirty-five pound draw longbows. When you consider the old archers used to draw upwards of seventy pounds, you should be all right. You've got longer arms than Sabina, so you'll need some longer arrows." He drew out several each from the quiver, then led his pupils to stand in front of the target, about five yards away. "The idea's to learn how to shoot, not damage arrows, so we start off quite close," he told them with a grin. "Can I borrow yours for a moment, Wolf?"

John showed them how to stand sideways on, knock the arrow onto the string, raise the bow, draw, aim and loose the arrow in a smooth action. He watched each have a go individually first, correcting errors of handling or technique, then left them to shoot their six arrows. A few went wild of the target until they adjusted their aim, but after several groups loosed, they found consistency of hitting the target, if not of accuracy.

"That's fun!" Sabina declared, handing back her bow when it had finally got too dark to see clearly in the barn. "I wonder if I can find an archery club in Dortmund."

"I'll ask my assistant, Silke, if she knows of one," Karl told her. "She's into archery, although I think she prefers field archery."

"I've heard about that," John said, intrigued. "They shoot at animal-shaped targets and pictures of animals don't they?"

"Yes. She told me that it developed in America for practice during the hunting closed-season, but it's taken off in it's own right now. She's trying to get more interest locally in Germany." Karl turned to Sabina. "We'll have to get Silke to take us along one weekend."

"As long as Ilse doesn't want to come too," she muttered under her breath to Wolf as they went to fetch the target butt.

Wolf glanced anxiously at Karl, but he had not heard. Sabina's attitude to Ilse concerned him, as he knew that Karl had spent a lot of time with her recently. Leaving Karl and John chatting happily, Wolf ushered Sabina back into the house.

EIGHT

Early in the new year Karl phoned Sabina to ask whether she and Wolf were free on January 24th to join him and Ilse for an archery session with Silke. Despite her misgivings about Ilse, Sabina accepted and entered it in her new engagement diary. The figure 1970 still looked very strange. She only vaguely remembered, aged eleven, the dawning of the sixties, but the world seemed to have changed so much in those intervening years. Now she was twenty-one, married, with a career both as a travel agent and a folk singer. She checked her bookings with the Brothers Grimm, as she called the singing pair. They were performing on three nights the following week, but then had arranged to keep the week of Sarah and Audrey's visit free.

When Saturday the 24th dawned crisp and clear, Sabina made a flask of coffee, dressed warmly in several layers and made sure Wolf had brought his woolly hat and sturdy boots before they set off on the drive to Iserlohn.

On the outskirts of the town Wolf reminded her gently: "You won't make any mutterings about Ilse, will you, Bina? It really isn't fair on your father."

She glowered theatrically before giving a grudging smile. "I'll try not to, but the thought of seeing them being all lovey-dovey together turns me quite queasy!"

They were picking up Karl first, then Ilse. Sabina ran up to her father's door, waving at the neighbour walking her children up the road. Karl had heard them draw up and was already waiting by the open door. He kissed Sabina on the cheek, picked up his small rucksack of provisions for the day then followed her back to the waiting Wolf.

"Couldn't be better weather," he declared. "It would be a bit difficult shooting in snow, I imagine."

"We'd want to be skiing then," Wolf said. "You haven't had a chance to try out your new skis yet, have you, Karl?"

"I told them not to buy me any! I could have done with the money for something else, like a washing machine."

"You'll get far more fun out of skis," Wolf chuckled.

"True," Karl agreed. "And Silke's laundry service is still operational, thank heavens. I don't know who's doing it, but they certainly do a good job. No tram lines in the shirt sleeves."

Sabina smiled at the reference to her mother's failings. It was good he could joke about her again.

When they arrived outside Ilse's apartment, Karl went up to fetch her, so Sabina did not see their initial greeting. When they eventually appeared, Ilse was dressed snugly in a padded jacket and fur hat. Karl held open the car door for her and they got into the back of the car together, Sabina gratified to see they kept to their own corners.

"Hello, you two," Ilse said cheerily, leaning forwards with a waft of perfume, totally unaware of Sabina's frosty mood. It was the first time she had seen them since Siegfried's funeral and she was keen to re-establish her relationship with them. "Thank you for the lift. I'm really looking forward to today. It should be a bit different, shouldn't it?"

"Yes," Wolf replied, sensing Sabina's reticence. He started the engine and realised Sabina was not going to make any effort at conversation. "Have you done any archery before?"

"No, but I've always fancied having a go."

Ilse kept up the friendly chatter all the way to the private woods where they had arranged to meet Silke and Mick O'Reilly. Their two cars were waiting by the gateway into the frost-canopied woodland. Silke was busy stringing a bow, with two other bows lying ready on the roof of her car. Mick was struggling to get a large, high-density foam boar out of his car. Wolf parked just beyond him and they all piled out.

"Greetings!" Silke called, putting down the bow. "You must be Sabina and Wolf," she said. "I've heard all about you both from Karl." She shook their hands. "I bet you're glad you've finished your exam project now, Wolf, aren't you?"

He grinned. She certainly had heard all about them. "Yes. I handed it all in this week, thank heavens. Now I can relax a bit."

Mick approached after dumping the boar over the gate, and was introduced to the two newcomers. It was going to be a problem as to which language was primarily used that day as Mick's German and Ilse's English were comparably poor. They fairly soon settled on Mick teaching Karl and Sabina in English, while Silke would instruct Wolf and Ilse in German. Once they were all equipped, they headed off into the woods, each with a paper target pinned to a straw butt under one arm, while Mick carried the boar across his shoulders. They walked a short distance into the wood, jumping across a small stream, until they reached a more open glade where Silke and Mick set up the targets, including the boar, at various distances and directions from where they were standing.

"It's easier today if we keep to this part of the woods," Silke explained, "but normally we would lay a trail of targets throughout the wood. Each target is shot from a peg an unmarked distance away. It's up to the individual archer to take account of dips in the ground, intervening trees and bushes or whatever and try to work out the range of the target." She pointed to where Mick was hammering two metal stakes into the ground over which he stuck the hollow legs of the boar. "You'll notice there's a nice bank behind the boar to catch any missed shots, otherwise you could be searching for lost arrows all day. But I hope we don't lose too many."

"Don't forget I've not done this yet, Silke," Ilse pointed out. "The others all had a go at Christmas."

"You'll soon catch up," Silke promised.

Sure enough, after they had stopped for a coffee break, Ilse was feeling more confident and able to join Karl with Mick, while Sabina switched to partnering Wolf under Silke's continuing tutelage.

After coffee the conversation was less on technique and more on general matters as they aimed at the pictures of pheasant, deer, squirrel and rabbit. Sabina finally asked Silke the question she had been waiting all morning to ask.

"So how come you speak English with an American accent? Did you live over there"

Silke laughed. "I sure did," she said in English, exaggerating the drawl. Then she grew serious again. "My mother died two years ago. Cancer. I didn't cope very well and I had to get away, so I rented out the house and got a visa to the States. There I really freaked out and joined a hippie commune on the West Coast. Flower Power, free love and all that. Fun for a while, but when my visa expired I was quite glad to return to sanity again."

Sabina was astonished at the revelation. Silke seemed so responsible now, from what her father had said. She couldn't imagine her with flowers in her hair, smoking pot and jumping into bed with anyone who came along.

"I can see you're shocked!" Silke laughed. "Don't tell your dad. He doesn't know my shady past yet."

And you don't know his, Sabina thought, but said out loud: "I won't." She cast a glance to where her father and Ilse were aiming for the boar. Try as she might, she hadn't been able to spot any overt signs of affection towards each other. They seemed to be treating each other simply as good friends, which surprised her, as she didn't think Ilse capable of such restraint.

By twelve-thirty they had all had enough and began packing up. The fresh air had given them all healthy appetites and they decided on a local hostelry used to hikers, where their outdoor clothing would blend in.

Karl had not managed to build up his funds since Christmas and was glad when Mick offered to buy everybody a drink. It was another matter when he came to look at the menu. Mick was clearly going to pay for Silke's meal, so Karl felt obliged to pay for Ilse's. He knew Sabina and Wolf understood his impecuniousness well enough to fend for themselves. He tried not to make it obvious he was choosing something from the lower price range on the menu, and fortunately Ilse made the same choice. A hearty stew served them both, washed down with a couple of bottles of red Bordeaux provided by Mick.

The wine loosened tongues and Sabina found herself caught out when the gruesome topic of the Sharon Tate murder cropped up. "Did you ever get to meet Charles Manson or visit his commune?" she asked Silke innocently, then clapped a hand over her mouth.

Silke took her gaffe in good humour. Her history was really not such a big deal, compared with what Margit had told her about her boss's murder trial. "No, California's a big place. No, my lot were as limp as old lettuce leaves, spaced out most of the time and tending towards the comatose rather than Satanism. I guess it was partly a reaction on my part against that side of things that got me into the archery. One of the older guys was also starting to realise the shallowness of it all and took me under his wing. Tom talked some sense into me about what I should be doing with my life, and we went off into the hills together and met these guys bow hunting. Or rather out-of-season hunting using these models. I suppose it combined my 'back to nature' urges with not killing anything, and Tom and I really went for it. It was Tom who sent the boar over here for me at huge expense, but he's worth it, don't you think?"

They had all been hanging on her every word, except Mick, who had not understood and who probably knew it all anyway. It was Karl who broke the astonished silence first.

"Yes, he's very lifelike, except he doesn't move and you're in no danger of him charging at you. Are there many other models available?"

Sabina let out the breath she realised she had been holding, as her father by-passed the subject of drugs. It was an awkward one for him, having had a very bad experience of them during the war through no fault of his own. Their effects had left him prone to depression and nervous of coming into contact with them again.

"Oh yes," Silke enthused, oblivious of Sabina and Karl's concerns. "But as I said, getting hold of them over here is the problem. If demand increased it would become cheaper, obviously. That's why I'm selfishly trying to spread the word about field archery. Until then we'll have to make do with the paper target faces most of the time."

"How easy is it to get hold of bows and suchlike?" Karl asked her, remembering the problems John Turner had with arrow shafts.

"It depends on what you're after," she replied. "Most of the equipment we use comes from regular sports retailers, but if you want the real traditional stuff then you have to make it yourself or find a specialist supplier somewhere."

Sabina noticed Mick was gazing out of the window, unable to follow the German conversation. She took pity on him and attracted his attention by first asking him to pass the wine bottle. "How long have you been in Germany, Mick?" she asked next.

"Nearly three years. I'm coming up to the end of my tour." He emptied the bottle into Sabina's glass. "I'm hoping for Hong Kong next, but you never know until that piece of paper arrives on your desk! They'll probably ship me off to Belfast, more like."

"I can see Hong Kong is the more attractive prospect," Sabina said, "but Belfast is probably more worthwhile. You're an anaesthetist aren't you?"

"Yes, so if I'm boring you and putting you to sleep, blame it on my job."

She laughed. "No, you're not boring! I don't actually know any anaesthetists. There must be far more to the job than just putting people to sleep though, isn't there?"

She knew she had given him a nice topic to keep him busy with, and let him ramble on while the others discussed the finer points of field archery. She was enjoying the day. She had even enjoyed Ilse's company, but then she had always liked Ilse until the incident with her father. Perhaps she could reconcile herself to them getting together eventually, but just not quite yet.

*

Sarah closed her bulging suitcase, convinced she had forgotten something vital. Karl had phoned to say there was snow in Winterberg, so skiing was on the cards. It had meant packing extra warm clothing at the expense of one of her smarter outfits, and she hoped she had made the right decision.

Having double-checked the house was secure, she picked up her bags and loaded them into her car. Audrey was eagerly waiting at her door and soon they were on their way to London's Heathrow airport. They were hardly under way before Audrey began speculating on the likely outcome of their visit.

"What if I can't get Karl interested? What do we do then? We can't report back to Robert that I've failed."

"He suggested we tried everything within our power to show him we don't mind who he has a relationship with. As I see it, that means if you fail, I must try, but it's going to be very awkward. We're ostensibly each other's chaperone for heaven's sake, but it does make things harder for us."

"We want things harder. Or at least Karl does."

"Audrey!" She returned to the matter at hand. "Our real problem is going to be persuading Karl he won't be showing favouritism by choosing you over me. He'll be the perfect gentleman all week and nothing will happen, you'll see."

"We'll make it happen!" Audrey looked at Sarah thoughtfully. "Let's make a pact, Sarah. We do whatever it takes, and I promise not to be embarrassed by anything if you promise not to be embarrassed. We make a full-on attack on him and get the job done – whether he likes it or not!"

"I'm not sure that's quite what Robert had in mind," Sarah pointed out, " but I do think we ought to make sure Karl likes it."

Audrey grinned. "You're on!"

The journey to the airport proved uneventful, and as they neared Heathrow they saw one of the new Jumbo jets coming in to land. The size of the beast astonished them. It seemed to hang in the air, rocking gently as the pilots adjusted the controls on the approach to the runway.

"Imagine living under the flight path of that thing!" Audrey shouted above the roar.

"Imagine flying in that thing!" Sarah countered. "We'll have to visit the States next."

"You bet!" Audrey agreed. "How about New York in the Fall? I can just see us debauching in Greenwich Village, gawking in Times Square, ogling the Statue of Liberty, chomping on all those lovely frankfurters!"

"Really Audrey! You're terrible," Sarah laughed. "I can see why Robert assigned you this mission."

"You too, Sarah. You're in on this as much as I am."

"Yes," Sarah replied, having further doubts now they were about to commit themselves to the flight. "I'm just not sure it's such a good idea." She hunted for the car park signs and headed in the right direction.

"Of course it's a good idea, otherwise Robert wouldn't have suggested it. He knows Karl well enough, and I think he's right. I know it seems a bit scheming, but don't forget, even Katherine asked me to help out when Karl had his … breakdown in nineteen forty-seven." She thought back to how he had been then: angry at his condition, superficially arrogant to hide his fear. He had treated her like a whore but she had never blamed him for it. She could remember only too well what he had been like before his mental breakdown. A smile crossed her lips. She was looking forward to experiencing him again.

"Well, perhaps we'll play it by ear and see how he is," Sarah said, unaware of her friend's musings. "I'd hate to upset him."

"I don't think we will," Audrey reassured her.

After the hour-long flight to Düsseldorf, they were relieved to find Karl waiting for them at the airport. Sarah hugged him close, hoping she was doing the right thing being here with Karl and leaving the boys at such a distressing time for them too. Then it was Audrey's turn to hug him. As they left the terminal building Audrey shivered and pulled the collar of her fur coat up higher.

"It's a lot colder here than at Heathrow," she said.

"There's more snow forecast," Karl replied, pushing their baggage trolley into the car park lift.

"I hope we don't get stuck anywhere," Sarah said anxiously.

"We'll be all right," he reassured them. "We're used to a bit of snow here."

The journey to Iserlohn took a little over an hour, plenty of time for both Sarah and Audrey to acquaint themselves with everything Karl had been up to since Christmas. They grew quieter as they approached the town of Iserlohn, concentrating more on the scenery around them.

"Here's my pad!" Karl joked, drawing up outside his quarter and giving a nod to Mrs Mitchell who was walking past on one of her missions. He had spread the word locally as to who his female guests were, to try to forestall the inevitable idle speculation.

Virginia Mitchell crossed the street to greet them. "Hello, Karl. Your guests have arrived safely, I see."

"Yes. Let me introduce my sister-in-law, Sarah Carter, and her friend, Audrey Kellett. Ladies, this is Virginia Mitchell, hostess of the street and maker of most delicious gourmet dinners."

Smiling modestly Virginia turned to Audrey and Sarah. "I do hope Karl will bring you for a meal next Thursday, unless you have anything else planned. It's always a treat to see some new faces over here."

Sarah looked over at Karl for his reaction to the invitation. Sensing his approval she said: "That sounds lovely. Thank you. What time would you like us?"

"Seven-thirty for eight, and I'll round up a few more bodies to make up the numbers. Anyway, I'd better let you all get in out of the cold. Enjoy your stay!" She departed in her usual brisk stride and Karl could not help smiling at Virginia's none too subtle nosiness.

"Looks like you've passed muster," he commented, hefting a suitcase in each hand. "Like she said, let's go inside."

He had made up a bed in each of the spare rooms. "You'll have to toss up who gets the bigger room," he told them, showing them where the bathroom and toilet were. "If you want to sort yourselves out a bit, I'll go and either put the kettle on or open a bottle. Which is it to be?"

Sarah laughed. "I think we'd quite like to see a bit of the place before we get too pickled, so tea would be lovely. I did remember to bring the tea you asked for, but I just need to find it."

"No hurry, I've still got some I brought back at Christmas." He looked at Audrey. "Tea, coffee or something stronger?"

"Coffee for me, please, Karl."

While he busied himself in the kitchen, Karl realised how good it felt not to be alone in the house. He could hear their footsteps overhead, a giggle, flushing water, all the normal sounds of an occupied house. Pouring Sarah's tea and coffee for himself and Audrey, he took the cups through to the living room, where his new picture had pride of place. It would soon be dark and he gazed out at his bare garden while waiting for the women to come down.

Sarah was first. She joined him at the window, looking out with him at the bleak scene outside. "Not much of a garden, is it?" she commented.

"Who knows what will appear, come the summer," Karl said optimistically.

Audrey made her entrance, flinging herself down on the sofa and bouncing up and down like a small child, testing its comfort. "They equip the house quite well for you, don't they, Karl? But they could have chosen nicer curtains and carpets! You could do with a few colourful cushions and rugs about the place to brighten it up."

He smiled ruefully. "I'm a typical male. I've not really put much into the house yet. When you go into Virginia's you'll hardly recognise it as a quarter, she's got so many knick-knacks, paintings and what-have-you."

"We'll have to find something for you. A plant or two might help, for a start."

"Perhaps I could bring some things back from Medebach," he suggested, passing round a plate of biscuits before sitting down to drink his coffee. "There's bound to be something lurking in a dark corner that nobody will miss."

After their refreshments, Karl took them on a brief tour of the area, before it grew too dark to see very much. They then passed the evening in a small restaurant that served plentiful, cheap food. Sarah was surprised how nobody seemed to even notice when they spoke in English, and the waiter took their order without a murmur.

"They're used to it, having so many British Army personnel around," Karl explained, once the waiter had left them. "Although it amazes me how few British people make any attempt to learn even a few words of German. I suppose it's because they live in their own little world here and only come out of it in a group or to places where they know they'll be understood. I'm exaggerating of course, but I do feel some of the British are unnecessarily timid about exposing themselves as foreigners here."

"I expect it's because we don't see all that many foreigners in Britain," Sarah said, "except in places like London. We're not used to being unable to communicate with our fellow man."

"Just speak loudly and they'll understand!" Audrey quipped.

"Well that's not so far off the truth," Karl pointed out. "I know when I was learning English it was infuriating when people mumbled away and I couldn't hear what they said. Speaking slowly and clearly certainly helps a foreigner who's struggling with the language."

"But you could speak as slowly and clearly as you like in German and I wouldn't have a clue!" Audrey said, knocking back her glass of wine.

"Oh, you'd be surprised," he told her. *"Noch ein Glas Wein?"*

Audrey had to laugh. "I see what you mean! Yes, please."

At the end of the meal Karl was very pleasantly surprised when Sarah took the bill off him and insisted on paying. The evening had gone well and they laughed their way back in the car.

The laughter continued the next morning, despite the very early start, as they headed for the slopes. They drove through Winterberg, already busy with weekend skiers, and on out towards the small town of Medebach a few kilometres beyond. Karl's family home was located outside the town, past the family-run sawmill and up a quiet back road leading towards the surrounding forest. Audrey had only briefly met Karl's family at Katherine's funeral, so wanted clarification of who was who and how to pronounce their names. She was determined to get the right vowel sounds, but her attempts left her in stitches when she could not hear the difference between what she was saying and what Karl wanted her to say, while the initial 'r' in Karl's brother Rudi's name stumped her.

"Never mind," he reassured her. "I expect they won't be able to say your name either."

It turned out as he had predicted, with Audrey hearing several versions of her name. She answered to all of them, and soon felt at ease in the large family, which grew even larger upon Sabina and Wolf's arrival at Haus Fichtenblick. After everyone had refreshed themselves with coffee and cakes, they headed off to the barn to kit out Sarah and Audrey with skis. Adele, Rudi's wife, had loaned hers, and Anna's proved suitable for Audrey. Rudi drove the sawmill lorry round to the house and Sarah and Audrey joined him in the cab, while Karl, Sabina and Wolf piled in the back along with Rudi's children, Andrea and Martin and all the skis. They drove to a nearby hill suitable for absolute beginners to learn on where Rudi dropped off Karl and his two pupils, then set off for more taxing slopes with the others.

Sarah and Audrey viewed the gentle slope with some misgivings.

"You'll think it quite tame by the end of the day," Karl told them. "Before the war, Rudi and I used to bring our non-skiing house guests here to start them off. I don't think I've been here since then. I must have been about sixteen or so - Paul's age," he added with a wistful smile. "It seems a lifetime ago." With a sigh he shrugged off the past and concentrated on the present. "Right, let's get your skis on and get moving!"

When he had taught Katherine to in the heavy snows of February 1947, she had been young and supple. Neither Sarah nor Audrey was as young or as supple, despite all their horse riding, but they made progress throughout the day without falling, mainly thanks to extreme caution. It was mid-afternoon, with confidence beginning to rise, when Sarah first took a tumble. After helping her to her feet Karl was uncomfortably reminded of doing the same for Katherine. Their eyes met and she saw his sorrow, but then he abruptly smiled as though determined not to be maudlin.

"Race you to the bottom!" he goaded her. "Just point your skis downhill and let yourself go!"

Caught up by his enthusiasm, Sarah did just that. With a shriek of excitement she careered off, picking up speed, Karl at her side all the way until she reached the bottom and ground to a halt at the gentle incline there. She then started slipping backwards and sat down quickly.

"Well done!" Karl congratulated her. "You looked quite confident there!"

"I think it helped having watched Jean-Claude Killy in the Winter Olympics."

"You'll be competing in it yourself next time," he joked.

"On my bottom!" she retorted. She untangled her legs enough to try standing but was facing uphill and the effort was too great. "Aren't you going to help me up then?" she asked, still looking up at him from where she was sprawled on the snow.

"Spin on your bottom and swivel your legs round to face the other way," he told her. "You've got to learn how to do it by yourself. I can't always help you up."

Making a face up at him, she did as he suggested and got to her feet just as Audrey came hurtling towards her. Audrey managed to stop by skiing into Karl, who held her upright.

"Right. It's a race between the two of you now," Karl declared, with Audrey still clinging onto him. "Make this the last run, and make it a good one!"

They took off their skis, hiked to the top of the hill then put them on again. This time Sarah was determined not to fall over at the bottom and managed at the end to turn sideways to the slope to see

Audrey following her in, with Karl at the rear like a sheep dog guiding them home.

"I won!" she shrieked up the hill, waving her arms and ski sticks in celebration like a six-year-old then waving at the lorry as Rudi pulled up to fetch them. "That was fabulous!" Sarah laughed, handing Karl her skis to stow in the lorry. "We'll have to come every year."

"Certainly you will! But you might not be so thrilled tomorrow when the stiffness sets in," he warned.

"Who cares about tomorrow when today was such fun?" she gaily replied.

"I'm so glad you could take a day's leave so we can stay another day here. You were right. That slope is tame. Tomorrow I want to try something steeper. Are you game, Audrey?"

"You bet!"

The weary skiers arrived back at Haus Fichtenblick to the welcoming aroma of ragout of pork.

"I think I could do with a soak in a hot bath first," Audrey told Karl. "Is that all right?"

"Of course! There's no hurry. We're not eating till later."

Audrey and Sarah retired upstairs. Their room had once been that of Anna and Stefan's daughter, Monika, who now lived in Winterberg with her husband Jens. Karl was staying in the room recently vacated by their nephew Uwe, who had just started an accountancy course. Lothar, the youngest, was doing his national service, leaving Haus Fichtenblick emptier than it had been for many years. It had seen many visitors come and go, and Sarah was sure they must all have felt as welcome as she and Audrey did now.

Refreshed after their baths they rejoined the family in the living room. Dieter was ensconced in his favourite chair near the cosy Delft-tiled stove, beer in hand. Karl was happily leaning against the stove, warming the backs of his thighs. He too was drinking a beer, as were Stefan, Wolf, Rudi and Sabina. Anna and Adele had a glass of white wine each, while Andrea and Martin were sharing a chair and drinking apple juice.

Sarah squeezed herself onto the sofa next to Sabina, while Wolf leaped out of it to give Audrey room to sit down. He poured glasses of wine for the newcomers then perched on the arm of the sofa. Sarah looked at Audrey and smiled, realising how much at home they both felt after only one day among the Drieslers. She knew it was really Katherine who had laid the groundwork for this easy relationship, and that to Karl's family she was almost, but not quite, Katherine herself. Except that Katherine had managed to learn some German over the years, Sarah thought ruefully, watching Dieter chatting away to his eldest son.

Karl did not allow them to feel left out, however. "My father was saying it's a shame we couldn't get Richard and Paul over here as well. I told him Vanessa's lot would be looking after them well."

"That's what this reminds me of!" Sarah laughed. "Christmas at Ledbury with the Turners. Another big, happy family." Her train of thought carried her further. "Just imagine what their wedding will be like when this lot get together with her lot!"

"At least you're a part of it, Sarah," Audrey said somewhat mournfully. "I'm not really a part of anything any more, especially since my parents retired and moved to Bournemouth."

"You're an honorary Carter-Driesler," Karl told her, "welcome at all and any family event and any time in between. Don't forget that."

"That's very kind of you, Karl. I shan't ever forget it."

Anna had decided it would be too much of a squeeze with twelve round the kitchen table, so they ate in the large dining room which had formerly been reserved for the guests, but which now doubled as a music and entertainments room. Its walls were hung with rather dark and sombre oil paintings of forested or mountainous German landscapes invariably with a group of hunters somewhere to be seen. In between the paintings were occasional trophy sets of antlers.

The pork was washed down with plenty more beer and wine, followed by coffee and schnapps back in the living room. The language barrier seemed to have disappeared for Sarah and Audrey. Karl or Sabina translated for them when absolutely necessary, but mostly they sat and listened to the flow of German and laughter around them, relaxing deeper and deeper into their chairs as the evening wore on.

When Sabina and Wolf had to leave to drive all the way back to Dortmund, Sarah and Audrey rose to see them off and discovered just how stiff they already were.

"I'm pooped," Sarah said to Audrey. "And it's up early in the morning, I think, so we don't miss a moment of daylight. Are you ready for bed yet?"

Audrey yawned. "There's your answer. Looks like everyone else is yawning too."

Rudi's family was next to leave for the short drive to their house in Medebach itself. When Dieter looked like he was making preparations for going upstairs, everyone followed suit.

"Sleep well, you two," Karl told them.

"You too," they replied.

The next day everyone else was back at work or school so it was only Karl, Sarah and Audrey who put the skis on Karl's car roof and drove to a more demanding, but still reasonably gentle slope for them to spend the morning on.

After reaching the bottom following Karl in a series of long turns, Audrey said to him: "I expect you wish you could go off without us and give your new skis a jolly good try out, rather than messing about on the baby slopes with us."

He began to nod then turned it into a shake of his head. "I don't actually. I need this gentle working out to get used to it again. My muscles are probably as stiff as yours at the moment."

"But you make it look so easy compared to us," Sarah protested. "I'm sure I'm putting far more effort into staying upright than you are."

He grinned. "Now you mention it, I am getting itchy feet to hurtle down a slope."

"Go on then. It's not fair for Audrey and me to stop you after you've spent all your time trailing around at a snail's pace for us. Is there a slope nearby you can use?"

Karl's eyes glistened. "Yes. Just over the next hill. If we walk back up this hill, there's a trail we can ski along that takes us to it. You two can come down slowly, making lots of long wide turns like we've just done, and I can have a good fast run."

Audrey shouldered her skis. "What's stopping us then? Let's go!"

The three of them set off back up the snow-clad hill, all three working up a fine sweat in the process. The trail through the trees was hard work in places wherever they met a gentle incline, but it was worth it when they arrived at the brow of the hill to see a long, inviting slope in front of them. It was quite steep at first but flattened off reassuringly at the bottom. Wide enough to give the two women plenty of time to negotiate their snowplough turns, it was also steep enough for Karl to let off steam and try out his new skis properly.

"Stop and rest half way, if you need to," he advised them. "See you at the bottom!"

He set off straight down for a few metres then began making a series of short, rhythmical turns, like he was swaying from side to side. It looked effortless and Sarah sighed.

"Gorgeous, isn't he?" Audrey commented, licking her lips.

"Mmm," Sarah breathed in reply, her eyes not leaving the tall figure now halfway down the hill. "I just hope we're doing the right thing. I'd hate to spoil things."

"We won't if we're careful. And don't forget it was Robert's idea. He ought to know what's good and what isn't for Karl. He seemed quite convinced this would be a good thing."

"I wish I was so sure." She saw Karl had reached the bottom and acknowledged his wave. "You first or me?"

Audrey grinned. "That's something we'll find out tomorrow. In the meantime, I'll follow you!"

NINE

The alarm clock woke Karl as usual at six. He switched on the light and his eyes met Katherine's. Today was the 3rd February. A year ago today, he thought, his hand moving from the bedside lamp to the photograph in its silver frame. He picked it up and held it in the pool of light, devoting a few intense seconds to her memory. That was going to be it, he had decided the night before when he went to bed. It would be the only way he could get through the day otherwise.

Carefully replacing the frame on the bedside table he threw back the covers, got out of bed and made his way to the bathroom. He hoped he would not wake Sarah and Audrey. They would probably sleep in, considering how late it was when they had got back from Medebach yesterday, and how tired they had been after all the skiing. There was no sound from their rooms or light visible under their doors when he came out of the bathroom.

Getting dressed in his suit he crept downstairs and put the coffee on to brew. It would be easier not to see them this morning. The quicker he got to work and put his mind on mundane matters, the better.

By the time he had eaten breakfast and tidied his room, there was still no sign of life from either of his guests. Leaving the table laid for their breakfast and a note wishing them a successful day's shopping and sightseeing in Iserlohn, he left the house and set off at a brisk walk to his office to ease the unaccustomed stiffness in his legs. A few more weekends spent skiing would be good, he thought.

He was early for work. Both he and Silke liked to be in and organised before the phone started ringing, but Silke prided herself on getting there first. This morning he had planned on inspecting the workshop stores and needed to clear any backlog from his day off yesterday before he could leave the office, but when she came in, Silke warned him that he was likely to get a series of visits or phone calls from people who had tried to get hold of him the day before.

"I'd better stick around in the office then," he told her. "Do you know what they wanted?"

"Major Pascoe called wanting to speak to you urgently, but said he'd call back later this morning. Another one was that woman whose hall carpet had moth in. I told her we were having to get a special delivery to match her existing carpet, but she seems to have the idea that if she speaks to you in person it will get here quicker."

Karl nodded. There were several occupants of married quarters with the same misapprehension. "Anything else?"

"Apart from that it was people returning your calls. I made a list." She handed it to him. "Did your visitors arrive all right?"

"Yes. No problems. The skiing was good and they both managed to make good headway without injuring themselves."

"That's a relief!" Silke laughed. "What are they up to today?"

"They want to try their hand at food shopping in German. They've offered to cook dinner tonight and want to experience being foreigners here on their own. I've lent them a dictionary and instructions on where to find a supermarket if it all gets too much for them to cope with."

"Good luck to them! I'm impressed."

Karl smiled. "There's nothing those two aren't willing to try." He turned back to his desk and the list of callers and began ringing the ones he knew would already be at work. He had dealt with the list, received several new phone calls and had checked on the progress of the replacement carpet ready for the physician's wife when she called by, which she did promptly at ten o'clock.

"She fancies you, you know," Silke muttered after the lady in question had finally left the office, confident her carpet was on its way.

"Yes, I'm aware of that."

"She used to give old Arnold merry hell, but you can't put a foot wrong."

"I'm sure there are others who don't feel the same way."

Silke nodded. "The big sergeant in the hospital kitchen. Don't eat there or he'll poison you or attack you with the meat cleaver."

"That bad is it?"

"Yes, but that's because his wife fancies you too."

"You're making this up, Silke. I'm forty-nine for God's sake!"

"So?" she teased, but said no more, keeping her head down filling in a batch of job instruction forms for the workmen for next week. The office was quiet for the moment.

Karl glanced at the wall clock and immediately wished he hadn't. Of all the times not to be busy, this was the worst. Ten-twenty, the time she had died. Once on that train of thought he could not derail himself and the events of that day sparked alight in his mind: seeing Kellet's car driving up to the farm; coming in to find him molesting Katherine; her threatening him with an umbrella and breaking the window; Kellet shoving her aside towards the broken window and making his escape through the front door. Now Karl heard Richard's cry for help and he pictured himself turning from chasing Kellett to see Katherine's head through the window with a cascade of crimson blood flowing down the wall. He felt again that sickening lurch in his stomach as he realised she would die, heard her gasping breath as she drowned in her own blood, felt her life slip away as he held her in his arms.

Fighting back the tears, he abruptly got up from his desk and blundered out of the office, avoiding Silke's curious glance. He made his way down the corridor to the gents' and shut the door behind him. The room was empty. Leaning against the door he sniffed hard, desperate not to break down, his throat tightening with the effort. Gradually his shuddering breath eased, the strangling grip on his throat relaxed and he was over the worst. He went over to the hand basin, looked in the mirror and decided to wash his peppery eyes. As he was doing so, someone came in.

"Are you all right, Mr Driesler?"

It was one of the corporals from the ambulance section. Karl nodded and began drying his face on the towel.

"It's just that Miss Sommer suddenly ran out and grabbed me and asked me to come in and check on you. She thought you might be ill."

"I'm all right. Thank you." He turned round and saw the young man's still anxious expression. He supposed he deserved an explanation. "It's the first anniversary of my wife's death. It just suddenly got to me, I'm afraid."

"Oh, I see. I'm really sorry, Mr Driesler," the young corporal muttered, embarrassed and unsure how to deal with the situation.

Karl gave him an exit. "Perhaps you could explain that to Miss Sommer and tell her I'll be back in a few moments."

"Sure, of course," he said, only too glad to be excused. "I'm really sorry," he repeated as he left the room.

Karl waited a few moments more to be sure his emotions were under control then set off back up the corridor to face Silke.

She was waiting for him. He cleared his throat. "I'm sorry if I -"

"Don't apologise. I understand totally. You sit down and I'll make us some coffee," she said gently, getting up to busy herself at the kettle.

Karl nodded and sat down at his desk, listening to the hissing of water as it heated and the clatter of teaspoon on mug.

"You were doing pretty well until then," she said to the kettle, not meeting his eyes, not wanting to intrude on his grief. "I found the same when my mother died. I learnt to cope, then suddenly, out of the blue, I'd think about her and that was me gone. I still do it sometimes, but not often now." She put his mug of coffee down on his desk. "I think we deserve a treat, don't you? I keep a special box of chocolates in my drawer for moments like this." She went over to her desk, rummaged in it and pulled out a large but half-empty box of liqueur-filled chocolates. "See, I've had quite a few moments already."

He took one and smiled up at her. "Thanks. It's a good idea. I'll have to get my own box in."

"We can share this one. Help yourself any time you need one." The telephone on Karl's desk rang and Silke looked anxiously at him. "Shall I answer it?"

"No, I'm fine now. Thanks anyway." He picked up the receiver, gave his name then relaxed as Major Pascoe announced himself. "Good morning, John. What can I do for you? I gather you called yesterday."

Silke soon realised it was not a personal call after all as she listened in to Karl's side of the conversation.

"As you know, I'd spoken to him about it on my first day ... Of course I'll deal with it ... No, he won't ... I agree totally ... I'll deal with it straight away." Karl put down the receiver. "Shit! That numbskull, Hussels, was caught smoking where he shouldn't yesterday. I suppose he thought since I wasn't around to notice he'd get away with it. Now I've got to sack him on the spot."

108

"Oh dear."

"Where's he working today?"

"Nurses' accommodation. Bathroom," she told him instantly.

"Blast. I'll have to get Matron or someone to haul him out so I can speak to him."

"Shall I do that? I can go up there myself and get him."

"I'll let her know you're coming, and that the job mightn't get finished today, unless I do it myself. What was he doing anyway?"

"Replacing broken tiles. You'll have to finish it if you can, as there's nobody else free today. They're all busy."

"It would be easier to let him finish then sack him, but Major Pascoe insisted he went immediately. Oh well, I'd better find myself a pair of overalls after I've done the deed. You go and haul him out and I'll speak to Matron about getting up there myself."

The nurses' rooms were above the wards on the top floor of the hospital, so Karl knew it would take Silke a few minutes to locate Hussels and bring him down. In the meantime he cleared it with Matron for him to go up and finish the job himself later on. He would need a female escort to enter the holy of holies.

When he arrived back with Silke, Hussels was aware he was in trouble as Silke had made him pack up his tool bag and bring it with him. It was confirmed when she retreated diplomatically to fill the kettle from the tap in the ladies'. He put down his tools and stood by Karl's desk, eyes meekly downcast.

"You know why you're here, Hussels?" Karl began.

"Yes, Herr Driesler. I was caught smoking by the oxygen cylinders."

"Why, after everything I said last time?"

"I forgot, honest. I've been smoking there ever since I first worked here. Herr Arnold never said anything and I just got into the habit, like."

"Habit? It's a very dangerous habit. So dangerous we can't risk you doing it again. I'm afraid I've got to ask you to leave immediately. You're fired as from now." He saw the look of dismay on the young man's face.

"But I support my mother and younger sister, Herr Driesler! How'll we manage?"

"I'll give you a good reference, Hussels. Apart from your stupidity with regard to smoking you're basically a good worker. I'll do all I can to help get you another position. You've just got to start looking." He noticed Silke had returned with the kettle. "Fräulein Sommer will deal with the paperwork, if you go and collect your belongings. You can leave your tools in here. I'll have to finish your job for you."

Hussells looked stricken and leaned on Karl's desk to plead with him. "Can't I have another chance, please? I promise I won't smoke there ever again."

"I'm very sorry. Apparently it's the commanding officer's decision. There's nothing more I can do."

Hussells scowled, but held his tongue, realising he would need Karl's reference. He stamped out of the office and Karl exhaled deeply.

"What a morning! How far had he got with the job, did you notice?"

"About half done, I should think, and too much of a mess to leave overnight. The nurses will be wanting to use the showers."

"Then the sooner I start, the sooner it will be finished. Would you mind getting me a sandwich or something for lunch? I won't have time to get out."

"Are your visitors not expecting you back for lunch?"

"No. They were going to have a snack in town."

"I'll get you something then."

Karl picked up Hussells' tool bag and headed for the workmen's stores where he found a set of overalls. Next he reported to Matron's office for an escort to the nurses' rooms on the top floor. Assured the bathrooms were unoccupied, he set about fixing the tiles in place that Hussells had left. It was mid-afternoon by the time he had finished. He tidied up, removed the warning notices from the doors to prevent any nurses barging in on him in a state of undress, and replaced them with others asking the nurses not to use the showers in question until the following day. He then returned to Matron's office to inform her the work was complete.

"Thank you for seeing to it yourself, Mr Driesler," she said. "We do appreciate it."

"My pleasure, Matron. I'm only glad it was something I could tackle."

By the time he got back to the office he was starving. Silke was on the phone but she pointed to the carrier bag on his desk. In it he found a box containing a cold chicken leg, one ham and one cheese roll, salad and an apple. He also found a bottle of apple juice.

He had nearly finished eating when he realised he hadn't thought about Katherine since the morning.

"Do you want a chocolate?" Silke asked, holding out the box.

"That obvious, was it?"

"Yes."

He smiled at her. "No, I'll be all right."

'Darling' Silke. The epithet was so true. It was the Silkes of this world who kept the wheels well oiled for everyone else. Like Katherine. He finished his apple and settled back to work.

*

The smell that greeted him when he opened the front door was mouth-watering.

"Hello!" he called out.

Audrey popped through the kitchen door, tea towel in hand. "Oh, hello, Karl." She came up and gave him a peck on the cheek. "How was your day?"

She looked and sounded just like somebody's wife, he thought, except for the significance of her question. "Oh, not too bad," he said. "I got through it. I just had to fire one of my workers, that's all."

Sarah had joined them in the hall. "All right, Karl?" she asked quietly.

He nodded. "And you?"

"Fine. We kept ourselves busy."

"Good." He hoped that was the end to the questioning. "That smells delicious, whatever it is. Can I get you girls a drink?"

"I don't suppose you have a gin and tonic, do you?" Audrey asked.

"I got some in especially for you," he told her. "You too, Sarah?"

He was in the middle of pouring their gins and a beer for himself when the telephone rang. It was Sabina.

"Hello, Daddy. Are you all right? I've been thinking about you all day."

"That's very sweet of you, Treasure. I'm not too bad. Aunty Sarah and Audrey are looking after me very well now. They've cooked something marvellous for dinner. We're going to open a bottle of wine, toast Mummy and enjoy the evening. How about you?"

"We're going out for a meal as I didn't want to sit at home and brood." She swallowed hard. "I'm so glad you've got company today. It would have been awful for you, if you'd been all alone."

He heard the tears in her voice. "I'm sure we'd have got together somehow," he said, stifling his own tears.

"Yes, we would have," she agreed. Her voice steadied as she continued: "I phoned the boys earlier, and they're both fine. The Turners invited them both round for the evening. They sent their love to you."

"Thank you. Well you enjoy your meal, Treasure, and I'll enjoy mine. Thank you for calling."

"'Bye, Daddy."

"'Bye, Beauty." He heard her gasp with the significance of the pet name. "Wasn't that Mummy's pet name from her parents?" she asked tremulously.

"Yes. It can be yours now."

"Oh."

He heard a click and the line went dead. He hoped he hadn't upset her. He turned to find Sarah standing in the hall with him.

"That was sweet of you," Sarah said, "calling her 'Beauty'."

"She deserves it." He looked at her. "You were 'Beauty' too, weren't you?"

"Yes. It was a thing of my mother's. If she couldn't remember our names in time, she just called us both 'Beauty'. Daddy tried to differentiate sometimes and called me 'Ladybelle', so we each had a pet name, but more often than not I got called 'Beauty' too. I liked it. I hope Bina does." She looked past him towards the dining room. "Is that gin ready? Dinner's not far off."

"I'll get it."

He had just handed over their drinks when the telephone rang again. This time it was Anna calling to see how he was. He drank his beer while chatting to her then joined Audrey and Sarah in the living room. "Hopefully that's it now. No more well-wishers. We can eat in peace."

The meal Sarah and Audrey served up astonished him.

"Where on earth did you get hold of the venison?" he asked, scraping the last delicious morsels off his plate.

"A butcher's, of course!" Sarah told him. "The word is *Rehfleisch*. We've learnt lots of words today, haven't we, Audrey? I think the shopkeepers were most impressed with our efforts."

"I'm sure they were," Karl said with a laugh. "You must have spent the whole afternoon cooking. And where did this casserole pot come from?"

"We borrowed it from Virginia."

"And had a cup of tea with her too," Audrey added. "She's very nosy, isn't she?"

"Bored, more like, but I know what you mean. So did you fill her in on all the gossip?"

"I'm afraid she wheedled out of us why we were here," Sarah admitted. "Still, it's best she knows. She sent her best wishes for you and promised to try to keep the conversation away from sensitive ground on Thursday when we go round there."

"That's very thoughtful of her." He topped up their glasses with the claret Audrey had bought then raised his glass. "To the cooks!" He took a sip then remembered what he had said to Sabina. "And to Katherine!"

There was a moment's silence before both women responded quietly. "To Katherine!"

What composure they had all managed to retain disappeared at that moment. Sarah's face crumpled, Audrey joined in and Karl felt the familiar prickling of tears. Blinking them back he stood up to clear the dirty dishes away while Sarah and Audrey blew their noses and got themselves under control. They joined him a minute later, red-eyed, in the kitchen where he had stacked everything neatly by the sink and told him to go back to the dining room while they brought in the dessert.

"Bread and butter pudding!" Audrey announced with a flourish, laying the piping hot dish on the tablemat.

"Delicious!" Karl declared, relieved to see their spirits raised again. Temporarily, probably. It was going to be a difficult evening after all, unless they were more careful. He noticed Audrey had brought out a

Sauternes as the dessert wine, so poured them each a glass. "It's strange how such an old standby as bread and butter pudding takes on a new dimension when served up with cream. The ugly duckling becomes an elegant swan of puddings!" He raised his glass. "To ugly ducklings everywhere!"

Audrey giggled. "To ugly ducklings!"

They tucked in to the fluffy white pudding, Audrey and Sarah arguing the meantime over which was the best fairy story. Audrey had always favoured Sleeping Beauty, while Sarah insisted that Rumpelstiltskin was a much more interesting tale.

"The peasant girl-turned-princess defeats the dwarf by finding out his name. That's far more fun than some soppy princess being woken up by a boring old prince." She turned to Karl. "What do you think? Which is your favourite?"

He sat back in his chair, twirling the stem of his wineglass between his fingers. "I don't remember many now, but I think I'd have to go for Little Red Riding Hood."

"Why?"

He grinned. "It's violent and the hunter kills the wolf."

"Typical male!" Audrey shrieked. "Not a spark of romance in him."

"You're saying we men can't be romantic?" he protested.

Sarah and Audrey exchanged glances, Audrey giving an almost imperceptible nod. "Prove you are!" she teased, looking up at him coyly from under her long eyelashes.

He was completely taken aback by the sexual energy unleashed by that look, by her seductive smile, her air of expectation. Her blue eyes held his, waiting for him to make a move, a move he was astonished to find he wanted to make. He had not been able to resist her charms back in 1947, and her magic still worked for him as forcefully as ever. She was a no-strings, pleasure-of-the-moment woman, who could offer him the solace he needed; had indeed offered it before, shortly after Katherine's death. It would not be difficult to accept her offer this time, except … for Sarah.

Sarah saw him hesitate, knew now they had to play him carefully, reeling him in slowly and gently, giving him time to consider. She wanted no regrets or recriminations. They must not force him into this. She stood up. "Who's for coffee?"

"Yes, please," Audrey murmured, accepting the delay, the teasing process all part of the gentle art of seduction.

Karl looked up at Sarah and saw an odd expression in his sister-in-law's eyes: one he was not expecting, one he had last seen a very long time ago on a visit to her flat in London. She too was offering her services. He nodded.

"You go on through to the living room, Karl," she said, quickly stacking the dishes together, "and I'll bring it in.".

Karl left them to clear the table while he went back to the lounge, perplexed but not alarmed by the turn of events. It had suddenly occurred to him that this was why they had come, sent by Robert in response to his letter. He switched on the radio, found some light music playing and placed himself deliberately on the sofa to see which of the two would sit next to him.

He understood exactly what it was they and Robert were telling him: he was free to love again. They were giving him their wholehearted consent and he should not offend them by refusing.

Sarah brought in a tray with the coffee, while Audrey shut the door behind her. Neither sat next to him, choosing the armchairs instead, and disappointment washed over him.

Was he wrong in his assumption? What he had thought they were offering, he discovered with some shock, he really wanted. It had been a year since he had physically loved a woman, a year when the idea of having anyone other than Katherine had been impossible. His feelings for Ilse had proved that. But now Audrey had come along. Sarah too. He would be happy with either one of them to make an official end to his year of mourning. They were trusted and reassuringly familiar. They posed no threat, no demands, just release, but he was wary now of making a false move.

"Would you like a chocolate, Karl?" Sarah asked him, leaning forward to pass him his coffee and pointing to the box of Swiss chocolates Audrey was holding on her lap.

He smiled, remembering Silke's ministrations earlier. "I'd love one," he said boldly. Audrey stood up and approached him, her fingers circling slowly above the chocolates in an effort to choose the right one for him. Selecting one she delicately picked it up and popped it in his mouth.

"A hard one," she warned him playfully. "Brazil nut."

He felt convinced now. They were playing with him, both of them, and he was loving it. As if in confirmation of his suspicions, Audrey sat down next to him but sideways on so she was facing him. The signals she was emitting were unmistakable now, but still she refrained from going further. The first time they had made love together she had made all the running. He had needed a lot of urging to take her in an act of illegal fraternisation on the same day Katherine's father had died. But it had been worth it. He knew it would be now. But what of Sarah?

He noticed she had moved round the coffee table and was standing next to him. Audrey leaned in front of Karl and passed Sarah the box of chocolates. She took one then held the box in front of Karl.

"Choose one," Sarah said, looking deep into his eyes, wanting to be as much part of this now as Audrey.

"You tell me which," he replied carefully, unable to risk offending either by choosing one over the other.

Audrey gave a girlish giggle. "If you can't make up your mind, Karl, have two together." She laughed again when she saw both Karl and Sarah's jaw drop in disbelief. She had never shared a man before, whereas Sarah had at least participated in a threesome, albeit with two men: her husband and his soon-to-be lover. If this was what it took then she was willing to give it a go. Now all she needed was for Sarah and Karl to agree.

Karl was first. "All right, I will." Taking them both by the hand he stood up. "I'm not making a mistake, am I?" he asked, just to double-check their intentions.

Audrey looked enquiringly at Sarah, who seemed distinctly shocked but nevertheless nodded her approval since Karl seemed game. "No, you're not," Audrey said, unable to control herself any longer. She stood on tiptoe and kissed him full on the mouth, his response sending a surge of excitement deep within her body.

As their lips parted Karl was aware of Sarah on his other side. He had never kissed her like this, hoped he would not try to compare her with Katherine. He turned to her to find out. He bent his head down and found her mouth reaching eagerly for his. As their lips met, he held her head in both hands, feeling that same hair, but knowing it was different. Her kiss was different, her taste too. She wasn't Katherine. As their lips parted he looked into her green eyes, like Katherine's, but also unlike, and smiled. He had no problems with this.

Audrey was already by the door to the hall. She nodded towards the stairs and Karl led Sarah up after her. Audrey opened the door to Karl's bedroom and waited, hand on hip like a whore. As he passed by her he reached for her hand too and drew both women into his room.

Faced with both of them he knew he had to make a choice at some point, but now was not the time for deliberating. Audrey was already peeling her clothes off, but Sarah was more hesitant. He put his hands on her waist and raised her soft woollen jumper up over her head, then felt her hands reaching for his jacket. Behind him Audrey groped blindly for his tie and undid the knot, while Sarah started on the buttons of his shirt.

This is crazy, he thought to himself. What are we doing? By now he had undone Sarah's skirt and Audrey was undoing his trousers. Sandwiched between them he could feel Audrey's hot breath and her nipples on his back while Sarah was stepping out of her skirt. Audrey's warm fingers were busy tracing the pattern of scars on his back as he helped Sarah with the rest of her clothing. Audrey's expert hands were moving towards his hips now and he turned towards her, relishing the attention she would give him, knowing they were doing this for him and that he should enjoy it. Now it was Sarah who warmed his back with her body, her hands caressing his chest, her lips kissing his shoulder blades. Audrey was doing her work too well and the time was approaching when he needed to make his choice. He drew them both over to the bed, and as they got in he found himself facing Audrey. Suddenly he knew which one he wanted. Deliberately he drew Sarah closer, kissing her long and hard to show his intent. Audrey would have to wait. He couldn't any more.

Sarah was more than ready for his embrace, accepting him eagerly, aware of just how long she had waited for this precious moment. His hot breath was beating against her stretched-back throat as he felt his own excitement mounting along with hers. As he clutched her shoulders with a groan she gave herself up to him, gasping her own release.

He lay still a moment, collecting his breath, then kissed her neck softly and whispered: "Thank you."

"My pleasure!" she murmured, smiling up into those so familiar grey eyes and kissing his lips, aware of Audrey waiting impatiently beside them.

Karl too sensed Audrey's anguish. "Excuse me, duty calls," he said to Sarah, moving off her.

"Thank God, I can't wait much longer!" Audrey moaned. "Watching you was such a turn-on, Karl."

He grinned and pulled her towards him so she was snuggled with her back against his chest. One hand caressed her breasts as the other made its way lower down her body. He had scarcely touched her before she was writhing and shuddering in his arms, moaning with far more gusto than Sarah had.

When her shudders had died down he kissed the back of her neck. "All right now?"

"You bet!" she drawled, reaching up behind her to stroke his hair.

They lay together for a while, warm and snug, chatting about nothing in particular until Karl realised all the lights were still blazing downstairs. He eased himself over Audrey's body, got out of bed and put on his dressing gown.

"We never had that coffee," Sarah murmured.

"Would you like some?" Karl asked.

"I'd rather have tea now, I think," she replied.

Karl looked at Audrey. "You too?"

"Why not? It's not often I'm waited on in bed by my lover!"

They waited, demurely covered, avoiding each other's gaze at first, until Audrey suddenly giggled.

"That was actually quite fun, wasn't it? Not as embarrassing as I thought it was going to be."

Sarah smiled back. "I agree. We've certainly seen a different side to each other, haven't we?"

"Do you think Patrick and Ron could be persuaded to try something like this?" Audrey asked.

Sarah considered it for a moment then pulled a face. "No. Far too square! I'm quite surprised Karl went for it, but I think he had no choice. It had to be two or nothing."

"Next time as well?"

"Yes. It keeps it impersonal; no favouritism, no commitment for him. Are you happy with that?"

Audrey nodded then put a finger to her lips as she heard Karl climbing the stairs.

Karl arrived with a tray of mugs, which he placed on the bedside table, moving Katherine's picture onto the dresser in the process. Hanging up his dressing gown on the door he crawled back into bed between Sarah and Audrey.

"I wonder what Katherine would think of this?" Sarah said casually, but wanting to make sure Karl was happy with the situation.

"Wholehearted approval, I'm sure of it." Karl passed her a mug of tea. "Do you think so?"

"Yes. You needed waking up and who better to do it than us?"

"Who said I needed waking up?" Karl asked, knowing he had her trapped.

Sarah smirked. "All right! It was Robert's idea. And a jolly good one it was too!"

"And did he ask for a three-page typed report with all the gory details?"

"I'll write that," Audrey offered. "I could turn it into a blockbuster novel and make a fortune. But I'd need to do some more research first." She giggled, pressing her warm body against his cooler one then licking his chest. "God, you're delicious, Karl. Like roast chicken. I could eat you!" She kissed his right nipple. "Tomorrow I get the main course, promise?"

"Promise."

It was still only half past ten by the time they had finished their teas and all used the bathroom. As first Sarah then Audrey rejoined him in bed, Karl glanced at Katherine's photo, which was still on the dresser. Audrey followed his gaze.

"She seems happy enough with the situation, don't you think, Karl?" She reached out and switched off the light.

"Yes. For the moment. For this week." Karl put his arms round both women, curled either side of him. "My future's here now," he warned them. "I'm not going back."

Sarah put her hand reassuringly on his chest. "Don't worry. We're

119

not expecting anything from you. We just wanted to help you get through today and move on."

"You've certainly done that," he told them with a kiss on each of their noses.

TEN

Margit rolled her lips together and looked in her compact mirror at her face. Nothing she did could mask the fact that she had not inherited her mother's beauty. She put away her lipstick and compact and glanced at the object of her envy. Her mother was sitting on the sofa, reading a magazine and looking bored.

"You haven't seen Karl for ages, have you?" Margit commented.

"You know he's got visitors this week. His sister-in-law and a friend."

"There's no reason why you can't invite them round," Margit pointed out, irritated by her mother's obtuseness. "They can get to meet you; potential family and all that. Silke's dying to see them too. She keeps hearing about them from Karl at work."

All traces of boredom were swept from Ilse's face. "That's a super idea!" she cried, her brain steaming into action. "But we'd have to invite some other people too, not just Silke. He sees enough of her at work every day. And besides, poor Karl wouldn't like to be the only male among a crowd of women!"

Margit had an easy remedy. "I'll invite my lot, Roslinde and Edeltraud can invite their boyfriends, Silke can bring Mick, if he's not on duty. There you are! A ready-made party."

"Well we haven't got much time to organise it. Today's … what … Wednesday and they're leaving on Sunday. Friday's possibly the best night. What do you think?"

"Friday sounds good. You'd better give the guests of honour a ring and see if they can come. Then I'll ask Silke and the others this evening."

Ilse put down her magazine and looked at her watch. Almost seven o'clock. Hopefully they would not have gone out yet if they were going. She went to the telephone in the hall.

Karl answered promptly. "Ah, Ilse. How are you?"

"Fine, thank you, Karl. How are you and your guests?"

"Fine. We were going out for a bite to eat shortly."

It was almost like she could read his mind. Should I ask Ilse too? No, she would be in the way. Ilse hurriedly cleared her mind of such thoughts. "I'm glad I got hold of you then. Margit and I were wondering whether the three of you wanted to come round here on Friday for a small party along with some of the girls' friends. I'd love to meet your sister-in-law, and it would save you cooking or whatever. Margit's going to invite Silke and Mick, if he can make it."

"Er, Bina and Wolf were coming down that evening to see us."

"Bring them too! The more the merrier!"

There was a pause while Karl thought about it. It might be interesting for Sarah and Audrey to meet some other Germans socially. "That would be lovely, Ilse. Thank you. What time?"

"When are you expecting Bina and Wolf?"

"About seven."

"Well, shall we say eight, then?"

"Fine."

"Good. It's a date then. I'd better let you get out for your meal and I'll start planning the party."

"You're good at that sort of thing. You'll like meeting Audrey. She's a born organiser too."

"I'll look forward to it," Ilse replied a little less enthusiastically. "See you Friday." Putting down the receiver she returned to the living room. "It's on," she told Margit.

"Good. I'll invite the others. I'll see you later."

Margit was meeting her friends for a few drinks in a bar. At twenty-four she was one of the few unmarried ones in the group, whose numbers were steadily dropping as babies came and responsibilities grew. She and Silke were the only unattached females left. Margit, who was spectacularly plain, had found herself ostracised for a while when all the drama of her parents' neo-Nazi connections came to the fore. Silke had had to deal with her dying mother then had upped and left for America. Now she spent much of her time with the married Irish anaesthetist, Mick, who was old enough to be her father. What a pair we are! Margit thought.

She walked to Bahnhofstraße, spotted Silke parking her car nearby and went over to meet her. "No Mick tonight?"

"No, he's working still. Anyway, this crowd's too young for him." Silke pushed open the bar door and they walked in to the blast of warm air. They hastily removed their thick woollen coats and hung them by the door before joining their group of friends. Two chairs had been kept free for them and they sat down while one of the young men ordered drinks for them.

"Right everybody!" Margit said. "Before I forget, we're throwing a small party this Friday and you're all invited. Sorry it's such short notice, but who's able to come?"

Two of the four couples seemed interested. Margit looked expectantly at Silke. "Karl's invited along with his visitors. I thought you wanted to meet them."

Silke's eyes lit up. "Yes, I would like to."

Margit gave her a hard look. "You know something I don't! Come on, out with it! What's he been telling you?"

"I think it's more like what he's not been telling me," Silke said vaguely.

"What on earth do you mean?"

Silke looked away. "Oh, nothing. Is Mick invited too?"

"Yes, of course. He'll be someone else for the Englishwomen to speak to. Mick's not got long here now though, has he?"

"No. Another two months."

"Will you miss him?"

"Maybe. I don't really know. We're not that close really."

"Get away! You and he seem to be always going off somewhere together."

"Hardly! Two archery competitions, that's all." She sipped her beer. "How are things going between your mother and Karl? Is that why she's holding the party, to get to know his family?"

"Well it was my idea actually, trying to chivvy things along a bit. But yes, I think she wants to meet Sarah, Karl's sister-in-law."

"You're keen they get together then?"

"Oh yes," Margit gushed. "I adore Karl. It would be great to have him as my new stepfather, so long as my mother can divorce Paul. Mind you, she's got enough grounds to ten times over, but she never wanted to until Karl became available again. We're really grateful to you for finding the job for Karl."

"Well, when you told me he was so wonderful, I thought he was worth catching."

"And was he?"

"Certainly. He's made a big difference already. Matron adores him too. I think she'd run off with him, given half a chance."

Margit nodded. "He's always had that effect on women. His son was like that too. The one who died last year," she clarified. "My half-brother, Siegfried. Mind-blowingly attractive, although he was a devil to live with. That wasn't really his fault, I suppose."

"Whose, Karl's?"

"No, Siegfried's. He had a tough childhood. Hated Karl and my father. He grew up bitter and twisted."

"That's a real shame. But what about Karl's other children? I've met Sabina already. She seems really nice."

"Oh she is. I was a bridesmaid at her wedding. Her two brothers are lovely as well. Both quite good-looking, though young Paul's got a way to go yet before he matures. When he does, watch out!"

Silke laughed. "Three lovely children. Isn't he lucky!"

"You sound quite jealous, Silke. Are you getting broody?"

She sighed. "I'll be twenty-six in August. Hardly an old maid, but no longer a spring chicken." Draining her glass she looked at her friend. "And what about you, Margit? Do you want children?"

"Yes, if anyone will have me, which I doubt. I'm hardly gorgeous to look at, am I? Not like my mother at all!"

"Looks aren't everything. You're a very charming person."

"Yes, but I only fall for the handsome men, and they don't want me."

"One of these days you'll find somebody."

"I wish."

"You want a handsome man, Margit?" one of the married young men in the group butted in.

"Any man will do, Ulrich!" she moaned theatrically.

"Can I bring my cousin along on Friday, then? He's fun. His name's Bruno. You'll like him."

Margit and Silke exchanged doubtful glances but proceeded to grill Ulrich about his cousin Bruno anyway. By the end of the evening Margit was hopeful that this Bruno might be worth a look, though whether he would look at her was another matter. ·

She mentioned him to her mother when she got back later that evening. Her sisters had gone to bed already but her mother was watching a late night show on the television. She sat down on the sofa next to her mother, gazing at the dancers on the screen as she described her evening in the bar.

"He'd have to be as blind as a bat to want me. How come Roslinde and Edeltraud manage to get boyfriends?"

"Perhaps they're not as conscious of their looks as you are, Liebchen," Ilse said. "You need to relax and smile more. You can get a bit serious sometimes."

"That's because I'm in despair all the time."

"Despair? You?" Ilse asked in surprise.

Margit studied her fingernails. She had never been one for confiding much in her mother before, but now she could not keep quiet any longer. "Because you've got the man I want!" she blurted out.

Ilse let out a gasp of horror. "You mean Karl?"

"Yes," Margit cried. "I've loved him ever since I was twelve, when they came to visit us that first time in Bavaria."

Ilse was shocked. "I knew you had a bit of a crush on him, but I thought you'd got over that."

"No. I just hid it. At least if I can't have him I want you to have him, then he'll always be around."

Ilse was frowning now. "That's not a healthy way to live your life, Liebchen, lusting after someone you can never have. You've got to try to look at other men – younger ones. Try giving this Bruno lad a good chance."

"I intend to, but I know he won't want me!"

"Because you're not letting yourself open up to other men, that's why. You're keeping yourself back for Karl and they sense that. Let him go, darling. It's your only hope."

Margit's eyes filled with tears. "If only I could!"

Ilse found her sympathy lacking. "Well, you're not having him," she warned her daughter firmly.

*

Virginia Mitchell put on a magnificent spread on Thursday

evening. She had invited Mick O'Reilly as a spare male to balance Karl's two female guests. He was seated next to Audrey, and Karl watched in amusement as Audrey proceeded to turn on her charm to the full. She couldn't help it, Karl realised, given the lure of an apparently unattached male. It was second nature to her, and Mick was responding. Come the end of the meal, he noticed their hands brushing in deliberate contact, and he began to worry what Silke would think.

Later that evening, as Karl was getting into bed with his two companions, he asked Audrey whether she knew Mick was married.

"Yes, and if that's a marriage then I'm a virgin," she replied. "And yes, I do know he's been seeing a lot of your young assistant, whatever her name is. One of the other guests very kindly informed me."

"Her name's Silke. She'll be with him tomorrow night at Ilse's, so be warned! I don't want a cat fight on my hands," he joked.

Audrey meowed and dragged a long fingernail slowly down his chest. "It's Ilse who needs to be jealous, don't you think?"

He did not answer her so she decided to dig deeper. "How do things stand between you and Ilse? Just so we don't put our feet in it tomorrow night," she added to explain her curiosity.

"I'm not rushing things," he replied carefully.

"You don't know, in other words?" Sarah suggested.

He shrugged. "I know she wants me."

"But you're not so sure?"

"I don't know. I'll have to see how things go since …"

"Since we helped you out?" Audrey purred. "Ooh! Lucky old Ilse! She doesn't know what she's in for."

"She does actually. Or had you forgotten Siegfried?" Sarah reminded her. Karl's hand, which was resting gently on her full stomach clenched suddenly as though he were in pain. She put her hand over his. "Sorry, I didn't mean to be frivolous about him."

She was beginning to understand just how much Katherine had taken care of Karl over the years. There always seemed to be some kind of mental pain lurking close to the surface. Sarah knew about Siegfried and Katherine of course, but she was also aware there was a huge mass of history she was not privy to. Now Karl had nobody to share that burden with, apart from Robert and possibly Sabina.

She curled up into his body, her fingertips stroking up and down his thigh. "It's our last chance for a bit of fun tonight. Bina and Wolf will be here tomorrow and Saturday." She felt Audrey moving on the other side of him, and found herself wishing that she was alone with Karl, but at least with the two of them there it kept things impersonal, if a bit weird. A bit of fun. That was all it was: fun and a means of restoring Karl's desire for a sex life.

Karl lay still between them. He realised he felt tired, but more than that, he felt depressed at the realisation he would be sleeping alone again. It had been good having someone, two people even, to hold in the night. He was lucky he hadn't had any nightmares during the week, but the occasional one would inevitably return and he would have to face the darkness alone.

On his right, Audrey had discovered his lack of response and set herself the task of righting the situation. It only took her a few seconds.

*

The plan in the morning was for Karl to drop off Sarah and Audrey at the station to catch the train into Dortmund. After shopping, they would meet Sabina at her travel agent's office and go for lunch together. Bina and Wolf would then drive the pair back in the evening to Karl's house for seven o'clock, where they could all get ready before going on to Ilse's. In his lunch break Karl changed the sleeping arrangements in the house for Bina and Wolf's visit. They would have his room, bringing their own bedding to save him on laundry; Sarah and Audrey would share one spare room, while he would have Audrey's original room. He just hoped that in the middle of the night, Sarah and Audrey would remember which room they were supposed to be sleeping in.

He returned to the office at three thirty, having first had the usual Friday meeting with John Pascoe and the other administrators.

"You look bushed!" Silke told him as he walked in. "Are you sure you'll make it to Ilse's this evening?"

"I'll be fine. I can snatch an hour's shut-eye before everyone arrives at seven."

"Oh yes, they're with Bina in Dortmund today, aren't they? Will you miss them when they're gone?"

"Yes. The house will be empty without them."

"I know the feeling," she replied heavily. "Still," she continued, brightening the gloom that had suddenly descended on them both, "they seem to have been good for you. You were remarkably cheerful on Wednesday, compared to the day before."

He grinned, saw her knowing smile and realised she had not missed much. A silent exchange of information passed between them and he knew he had just confirmed her suspicions, but he made no comment. She could think what she liked. He didn't mind.

As they were leaving the office at the end of the afternoon, Silke reminded him: "Make sure you get that bit of kip. We don't want Ilse finding you asleep on her sofa this evening, do we!" She picked up the bag of laundry he still brought on Friday mornings and hurried out.

*

Wolf's car drew up outside the house promptly at seven and disgorged its passengers with their shopping.

"We had to buy something to wear for tonight as we'd run out of clothes," Audrey explained, dumping several carrier bags in the hall.

"I've put you in with Sarah now," Karl reminded her.

Audrey grinned. "Right-ho. I'll try to remember."

Wolf was struggling with an armful of bedding, heading upstairs. "Bina says we're in your room?" he asked Karl from halfway up.

"Yes, that's right."

While the others got changed, Karl poured out drinks for them and took them into the living room. He felt anxious about the evening ahead, and was beginning to wish he had not accepted Ilse's invitation. Somehow having Ilse, Bina and Sarah all in the same room, not to mention Audrey, Silke and Mick, seemed to be tempting fate.

Wolf was the first one ready. "You look worried, Karl," he said, finding his father-in-law sitting staring into space.

"Do I? I was just wondering what fireworks the evening will bring." He handed Wolf a glass of beer.

128

"If you're worried about Bina and Ilse, I've already told Bina to mind her manners. She's better than she was about Ilse, though. That archery day helped a lot."

"Yes. It was fun, wasn't it? We'll have to do it again some time, once the skiing season's over."

"You liked your new skis, then?"

"Wonderful." Karl studied his glass of beer. If Silke had spotted what was going on, would Ilse?

Wolf could see Karl was lost in thought again. He decided to leave him to it and drank his beer quietly while he waited for Bina and the others to appear. Their chatter upstairs warned him he was in for a bit of a wait

In Karl's bedroom, Audrey was begging Sabina for more information about their hostess for the evening.

"Is she really beautiful?" she wanted to know, sitting smoking on the edge of the bed while Sabina sat on the dressing table stool, brushing her hair in front of the mirror. "Sarah says she always got the impression she was."

"Considering she's in her late forties, she's still quite attractive," Sabina said rather tactlessly. "But yes, I believe she was a stunner in her time. I've seen a photo of Daddy and her together during the war, him in his uniform and all. It's a bit weird, seeing that side of his life, but they certainly looked made for each other."

"And Katherine never liked her because of that?"

Sabina gave a careless nod and stood up. "Right, I'm just about ready. You'll be seeing her shortly. You can judge for yourself what you think of the potential new Mrs Driesler. Although Vanessa will most likely be first with that title." She picked up her handbag and coat from the bed then stooped for one of her gloves, which had fallen on the floor. As she did so she noticed a discarded stocking lying under the bed. Shocked, she turned her back on Audrey, hiding her face, wondering how long the stocking had been there. Only since this week, or longer? Did it belong to Audrey, or even Aunty Sarah, Ilse or someone else altogether?

Whoever it belonged to, she had no right to comment or pass judgement, but she could not hide the hurt she felt that her father had moved on already. As she joined him in the living room, she saw him

129

again as she had once before: not as her father, but as a man with sexual needs. It was an image she found distasteful.

Wolf drove them all to the Zopfs' apartment block and managed to park nearby. Sarah and Audrey were both on tenterhooks as they walked up the two flights of stairs to Ilse and her daughters' apartment. Ilse opened the door to them and Audrey discovered how right Sabina had been. Ilse was beautiful, with her oval shaped face, blue eyes and silver-blonde hair, high cheekbones and delicate nose. A classic beauty and a fitting companion for Karl. She watched Ilse attach herself to Karl as he greeted her with a kiss on the cheek, noticed her possessive hold on his arm as she bade him introduce his guests.

"Welcome, Sarah, Audrey," Ilse said in English, paying particular attention to Karl's sister-in-law, who struck her as a confident woman of the world, unlike Katherine, who had always seemed in awe of Ilse. There was some family resemblance in the auburn hair and green eyes, but not overly much to be a constant reminder of Katherine. Her friend, Audrey, with her dyed blonde wavy hair, blue eyes and coquettish mouth was an immediate threat. Ilse sensed instant rivalry in Audrey's forthright stare.

*

Silke had arranged to pick up Mick from the Officers' Mess. She usually drove them, as she lived somewhat out of town and it was more convenient that way. It also meant he could drink as much as he wanted, which was usually a lot.

"How was last night?" she asked him as he settled himself in the passenger seat beside her.

"Last night?" He had temporarily forgotten. "Oh, at the Mitchells'. A right royal spread as usual. Virginia certainly knows how to cook."

"Did you meet Karl's guests?"

He smiled. "Phew! Did I just!"

"And what's that supposed to mean?" she chuckled.

"His sister-in-law's friend, Audrey, is quite something. You'd better watch out for her this evening, before she snatches me away from you."

130

It was a measure of their friendly and light-hearted relationship that Mick could joke with her so easily. "Is that likely?" she asked.

"Not with Karl around," he replied sourly.

Silke discovered what he meant after they arrived at Ilse's. The apartment was nearly full with about twenty or more people, she guessed, mostly youngsters like herself. Standing in the corner by the record player were Sabina and Wolf. Or rather Sabina was standing, while Wolf seemed to be surreptitiously tweaking the bass and treble settings on the amplifier while the Beatles' 'Sergeant Pepper' LP reverberated round the room. With the couple were Margit, her sisters and their group of friends, including Ulrich and his cousin Bruno. She waved to them, but Ilse was leading her and Mick towards the drinks' trolley in the dining area. Here she recognised Hans and Corinna Münzel from the furniture shop talking with Karl and his two female companions. Ilse fussed over her latest arrivals, handing out cocktails, made the introductions then regained her place at Karl's side.

Silke watched and listened to the conversation around her, but it was the watching that was the most fascinating. During her days in the West Coast commune she had grown adept at spotting who was partnering whom that day by their little gestures and careless intimacies. Whereas Ilse made the obvious claim to Karl, standing closest to him, touching his arm to emphasise a point, there was no doubt in her mind that Audrey felt she had the stronger claim. Then she saw Sarah give Karl a glance and saw the same claim. So it was both of them!

Silke grinned and watched the scene unfolding. She knew both Ilse and Margit were infatuated with Karl, but when she looked round the room, nearly every female except Sabina, of course, was behaving like a mare in season. Eyes were rolling, nostrils flaring and rumps quivering in every direction. Even Corinna Münzel was not immune as she smiled at the stallion in their midst. Yet he was doing nothing to encourage this extraordinary behaviour. His mere presence had set them all twitching and she could not explain why it was. She remembered Margit's observation in the bar on Wednesday night. 'He's always had that effect on women', she had said. It set Silke wondering why.

He was handsome, sure enough, in a mature kind of way, and that made heads turn, but there was that something extra that she herself had felt strongly: he exuded masculine strength but she felt an instinctive urge to look after him, almost as though he were a small and vulnerable child. Vulnerable. The word fitted him perfectly, but she did not know why.

She sensed Mick drawing away from her, shifting closer to Audrey who was chatting animatedly to him. Perhaps he needed a little freedom, she thought.

"I'm going to say hello to Margit and the others," she said quietly in his ear. "Are you staying here?"

He nodded, seeming happy to be left with the other oldies, while Silke made her way over to the younger generation.

"So that's Silke," Audrey said to Mick when she had left them. "She seems a pleasant girl. Into archery, I gather," she added, inclining her body in Mick's direction and effectively excluding Sarah from their conversation.

Mick took up the challenge. "Yes, she's pretty good at it. Have you ever tried it?"

Ilse was asking the Münzels about their recent skiing holiday in Italy, drawing Karl in too, and Sarah now found herself excluded from any conversation, so she contented herself with quietly observing the infamous Ilse.

She was very different from what Sarah had been expecting. Katherine had tried never to speak ill of her, so it came as a shock to discover that Ilse was a self-centred bore, a sophisticated hostess dominated by her own self-interest. She knew what she wanted in life and how to get it. Sarah could now see from where Siegfried had inherited his scheming nature. Whereas Katherine had cared intensely about others, Ilse cared only for herself. It would be a disaster for Karl if he were to rely on her for strength and help in the years to come.

Karl caught her eye, silently asking her if she was all right. Sarah smiled in return. She was finding the evening very useful.

Over by the record player Silke watched the exchange with interest. While apparently holding a conversation with Ulrich and his wife, Jutta, she saw Sarah's growing dislike of Ilse. She noticed Sabina too was watching her father's involvement with Ilse with a curious mixture of distaste and resignation. Oh, this is interesting, Silke thought to herself. Very interesting.

With so many people to seat, Ilse had opted for a buffet supper. Edeltraud and Roslinde helped her bring the food out from the kitchen, while Margit got Bruno to help her with everybody's drinks. It was proving almost impossible for her to concentrate on Bruno with Karl in the same room, but she had to acknowledge he was fun, if severely lacking in the looks department, with his baby-faced chubby cheeks and rosebud lips. She knew her mother was right about letting go of her fixation with Karl, and seeing her mother's arm tucked under his only emphasised her claim to him. Nevertheless, when Margit topped up Karl's glass of wine for him she felt that familiar flutter of excitement she had felt since she was twelve. Stupid girl, she told herself. Get over him! In a deliberate measure designed to commit herself along a new path, she grabbed Bruno by the arm and dragged him towards the food.

"A new boyfriend for Margit?" Karl asked Ilse as they waited for the queue to die down before taking their turn at the table. She handed him an empty plate to fill.

"I hope so. She's not been very successful in that department yet. I always hoped she and Wolf would hit it off, but once your Sabina came on the scene there was no possibility of that."

"That's life," he commented, looking around for Sarah and Audrey, not wanting them to feel left out. Audrey had wedged herself between Silke and Mick, while Sarah was being looked after by Sabina and Wolf. Corinna Münzel smiled at him as she passed by, her plate comparatively empty next to her husband's mountain of food.

Karl helped himself to the herring in dill sauce that Ilse had prepared, adding a generous helping of noodle salad, egg mayonnaise and tomatoes. He really had eaten well this week, and felt he had regained some of the weight he had lost the previous year. There was a vacant chair next to Silke, and he sat down with his plate balanced on his knee, while Ilse found a place on the far side of the room with Hans and Corinna.

"I hear Mick's off to Hong Kong soon," Karl said after eating a few mouthfuls.

"Yes," Silke replied. She lowered her voice so Karl had to lean closer to hear her. "He's really glad. Even further from his wife, more chance to stray."

"Hmm," Karl commented, chewing thoughtfully. "Why don't they just call it a day?"

"He's Catholic. He can't divorce her."

"I see." Although he and Silke chatted to each other in the office, they seldom had the chance to engage in long conversations with each other. Now seemed a good opportunity to find out more about her. "Are you likely to visit him there?"

"Me?" she asked in astonishment. "No. Why should I?" She smiled. "Why does no one believe me when I say there's nothing going on between us?"

"Because it's not true."

"There's as much between us as there is between you and Audrey," she said, grinning broadly when she saw his look of horror. "And Sarah," she added louder, just to tease him.

"Shhh." Fortunately the brass section of James Last was blasting out from the record player and no one seemed to have overheard.

"But not with Ilse," Silke persisted in her search for enlightenment. "Not yet, anyway." She picked at her herring. "Did you know Margit's infatuated with you?"

"Still?"

Silke nodded. "They all are. Funny, isn't it?"

"Not really. Awkward, more like."

She eyed him up carefully. "Yes. Apart from at the moment, I can see you're a one-woman-man."

"You're very perceptive. You don't miss much, do you?"

"I try not to. Sabina doesn't like Ilse, you know?"

"I am aware of that."

"Nor Sarah. It makes you wonder why."

Karl looked at her crossly. "I'll handle my own love-life, thank you, Silke."

Not put out by his harshness, she smiled beatifically. "I'm sure you will. We'll have to start placing bets on who the lucky woman will be!"

Karl had to smile too at her ingenuousness. "An American accent wasn't the only thing you picked up in California, was it? You learnt to say what you think, too."

"Well that's right," she admitted. "I can't stand all this European diplomacy and hiding of feelings. Say what you think and be done with it!" She scraped the remains of the herring up with her fork and popped them in her mouth. "Up to a point, of course," she conceded.

Their eyes met and he felt a sudden jolt deep within like a kick in the guts, a kick that shocked him to the core, disorientating his senses. His head seemed to be swimming, his limbs felt heavy and uncoordinated. He turned round slowly to set his plate down safely on the table beside him and saw Margit and her friends smoking – and it wasn't tobacco, he realised in alarm.

Silke saw his look. "You object to them smoking a bit of hash?"

"Not in their own space, no, but in mine, yes."

"Haven't you ever tried it?"

"You have, obviously."

"Yes, but I was asking you."

It was a question he found hard to answer. With an effort he managed it. "No."

"But you've tried something else?"

Silke really was too perceptive, he thought wretchedly, waves of panic mounting inside him. He searched around the room for an escape and managed to catch Sabina's eye. She would understand this problem only too well. He beckoned her over. Leaving Wolf chatting to Edeltraud and her boyfriend, Sabina wandered over to him and leant over him. Fortunately Wolf had turned the music down a few notches and she could speak reasonably normally.

"What is it, Daddy?"

"We were talking about drugs, Bina," he said carefully, seeing her eyes fill with alarm. "Silke wanted to know what my experiences with them were."

Sabina thought quickly. She knew her father did not want to tell the truth and was asking for her help in avoiding it. Suddenly she had the answer. "Well, it's hardly your experience of them, more like Alex's." She lowered her voice and put her mouth near Silke's ear. "Audrey's son, Alex, died of a heroin overdose. It's always been a bit of an awkward subject in our house, since I was the one who introduced him to smoking cannabis and it led on from there."

Silke looked stricken and searched for Audrey. She was giggling with Mick safely on the other side of the room, refilling their plates from the buffet table. "I'm sorry. I shouldn't have been so nosy. Poor Audrey." A thought occurred to her. "Do you think she'll mind the others smoking? I can ask them to stop, if you want?"

Sabina shook her head. "I don't think she's noticed. She's probably used to the smell of it, actually."

"Are you sure?"

Sabina nodded, her job over, or so she thought until she noticed her father's still anxious face.

"Are you all right, Daddy?"

"It's getting a bit hot in here. I'll just go out for some fresh air."

"I'll come with you."

Silke watched them leave the room together, puzzled.

Outside on the communal stairway, Sabina made her father sit down on the steps. He had turned quite pale and was shaking visibly.

"What is it, Daddy?" she begged, sitting beside him and putting an arm around him.

"The smoke – drugs. I can't cope with it," he gasped, holding her hand tightly.

Sabina felt her own panic rising now, realising her father was in danger of losing control. What should she do? She tried to think what her mother would have done but could only hold his hand and stroke it. He had closed his eyes now and seemed to be concentrating hard on something, going through a well-practised ritual in his mind that calmed him quite quickly. She could feel his hands steadying, his pulse slowing until his face relaxed as though he were asleep. She sat with him waiting and after two minutes he slowly opened his eyes.

His voice was steady when he spoke. "I'm sorry to have burdened you with that, Beauty. I'm all right now."

"Are you sure? Can you go back in now, or shall I ask them to stop smoking?"

"No. I don't want to make a fuss. I'll be fine now. I was just taken by surprise. Now I'm prepared."

"Well, if you're really sure, but if you find you can't cope with it we can go."

"Thank you, Beauty. You're so like your mother, watching over me still." He kissed her forehead then stood up. "We'd better go back in before someone comes out to find us. You go first and I'll follow in a moment."

Silke watched first Sabina then Karl come back from the hall, saw Karl rejoin Sarah in the oldies' end of the room away from the pot smokers, and particularly noticed how Sabina kept a careful eye on her father for the remainder of the evening.

ELEVEN

Audrey rang on the doorbell at twelve the following day, looking suitably contrite. The others had waited in for her all morning, not wanting to abandon her totally to Mick's care.

"I'm so sorry, Karl," she said, hurrying inside out of the cold and the neighbours' view. "You must think me a right trollop going off with Mick like that last night and leaving poor Silke alone. He assured me she wouldn't mind, but when you see her on Monday, please give her my deepest apologies. I don't know what got into us!"

"Cannabis smoke I expect," Sarah suggested equably. "The air was pretty thick with it until Silke seemed to have a word with Margit's friends."

"Yes, it was rather," Audrey agreed, deciding to make light of it. "So, what are the plans for today? What's left of it, that is."

"A brisk walk in the woods to burn off some of the food we've eaten this week," Sarah told her, patting her stomach. "I don't know about you, but I'm feeling like a stuffed pig at the moment. Although I expect you got some exercise last night," she added cheekily. "We had quite a late breakfast, so we won't be eating until much later. Is that all right for you?"

"Yes, I'm fine. I'd better go and get changed then."

Audrey hurried upstairs, just remembering in time that she was now sharing the larger spare room with Sarah. Talk about musical beds! She would have slept in every room in the house by tomorrow. She turned to find Sarah had followed her up.

"That wasn't very clever, Audrey. You've probably made things very awkward for Karl now, going off with Silke's boyfriend."

"But he's not her boyfriend," Audrey protested, hunting in a drawer for some slacks. "They just … hang out together sometimes. Besides, she was talking to Karl for a lot of the evening, as you well know. I saw you sitting with Ilse and her friends, looking as bored as hell until Bina rescued you."

"Because you'd already abandoned me for Mick," Sarah argued.

"Well, Karl had abandoned you too." Audrey paused as she bent double to put on some warm socks. "Why did he suddenly go out with Bina like that?"

"I don't know. She looked worried, didn't she?"

"Yes. Do you think Silke had said something already to him about me that had upset him?"

"No, she didn't seem cross," Sarah reassured her. "Maybe Karl just wanted a private word with Bina about something." She studied her friend's change of clothing. "Are you going to be warm enough in that thin jumper? It's jolly cold out."

"Yes, mother," Audrey teased her. "You go on down. I'll be ready in a tick."

After Sarah had left the room, Audrey rummaged in her handbag, removed the piece of paper Mick had given her bearing his new address in Hong Kong, carefully folded it up and tucked it out of sight in her diary.

Iserlohn was surrounded by forest and they were spoilt for choice for somewhere to walk. In the end Karl drove them all up to the Danzturm, a stone-built high tower with a viewing balcony and windows looking out over the surrounding hills. Here he parked, and they set off at a brisk pace down one of the main routes through the silver-frosted woods.

"This is more like it!" Sabina laughed, chasing Wolf round a large beech tree until she was too puffed to continue and Wolf let her catch him.

"I expect you miss the outdoor life, don't you, Karl?" Sarah asked him, as she and Audrey walked sedately along either side of him.

"I suppose so, but I don't miss being up all night for lambing. I was beginning to get rather exhausted by it all, as you may remember. You've got all that to look forward to when you get back, haven't you?"

Sarah groaned. "Yes, I suppose I have. Although between them Richard and Paul seem to be managing things pretty well. I don't really get involved that much with the farming side of things, fortunately." She caught hold of his arm and walked closer to him, feeling the biting cold of the sharp frost that lay around them. So much for warning Audrey to wrap up warmly, she told herself. "Has Richard given any clues yet as to when he and Vanessa are hoping to get married?"

"I thought you might be able to tell me that. But there's no rush, surely?"

"No, of course not. I was just wondering when all your family would be coming over next, that's all."

"God knows what'll happen when my two want to get hitched," Audrey chipped in, clutching hold of Karl's other arm. "Angela will want a grand family wedding and I'll have to be there and stand alongside that beast, Andrew, for the photographs. I don't think I could bear it!" She looked up at Karl. "Sorry to mention his name. I expect you hate it more than I do."

He shrugged, not wanting to talk about her soon-to-be-divorced husband.

"How can you be so calm about it?" Audrey went on. "Why didn't you insist on him being charged with attempted rape? I could never understand how you let him get away with it."

"I left things up to the police. If no charges were brought, it was their decision. I couldn't face any more hassle in the courts anyway."

"But it meant he got away scot-free!" Audrey protested. "He's got friends in high places, that's the trouble."

"He's got his conscience to live with, hasn't he? And he lost you."

"He'd lost me already!" she retorted loudly. "Perhaps that was the trouble," she added a moment later, more reflectively. "Was that why he was hunting out Katherine? If so, it's all my fault!"

"Don't go upsetting yourself, Audrey" Karl said, stopping to face her so she could see he bore her no malice. "It was nothing to do with you, and all to do with me and ancient history."

"I can't help it," she cried wretchedly. "I do blame myself."

"There's no need," Karl reassured her with a squeeze.

"The worst of it is," Audrey went on, "that I don't even like my own children very much. They remind me too much of him. I'm not sure I even want to attend their weddings."

"Of course you do," Sarah told her sternly. "It's just the thought of having to see Andrew again so soon that puts you off the idea. It'll be different when the time comes, you'll see." She clapped her frozen hands together and stamped her feet. "Come on, it's too cold to stand about. Wolf and Bina are miles ahead."

Karl took hold of Audrey's hand and placed her arm around his again. "Don't fret about Andrew ... or Mick. You do your own thing, Audrey." He scooped up Sarah's arm as well and set off with them in pursuit of his daughter.

*

Sabina and Wolf were driving Sarah and Audrey to the airport on Sunday morning. As they said their goodbyes out of Sabina and Wolf's earshot, Karl thanked them both for their generosity.

"I'm so glad we were of help, Karl," Sarah said, hugging him close to her and realising how much she was going to miss him. She was close to tears but dared not show how much her feelings for him had grown over the past week.

Audrey on the other hand was quite chipper as she sidled up to Karl, lips pursed for the formality of a parting kiss. "We've all had a great time, haven't we? Now we must all move on. And I think I know where I'm going."

Karl hazarded a guess. "Hong Kong?"

"Do you know," she said with artful innocence, "I've always wanted to go there. Perhaps I might manage it this year!"

Karl could not help smiling. Irrepressible as ever, was Audrey. "Good luck," he wished her sincerely, kissing her on the cheek.

They got into the back of Wolf's car and Karl shut the door for them, waving them off as a rush of loneliness engulfed him. He went back indoors to the empty house.

Sarah had already stripped her and Audrey's beds, while Audrey had run the vacuum cleaner around the whole house. He set about making his own bed, unavoidably recalling what had gone on there over the past week. Without warning another image flashed into his brain, an image so startling that he sat down on the bed in shock.

The image was fleeting but clear, the result, no doubt, of his re-awakened sexual desires, but it disturbed him with its implications. Instead of seeing Sarah or Audrey lying in his bed he had clearly seen a naked Silke looking up at him, waiting for him expectantly. Erotic as the image should have been, it puzzled him more than aroused him. Why Silke? Why a naked Silke? His imagination had had to supply a lot of detail for that scenario.

Could it be a residual effect of the cannabis from last night? Before becoming aware of the smoke, he remembered the strange jolt he had felt when Silke had looked at him. If it were not such a stupid idea he would have likened it to being shot … by an arrow.

He sought to make sense of it all. What had she done with that look of hers? Had it even been anything on her part? He had been disorientated by the smoke, overly susceptible to its influence, was hallucinating even now. It was simply that he had been with Silke at the time. If he had been talking to Ilse, he would be seeing her now instead. Surely that was the explanation? It had to be.

The image would not leave him the entire day. He tried reading a book, listening to the radio, even washing the kitchen floor, but Silke kept looking up at him with her molten brown eyes, her dark hair flicked across her cheek, her soft lips parted to form his name.

"Damn!" he cursed, throwing the floor mop into its bucket. "I'm obsessed … or possessed. She's a witch!"

In the end he decided to phone Ilse as a means of distraction. Edeltraud answered and Karl spent the time, while he waited for her to fetch her mother, picturing Ilse's face.

"I wanted to thank you for the party on Friday," he told her when she got to the phone. "It was very good of you to invite us. I hope there wasn't too much clearing up to do."

"The girls did most of it," she replied cheerfully. "It was nice to be able to meet Sarah … and Audrey, of course. I hope we'll be seeing more of them some time." There was a brief pause. "They'll be on their way home now, won't they?"

"Yes." He looked at his watch. "They should be in the car and well on their way to Hereford by now."

"So you're all on your own again," Ilse pointed out, "and lonely?" When he made no immediate reply she knew she was right. "Why don't you come round for some supper, Karl? There are still some leftovers. We've got to get them eaten up today. Do come."

It was probably what he needed. "That would be lovely, thank you."

"Come now, then."

He arrived thirty minutes later and met Margit on her way out of the main entrance, dressed up for an evening out.

"Bruno?" he asked.

She nodded. "He's surprisingly sweet, actually."

"Have fun then." He carried on up the communal stairs to where Ilse was waiting for him at her door. He greeted her with a kiss that was somewhat warmer than he had been giving her lately and she responded by putting her arms around his neck and drawing his mouth down to hers. He did not freeze or withdraw but she sensed she had rushed him yet again in her desperation to have him back. But it had been an adequate kiss, she told herself, taking his overcoat from him to hang up in the hall. A starting point.

The apartment always smelt of tobacco smoke, but he could detect a different, lingering odour from the party. A rush of panic engulfed him, just as it had on Friday. His heart pounding, he tried to breathe slowly and calm himself as he entered the living room. Roslinde was sitting in an armchair with a book, while Edeltraud was writing in a diary at the dining table. They both looked up and gave him a cursory nod before resuming their pastimes. He sat down on the sofa and Ilse settled herself beside him.

"That Audrey's a fast mover, isn't she?" she commented immediately. "When she and Mick went off together at the end of the evening, I was astonished, not to say sorry for poor Silke."

Silke's was the last name Karl wanted to hear but he had to try to forget about her. "That's Audrey, I'm afraid. She's always been like that. No doubt I'll hear Silke's views on the matter tomorrow."

"Well, if I were her, I'd be fuming at some other woman going off with my date like that."

"I don't think she minded too much," Karl said lightly, wishing they could talk about something else. He said the first thing that came into his head. "Sarah was asking me yesterday if I missed the outdoor life, and I don't, yet, as much as I was expecting. It'll probably be different come the spring, but I'm surprised how well I've adjusted to working in an office. I must be getting old, I suppose." He chuckled then added: "I think I'm going to need reading glasses soon."

"I'm sure you'll look very dignified in them," Ilse said deftly. "I'm going the same way myself. Why don't we book an appointment at the optician's together?"

"And order our walking sticks at the same time?" Karl laughed. "Then we will look like Opa and Oma!"

Ilse edged closer to him. "We could go up to see Sophie next weekend, if you like. We haven't been since before Christmas. The twins will have learnt at least fifty new words since then."

Karl had other ideas, however. "I was hoping you and I could go skiing next weekend. While there's still plenty of snow around," he added.

It was the break Ilse had been longing for. "You're on!" she beamed at him. "I'll have to get my legs in training right now!"

For the remainder of the evening, Ilse was like a little child given the promise of a trip to Disneyland. She seemed to float above the carpet as she brought out the leftover food and put it on the dining table. Roslinde and Edeltraud filled their plates and put them on trays to eat in front of the television, leaving Karl and Ilse to eat at the table alone.

"I think it's about time I got my own flat," she said, pouring them both a glass of wine. "I'm sure I must get under the girls' feet most of the time and stop them doing what they want, or inviting whoever they want round."

"Good idea," Karl agreed. "And what's Heinrich going to do when he finishes his national service? I don't know that he'll fit in here any more."

"True, but I'm not sharing with him!" Ilse laughed.

"I wasn't suggesting it." He grew more serious. "Have you heard from Paul at all since you've been here?"

"Once or twice. Why do you ask?"

"Well … I just wondered."

He did not need to say any more. She realised where his thoughts were leading. "Are we getting divorced, do you mean?"

He looked embarrassed at having suggested the subject. "I don't mean to pry."

"You have every right to," she said softly. "And yes, I have asked him for a divorce on the grounds of his persistent adultery. He's not disputing it."

Karl nodded. "I see."

"The way is clear for you," she told him, lest he should be in any doubt.

*

Karl arrived early at his desk on Monday morning. He had wanted to be busy when Silke arrived. Despite his evening spent with Ilse, the moment he had returned to his empty house the image of Silke had returned to haunt him. He had lain in bed tormented by the sight of her lying naked before him, and now he was not sure how to look her in the eye.

She arrived in a cloud of turquoise Indian silk scarf, clutching his washed and ironed shirts as usual on a Monday. She deposited the bag carefully at the side of his desk.

"Morning, Karl! Did Sarah and Audrey get off all right?" She chortled at her unintentional joke. "Get off! Audrey got off with Mick!"

"I'm glad you can laugh about it," he told her, not looking up from the report he was writing. "We were all worried about what you would think."

"Me? I couldn't care less. Really."

He looked at her now. "Sure?" The top half of her was well covered by the scarf and a skinny-rib yellow jumper, but her turquoise skirt revealed a considerable amount of leg. He returned his gaze hastily back to his report.

"Of course I'm sure." She picked up the kettle to fill. "Well, did they get off all right?"

"Yes, the plane was delayed a quarter of an hour, apparently, but I assume they got back all right."

"Good. They're fun, aren't they? Like a couple of schoolgirls rather than middle-aged women. They did you a lot of good, I think."

Despite himself he looked up and caught her eye. Again that bolt of energy hit him full in the stomach. He got over it quicker this time and was just able to reply. "You could say that."

"Oh, there's no need to be embarrassed, Karl," she chuckled. "It's exactly what you needed."

145

"Silke!" he protested mildly.

"Sorry. West Coast manners," she grinned on her way out with the kettle.

He shook his head in amazement. What a girl!

Karl was still staring into space when Silke returned with the filled kettle. "No inspiration for that report?" she asked him as she plugged it in to boil.

He couldn't possibly tell her that she was all he had thought about since she had left the room. He sighed. "I'll get there. Some coffee might help."

"It's on its way!" she said, saluting him snappily in the US army manner.

The unwritten report on the state of the drains from the hospital sluices sat on his desk all morning. No sooner had Karl got his coffee than the telephone had rung with Matron reporting an emergency in the nurses' quarters. A pipe had burst in the roof and water was pouring through the bathroom ceilings. It was late afternoon before Karl had inspected and was satisfied with the repair work on the pipes and the temporary repairs to the collapsed ceilings. He made a note to get the pipes properly lagged, told Matron the bathrooms were usable again for the moment then ambled back to the office to find a bag of provisions sitting in the middle of his desk.

"I thought you'd be hungry," Silke said.

"That's very thoughtful of you. Thank you." He sat down and inspected the contents of the bag: liver sausage, salami, a tub of potato salad. Silke had gone to some expense to feed him. "How much do I owe you?"

"Don't worry. You can buy the next jar of coffee when we need it." She put away one file and drew out another. "While you were out I found the relevant plans for the drains, and I've jotted down a few notes you might find useful. There's also a copy of a previous report made a few years ago about an incident with one of the Mess's drains after a rather wild party. Don't ask me what they found blocking it! Anyway, I thought it might help you with this report."

"Right, I'll get cracking on it. Sounds like you've virtually written it for me!"

The day's events had cleared Karl's head of his earlier problems and, with the aid of Silke's notes, he had the report drafted and ready for typing by six o'clock.

It had been a long and hectic day, and by the time he got home, had cooked himself something to eat and tidied up, he felt almost ready for bed. He remembered the shirts Silke had laundered and took them upstairs to hang up in his wardrobe and he found himself thinking about her again, although this time his thoughts were practical rather than lewd. He recalled her saying she lived alone, that her mother had died. He already knew her father was long dead. She had denied washing his shirts herself, so who was doing his laundry for him? The puzzle perplexed him until sleep finally came.

*

The morning was dragging for Sarah. Little seemed to be going on in the office for a Monday. Despite her recent absence, she only had a couple of letters to type and that was all. The telephone stayed resolutely silent and the clock ticked monotonously on the wall. Once the letters were typed she only had the secretary's fallback of nails to file. Instead, she got out her notepad and began writing a letter to Robert Murdoch. She hardly intended writing the three-page report Karl had joked about, but nevertheless, she had plenty to say.

Dearest Robbie,

Firstly, I hope that you, Alice and the boys are well, as we are. Richard and Paul are pleased to see me back safe and sound, although Vanessa seems to have kept them in hand very well while I was away.

Secondly, may I say what a clever boy you are! It needed both Audrey and myself to get Karl over the hurdle, but we made it – very successfully I might add. Without going into graphic details, I can safely say that Karl has no problems in that department any more. At least, not with us. Whether Ilse is the problem, I couldn't say. You'll have to wait until he confides in you again, or not, as the case may be. We all went round to Ilse's for a party last Friday and I met her for the first time. I know you've seen her before, but she was not what I was expecting at all. I just can't see Karl with her, somehow, and I don't think she's the right person for him, bearing in mind all his problems in the past. Is there anything you can say or do to put him off her? I know that's an impossible thing to ask, really, but I'm concerned he's going to make a big mistake with her. Sabina feels the same, but then she just doesn't like Ilse all that much any more, for some reason I'm not quite sure of.

A bit of gossip! Audrey disgraced herself by going off with the boyfriend of Karl's office assistant! Can you believe it? And it's not as if she was remotely sex-starved either. Karl had seen to that. Audrey's gone all secretive on me about it, but I'm convinced she's fallen hard for this chap. Watch this space!

In the meantime I've had trouble facing Richard and Paul and trying to keep secret what I've been up to with their father. However, I feel I must confess to you what I daren't to them, and that is I'm tempted to buy a Valentine's Day card this year and send it to Karl. Please tell me I'm being very foolish and that I must put him out of my head now that our job is done, otherwise I'm going to end up a very frustrated old woman.

As for Karl, he seems happy enough with his new life. He has plenty of family and friends to keep him busy, and now that the first year is over he'll be able to think about finding someone else to share his life with. I can't see him staying single now. He does need company, and most people seem to fall over backwards to look after him. Just please let it not be Ilse he chooses.

By the way, he would love it if you and the family paid him a visit. How about this summer?

Must stop now as finally some work has dropped on my desk.

All my love,

Sarah.

P.S. I'm going to buy that Valentine's card anyway just to make Ilse jealous.

In her lunch break she bought a soppy card and posted it off to Karl along with the letter to Robert. She had meant the big kiss she had drawn on the card, but had to resign herself to the memory of the real thing. She doubted there would be any more. In fact, how would she face him when she next saw him? She shuddered. Now she knew how Ilse must have felt every time she saw him with Katherine.

After posting the card she popped in briefly to Audrey's work place in a solicitors' office. Audrey had plenty of work, and had cut short her lunch break to try to catch up on the mountain that was awaiting her on her return from their trip.

"I've sent Karl a thank you note," she told Audrey, "inside a Valentine's card, just for a laugh. Are you going to send one to Mick?"

"I might."

"I'll take that as a 'yes'." Sarah perched herself on the edge of Audrey's overflowing desk. "I've also written to Robert. I said no doubt he would hear from Karl whether all was well with him and Ilse now, or not. I wanted to ask him to let us know, but of course I couldn't do that."

"Hardly!" Audrey laughed. "That's men's talk. Although you would have thought that being made privy to it earlier would entitle us to hear the final outcome, wouldn't you?"

"I don't actually think I want to know. I'd be too jealous."

Audrey looked pityingly at her. "Don't get heavy, Sarah. That's why we were there together, to keep it light-hearted."

"I know, I know. Easier said than done, and all that." She edged closer to Audrey, even though the office was empty. "You didn't say anything to Mick, did you, about … you know?"

"About what?"

"About Karl and us."

Audrey hesitated. "Well … I can't be too sure."

"You were drunk, you mean."

"Maybe, but the chances are he wouldn't remember anyway. Don't worry, Sarah. Nobody's going to find out, unless Karl tells them. I promise you, I won't brag about it."

"Well, I just don't want Bina, Richard or Paul finding out." She moved slightly and only just saved a stack of correspondence from falling on the floor. "I can see you're busy. I'd better leave you to it."

After doing a bit of grocery shopping Sarah returned to her office. Perhaps she shouldn't have sent that Valentine's card after all.

*

Karl too was looking at Valentine's Day cards. He had popped in to the Naafi shop to buy a jar of Bovril, a product unobtainable in German shops. The cards caught his eye and set him thinking about whether to buy one for Ilse. If he saw a decent one, he would. He began to flick through them, finding the usual red roses and hearts, and had selected a not too slushy one when he noticed the jollier ones below. A cute teddy bear with molten brown eyes looked up at him, begging him to 'Be My Valentine'. He bought both cards.

On Tuesday evening Karl visited the Mess, feeling in need of company. Mick was on his usual bar stool and, after Karl had bought him another Irish whiskey, he commented that Karl's name was not on the list yet for the Valentine's Day dance on Saturday.

"You'd better be quick about it," Mick added. "The list closes tomorrow."

"Are you and Silke going?"

"No. I'm on call. Not much point. Silke's going to have to find another partner if she wants to go."

Karl's thoughts set off on an unexpected track. Two Valentine's cards, two women. One a rational choice, the other, crazy. Too crazy, he knew. One was the woman who was finally destined to be his after nearly thirty years of waiting. The other was a middle-aged man's fantasy figure. Thoughts of his age reminded him of how stiff he had felt after skiing, which prompted his memory further.

"I can't sign up for it. I'm going skiing with Ilse this weekend," he told Mick. "Otherwise she would have liked the chance to dress up."

"My wife's the same. Trouble is, the events she dresses up for aren't the same as the ones I go to. Still, that's life for you. No doubt she'll manage to get a free visit to Hong Kong out of me at some point."

"You really don't get on with each other, do you?"

"Nope!" Mick said succinctly, downing his whiskey. "And I'm stuck with the Gorgon. No hope of shedding her, unless she snuffs it." He suddenly realised what he was talking about in front of Karl and looked contrite. "Sorry there, Karl. Didn't mean to -"

"No problem. It was your wife we were talking about, not mine. It's getting a lot easier for me these days, fortunately."

Mick smiled warmly. "Good. Ilse looking after you is she? And Audrey?"

Karl blinked.

"It's all right. It's a secret with me," Mick assured him, tapping the side of his nose.

Silke! Karl thought angrily. What had she been blabbing?

TWELVE

When Karl arrived in the office next morning he gave Silke a curt nod. Without bothering to take off his overcoat, he checked his diary, shuffled a few papers around then headed off back out without a word, leaving Silke speechless with bewilderment at his lack of courtesy. She went over to his diary, checked what his schedule was that morning in case she needed to contact him, then resumed her form-filling wondering what on earth she had done to offend him.

When he reappeared shortly before twelve, his attitude to her had not changed. He took off his coat and hung it up, still without a word to her. She decided to tackle him about it immediately and stood up to confront him.

"Is something wrong, Karl?"

He gave her a sharp look. "Yes. I don't like being gossiped about." He turned his back on her and sat down at his desk to check the messages she had left.

Silke stood open-mouthed in astonishment at the unjust onslaught. Karl had clearly got hold of the wrong end of the stick somewhere along the line but her sense of outrage was tempered by her desire not to provoke him. She approached his desk and perched on the edge of it. "What am I supposed to have said, and to whom?" she asked gently.

He pretended to ignore her for a moment while he carried on reading the messages, leaving her to dwell on her misdemeanour. His attitude was so like that of a sulky child that Silke almost broke into a smile, but managed to catch herself in time. Eventually he looked up at her.

"My private life is of no concern to Mick."

Silke looked innocently back at him. "Can you be a bit more specific, please?"

Her tone of voice told him he was sounding petulant. He should explain himself better. "I like you, Silke," he said more reasonably, "and so far I have accepted your very … candid comments with good grace. But I draw the line when you go blabbing to Mick about …" He was not sure how to phrase such a delicate topic, but she continued to look blankly at him. He must be more specific. "… about my activities with Audrey and Sarah," he concluded brusquely. He felt himself blushing like a schoolboy under her gaze. Those brown eyes did so remind him of the teddy bear on the card he had bought for her.

Comprehension began to dawn on Silke. "Have you been speaking to Mick? Did he say I told you?"

"Yes to the first, not in so many words to the second, but he mentioned Audrey's name."

"Then maybe Audrey let something slip when she spent the night with him last Saturday," Silke said with a flash of inspiration.

Slowly Karl nodded. It was certainly a possibility; one he preferred to the alternative. "You promise me you said nothing?"

"I promise," she said earnestly.

Those big brown eyes proved overwhelming for Karl. "I believe you. It must have been Audrey. I'm sorry for blaming you."

She smiled. "That's all right, Karl. I don't blame you for being cross. I would have been." She laid a soothing hand on his shoulder. "I'm just glad we've been able to clear the air and this cloud hasn't hung over us all day."

"You cleared the air, not me." He felt really bad now. "Can I buy you lunch by way of an apology?" he begged. "I think I owe you a few lunches, anyway."

She grinned. "That would be lovely."

They set off a few minutes later, wrapped up well against the cold. Light snowflakes were beginning to fall, but the crisp air was invigorating after the stuffiness of the office.

"I hope it's snowing well in Winterberg," Karl said as they negotiated the slushy road and set off into town. "I'm off skiing at the weekend with Ilse."

"Oh. That's nice."

They walked on a few more paces in silence, their breath steaming in front of them. Silke seemed rather quiet all of a sudden, Karl thought, and broke the silence. "Do you ski?"

"Yes. My mother and I used to go each winter to Switzerland, before she became ill, of course. I haven't been since then."

"Not even to Winterberg?"

Silke shrugged. "It reminds me too much of her." She looked up at him and smiled, her brown eyes suddenly shining with newfound resolution. "But perhaps I could now. Margit and I could plan a trip. I believe she skis well."

"I believe so." Karl grew thoughtful. "Perhaps you could both come this weekend with us."

Silke laughed. "That's very kind of you to suggest it, Karl, but I don't think Ilse would be very thrilled to have us tagging along!"

"Perhaps not," he agreed.

The walk to the town centre worked up their appetites. They found places in a shoppers' restaurant and placed orders for a hearty dish of *Schweinebraten*. While they were waiting for it to arrive, Silke exchanged greetings with a portly lady she recognised.

"One of my mother's friends," she explained to Karl. "They're very good to me still, inviting me round to meet their sons or nephews, trying to get me safely married off and taken care of, poor little orphan that I am!"

Karl was astonished she could be so light-hearted about her situation. "Don't you have any family of your own?" he asked.

"Only some distant cousins on my father's side who live in Italy. I'm an only child and my mother's family was from the Sudetenland. She's had no contact with them since the war."

"So you really are alone."

"Yes, but it's not that bad, really. I've got plenty of friends around town, as well as my archery club." She grinned at him. "You make me sound like some poor foundling." Her smile faded as she added more wistfully: "I do miss having a family though. I often daydream about being part of a huge family Christmas celebration, with grannies and uncles all reminiscing, and little children running around screaming."

"That sounds like my last Christmas."

"Really?" Silke looked intrigued. "In England? I didn't know you had so many relatives there."

"I don't – yet. This was my future daughter-in-law's family. There are hundreds of them, just like you described. They invited us over to

154

join them on Christmas Day. Actually, I think it was as much to get us into different surroundings for Christmas as anything, so we wouldn't miss Katherine too much."

"How thoughtful of them. And did you?"

"Did I what?"

"Miss her?"

He looked down at his plate but only for a moment. "Yes. We all did, but we were all very brave and got on with enjoying ourselves surprisingly well." He looked deep into her eyes, enjoying opening up his feelings to someone so honest and non-judgemental. "It sounds odd, but it helped that my son had died the year before. Not immediately, of course, but I think I handled it better with Katherine."

He realised immediately he had spoken too soon as the familiar pain kicked in. He may have handled it better but the effects were longer lasting. He no longer had Katherine to unburden himself to, and Robert was too far away. Here, in the middle of a busy restaurant, it seemed right to be talking at last.

"You said when your mother died you went off the rails a bit," he said cautiously, watching for her reaction. Encouraged by her nod, he continued: "I did too with Siegfried, but then I've done that before." Her sympathetic brown eyes urged him to confide in her. "I had a mental breakdown in nineteen forty-seven. I still get a bit wobbly at times."

He expected her to be shocked but she appeared totally undaunted by the information, calmly commenting: "You relied on Katherine, didn't you?"

Karl just stared into her perceptive eyes.

"And now you've got to find someone else to take on the role," she told him. "I hope Ilse's up to the job."

His gaze dropped.

"You're not sure about her, are you?"

She was watching his response intently and suddenly he felt she was seeing too much. His barriers shot up and he broke into a grin. "What is this – the Spanish Inquisition? Enough of me! What I really want to know from you is, who's doing my laundry every week?"

"You're changing the subject! Answer me first!"

"Shan't," he retorted playfully. "Not until you've answered my question."

"Well then, neither of us is going to get an answer, are we?" she giggled, having hers already.

*

It took Ilse two hours to pack her weekend bag. They would be staying at Haus Fichtenblick, and Anna, no doubt, would give them separate rooms, but she lived in hope that somehow she would find an opportunity to remind Karl of what they felt for each other. The signs were good that he was turning the corner at last, his suggestion of a weekend away together proving his intentions. Her packing was not helped by Margit coming into her room and criticising her choice of clothing.

"You can't wear that dress, Mutti! This isn't the Reeperbahn." She removed the flimsy item from the bag. "Just something understated and sensible will do. You don't want to frighten him off."

She was right of course. Ilse hunted through her wardrobe and pulled out a burgundy-coloured jersey dress she had bought recently.

"That's better," said Margit approvingly. "Your pearls would go well with that, but it's not too dressy. If you go out anywhere, you'll probably be in your ski slacks and jumper anyway."

Ilse gave a heavy sigh. "Why do I feel so nervous about this now? I was so excited when he asked me, but suddenly I'm feeling a lot's going to depend on this weekend."

"You'll be fine," Margit reassured her. "Just don't expect too much still. Let him do the running."

"Thank you for that kind advice, dear," Ilse managed to laugh. "And here's some for you and Bruno. While the cat's away…"

Edeltraud popped her head round the bedroom door. "What's going on in here?"

"Mutti's having kittens and I'm just trying to calm her down," Margit explained.

Edeltraud chuckled. "Oh, it's the big weekend, isn't it? Catch yourself a new husband. What time's he picking you up?"

"Eight o'clock tomorrow morning, and at this rate I won't be ready, so clear off both of you and let me get on with my packing!"

"Have fun!" Edeltraud said cheekily, beating a retreat.

Hunting through her wardrobe, packing and re-packing, Ilse kept finding her attention wandering, wondering when and if Karl would allow himself to love her fully again. Of course she respected Katherine's memory, and of course she would never do anything to hurt Karl, but she was so impatient to have him back, to feel him as a part of her in that unity of being that had been so noticeably lacking in her relationship with Paul. Karl was her all-time love: the first and the greatest.

After a restless night spent in happy anticipation, she opened the door to Karl and, remembering Margit's advice, greeted him with a light kiss on the mouth. "Hello, Schatz. Prompt as ever, aren't you!"

Karl still found it disconcerting to hear Ilse calling him 'Schatz'. She had been the first to do so, but for the past twenty-two years it had been Katherine's prerogative to use that term of endearment. "You know me," he replied. "Always on time. Are you ready to go?"

"Of course! Let's away!" She called out 'goodbye' to her daughters, got muffled grunts from behind their bedroom doors and led Karl out and down the stairs to the cellar to fetch her skis. Leaving him to secure them on the car, she opened the passenger door and saw an envelope with her name on it lying on the seat, and next to it a single red rose. She picked them up, sat down and opened the envelope, drawing out a card with a picture of more red roses. Inside Karl had written the message: *To Ilse, with my love.* He had not signed it, but there was no need.

"Happy Valentine's Day," he wished her, sitting down beside her and kissing her gently.

She held the rose up to her nose and sniffed it delicately. "Thank you, Karl. I'm sure it will be."

Throughout the drive through the snowy hills of the Sauerland she felt as excited as a new bride going off on honeymoon. She had to keep telling herself not to expect too much from Karl, but hope kept bubbling up like marsh gas, and she felt absurdly happy as they drew near Karl's home in Medebach. The hills were looking spectacularly beautiful under their blanket of deep snow and the traffic in the ski resort of Winterberg was already getting busy as they drove through. Passing the station on the road out to Medebach, she could not help picturing the day she had first seen Karl again after the war; the day she had brought the six-year-old Siegfried to live with the father he had never seen; the day she had realised she still loved rather than hated Karl.

"I was just thinking about that day," she said, guessing he would know which one she meant.

"Me too."

"Very awkward, wasn't it?"

"Very."

"I was such a fool not to find you or your parents earlier after the war. Did you know I actually stayed in Medebach one night with Margit Witter and her family on my way to Dortmund? I could so easily have stopped at Haus Fichtenblick instead. Everything would have been different then."

"Yes, I know." Karl felt uncomfortable. Talking about what might have been denied Katherine's place in history. But it was Siegfried, he told himself, who had brought him and Ilse together again, and he could not deny Siegfried his place in history either. History had come full circle. He smiled. "Maybe it'll be different now."

Ilse risked a gentle pat of his thigh. "I hope so."

Anna certainly seemed to think so when she greeted them at the door to Haus Fichtenblick. "Ilse! Welcome back!" she cried, hugging her close.

"It's good to be here," Ilse replied, stepping inside the house that held such happy memories for her.

The hall had not changed at all since her last visit: the heavy carved dresser with its display of hunting trophy animals to the right of the door, the dark wooden floor and wall panels, the elaborate wooden banisters of the staircase ahead of her. The smell of tobacco smoke from Dieter's pipe still pervaded the air, reminding Ilse strongly of the first time she had visited Karl's family in those dim and distant glory days. She looked up at the man by her side, seeing the changes thirty years had wrought in him: still lean but more rugged and beaten about the edges than the god-like youth of before, yet he was also softer now, gentler, less arrogant. She wondered how she compared with her previous self in Karl's eyes. Fuller-figured, naturally, but still managing to remain reasonably trim. She had not allowed herself to go to seed, having always to compete with Paul's succession of young mistresses. Otherwise she felt she was pretty much the same as she had been in nineteen forty-one. More tolerant though, she had to admit, out of political necessity.

All these thoughts whisked through her mind as Karl helped her off with her coat and she was led through to the living room where Dieter stood waiting to greet her. She had last seen him at Siegfried's funeral, when she had been too distressed to take much in, but she noticed he seemed robust in health, his charm and courtesy as striking as ever.

"Ilse, dearest, welcome back to Haus Fichtenblick," he said, kissing her warmly on both cheeks. "However long is it since you were last here?"

"Before I married Paul. 1953, probably."

"My word, is it really that long? It seems like yesterday," Dieter said, adding chivalrously: "I still remember the very first time Karl brought you here. You've hardly changed a bit. As beautiful as ever!"

"And I could say the same about you, Dieter," she laughed. "As charming as ever."

Karl noticed his father's acceptance of Ilse, despite his earlier reservations concerning her marriage to Paul. His whole family seemed prepared to accept her back into the fold, even Sabina, if that was what he wanted. And that was precisely what he had to decide.

Ilse certainly felt at home here, he noticed. She was already chatting away to his father about the changes in Medebach over the years. Anna brought in a tray of coffees and they gradually found themselves slipping back in time to the war years, when Ilse had been a welcome visitor to the house during Karl's rare periods of leave. Anna even found the photograph album, which Ilse pored over but Karl only glanced at. He did not like seeing himself in that uniform, when he shared that idealism.

For Ilse, however, it was another matter. Not only did the photos bring back such wonderful memories, but also she could see Siegfried so clearly in his father at that age. She looked at Karl, saw his discomfort, and it brought home to her just how much his views had changed since those halcyon days. But none of that was important now. She closed the album and finished her coffee.

"Well, I don't know about you, Karl, but I came here to do some skiing. How about it?"

"My thoughts exactly." He turned to Anna. "Is Rudi coming with the family?"

"Later. You and Ilse can crack on. You probably haven't skied much recently, have you, Ilse?"

"No. It'll probably take me a while to get what confidence I had back. Karl's going to have to be a bit patient with me."

"Don't worry," he grinned. "I'll be taking it easy too."

Every time he spoke to her, Ilse hoped to hear him address her as 'Schatz', but she must wait a bit longer, it seemed.

Once they were dressed and ready, Karl and Ilse got back into his car for the short drive to the nearest suitable hill. They had decided to start Ilse out somewhere quiet before tackling the busier slopes of Winterberg. At least she wasn't a novice like Sarah and Audrey, Karl thought thankfully, as she followed him carefully down a gentle slope.

"All right?" he asked her at the bottom. "Not too rusty?"

"I'm fine. It's strange to ski with a male who waits for me. Siegfried and Heinrich always went bombing off." She stamped the snow off her skis and began undoing the bindings.

"Paul used to ski well. Did he never try again after he lost his arm?" Karl asked her, steadying her as she wobbled while stepping off her skis.

"No. Our skiing weekends were always a chance for him to catch up on paperwork or … other things."

"I see." He looked at her. "Did you mind?"

She saw the pity in his grey eyes and wanted to revel in it. "Yes, of course, but what could I do? I loved him and didn't want to leave him."

"But you've left him now."

"Yes."

They stood alone in the snow, surrounded by silent white hills and creaking black forests and suddenly the time felt right. He cupped his gloved hand under her chin and drew her mouth closer to his.

"For me?" he asked, finding her warm lips with his. He dropped his ski sticks so he could embrace her as he kissed her, but although he felt her eagerly respond, he still felt no spark of desire within himself. He tried to put as much passion into his kiss as he could, to lose himself in her presence, but his emotions met a resolute barrier they could not yet cross. He ended the kiss, drew back, hoping she had not felt his distance from her. She had not.

"Oh, Karl," she breathed, clinging to him. "That was so good." She reached up and stroked the under side of his jaw with her ice-encrusted woollen mitten, making him flinch. "Sorry," she laughed and moved her hand to the back of his head, drawing his face down towards hers for another kiss.

He tried again to respond, putting on a show that fooled her enough to have her eyes brimming with tears of joy. It will come, Karl told himself. I'm sure it will come.

"Are you ready for another gentle run?" he asked, picking up his sticks and skis and shouldering them ready for the climb back up the hill.

"You bet!"

They spent the morning making increasingly more daring runs, interspersed with a few more kisses, and by the last run before lunch Karl felt the iciness thawing from his passion at last. His training with Sarah and Audrey was finally paying off, although he was surprised how long it had taken that morning to get himself warmed up.

For lunch they drove into Winterberg where there was a selection of establishments catering for hungry skiers. They found a table with a view over the ski slopes and had an entertaining meal watching the antics of the other skiers. They took their time over the meal, enjoying each other's company but feeling their muscles beginning to stiffen.

"We'd better not sit too long," Karl said. "Do you think you can manage to ski for a couple more hours?"

"Just about, but we'd better see how it goes."

"We're not as young as we used to be, are we?" He gave a rueful smile and saw her eyes sparkle in return.

"No, we're certainly not, but what we lack in energy we make up for in experience, don't we?"

Her coquettish smile told him in no uncertain terms what she had in mind. "Yes," he replied blandly. "And experience tells me I won't be able to move unless I get on my feet again right now."

He heaved himself up from his chair and helped her up.

"Oh dear, I do feel creaky!" she moaned.

In the end they managed just another hour before they both admitted defeat and took a break for a cup of hot chocolate before driving back to Haus Fichtenblick. Everyone else seemed to be out when they got in, and Anna had left a note telling them to meet them round at Rudi and Adele's when they were ready, as they were all eating there that evening. Karl suspected they had left the house empty on purpose in their efforts to help him develop his relationship with Ilse. He showed her the note and saw by the flush of colour to her face that she too understood the significance of it.

"Well," he said slowly, taking the note off her and fingering the top button of her blouse before slipping it undone. "Do we make the most of it?"

Ilse's heart leapt into action, pounding with the rush of excitement brought on by his suggestion.

"Of course," she whispered huskily.

Reaching for her hand he drew her upstairs to his room, shutting the door carefully in case anyone happened to return unexpectedly, although he knew they would not. Ilse stood waiting expectantly, not rushing him, content to follow his pace now she was sure of what was coming. For a brief moment Karl felt the familiar flicker of doubt, but he overruled the thought, concentrating on the woman who stood happily in front of him now. If only he could lose himself in her this time. He must try.

Ilse was a more than willing helper. When they lay afterwards in each other's arms in his bed she seemed perfectly content with his performance. In fact she was more than content, brimming over with happiness, her arms enveloping him as she lay curled up beside him, her head on his chest. But Karl felt empty. His fingers fondled her arm absently as he struggled to explain his lack of feelings towards Ilse now that he had her back. He certainly loved her in some way, but it was blatantly not the right way, he had now discovered. He felt no more connection with her than he had with Sarah and Audrey.

He lay with her as long as he felt was polite but then had to get up. "We'd better get dressed and off to Rudi's or they'll be wondering where we've got to and be sending out a search party."

"They wouldn't," Ilse protested. "They jolly well know where we are!"

"Perhaps, but it would be rude to make them wait any longer."

Ilse sighed with ill grace and moved out from under the covers. "I'm going for a very quick bath, Schatz. Can I borrow your dressing gown to get there?"

He nodded, handing it to her from the back of the door where it hung. As she took it off him she paused, admiring the body she saw in front of her, trying to ignore the various scars on abdomen, back, right arm and leg he had acquired over the years. Somehow the imperfections only enhanced the perfection elsewhere, she decided, donning the overlarge robe and heading for her room in a cloud of happiness.

Karl watched her progress up the landing to the guest room with its own bathroom. Is it still too soon to be looking for love, he asked himself, or are brown eyes better than blue?

Instantly he felt that electric jolt deep inside and he finally acknowledged what it was he wanted. Slowly he headed for the family bathroom and turned on the shower. He thought about the Valentine's Day card and chocolates he had bought for Silke and left on her desk almost as a joke for her to find at the end of Friday afternoon. She had picked it up, given him a searching look, and declared she would open it tomorrow. He wondered as he soaped himself down, whether she would have been disappointed or pleased with what he had written inside. *Chocolates are meant for sharing.* He had been deliberately ambiguous, unable to acknowledge what he felt for her because of their huge age difference. Until now. As the hot water ran down him, he felt the void in his emotions filling. Silke was the answer. Now he had taken off his blinkers, he yearned for her with a longing that was growing by the second.

"Are you still in there, Schatz?" he heard Ilse calling to him impatiently from outside the bathroom door. "I thought you were in a hurry to get to Rudi's!"

"I won't be a minute," he called back.

"I'd have had a longer soak if I'd realised you were going to be so long."

Have I been so long? Karl wondered. He stepped out of the

163

shower, grabbed a towel and hurriedly dried himself. As he went back to his room he could smell cigarette smoke coming from downstairs. Ilse was peeved at having to wait for him. She would be even more peeved when she realised she had lost him to a younger woman.

That was assuming Silke wanted him. Perhaps she wouldn't; she just liked the company of older men. Mick had always sworn there was nothing between them. Maybe she just wanted a father figure to hang around with. The thought left him depressed.

He found Ilse sitting at the kitchen table, legs crossed and foot bouncing in irritation. The moment she saw him, however, she stood up and stubbed out her cigarette.

"Don't you look as fresh as a daisy now," she said, kissing him and pulling his shirt collar out of his jumper.

"You look very smart," he told her, admiring her burgundy dress and pearls to placate her. "I'm sorry I kept you waiting. I hadn't realised I was taking so long, or else you were incredibly quick."

"The latter. I didn't want to be away from you a moment longer than necessary," she said.

Karl found himself faced with a dilemma. Should he say something now before her hopes got even higher, or was it too late already and he might as well let her enjoy the evening ahead before spoiling everything for her? Making a snap decision, he chose the latter.

"Well, here I am, so let's get going. Where did I put my car keys?" He knew perfectly well but it was an excuse to move away from her.

It was snowing gently when they went out to the car and he had to drive carefully along the clogging roads to Rudi and Adele's small but modern house on the edge of Medebach. Stefan's car was already parked outside and the family were all onto their second glass of *Glühwein* by the time Karl and Ilse joined them.

There were knowing looks as Ilse clung onto Karl's arm, and, when Ilse disappeared off to the toilet later on, Anna whispered in Karl's ear: "You appreciated an empty house then, brother dear?"

He gave her a steady look. "Don't jump to conclusions please."

Anna looked disappointed. "Oh. Sorry. I thought from the way Ilse was -"

"Maybe, but just ... steady on." It was not only Anna, he noticed. They all thought the same, but he could say nothing until he had spoken to Ilse. And Silke. For if Silke didn't want him, then he was left with Ilse. And would that be such a bad thing? He had to keep his options open for the moment.

THIRTEEN

Footsteps on the landing told Karl his father was already getting up. Having been awake much of the night, Karl was glad of some company at last, as he urgently needed someone to confide in. He had never had to ask his father for advice in his teens. Popular with the girls, confident in his politics and outlook, Karl had found all the guidance he needed in the Hitler Youth. Then the war had come and with it the inevitable separation, distancing him from his parents as life wrought its new destiny for him. He had had nobody to confide in for several years until he met Robert Murdoch, and that bond was instantaneous. Since then the only time his parents had given him an opinion was in his dealings with the young Siegfried. They had been right then and he had been wrong. Now he needed to talk to somebody and Robert was too far away.

Karl quickly got out of bed, dressed and went downstairs where his father was setting the kettle on the stove.

"Morning, Karl. Did you sleep well?" Dieter asked, seeing the answer in Karl's bleary eyes.

"No. I've got something on my mind and I'd like to discuss it with you."

Dieter frowned. "Relationships?" he guessed.

Karl nodded. "Perhaps we could go out to the barn and talk before the others get up."

Now it was Dieter's turn to nod. He took the kettle off the stove and went to the hall to fetch his and Karl's coats to face the cold outside. They crunched through the crisp snow in the yard in silence until they reached the comparative warmth of the barn at the end of the house. The household cats mewed expectantly at their arrival but were ignored.

Dieter sat on an empty crate while Karl chose to lean against the side of his father's old car.

"Well?" Dieter prompted him gently.

Karl looked at his father, at his hands, at the three cats busy washing themselves, finding it difficult to put his thoughts into words. "It's Ilse," he finally began, "or rather how I feel about her, as you've probably guessed."

"Go on," Dieter encouraged him.

Karl gazed at the straw on the floor. "You saw how things were between us at Siegfried's funeral, how jealous it made Katherine – with justification, I might add." He paused, realising he could not tell his father about his adulterous night with Ilse two summers ago. "I've never left off loving her. She meant so much to me during the war. Katherine understood to some extent and lived with it. When Siegfried died I needed that link, that bond with Ilse even more, but now Katherine's gone everything's changed." He looked up at his father at last, finally meeting his eye. "I'm not sure I want Ilse now I can have her. It may be that it's just taking me longer than I thought to recover my old feelings for her. Should I persevere, even if it means deceiving her at the moment as to how I really feel, or should I pull out now before I hurt her more than I will have done already?"

"It depends how far things have gone," Dieter pointed out.

"Quite far," Karl said carefully.

"I see. So she thinks she's got you but you're not sure yet. Do you know what's holding you back? After all, you did feel strongly towards her a year ago. It's not *just* losing Katherine, is it?" Dieter said, scrutinizing his son's face for the truth of the matter.

Was he as transparent as all that? Karl baulked at the idea of mentioning Silke by name. It was too early, too tenuous to risk jinxing, but he ought to give his father some idea of the real situation.

"No," he agreed. "There may be someone else - there *is* someone else," he corrected himself, "but ... I don't know if she's interested in me. The chances are high that she won't be."

"Why?"

Karl took a deep breath then committed himself. "She's twenty-three years younger than I am."

"Ouch!" Dieter gasped. "Not good, Karl. Don't go there. I'm sure she's a lovely girl, but that's it, isn't it. She's scarcely more than a girl. It couldn't work in the long run."

"I know. It's stupid of me even to consider it, but I can't get her out of my head. And she *is* a lovely girl."

"Leave her to someone else, Karl, please," Dieter advised sternly. "Ilse at least knows you and your … problems."

"I think she's largely forgotten about them," Karl said, "or at least she doesn't understand the full extent of them." He realised he had an example of what he meant. "Take recently, when Sarah and Audrey were here and we all went round to Ilse's. The youngsters there were smoking cannabis and it rather shocked me. Bina noticed something was up and helped me cope with it – she's learnt that from Katherine over the years - but Ilse didn't seem to notice a thing. To her I'm still the strong, brave hero from the war. I'm the one who has to carry her through all her troubles. I don't know how well she'd cope if I needed her help."

"Test her then," Dieter suggested." I don't mean simulate a breakdown," he added hastily, seeing his son's appalled expression. "Just don't be so nice to her. See how she reacts in adversity, whether she backs you up or plays the spoilt child. If it's the latter then leave her be and look elsewhere, but not at Silke. It is Silke, isn't it?"

"How did you know?"

"Oh, the way you've spoken of her: so competent, so helpful, so understanding."

"There you are. You can see why I love her."

"Do you really love her, though? Isn't she just a young bit of skirt flirting with a middle-aged man?"

"I don't know yet. That's what I said; I don't know what she feels for me, although she must like me a lot. That is genuine."

"My advice is still to stick with Ilse. You've got grandchildren together, you loved her until very recently. It's probably just too soon for you to commit yourself to her -"

"But I already feel I want to commit myself to Silke!"

"Do you? What happens when you're sixty and she's a mere thirty-seven and casting her eye over someone much younger? You'll be left to a lonely old age, just as I am. Don't go there, Karl. Please don't. Give Ilse a second chance."

Karl sighed heavily, knowing his father spoke sense. "All right. I'll try. But I will test her out. I need someone who'll support me as much as I'll support her. Ilse must pass that test."

"I hope she does, Karl. We all like her, and she adores you."

"That's not enough! She must love me for who I am now. I'm not strong enough to carry both of us through life; Dachau saw to that." Just saying the name brought back the memories. Thoughts of Katherine saved him now. "Katherine used to say that I was like an old and battered but well loved teddy bear, whose seams occasionally came adrift and whose stuffing fell out. She had to push it back in every so often and sew up the seams again, but she and Robert knew how. Bina does too to some extent, but Ilse?"

Dieter understood his son's fears. "I know, but give her a fair test. Don't be too harsh on her."

"I'll try."

*

Despite being alone, Ilse had slept well that night. Exhausted by skiing, drugged by alcohol and physically satisfied by Karl, there had been little to keep her awake except her jubilation. She had hugged the pillow close, giddy with ecstasy, and thought of Karl, probably asleep by now, a few doors down the landing. He had seemed subdued after their lovemaking, and she guessed he was still overcoming his grief. She could excuse him this time but hoped to spark him up a bit in the months to come. They could go away on holiday together perhaps, to Italy or the South of France. Karl might even take her to visit his sons in England, although she envisaged that could be rather awkward, setting foot in Katherine's family home. No, best to leave England out of it, she had decided.

Just for good measure she had relived their lovemaking until she finally succumbed to the warmth of her bed with a smile still upon her lips.

Now it was morning and she realised she was the last one up. She glanced at her watch and discovered it was nearly eight o'clock. The family would be heading off for church later, while she and Karl tackled the slopes again. Dressing hurriedly in her ski slacks and jumper she went downstairs to find everyone.

Anna and Stefan sat in the kitchen, but there was no sign of Karl or his father.

"He's outside, Ilse," Anna told her on seeing her anxious face. "He and Papa must have gone for a stroll. I don't expect they'll be long. Do you want some coffee?"

Ilse settled herself down to wait, chatting amiably to Anna about their various offspring.

"Any sign of Monika producing a grandchild for you yet?" Ilse was asking when Karl and Dieter walked in through the door.

"Morning, Ilse," Karl greeted her, coming up behind her and laying his hands on her shoulders. He kissed the top of her head, but that was all. Perhaps he doesn't want to be too familiar in front of his family yet, she thought, remembering how uninhibited they had been during their former romance. She put a hand up to her shoulder to cover his, but he had slipped away to get a cup of coffee.

"How are your legs this morning, Ilse?" Dieter asked her, settling himself down on a kitchen chair beside her.

"A little bit stiff, but not too bad. What's the weather like out there?"

"Overcast. We might get more snow, I fear. I hope it doesn't stop you enjoying the day."

"I'm sure it won't," she replied, smiling confidently.

Now that everybody was gathered they could begin eating the breakfast of boiled eggs and cold meat that Anna had laid out on the table. Ilse stoked herself up, anticipating an active morning but noticed Karl not eating so heartily. It had been the same last night at Rudi and Adele's. Perhaps he's lovesick, she thought tenderly.

"So where are you off to today?" Dieter asked his son.

"Winterberg again," Karl replied. "There are plenty of different slopes to keep us amused there and ski-lifts too, more importantly. Trudging up the slopes around here isn't so much fun these days."

Ilse felt disappointed. Winterberg was busier. There would not be so many chances to sneak a quick kiss as they had found the day before. Never mind. There would be plenty of other occasions.

After breakfast she helped Anna clear away while Karl fetched their skis and boots from the barn where he had stored them overnight. Soon they were off on the road to Winterberg to join the merry throngs on the slopes. Ilse found Karl pushing her harder today, skiing faster and more aggressively now that she had found her ski-legs again. By midday she was flushed and weary and ready for a good long break.

The restaurants were beginning to fill up, and as they were finding a table to sit at, Karl spotted some familiar faces and led her over to meet his friends from Medebach's shooting club. One of them remembered Ilse from the old days and greeted her heartily.

"So you got him at last, Ilse! About time too!"

Ilse smiled back at the ruddy-faced farmer, who seemed more than a little drunk already, hoping Karl would find somewhere else to sit. To her dismay he pointed to a spare seat, indicating she should sit down. Reluctantly Ilse did as she was told. This was not how she had envisaged the day, watching a load of peasants drink themselves stupid. Karl bought himself and her a beer, ordered some food for them both, then squeezed in beside her at the table. Apart from initially acknowledging Ilse's presence, the conversation revolved around the various shooting competitions and likely candidates to become the championship king that year. Ilse's attention soon began to wander from their table, and she began to feel angry with Karl for ignoring her. When he finally dragged himself away from them after they had eaten, she made her feelings known.

"Honestly, Karl. I thought we were here for a romantic weekend, not a rifle-club reunion!"

"Sorry. I hadn't seen them since the summer and I could hardly ignore them, could I?" He hugged her to him and kissed her cheek, but she was not yet mollified.

"That's not good enough. I want a proper kiss."

They were surrounded by people on Winterberg's main street. It was not the place to indulge in a passionate embrace.

Karl looked around awkwardly. "Later. Somewhere more private," he promised her.

She had to make do with that.

They spent the early afternoon negotiating the ever busier slopes and gave up at three o'clock to return first to Medebach and then to Iserlohn. As they sat down in Karl's car he turned to her and reached for her face, drawing her closer to kiss her full on the lips, but not close enough to embrace her. She felt the distance between them and still Ilse felt cheated but refrained from comment. Somehow today just wasn't working out how she had expected it to.

"What's the matter, Karl?" she asked him eventually, when they had been driving in silence for some minutes.

"Mm? Oh, nothing," he said vaguely.

"There must be. You've suddenly gone all strange on me."

"Have I? It's probably just a mood. It'll pass."

"But it must be about something, surely. Have I done something wrong?"

"No." Karl decided to be uncommunicative to see how far she would go to discover the truth.

"It *must* be something I've done! Why would you be in a mood with me otherwise?"

"I'm not in a mood with you," he snapped.

"But you are! You just said you were!"

"Not with you."

"Then with what?" she demanded, annoyed by his sudden reticence.

He could see he was upsetting her and took pity on her, unable to taunt her any more. "I just get strange moods occasionally, that's all," he explained with a smile of apology.

"Hmm. I thought only women were allowed to do that," she responded with a hint of a smile herself. "Just don't go getting them too often."

"Why not?"

"I don't like it!"

"I don't either, but I can't help it," he protested quite genuinely now. "I thought you might be a bit more understanding."

"I see." Ilse did not like the implied reprimand, but she was more puzzled by his behaviour than angered. "Karl, why are you talking to me like this? It's like you want my sympathy or something."

"Perhaps I do."

"But you've got it – had it ever since I heard about Katherine's death. I've never expected any more of you than you've been willing to offer. Yesterday you gave me everything, or so I thought, but you were strangely quiet after that, weren't you? Is that it? Don't I match up to Katherine?"

"It's not about you, it's about me," he retorted, turning into the lane that led up to Haus Fichtenblick.

"But it must be. It all changed after we made love. You took ages in the shower. What did I do that you didn't like, or that you wanted me to do?" She gripped his thigh hard in her anguish. "I'll do anything you want, Karl, I promise."

He stopped the car short of the house, needing to finish this conversation before they arrived. "I want you to listen, Ilse. I'm telling you it's not so much about you as much as it's about me and my problems. I want you to understand me, to make allowances for me when I may seem offhand or moody; to just be there for me and accept that it's not necessarily anything that you've done."

He looked into her pale blue eyes and saw that although she had heard, she had not understood. She was still focused on her own part in events. Maybe she would never see beyond her own boundaries, he thought sadly. Then she surprised him.

"I knew exactly where I was with Paul," she said, suddenly wistful. "I don't think I understand you at all any more, Karl. I've got a lot to learn, haven't I?"

He smiled. "That's a start, anyway." He drove up to the house, parking outside, wondering whether he had achieved anything by his day of gentle testing. For the most part she had passed reasonably well, but it did not make up for the fact that his earlier talk of teddy bears to his father had prompted thoughts of Silke that had lingered all day. Ilse had a right to feel aggrieved. Although she may have won back some ground, Silke was still way out front.

When he dropped Ilse and her skis off at the apartment later that evening, he was still in a quandary about his feelings towards her and how far he should continue to keep her hopes up. When the time came to kiss her goodbye, he knew he was leading her on with his practised response to her eager lips. He still felt no emotion, no connection with her whatsoever. Katherine's death had severed it totally, but he still needed Ilse. He could not afford to let go of her yet. As he finally bade farewell to her, he saw Margit peeking at them through the crack of the door, and realised how much he owed Margit for finding him his job and Silke. It occurred to him that Margit and Silke were of similar ages, yet he would never countenance going out with Margit. What was so different about Silke then?

*

It had not been a good Valentine's Day for Sarah and Audrey. Ron and Patrick, feeling neglected recently, had decided to attend a dance nearer Birmingham without them, leaving them with no plans for their own entertainment. Audrey was not feeling very well either, succumbing to a cold that was doing the rounds, so Sarah decided to spend the evening alone in front of the fire with a good book and a cup of tea.

The evening proved tedious. She kept losing the plot of the book, finding her mind elsewhere, wondering what Karl was doing right now. For the first time since divorcing Perry she was feeling the need for a long-term commitment, for some stability in her previously frivolous love life. Her feelings for Karl showed her she was not immune to love, that she could desire a man's presence as much, if not more than his body. She had missed out on so much as a result of choosing the wrong man initially. For years she had been glad to be free, glad of her independence, but now what did she have? Nothing except loneliness. She was bored with her job, bored with everything, jealous of Ilse.

There was not much she could do for the moment, committed as she was to caring for her nephews. She had promised Karl she would, and she meant to keep her promise. Paul still needed her advice and presence in the home occasionally, even if Richard was reasonably self-sufficient now. A prospective partner for herself must be local but she would not find him by sitting at home moping.

She got up from her armchair to shovel more coal on the fire and refresh the teapot. Perhaps finding a more stimulating job would be a start, she thought on returning to her chair. She had rather undervalued her talents by opting for secretarial work, but what did Hereford have to offer a career woman? She would have to scout around. Maybe the Civil Service would take her on in the DHSS or the local tax office. Perhaps a shop needed a manager. She would turn her hand to just about anything to keep her mind off Karl.

*

After his previous sleepless night Karl went out like a light, waking on the Monday morning to the knowledge that today he must confront

174

his feelings for Silke. She would no doubt mention the St. Valentine's Day card and chocolates he had given her, and he would either have to bluff his way out or, depending on her response, do what his heart commanded and let her know how much she meant to him.

He called in at the Mess on his way in to work to check on his post and found an envelope with a British stamp and Sarah's handwriting that looked suspiciously like a card: a thank you card in all probability. Sarah was a stickler for such niceties, although he did not really expect family to bother with such a thing. He was the one who should be sending the thank you note for the way she and Audrey had helped him get through that evening. But Silke had done more. She had been the one who had truly lifted his spirits that day.

He tore open the envelope and glanced at the card, suddenly shocked by what he saw. Sarah had sent him a Valentine's card. Opening it, a note fell out and he hesitantly picked it up off the floor. Glancing at the single kiss mark on the card he read the note with trepidation, but by the end he felt relief. It was a thank you note after all and the card was clearly just a brief reminder of what fun they had had. Or he sincerely hoped so. He stuffed the card back in its envelope and ambled off to his office, his mind already back on Silke.

She smiled as she always did when he entered the room. "Morning, Karl. Good weekend was it?"

Her smile turned into a grin, her eyes twinkling mischievously. Something about her tone of voice also set Karl wondering whether the jungle drums had already been sounding. Had Ilse said anything to Margit who might then have told Silke? Surely not!

"It was all right, thank you, Silke. We had some good skiing. How was yours?"

"Fair to middling. Went swimming with Margit, did some shopping, all the usual mundane things. Mick was on call, of course, so I just spent Saturday evening in the pub with the others. Not very exciting, really."

"You must try skiing again before the snow melts."

"Yes. I must." She was switching on the kettle to boil, with her back to him, when she added: "Thank you for the lovely card and the chocolates. I've put them in my drawer in case we need them. You did say they were for sharing."

Damn! He couldn't see her face to see what she really felt. He had been counting on getting some clues as to how she regarded him, but her voice was studiously neutral. On balance he thought she was pleased with his gift, and she had said the card was lovely.

"The chocolates are meant for you, really," he told her, waiting for her to turn around. She was spooning coffee into the mugs now, but as he watched she finally turned to face him.

"And what did you give Ilse?" she asked quietly, arms folded across her chest.

It was a loaded question, and he sensed she already knew the answer to whichever way it could be interpreted.

"What did Margit tell you I gave her?" he countered.

"Touché!" she laughed. "All right, I admit I know you gave her a rose and a jolly good ... time," she said decorously. "Margit phoned me shortly after you dropped Ilse off. Your rose was installed in a crystal vase and Ilse looked like the cat that had got the cream. She didn't need to say anything to Margit."

"So why did Margit phone you? What business is it of yours? Unless you had a bet on or something?"

The kettle boiled and Silke turned her back once more to pour water into the waiting mugs. "Oh, girl-talk, idle speculation, gossip, call it what you will," she said casually.

"Maybe I don't like being speculated about, Silke."

She handed him his mug of coffee. "Then you should make your intentions plain, Karl." The tone of the conversation had become rather tense but Silke remedied that with her next comment. "Plain talking, West Coast style is what's needed, don't you think? None of this shilly-shallying and beating about the bush! People like to know where they stand."

She meant herself, Karl knew, but he dared not risk declaring how he felt about her if she didn't feel the same. He needed openness from her too.

"That works both ways."

"And we're still beating about the bush," she retorted. "I tell you what. At lunchtime you and I can go for a walk and a talk. That'll be fun, won't it? We can tell each other exactly how we feel about people."

Karl had to smile. "At the moment I think you're a bossy little thing."

She smiled back. "Someone has to take the initiative." She looked at him intently. "Are we on for our talk?"

"I suppose so. I won't get any work done unless I agree, will I?"

"Nope! Lunchtime it is, then." The conversation over, she sat down and turned to the folder on her desk.

Karl sat down at his and consulted his diary. He had plenty to do this morning. No chance to ponder on what he would say to her. His first job on a Monday morning was to speak to the workmen, to make sure there were no problems, although Silke's blackboard and worksheets usually prevented the likelihood of those. He downed his coffee, made sure he had pocketed his notebook, then headed off to the workmen's room where the men were still sitting having a final cigarette together before dispersing on their respective tasks. The replacement for the sacked Hussels was due to start today and Karl needed to meet him, introduce him to the others and settle him in working alongside one of the old hands to start with.

Throughout the morning his work took him around the site, including a call on the commanding officer's house to assess the refurbishment needed in the kitchen. The housekeeper had a long list of requirements and Mrs Seares, the CO's wife, wanted her say too. By the time he had rid them of their more fanciful notions and negotiated what was possible within the budget, as well as drunk two cups of coffee at Mrs Seares's insistence, the morning was over. He headed back to the office to find Silke impatiently waiting.

"At last!" she said. "I was beginning to think you'd chickened out."

"Are you calling me a coward? Me, who was awarded the Iron Cross, First Class!" he joked.

"Were you?" she asked, sounding impressed.

"Well, yes I was actually, but ..." He was going to add that he had not been allowed to keep it long, but that was history she did not need to know.

She misunderstood his reticence. "Don't worry. My father had medals too. What you did in the war is no concern of mine."

He realised his previous thought was wrong. "It should be, really. Your generation must know what we did."

"We do. They were at pains to teach us at school. Don't worry, though. I don't hold it against you personally. It's history I blame, not you."

"That's a nice way of looking at it."

"Well I have to, otherwise I would hate my father for some of the orders he was forced to give, and I can't do that, can I?"

"No," he agreed. "My daughter still loves me, despite what she knows about me."

He could see she would have loved to have asked what that was, but knew it was none of her business. "The past is long past and should lay buried now," she told him. "We don't need to open old wounds, just recognise the scars for what they are."

"I've plenty of those," he told her. He reached for his coat hanging by the door. "Well, we'd better get going for our great heart-to-heart talk. Just promise me that you'll go first, then I can see how it's done."

They headed for one of the paths that led through the parkland surrounding the hospital. It was cold outside and they set off briskly, but once they were a safe distance from any buildings they slowed their pace a fraction, their breath steaming in front of them as they walked.

"Right. You begin," Karl told her. "What is it that's on your mind?"

Silke looked up at him from under her purple velvet hat. "I'm going to be totally honest, say exactly what I think and damn the consequences, OK? If we don't agree or we find ourselves at odds, then we put it all totally behind us, like the war," she added with a smile, "and carry on as if nothing had been said. Agreed?"

"Impossible!" he told her. "You can't ignore something like that!"

"Like what?" she quickly probed.

"Ah! No," he said, laughing at her manoeuvre. "You first. Come on."

They had reached the woodland now and carried on up the hill at a gentle pace, enabling them to talk without getting too puffed.

"I've spent most of the morning planning this," she began, "so I hope it comes out right. I thought you would find it impossible to speak openly, so I'll pave the way. Here goes." She paused to draw breath. "Firstly, we've only known each other for three months, but I've seen you change over that time. I think I can read you quite well now. To begin with I was just Margit's friend, as far as you were concerned, and an efficient office worker. Then you thought I was an easy lay for half the hospital staff, Mick especially – no don't interrupt, just let me say my piece – since they all called me 'darling' Silke. By Christmas you realised they only call me that because they rely on me and like me so much. I'm friendly, efficient and caring by nature and you're starting to respect me for who I am, although you think my preference for the company of older men is because I lost my father when I was so young."

She stopped by a large tree, looked around to check that nobody else was in sight then carried on walking, knowing she had his total attention. "At the Christmas Ball in the Officers' Mess when you danced with me, you discovered how nice it was to be so close to me. Over Christmas, while you were away in England, you realised you missed me slightly. You made sure your archer friend let you have a go at archery so you could have an excuse to spend time at the weekend with me, safely chaperoned by Bina and Ilse. Now Ilse is the problem. You are sort of committed to her, and she expects to end up marrying you, especially after last weekend when you finally managed to overcome your feelings about your late wife. That was thanks, in part, to the help your sister-in-law and her friend gave you. However, before that you discovered someone else who really understands you, who would care for you if only you would let her. The problem is, you are worried about how young she is, that a relationship with her would prove unworkable in the long term because her love would prove fickle as time passed."

She stopped and turned towards him, standing close. "How am I doing so far?"

He looked down into her warm brown eyes and felt the now familiar kick as love struck him the same body blow he had felt before. Still he had to hold back. It was unnerving how well she had read him. She was a mind-reader with psychic powers. But he had to hear more. "It's interesting. Carry on."

She nodded, a smug smile playing around her lips. "You see how well I understand you, Karl. I know that Sarah and Bina don't approve of Ilse as a future wife for you, and for my part I don't approve of her either. She's shallow, self-centred and can't see the real you, the one who needs help. I saw how much both Sarah and Bina watch out for you, try to protect you. At Ilse's party, Bina was very concerned about you at one point, but Ilse never noticed a thing. It had something to do with the joints being smoked. You have a huge problem with drugs for some reason." She saw him look away and knew she was right. "I guess you were addicted yourself once."

He flinched, again confirming her suspicions, but she had gone too far. He was drawing away, retreating from her scrutiny and she cursed herself now for being too frank. Making amends she said: "Tell me what you know about me, then, Karl. Get your own back. Say whatever you like or think is true."

Karl was too shocked to think for a moment, but then he realised just how right she was, how well she understood his needs, and how much he loved her. He wanted to kiss her right there and then but she was waiting expectantly for him to speak and he knew he must fulfil his side of the bargain.

He set off slowly up the hill again, preparing what he would say and she quietly followed, patiently waiting for his analysis of her, which would enable him to voice at last what she knew he felt for her.

"What I know about you, Silke, is very little. I know both your parents are dead, that you are an only child and that you enjoy archery. I know that you are a very kind and considerate person, with an uncanny ability to read people. What I don't know is why you should be interested in a man nearly twice your age, or even if you are interested in me. I know why I love you ..." He smiled as he realised what he had just said to her, then said it again because it sounded so nice. "I do love you, Silke. You're right. I realised it at the weekend, when Ilse paled into insignificance compared with you."

Her brown eyes staring up at him were proving too hard to resist and he moved closer, searching her face for the signs that would give him permission to kiss her. They were all there: the tilt of the chin, the sparkle in her eyes, even the running of her tongue over her cold lips. He needed to kiss her now. He leant forward, his hands bringing her shoulders closer and their mouths met in a soft and gentle embrace. A warm shiver ran right through him at the taste of her, at the feel of her breath on his face. He raised his hand to stroke her cheek, then abruptly broke off the kiss to hug her, laying his face on top of the soft velvet of her hat, drawing her body as close to his as he could. The emotion he felt was unmistakeable, the strength of it powerful enough to moisten his eyes.

"Darling Silke," he said, stepping back then so he could see her face once more. "Darling Silke," he repeated, overwhelmed by what he was allowing himself at last to feel.

Silke beamed up at him, tears in her own eyes now. "It sounds so different when you say it," she smiled.

"That's because I mean it." He kissed her again, this time with all the passion that had been locked inside him for so long, and she responded with equal measure. He had no thought of Katherine to distract him now. Her ghost had been safely laid and he could commit to Silke fully.

As they stood in their close embrace, experiencing the joy of each other's presence, Karl had to ask her: "Why me? Why do you want me?"

"You're the man I've always envisaged for myself. You fit every particular in every way. You're kind and considerate but tough when you need to be. You're honest, strong, a good father – and grandfather -"

"All right, that's enough!" he laughed. "You'll make me big-headed." He took her by the hand and began to walk slowly back down the hill the way they had come then said more seriously: "But I'm not perfect, by any means. You've said so yourself that I need looking after. And I do. Also I can be moody, depressed even, violent on occasion. Please don't think I'm perfect. I'm too old for a start!"

"It's all right, Karl. I know you're not perfect, and your age is immaterial, or rather not so immaterial. You've proved what a perfect husband you would be. With a younger man, I wouldn't have that guarantee, would I? Your children are all well-adjusted, healthy and loving -"

"Siegfried wasn't, and it's thanks to Katherine that the others turned out so well."

Silke stopped in her tracks. "You do yourself an injustice, Karl. You're a wonderful father, and I'm sure you were a wonderful husband too. But I've made myself sound too clinical, as though I've chosen you for your reproductive capabilities rather than love, haven't I?"

"And haven't you?" he asked in all seriousness.

She thought about it. "You're the lead stallion, Karl. Women can't help falling in love with you. It must be your chemistry."

He was puzzled now. "Stop talking in scientific riddles, Silke, and just tell me whether you love me or my body."

"I loved you from the moment I first saw you. I've never felt that way about anyone before. But it's not just the way you look. I know it isn't, but I don't know what it is. My heart just leapt out to you."

He looked down at her. "Actually I know what you mean. It was the same for me. Everything about you seemed perfect."

She heard the proviso in his voice. "Except my age."

He laughed. "Well, if we're talking reproduction, I shouldn't choose an older woman to be my wife, should I?" He stopped abruptly, appalled at what he was saying, discussing marriage and children already.

"I would want children," Silke said, expertly smoothing over his anxiety. "But at the moment I want food. Let's find somewhere to eat."

Karl felt they had said everything: their future together mapped out and settled in a matter of minutes. It felt good. He reached for her gloved hand again, kissed it then kissed her lips very tenderly. She was his.

FOURTEEN

The lambing sheds were a refuge for Paul. Dark, confined and associated with birth, their womb-like quality reminded him of the mother he missed so much. He had spent many hours with her here, learning the shepherd's craft, soaking up the wisdom of generations gone before.

Around him ewes chewed noisily on chopped beet or sat patiently awaiting events. Paul chewed on his breakfast toast and Bovril, reflecting on what life offered him now that Dad had abandoned them to their fate. There were a hundred and one chores he should have been doing now, chores his parents used to do but which were now his to fit in around his schoolwork. He had hoped to go to college, been encouraged by Mum to consider it, but it was impossible now. His fate was sealed.

He finished his toast and fished in the pocket of his scruffy jeans for a packet of chewing gum and popped a piece in his mouth. He knew exactly what had caused his mood. It was all Liz Goddard's fault for laughing at his dancing on Saturday, then for poking fun at his garden furniture business, making light of his craftsmanship and entrepreneurial skills. She had told him he was square, un-hip and boring, that no girl would be seen dead going out with him. He knew she was wrong, that there were plenty of girls apart from Liz and her gang who liked him, but her comments had struck a nerve. What could he do with his life?

Richard had Vanessa and ultimate responsibility for the farm; Bina had her new singing career with the 'Leuchtleute' as the trio now called themselves. She had rung yesterday in a state of high excitement to tell them that, after performing at a student gig on Saturday night, they had been approached by a talent scout, who had talked about signing them up for a possible record deal. Paul was pleased for her and had told her he hoped it would all work out, but it had left him feeling even more fed up than before. Even Dad had moved on to a new life – a new wife even, if what Bina had said about Ilse was true. Mum would have been horrified at the idea. How dare Dad even think of it!

He spat out the chewing gum onto the straw, but his rebellion was short-lived. Realising what he had done, he picked it up and wrapped it tidily in its silver paper to dispose of properly later. He could never be a rebel. He had been brought up to be too law-abiding a citizen. His father had never dared put a foot wrong, lest people would say it was because he was German. When Richard had punched Mr Kellett, Mum had been so fearful of a son of hers having a criminal record that she had sacrificed herself. He could never let Mum down now. But what could he do with his life stuck here?

He hurled a lump of beet at a nearby bucket, knocking it over. The ewes bleated anxiously as he strode out to the woodshed, grabbed the long-handled axe and began furiously chopping logs.

Richard found him there, half an hour later.

"You should have left for school ten minutes ago!" Richard shouted. "I've been hunting all over the place for you. Didn't you hear me calling? You'll have missed the bus."

"Damn! Sorry. I've just got too many chores to do." He sank the axe into the chopping block, wiped his palms on his jeans and looked imploringly at his brother. "Can you give me a lift? I don't want to miss Biology Practical."

Richard was annoyed. It was a forty minute round trip but he sensed Paul was upset about something. He never usually complained about the chores. "All right, just this once. You can tell me what the problem is on the way. You'd better hurry up and get changed."

Paul dashed indoors and up to his room, tore off his jeans and shirt, exchanging them for his school uniform, then hurtled downstairs, almost colliding with the grandfather clock in the hall. He grabbed his school bag and coat from the kitchen and ran out into the yard where Richard had the Land Rover warmed up, ready and waiting.

"So," Richard asked him as they sped off down the valley towards Penchurch. "What's on your mind?"

"Applying for my provisional licence just as soon as I'm seventeen for a start," Paul said glibly, hanging on to the sides of the seat as they hurtled round a bend, "so I'm not stuck on the farm."

184

Richard guessed where this was heading. "You want to go places?"

"Yes. I had hoped to go to college and make something of myself."

"Like what: Chief Panda-counter?"

"Don't be facetious!" Paul knew his brother was winding him up, but suddenly it seemed relevant to how he felt at the moment. "I don't want to make furniture all my life. Caring for the environment is important now. Those photos of the earth from space have really brought it home to me. I agree more and more with Joni Mitchell. I'd rather still have the birds and the bees than rid the world of spots on apples."

"I would agree but people want perfect apples."

"I don't see why. If people only knew what we put on them! I can see now why Dad took all those precautions when we were spraying the orchards and dipping the sheep, especially with all this worry about DDT. I can't understand why it's taken everyone else so long to realise the harm they do."

Richard sensed an opening into more personal concerns. "At least some good came of his time at Dachau."

"Dachau? You mean the concentration camp?"

"Yes." Richard kept his eyes on the road as a milk lorry negotiated a tight junction in front of them. "Don't you remember him telling us about what they did to him there, injecting him with different substances?"

Paul thought hard. "Did he tell us on that holiday at Ilse and Paul's hunting lodge in Bavaria? I vaguely remember the name being mentioned, but I must have been too young to grasp what he was saying. I was only … what … seven or so?"

"Probably. Well, I'll have to remind you some time. Perhaps then you'll understand Dad a bit better."

"Do you understand him?"

Richard frowned. "No. I suppose I don't. All that business after Siegfried died was scary. Mum understood him – and Robert does, of course. Thank heavens there's still Robert if we need him."

"Are we likely to, do you think?"

Richard shrugged. "No idea."

After he had dropped off Paul at his grammar school in Hereford, Richard decided to make the most of his journey and buy some provisions before calling in on his aunt at her office to discuss Paul's worries. Perhaps she would have words of wisdom to offer him.

As he walked through the street door into her office she was busy typing a letter. She looked round startled and her hand flew to her chest in relief.

"Thank goodness it's only you, Richard! I thought for one moment it was my boss coming in early. I'm busy typing my letter of resignation, you see."

Richard peered over her shoulder at the typewriter. "Whatever's brought this on?"

Sarah leaned back in her chair. "I'm frustrated and bored with this job, and know I could be doing something more worthwhile."

"That's strange. Paul's feeling just the same about his life. He's never really wanted to stay on the farm, had even spoken of wanting to work in Opa's sawmill at one time. Now he's bemoaning the fact he can't go off to college any more and count pandas. Paul's like Dad, I think. Dad's always had a touch of wanderlust and tried to get off the farm whenever he could."

"And you reckon Paul's the same?"

"Yes, but he realises he can't leave me to work the farm alone."

"You could employ somebody."

"True. Bill, Vanessa's brother, would come, I know, but Paul feels too loyal to leave me in the lurch."

"Well he shouldn't. It's his life to do with as he wants. You hurry up and marry Vanessa, employ Bill and let Paul go to college, if that's what he wants."

Richard perched on her desk. "That's what Mum would have said. And Dad will say the same thing, I know, but I can't bring myself to suggest it to him. I want him to stay and help run the farm. It's an awfully big thing for me to manage on my own."

Sarah nodded sympathetically. "I know, love. You're young to have such a burden already, but Vanessa's a clever girl. Between you, you'll make a good go of it."

"But everyone thinks we're too young to get married just yet! I'm only twenty on Friday."

"There's no doubt you love each other and that you understand each other well," Sarah observed. "You're well matched, so why wait? You might beat your father to it if you act now," she added wistfully.

Richard raised an eyebrow at his aunt as the incredible realisation dawned that she fancied his father. There was nobody else in the office but he lowered his voice nevertheless. "Is that why you're feeling fed up? Because of Ilse?"

There was no need for her to say anything. They both knew he was right.

"Well, I think we'd all prefer it if he married you rather than Ilse," Richard said a few moments later. "We all feel she'd take him away from us, that she'd never want to come over here and that she'd make him visit Sophie and the twins endlessly rather than be bothered with us."

"I'm sure that wouldn't happen!" Sarah protested. "Your father would never forget you. But ..." She looked pointedly up at him. "I agree with the bit about his grandchildren. Their grandchildren," she corrected herself. "That's the big issue, isn't it?"

"Bina had jolly well better get a move on in that department to even things out a bit," he remarked, "but I can't see her wanting to now she's got this new career about to open up - possibly." He glanced again at the letter in the typewriter. "Talking of which, what have you in mind?"

"Nothing much at the moment, but our little talk has made me think perhaps I should delay doing anything about it until Paul's finished his A-Levels next year. Then I'll feel freer to look further afield than I was going to."

"Further than Dad, you mean?" Richard teased her.

Sarah took a friendly swipe at him. "Get away with you!" Her eyes took on their wistful expression again. "No, I might take up teaching or something. Or even do Voluntary Service Overseas. Now that would be different! Your talk just now of panda counts has got me thinking!"

Richard smiled. "Well, I'd better leave you to your thinking. I've got work to do and some thinking to do myself!"

"About weddings?" Sarah hazarded a guess.

"Possibly."

*

187

The red squirrels skipped from branch to branch in the wood at the end of the garden. During the winter Sophie had got into the habit of putting out hazel nuts on the lawn for them, which they duly took off and buried somewhere. The squirrels were stark reminders of when she and Siegfried had first bought the house in *An der Waldecke*. They had nicknamed the pair Hans and Lotte, after the underwater filmmakers Hans and Lotte Hass, though whether these were the same pair, she could not say.

Little Friedrich was watching the squirrels too, and chuckled heartily as Hans, or was it Lotte?, fell off a twig, managing to twist and turn to a firmer foothold. Sophie smiled at her son.

"Wouldn't you like to be able to climb trees like that, Schätzchen? Wouldn't it be fun?"

"Me too!" squeaked Freia, banging her little fists against the windowpane.

"Careful, you'll frighten them off," Sophie warned her daughter.

Freia was proving a tomboy already in her choice of playthings and in her competitive streak, but Sophie had to acknowledge that she herself had always had a strong urge to outdo anyone. Siegfried had been just as bad. No wonder their offspring fought so hard. It made life extremely tedious at times when neither twin would give in to the other. At twenty months they were developing a strong sense of identity, but not only as individuals. When the need arose they would unite in simultaneous tantrums to get their demands met.

"Come along now. It's time to get ready to go to Oma and Opa's house. You're staying the night there; won't that be fun? You can take your teddies with you too. They'll like that."

The teddies went everywhere with the twins. As she helped her offspring into the car, she remembered how Gustav Halstrup had sent the teddies shortly after the twins were born. She had mixed feelings about them now, but the twins loved them and she could not get rid of them. Many were the long and empty evenings when she had wondered just what exactly Siegfried had been doing with Gustav on that fateful day of the twins' christenings. There was no denying Gustav had been watching Siegfried, uncertain as to his commitment to the neo-Nazi movement. He had got her to spy on Siegfried, threatening her, even, in that ambiguous way of his. Now she was left with this vacuum of knowledge and niggling doubts about her dead husband. To begin with she had been absolutely certain there had been nothing unsavoury going on between him and Gustav, but the more she thought about it, it seemed a plausible enough explanation for their clandestine meeting, why Gustav had also been in the car when Siegfried died. It tainted her memory of them both now, and when she looked at the twins' teddies, Gustav's brown eyes haunted her.

Lisl Wendt saw her daughter struggling to unload the car and hurried out to help her. "What can I take?" she asked Sophie, giving her and each grandchild a kiss.

"These damn bears!" Sophie grunted, reaching onto the floor of the Mercedes for the teddies dropped there by the twins during the short journey to their Oma's house. She thrust them at her mother, who in turn passed them carefully on to the twins' eagerly outstretched hands. She understood her daughter's feelings about the teddies … and Gustav.

"Liebchen, it wasn't what you think, I'm absolutely sure of it," she tried yet again to console Sophie. "Siegfried and Gustav had a mission of some kind. That's why they were together."

"So why does nobody know anything? That's why I've got to go to Berlin and talk to our people there – to find out something, anything! Somebody must know something!"

"But they don't." Lisl picked up a bag of nappies and hurried the twins inside out of the freezing air. "We asked everyone we knew at the time and nobody had the slightest clue. It's pointless you going all that way for nothing."

"Well I need a break, anyway, and Berlin's as good a place to go as any. At least I know plenty of people there." Sophie dumped a pile of baggage on the polished wood floor of the hall then returned to the car for another load. She would only be gone a week – a week of bliss away from the incessant demands of the twins – but she had had to pack enough baby equipment worthy of a trip up Everest. Her mother had her own supply of many items for the twins, catering for their frequent visits and occasional overnight stays, but even so, she was glad the new Mercedes had a capacious boot.

She stayed for an hour to let the twins settle with their Oma, then set out on the long drive to Berlin, with all its attendant delays and annoyances at the border checkpoints.

Markus and Sonja Fiebrantz, the friends she was staying with, lived in a smart district near the Charlottenburg Palace. She had known them since her days of living and working in Berlin, and been introduced by them to Gustav. It was Gustav who had first told her about the Wunderkind, Siegfried, so she supposed she had Markus and Sonja to thank for her marriage and children. Now she hoped they might help her find answers to her questions about Gustav and Siegfried.

Entering the city later that evening was like coming home. She had loved living here; loved the bustle and excitement of the metropolis; loved the stark reminders of the battles that still needed fighting.

Markus and Sonja had been watching from their apartment for her arrival. As soon as she drew up outside, they were out on the pavement to greet her with kisses of welcome and commiseration for her new circumstances. Markus, a flamboyant yet elegant art dealer in his mid-thirties, carried her case in from the car while Sonja hung on to Sophie's arm as they negotiated the steps into the spacious ground floor apartment. Evidence of Markus' business graced every surface and wall space. The hall acted as a gallery for a pleasing selection of oil paintings depicting views of Berlin before its destruction. Sophie knew these had comparatively little monetary value, painted as they were by his grandfather, but they had been hugely inspirational in his choice of career as well as his politics. The living room, however, could not have been more different. Here Markus' professional interests dominated, currently with a display of Op Art. Sophie recollected that previously it had been done out in the bold and brash style of Fauvism, but she discovered some of these works relegated to her bedroom when she was led there by Sonja.

"I do hope you'll be comfortable," Sonja was saying as Sophie studied the paintings on the walls. "Just let me know if there's anything you need. I'll go and pour us some cocktails and you can join us when you're ready. We've invited some of your old friends round this evening for dinner." She glanced at her watch. "They should be here soon. I hope you don't mind, but there's so many people for you to see, you'll never fit them all in otherwise."

"That's fine!" Sophie beamed. "It's just so lovely to be here again – and not have the twins to worry about. I hope my parents are coping with them!"

"You can telephone them, if you like," Sonja said on her way out. "There's a phone by your bed."

"Thanks. I might just do that. Let them know I've arrived safely."

After sprucing herself up and changing into more suitable evening wear, Sophie gave her parents a quick call, heard that the twins were safely tucked up in bed asleep and was told not to worry but enjoy herself. Sophie intended doing just that.

*

Over lunch they had agreed to keep their new relationship secret for the time being. Much as he wanted to, Karl did not kiss Silke goodbye after work, while she only gave her usual smile and wave of farewell as she headed for her car. Karl set off on foot to his house with an inward glow and new lightness of step in the certainty that his life had irrevocably changed today. Silke gave him a future filled with her youth and vitality, so different from his outlook only a few days ago. Talk of opticians, jokes about walking sticks and visits to grandchildren with Ilse had seemed the natural progression for himself, but suddenly he felt younger again; younger and more alive than he had felt for a long, long time.

It was only when he had let himself into his empty house and he longed to hear her voice again that he realised he neither knew Silke's address nor her telephone number. He had no means of getting in touch with her except at work. He could hardly ask Mick for her number, assuming he knew it, nor could he ask Margit or Ilse.

He took off his hat, scarf and coat and headed for the kitchen to make tea for himself. Silke was probably still driving home, but he would have liked nothing better right now than to curl up in front of the fire with her and toast crumpets together. She was uncomplicated, easy company, with no airs or graces or pretensions to be other than she was. Just like Katherine.

But she wasn't another Katherine, he told himself as he poured out his tea and spread butter on a few slices of bread, topping them off with ham and cheese. Silke had seen the world, experienced things Katherine would never have dreamt of. Whereas Katherine had run the farm efficiently all her adult life, Silke had messed up after her mother died, had bombed out then recovered, older and wiser. It had given her an insight into life that Katherine had never experienced, enabled her to empathise with his own history without knowing any of it. What was more, she was German. He had no need to explain anything to her. She understood the guilt.

He switched on the radio and sat down at the kitchen table to eat his sandwiches, but his thoughts drowned out the newsreader's voice. The person he did have some explaining to do to was Ilse. She had left her husband for him, he had led her on, now he would be rejecting her for a younger woman. That would hurt.

Silke was so much younger; that was the trouble. She had talked about children, but how could he provide for another family at his age? Assuming they got cracking right away, which they would not, it would mean he would be seventy or more by the time their first child was, at best, finding a job or, at worst, starting college. His own grandchildren would be older than his children. It was a ridiculous notion.

Suddenly he had no appetite. He pushed away his uneaten plate of sandwiches and stared at the white emptiness of the kitchen cupboards. Silke wanted children, most definitely. She would need a husband she could rely on to provide for them, a husband who would be an active father. How could he give her that?

The burden was already weighing him down and it did not even exist yet. Ilse would not want more children at her age. They had their grandchildren to look after. Surely Ilse was the more sensible choice? She was good company and he liked her well enough, even if his love for her seemed to have faded a little. A future with her would not be so bad and they could grow old gracefully together, whereas a life with Silke would be fraught with increasing difficulties as she found herself stuck with an old man. It could never work in the long term.

The telephone ringing in the hall jolted him out of his despondency. Perhaps it was Silke ringing! He hurried out to answer it.

It was Ilse.

"Hello, Schatz. I was just looking at that lovely rose you gave me on Saturday and I started to miss you. How are your legs now? Mine are still a bit stiff but not too bad."

"Hello, Ilse. I'm fine." He struggled to find something else to say. "How was work?"

"Quiet. I managed to sell a bookcase and that was about it! Typical Monday in February, I suppose. Which reminds me. Hans and Corinna have invited us to dinner next Saturday. I provisionally accepted for us both since the twins are at Peter and Lisl's while Sophie's away. We can visit them the following weekend perhaps."

Karl felt trapped. He had to make a decision on the spot. It was the topic of visiting the twins that swayed him. "What time shall I collect you on Saturday?"

"Come for the day! We could go for a walk if the weather's nice."

The trap was closing in on him. He needed more time. "I've got some chores to catch up on, I'm afraid. Can't leave them another weekend. What time's the dinner?"

"Eight." Ilse's disappointment was audible. "Well, if you can't manage a whole day, perhaps we can get together of an evening. How about tomorrow? There's that pub Margit's always going to near the Town Hall that I've never been to yet. We could go there."

Karl found himself agreeing to her idea. Ilse's continued friendship was vital while he was so uncertain about the wisdom of loving Silke. As he put down the phone, Karl thought about what would happen if he decided he could not stick with Silke. How could they continue working together? It could prove most awkward.

He desperately wanted to talk to her, to explain his misgivings and be reassured by her not to be so foolish, that of course she would love him for eternity and that there would be no problem over financing a family into his old age. He stared at the telephone, willing it to dial her number all by itself. Then the answer came to him. The hospital switchboard would know her number for an emergency when he was not available. He could ask them for it, and damn the gossip! He needed to speak to her again.

A minute later he heard her phone ringing then her soft voice, warm and dark brown as her eyes. "Sommer."

"Silke, it's Karl. I hope I'm not disturbing you?"

"Karl! How lovely to hear you. I was just about to go out to my dancing session, but it doesn't matter if I'm a few minutes late."

"Are you sure? It's just that ... well ... I've got a slight difficulty I wanted to discuss with you, but if you're in a rush I can wait until-"

"Is it to do with Ilse?"

Once again Karl found her astuteness uncanny. "Well, yes, it is, actually."

"It's all right, Karl. You do whatever you like; see her for a bit longer or whatever. I realise it's not so easy splitting with her, and if you want to do it slowly and gradually, that's fine by me."

"It's all been a bit sudden," he explained hesitantly. "This morning, when we were talking about children, set me thinking. I love you, Silke, I really do, and there's nothing I'd like more than to be with you for ever and have children, but ..."

His silence was unnerving. "Karl, listen to me. I know all the arguments against our age gap, but ..." Now Silke was hesitant to go on.

"You see?" Karl pointed out. "There's no way round the problem. We love each other now. But in ten or fifteen years' time? I would need to work until I was over seventy to support you."

"Is that the only thing that's worrying you, the financial side of things?" Silke asked in relief. "Money's nothing. Love is everything. I'm still enough of a hippie to know that!"

Karl had to laugh. "Well, all right, I'm making mountains out of molehills perhaps. We can all live in a tent on a beach somewhere. We'll survive, no doubt."

"That's right, Karl," she agreed. "We'll survive!"

Her optimism was contagious and Karl was glad he had spoken to her. "I'd better let you get off to your dancing then. See you in the morning."

"Right. Have a pleasant evening and don't worry about anything. Take your time with Ilse. I understand. I like her and I don't want to hurt her any more than you do."

"Thank you, Schatz. It's going to be difficult not to, though."

"And Margit's going to hate me for it," Silke added. "A tent on a far away beach might be the best place for us!" she laughed. "Where do you fancy? Mediterranean? South Pacific? Caribbean?"

"Mediterranean will do for now," he decided, joining in the fun.

194

"You can choose where exactly. Think about it while you're dancing."

"You're on! Bye for now then. Love you."

"I love you too."

Karl put down the receiver but stayed standing by the phone, overwhelmed for a moment by the emotions Silke wrought in him. Their kisses earlier in the day had proved unequivocally how much he loved her. He could not give her up, whatever people might think.

*

"Cyprus." Silke declared the moment Karl walked through the office door. "Land of Aphrodite. What could be more appropriate? You can ski there too," she added with a sly grin, knowing it would interest him. "On snow in the morning, on water in the afternoon. But only in winter of course."

"Great! Let's go. All we need now is our tent."

"If only," Silke sighed, plugging in the kettle.

Karl settled down to his morning's work, dealing automatically with the paperwork and telephone calls while his mind was in a tent on a Cypriot beach. It was a pleasant daydream but couldn't be more than that. A holiday with Silke was out of the question. They couldn't both be away from work at the same time. Besides, he had neither the funds nor enough leave, if he wanted to visit the boys in the summer.

At lunchtime they headed off into town together, having decided that was innocent enough. The fifteen-minute walk around the Seilersee gave them time to chat about more intimate things than work, provided nobody was nearby. At times it was nearly impossible not to hold hands or walk arm in arm but somehow they managed to restrain themselves.

As they were nearing town Karl mentioned his meeting with Ilse that evening.

"I'm dreading it," he told her. "I just don't know how I'm going to give her the gentle brush off. For the twins' sakes, as much as anything, I want to keep on good terms with her."

"I don't really know what to suggest. Perhaps if you just stay cool long enough, she'll realise herself that nothing's going to come of it and start looking elsewhere."

"You don't know anybody who'd be interested in her, do you? Someone with more to offer her than I've got."

Silke chuckled. "She's well known around these parts. If the word got out that she was free, I'm sure men would come running!"

"Really? Perhaps you could spread the word. Are there many men at your dancing evenings? What sort of dancing is it, anyway?"

"Ballroom, old-time, whatever you want to call it. Just the steps, not competition stuff," Silke explained. "You ought to come as my partner. There aren't enough men there."

"But how old are the ones who are there? My age?"

"Two of them are about your age, the others older. All my generation seem to want now is disco-dancing."

"So why do you go?"

"I like it. I've been dancing since my early teens. Didn't I impress you at the Christmas Dance in the Mess?"

Her words struck him. "You fancied me even then?"

"I knew from the first day you came that I wanted you," she reminded him.

"I see." Again he found himself reaching for her hand and again he had to restrain himself. "I'll come and be your partner. That way we can see each other innocently of an evening."

"Good! They'll be pleased to have another man there. You'll have to dance with some of the other ladies though. We all share the men."

"As long as I get to dance with you, I don't mind. Can I join you next week?"

"Of course! I can pick you up on the way."

"I ought to be the one to collect you," he said chivalrously.

"Why? It's out of your way. It's easier if I drive."

"You're certainly a liberated woman, aren't you, especially when you won't let me pay for things. I insist on buying lunch today."

Silke smiled indulgently. "Very well. As long as we take it in turns."

They walked on companionably up into the center of Iserlohn. Karl called in at his bank first then they chose somewhere to eat. They recognized no one there so chatted freely over their meal of herring, which reminded Karl of the sea.

"I've never been on a beach," he said. "Not by the sea, anyway. Only at lakes."

"Haven't you?" Silke asked in astonishment. "Not even during the war?"

"No. I was sent to Norway, Russia, then Yugoslavia, always inland. Then it was the Ardennes and the Dutch border. No beaches."

"And since then?"

"If we went anywhere it was to Medebach and once to Ilse and Paul's place in Bavaria. How about you?"

Silke stabbed at the chicken breast on her plate. "Oh, my mother took me several times when I was little, and in California I toured about a bit, saw the Pacific Ocean."

"Would you like to go back to America?"

Silke chewed thoughtfully for a moment. "No. Or rather only to visit Tom and do some archery. How about you? Would you like to go there?"

Karl pursed his lips. "Not especially. I'm sure there's some lovely scenery, but I can't see myself ever going there. Way too expensive. Even getting to Cyprus is out of the question at the moment."

Silke smiled. "One day, perhaps. We can but dream, can't we?"

"Of course."

FIFTEEN

Sarah was worried about Paul. It was probably just the whole teenage thing, but he had seemed even more withdrawn than usual. Bearing in mind what Richard had told her that morning, she decided to head up to the farm after work and spend the evening in, hopefully, fruitful conversation.

She went home first, changed out of her office clothes into a pair of slacks and warm jumper, shoved some groceries from her kitchen cupboard into a bag which she stowed in the Mini then set off up into the dark hills west of the city. Twenty minutes later she found him at the kitchen table busy with his homework, annotating his drawings of mosses and liverworts from the Biology Practical that morning.

"Evening Paul. How's things?"

He looked up and smiled. "OK."

Well that was a good sign, Sarah thought to herself, dumping the bag of groceries on the table away from his books. "Fancy risotto for dinner?"

"Great," he replied, his attention already back on his school work.

Richard appeared at the door, shedding his Wellington boots. "Risotto certainly beats cheese on toast!" He gave his aunt a conspiratorial look. "We weren't expecting you this evening. I just came in to start cooking."

"I decided I had nothing better to do than see that my two favourite nephews were properly fed." Sarah heard Paul's sigh of exasperation at the interruption to his studies. "Anything need doing out there, Richard?"

"Oh, er, you could feed Molly. I'll crack on with some paperwork then, if you're going to cook."

Sarah settled herself into the business of the farm, gave Molly her dinner in her kennel, one of Paul's creations, checked the chickens were shut in for the night then found herself wandering across to the work shed. She opened the door and stepped inside, switching on the fluorescent light. It sparked into life, revealing the neat racks of saws, chisels, screwdrivers and all the other many accoutrements necessary for the accomplished carpenter. Karl's presence in here had long since superseded her father's, and Paul had not yet totally imposed himself on the place. She was as near to Karl here as anywhere.

She sniffed the sawdust-scented air, immediately soothed by its evocative smell of patient creativity. The workbench was clear at the moment, Paul being too busy with the farm and his schoolwork to have embarked on any new projects recently. The lambing season dominated the next few weeks and they would all be too bleary-eyed to concentrate on much else. Vanessa was coming to help out, once things got going, and Sarah envisaged her and Richard spending many a cosy evening together out with the ewes in the sheds. But what of Paul?

The farm only had room for one family to live in, and Paul had always known Richard would be the one to inherit the farm. It had just happened sooner than anyone had imagined, leaving Paul, as yet, unsettled in his own home and career. He was keen on carpentry, but he also had a keen intellect. Katherine had been determined he should make the most of himself, especially after Richard had had to miss out on agricultural college.

She sat on the stool by the workbench for a few minutes, pondering on possible career options for Paul, before deciding she really should get back into the kitchen to prepare the meal.

Creeping round the back door she made a point of not talking to him, but within a few minutes he was clearing away his folder and pencils.

"All done?" she asked him, setting the chopping board down on the table.

"Yep." He shoved his work into his school bag then pulled out a college prospectus. "I borrowed this from school. I wasn't supposed to but I wanted a good long look at it. Here, see what you think."

Sarah had been about to chop an onion, but she laid down the knife and took the prospectus from him. He had opened the booklet at the page detailing the nearby agricultural college's arboriculture course.

"I've had that song on my mind," Paul explained. "The Joni Mitchell one – 'Big Yellow Taxi'. Do you know it?"

Sarah nodded. "I think I've heard it."

"I was talking about it to Richard this morning. All of it's relevant, but it's the bit about taking away the trees and putting them in a tree museum that's got me interested. So at lunchtime I decided to have a look through the further education filing cabinets at school and see what they had. I came up with this."

"You want to save the trees, you mean?"

He looked bashful but sincere. "Yes. I might even decide to take it further and do some research after I've graduated."

"You're certainly keen, aren't you?"

"Yes," Paul beamed.

"Well, I think that's a wonderful idea. You go for it."

Paul's smile faded. "But what about the farm? How can I leave Richard to cope alone?"

"He'll find help," Sarah assured him. "But you must make sure you fulfil your dreams or you'll regret it for the rest of your life."

Paul's grin nearly split his face. "Thanks, Aunty Sarah. You're the best."

Sarah could not help herself and gave him a big hug. She felt him return it, a little self-consciously at first then with increased vigour.

When he broke away he looked at her, trying to say what he felt. "Thanks for being here," was all he managed, but it was enough.

"My pleasure," Sarah told him, knowing that it was indeed her pleasure to have a family to take care of. She was going to see this through, for Katherine and Karl's sakes.

*

Ilse sprayed on her favourite perfume, tweaked her hair once more then picked up her handbag off the bed, feeling a fluttering of anxiety about how the evening with Karl would progress. She had sensed he was disappointed with their lovemaking last Saturday, and she hoped that tonight she could reassure him on that count.

As she headed out of her bedroom, she heard the doorbell buzzer and knew he had arrived. She heard Edeltraud letting him in the downstairs entrance and went to the apartment door ready to open it as soon as he had climbed the stairs.

200

"Hello, Schatz," she said brightly, reaching up to kiss him.

"Hello," he replied once his lips were free. For a moment he found her perfume overpowering and stepped back. He nodded to Edeltraud as she moved from the kitchen to the living room carrying a mug of coffee. "Well, you look as though you're ready, Ilse. Shall we go?"

Ilse. He still wouldn't call her 'Schatz'. What tripped so easily off her tongue seemed frozen on his. She nodded, then called out to Edeltraud: "Don't forget to do the washing up!"

"I won't," came her daughter's peeved reply.

Ilse followed Karl downstairs and out into the breezy night. Her skirt flapped at her knees and she held it down as she headed for his car. Once settled inside she checked her hair in the driving mirror, leaving it for Karl to readjust.

As he drove off, Ilse commented: "You're quiet this evening."

"Am I? Sorry. I suppose I've not got much to say. Work was pretty much the same as usual today. How about you? Did you sell much?"

Ilse smiled. "No, but we had a sales rep from a new manufacturer who called today. There was some wonderful stuff in his brochure! You should see it, Schatz. It's modern but traditional at the same time. The fabric designs are fabulous. Hans went wild about them."

"Really," Karl commented. "I'll have to mention the firm to the Ministry of Defence. They could do with some decent furniture."

Ilse looked at him in astonishment, then laughed. "You're joking."

Karl smiled. "Yes, I'm joking, but not about the MoD. They're replacing all the solid old furniture with strictly utilitarian stuff."

Ilse could not help herself asking: "Is your bed comfy?"

Karl did not bat an eyelid as he replied: "Not long enough, but otherwise all right." He knew exactly what she was angling for, however: an invitation to try it out. Things were getting awkward already.

Ilse was not prepared to let him off the hook. She snuggled up to his right arm, stroking his hand on the steering wheel. "Perhaps I can try it out tonight?"

It was impossible to give her a downright refusal. The only thing he could do was shrug as he negotiated the next road junction and headed up to the Town Hall. How was he going to put her off? Did he even want to? Should he perhaps give her another chance, just in case it jolted him back on course with her this time? Then he thought of Silke and knew he wanted nobody else. He could not lead Ilse on like that.

They arrived at the pub and entered its smoky confines. He ordered a glass of wine for Ilse and was about to order a beer for himself when he hesitated and decided upon a double Scotch. This was going to be an expensive evening, but necessary, he thought, directing Ilse to an empty table.

He listened to her enthusiastic descriptions of the new furniture, her latest letter from Heinrich, her choice of outfit for next Saturday's meal with the Münzels and her views on Roslinde's latest boyfriend as he ploughed his way through another double. Ilse was too busy talking to drink much and was still quite sober by the time he noticed his speech slurring. He couldn't keep this up without making a spectacle of himself in public, so would have to time the next step precisely to be sure it didn't backfire on him.

They had been in the pub about an hour, long enough Karl thought, as he suggested they went back to his house. He noticed Ilse's eyes light up, but once outside the fresh air hit him and he staggered, clutching hold of her arm.

"Perhaps you had better drive," he said, handing her his car keys.

"If you like," Ilse said, somewhat surprised by how much he had drunk already.

She drove the short distance to his home and found the house key on the bunch, letting them both inside. Karl helped her off with her coat, rubbed his cold hands then asked: "Right, what can I get you? Some more wine or a schnapps?"

Ilse felt she had some catching up to do. "Schnapps, please. Whatever you've got."

She followed him into his living room and watched as he found a nearly full bottle of *Apfelkorn* in the standard issue sideboard.

"*Prost!*" he said giving her a glass, then switching on the radio for some background music.

"*Prost!*" she replied, sitting down on the sofa. It had been a while since her previous visit there before Christmas. Karl had brought back several ornaments, a rug and pictures on his visits to Medebach and now the house looked more homely. Ilse kicked off her high heels and tucked her feet up under her legs on the sofa, leaning against Karl next to her.

A short time later a concert began on the radio, one of Ilse's favourite works: Brahms's 'Symphony No. 4'. They listened to the whole of it, Karl occasionally topping up their glasses. By the end, Ilse realised she could hear Karl's deep breathing next to her. He was sound asleep.

She glanced at her watch. It was only ten-thirty. She shifted heavily against him, hoping to wake him up but all he did was move his head slightly and begin snoring gently.

She debated whether to call a taxi but was unwilling to abandon all hope just yet. Instead she went out to the kitchen, made herself a cup of coffee and took it upstairs to his bedroom. She thought about taking a blanket downstairs to cover him over, but still hoped for something more than just drinks from him. If he got cold in the night he could join her then.

Downstairs Karl waited until he was sure she was settled in bed then got up and fetched his overcoat from the hall to try to keep warm. He felt mean, a real cad doing this to Ilse, but he wanted to put her off him gradually, make himself less attractive to her. It had to be her decision, not his. Once Ilse was off his hands, he could let himself be seen with Silke.

*

Sophie was trying to enjoy her freedom from responsibility. Markus and Sonja had invited nine guests, all old friends of Sophie's, four of them couples and the obligatory single man. But whereas Ilse's attempts at matchmaking for her and Siegfried had worked perfectly, Kristof Kemphausen did nothing for her. His looks were average, his height was average and his conversation was just that too. She supposed it was going to be difficult finding any man to match up to Siegfried, let alone one who was willing to take on the twins as well. She would probably have to lower her expectations.

Kristof sat next to her when they all adjourned to the living room for coffee, so she made a point of chatting about the twins to try to put him off. It did not have the desired effect: rather the opposite.

"A woman of proven fertility is highly desired in some cultures," he enthused, guessing her motives for her choice of conversation. "Besides, we need more like you and Siegfried. Young Friedrich will grow up to be like his father, with any luck, and little Freia will be a credit to her mother."

"You consider Siegfried a hero, do you?" Sophie asked as lightly as she dared.

"Of course! Killed in action; what more do I need say? It would be an honour for any of us to provide succour for his children."

"Is that what the word is?" Sophie asked carefully. "That he was killed in action?"

"Of course!" Kristof declared. "Didn't you know?" He saw she clearly did not and went on to explain. "Why else would he have been with Gustav?"

So he didn't know any more than she did, Sophie realised. It was all supposition. She still needed to get to the facts.

"I'd like to know what he was doing," Sophie said slowly. "Just to put my mind at rest. Do you know anybody I could speak to? Anybody who might know what Gustav was up to that day, or why he wanted Siegfried's … services?"

Kristof thought hard then turned to the man sitting on the armchair to his right, a printer by trade, whose profession gave him access to some of the undercover work that went on amongst their group. He tapped him on the shoulder. "Kurt? Do you know who could tell Sophie anything about Gustav's last assignment, when he and Siegfried were killed?"

Kurt looked hard at Sophie. He knew her well, but still he seemed dubious about revealing any information she was not privy to.

"Please, Kurt," Sophie pleaded. "I just want to know why they died, what my husband was doing. It would help me deal with it."

Kurt was moved by her appeal. "I'll ask around. I'll try to get back to you before you leave, but I can't make any promises."

"No, of course not, but I would be so grateful if you could try."

Kurt smiled. For a woman like Sophie he would walk over fire.

*

Ilse was woken by the alarm clock she had set the night before. To her dismay, the bed beside her was empty. So Karl hadn't made it upstairs. Disappointed, she got out of his bed, pottered to the bathroom enveloped in his dressing gown then made her way downstairs. She noted immediately that the lights were off and when she went into the living room, saw him asleep on the sofa, his knees poking out a long way over the edge. He had clearly got up at some point to fetch his coat as a cover, but had not bothered to join her upstairs.

He stirred as she watched, as though he sensed her presence. Going over to him, she kissed him on his bristly cheek.

"Wakey-wakey, sleepyhead!"

Karl tentatively opened one eye. His head hurt a little but a drink of water would soon sort that out. "Morning, Ilse," he mumbled, propping himself up on one elbow only to find his neck was painfully stiff.

"You seem to make a habit of sleeping on sofas," she told him, massaging his neck for him. "You should have come up to bed."

"I didn't want to disturb you," he replied, twisting his neck as she rubbed, and finding mobility partially restored.

"I was rather hoping you would," she pouted, abruptly ceasing her massaging.

"Oh. Sorry." He looked at his watch. "I'd better get up and drive you home or we'll both be late for work. Can I get you some breakfast?"

"No, don't worry. I'll have some at home."

She sounded put out. It was what he intended, but he hated doing it. Perhaps it would be kinder to finish this quickly, he wondered then thought of her devastation. No, it had to be slow but sure. "Have you finished in the bathroom?"

"Yes. It's all yours," she said resignedly. "I'll go and get dressed."

She was silent on the journey back to her apartment, and Karl, for his part, was not keen to liven things up by conversation. She seemed very subdued by the time she got out of his car, giving him a brief wave of farewell and a reminder of their date at the Münzels' on Saturday.

Karl returned home, fed himself and tidied up the place a bit then headed into work. His mood was not good.

Silke's smile changed all that.

Despite their resolution the day before not to be intimate at work, he stooped and planted a kiss on the top of her head.

"Do I sense a chocolate is needed?" she asked him, reaching for her desk drawer.

"No, just a cup of coffee as usual. It was bad, but not that bad. Ilse's peeved with me for not going to bed with her, and I feel rotten about it." He went over to the kettle, found it already filled, and switched it on.

As he turned round again, Silke asked him: "Did you want to sleep with her?"

Karl smiled. "No. There's only one person I want now, and that's you."

Silke fixed him firmly with her gaze. "You've got to get to know me better first, Karl. Contrary to what you might think, I don't jump into bed at the drop of a hat any more. I had too much of it in California. Now I want it to be special."

If he felt disappointed, Karl did not show it. "And I respect you for that. We'll take our time. No rush," he promised her.

"Good. I'm glad you understand." She softened her gaze, allowing a smile to play upon her lips again. "But I won't keep you waiting too long. I just want to choose the right moment."

The way she was looking at him, Karl thought, the right moment was here and now. He nodded hastily before turning his attention to making the coffee.

*

Margit said nothing when her mother came home after her night spent with Karl. She had wanted to make a lewd comment, but her mother's expression stalled her. It had not been a night of passion, by the look of things. A lovers' tiff, possibly. Oh well, she thought, these things happen, as she was finding from her relationship with Bruno. Lovely as he was, she found his politics diametrically opposed to what she had been brought up to believe. And yet his arguments sounded so convincing at times, she was ready to forgive his arrogance.

"Do you want some coffee, Mutti?" she asked as her mother disappeared into her bedroom.

"No."

The door shut behind her and Margit was left pondering on the nature of the tiff. Fairly serious, she guessed, but felt sure her mother would disclose nothing. Perhaps she could ask Silke that evening at the pub if she could glean a hint of anything from Karl tomorrow and report back. Silke was adept at getting people to confide in her. It was a skill she had honed while helping out at the old people's home on Thursday evenings. Though Karl was hardly a pensioner. Not yet, anyway.

Her day at work passed slowly as usual, and when she returned home Margit was pleased to find her mother in a better mood. She was still determined to find out what had happened the previous night, in case there was any way she could help or advise her mother, who tended to suffer from myopia when it came to Karl.

Bruno called to collect her at seven-thirty and they made their way to Heini's Bar. Silke arrived a few moments later accompanied by Mick. Not for the first time Margit wondered why Mick bothered to come here with Silke when he spoke so little German, but it got him out of the Officers' Mess, she supposed, which must become rather claustrophobic after a while.

"Not long till you go now, is it, Mick?" Margit asked him as the waiter marked their beer mats with the first round order as he served up their beers.

"No. Only another month and I will be in Hong Kong," he replied in his hesitant German.

"Whatever will Silke do without you?" Margit asked him.

"Oh, find another old man to hang about with, I'm sure," Silke laughed, punching Mick playfully on the arm in jest.

"And who will you find, Mick?" Margit continued. "Some delightful little Chinese girl?"

"Maybe," he grinned.

Talk of China launched Bruno off into a discussion of the benefits versus the horrors of Chinese-style Communism. While he and the others in the group hotly debated the topic, Margit took the chance to sneak a quiet question to Silke.

"Does Karl ever mention my mother at work?"

"Sometimes," Silke replied. "Why?"

Margit took a sip of beer. "Oh, she seemed a bit off when she came back from spending the night with him yesterday and I wanted to find out why."

Silke had to smile. "Your poor mother wouldn't like her secrets being disclosed to all and sundry, Margit!"

"No, I know, but you're a whiz at wheedling things out of people. I just wondered if you might be able to probe Karl gently and find out for me what happened."

"Margit, really! I couldn't ask him such a personal question."

"I'm sure you'd find a way. Please, Silke. I want to know if things are turning out the way she hoped."

It occurred to Silke that this might be a way of letting Ilse down gently, by passing hints down a chain of accomplices.

"Well, all right. I'll do my best. But I can't promise anything."

"Thanks, Silke. You're a brick."

Mick tapped her arm. "What was all that about Karl and Ilse?" he asked in English.

"Margit thinks there is a problem with their relationship," Silke explained.

"I'm not surprised," Mick declared, "if he's been cheating on her with Audrey." He saw Margit's look of horror and realised she spoke enough English to have understood. "Whoops! Sorry. I rather let the cat out of the bag there."

Silke was secretly pleased at Mick's indiscretion. If Margit had doubts about Karl now, then they would be picked up by Ilse eventually. Enough had been said for the moment, so Silke made an obvious change of subject to underline the awkwardness of the moment. "Just listen to Bruno, Margit! He's saying we should all read chairman Mao's 'Little Red Book'. How can you let him say things like that and get away with it?"

Bruno broke off from his preaching in exasperation. "I only said read, Silke. I didn't necessarily say implement!" He spoke in English to Mick. "You'll find Hong Kong a gross example of the capitalist system; sweat shops producing cheap toys for the West."

"While China has sweat shops producing cheap goods for itself," Mick countered. "Whichever system you have, the workers get a raw deal."

Silke sat back in satisfaction as the debate raged hotly around her, now in English, now in German. Margit was strangely quiet throughout, and she knew why.

*

It was good to have a quiet night in for a change, Sabina thought, as she soaked in the bath while Wolf watched a television documentary about the Vietnam War. Life seemed so hectic now, what with her day-job and now her singing gigs. Wolf had taken on the job as sound engineer for the Leuchtleute, working on a sound system for them now that they were performing in larger venues. Yesterday he had even made a demonstration recording of them for the talent scout, who would tote it around the record companies for them. Thorsten and Jörg, the Brothers Grimm, had splashed out on some new clothes at the suggestion of the talent scout, presenting a more traditional German look as their new image. They should not try to compete with the American and British groups but should tap into the rich vein of local work and appeal to German tastes. The television networks clamoured after that sort of thing, he had promised them, his eyes firmly on Sabina's youthful figure and flowing auburn locks.

She thought about their latest booking, which was at an outdoor spring festival in the nearby town of Hagen, and began to sing from their new repertoire, which featured more German traditional songs. Thorsten and Jörg knew many more of them than she did, and she had some catching up to do.

After a few verses, Wolf walked into the bathroom.

"That echo sounds good. I might try a touch next Saturday. See what T and J think."

"Don't call them that! It makes me think of Tom and Jerry." She laughed. "Now I come to think of it, they do look like Tom and Jerry. Thorsten's got big, round eyes and a pained expression when he sings, and Jörg's got buckteeth! But don't tell them I said that."

"I won't," Wolf promised. His eyes slowly followed the length of her body and back up again. "How about making some room for me in there?"

"I thought you were watching that documentary."

"Which would you rather: that I join you or watch TV?"

"No competition. Get in here now, Wolf Garisch!"

"Oh, I do love bossy women," Wolf groaned as he felt her wet hands unfastening his shirt.

SIXTEEN

The phone was ringing in the hall at Lane Head Farm and Karl prepared himself. He had phoned countless times since Katherine's death, yet still he associated the hall with where she had died, could not think of the place without seeing her lying in a pool of blood. Each time he phoned he hoped it would be different, and each time that image would flash through his brain no matter how hard he tried not to think about it. Once the image was there he could shift it by having ready an alternative image to focus on, but he was unable to stop it coming initially. Next time he saw Robert he would have to ask him to help sort it out, but for now he had a new distraction. He moved his mental picture from Katherine's body by the window to the hall table, where a brown-eyed teddy bear sat by the phone. He was able to smile again and as he did so, the phone was picked up and Richard's voice answered.

"Happy Birthday, Richard!" Karl greeted him warmly. "No longer a teenager, eh?"

"Thanks, Dad. Twenty seems ancient!"

"Don't say that! I'll be fifty in November. But I can promise you, you're only as old as you feel."

Richard detected an unusual note of optimism in his father's voice. "You sound happy," he commented.

"I am. You'll find out why soon."

"Why not now?" Richard asked, his curiosity roused.

He was right, Karl thought. Why not now? There was no need to keep Silke a secret from his family. Ilse would not hear anything from them. Besides, he was bursting to tell somebody his news.

"All right. I'll tell you." He paused, keeping Richard on tenterhooks for a few seconds longer. "I've found someone to share my life with."

Richard was caught off guard. "Gosh, that's sudden!" That might have sounded critical, he thought, and quickly went on: "Who is she?

Not Ilse by the way you said it."

"Would that please you?" Karl asked. "That it's not Ilse," he clarified.

Richard remembered his recent conversation with his aunt. "Well, yes, actually, and I know Bina wasn't too thrilled about you seeing her again." He realised his father was holding out on him. "So who is it, then? Have I met her?"

"No, you haven't met her, but you've heard me speak about her enough, I think." Karl waited for Richard to have time to ponder. "Any guesses?"

"Oh, come on, Dad, don't be so infuriating! The only person you've talked about really is that girl you work with, Silke, but it can't be her!"

"Why not?" Karl knew what the answer was but he wanted to hear his son say it.

"Because …" Richard suddenly grinned at the picture conjured up, of his father with his new dolly-bird, someone who was fun and lively; someone who would brighten up his life again and give him something worth living for. "No reason," he chuckled. "Good for you, Dad. I can't wait to meet her. You'll have to bring her over to our wedding."

"Wedding? Have you and Vanessa finally set a date?" Karl exclaimed, his turn now to be surprised.

"Not exactly, but we're thinking about it now. When would be a good time for you and all the Medebach crowd to come over?"

"Whenever. It's up to you and Vanessa and the farm. Is she there with you now?"

"Yes, and Aunty Sarah and Paul. We were all about to sit down to a birthday dinner."

"Oh, well, I'd better not keep you, then. I'll speak to Paul another time. Give everyone my love and have a lovely evening. No lambs yet?"

"Not yet, but imminent."

"I hope it all goes well."

"Thanks, Dad. 'Bye then. Oh, and give our love to Silke!" he laughed.

"I will. 'Bye."

Karl put down the phone and picked up his keys. He was meeting Silke at the ice rink shortly. They had quickly decided it was unthinkable not to see each other of an evening, but Silke was busy most nights: Mondays dancing, Tuesdays with her friends, Wednesday was her art class and on Thursdays she helped out at the retirement home. Now it was Friday and they could finally see each other outside of work.

The ice rink was just across the road from the Seilersee. Karl walked there briskly and cast an eye around for Silke's car. Like him, she drove a VW Beetle, but so did nearly every other German it seemed – that or a Mercedes. A scan of the number plates showed she had not arrived yet, so he waited in the entrance hall. He saw some of the hospital staff arriving in a minibus for a night out. As the group made its way into the building, one of the senior nurses from the medical ward tipped him a wink and said with a sly grin: "She's just coming!"

Karl nodded his thanks, trying to hide his astonishment. Somehow they were already acknowledged as a couple. How on earth had that come about?

Sure enough Silke hurried in through the doors a few moments later, a pair of ice skates clutched against her chest. She smiled but they did not embrace each other. "I hope you haven't been waiting long," she said, unwrapping a long multi-coloured scarf from around her neck.

"No. Just got here. That lot told me you were coming," he said nodding towards the hospital crowd at the pay desk.

"However did they know we were together? This is only our first date." Silke muttered, heading to the back of the queue.

"Maybe it was the switchboard operator. I had to get your number off her the other day."

"But that wouldn't necessarily mean anything," Silke pointed out. "It could have been about work."

"Perhaps we've been seen having lunch together," Karl said. "Who knows? We'll just have to assume that speculation is out about us."

"How nice," Silke beamed. She reached in her bag for her purse but Karl stopped her.

"My treat."

Silke scowled fiercely. "I pay my own way, thank you. I don't believe in men having to fork out for everything. I earn money too!" Then she smiled. "Besides, that will set them wondering, if they notice."

They noticed all right. Karl saw the glances from the nurses as Silke paid for herself. She was right. It made it look less like a date. He wondered how long they could fool people they were just work colleagues spending an evening together. Not long, he suspected.

While Silke put on her own skates, Karl joined the queue to hire a pair. He had not skated since he was a youngster, whenever the small lake near Haus Fichtenblick froze hard over. He assumed it was much like riding a bicycle and that he would remember how. Sure enough, as he joined Silke on the ice, he found he could keep up with her, though not so gracefully.

"You've done this before!" he complimented her.

"I've had lessons," she admitted. "I can dance better on ice than in a ballroom, would you believe!"

"Well, don't expect me to dance with you. I wouldn't have a clue," he warned her.

As if to disprove him, she abruptly turned to face him, skating backwards, and held out her hands to him. "Come on, try!"

"Go on, you can do it!" came an encouraging English voice as they passed one of the struggling nurses.

With a shrug of capitulation, Karl grasped Silke's hands and allowed himself to be led around the rink, skating in time to the background music. He was beginning to get the hang of things when they stopped for a breather half an hour later.

"Phew! It's hot work. Do you want a drink?" he asked his dancing partner.

"I'd love one. Coke please."

"Does that mean you're letting me pay?" he asked, eyebrows raised in exaggerated astonishment.

"It might," she admitted, laughing at his expression. "But only because my purse is in a locker."

"Well, that's as good an excuse as any," he grinned.

They tottered over on their skates to a table near the bar. When he came back with their drinks he remembered his conversation with Richard earlier. "It's my son Richard's birthday today. I gave him a ring before I came out and couldn't help telling him about us. He seemed pleased. Sent his love to you."

"Really? That's a relief."

"Well, he's in love himself, so I suppose he understands. He and Vanessa are trying to fix a date for their wedding. He asked if you'd be coming!"

Her face fell. "We can't take leave at the same time, remember?"

"Damn! I'd forgotten."

She smiled. "There's always a way around it. I could change my job."

"But then I wouldn't see you!"

"Romances at work are often not a good idea. Besides it would give us more flexibility to go away together. Wouldn't that be worth it? We can't even go to your family in Medebach together as it is."

"Yes, but what would you do?"

"Start a family?"

He stared at her, wondering whether she was serious. She clearly was.

"Karl, I realise our relationship is hurtling along with the speed of an express train, but I can't help that. I've wasted so much time – not wasted, no, that's not the right word – lost is better. What with my mother's illness, then my time out in America. Suddenly I feel everything's fallen into place with you and I'm impatient to get on with it. But I don't want to frighten you off. I know you've already had four children. You're obviously not in so much of a rush to have more."

"That would have been true until a week ago," he admitted. "But when you started talking on Monday about wanting my children, it just seemed so right. I couldn't expect a long-term relationship with you without them." He hesitated. "It's just this financial thing …" He saw her start to scowl and abruptly left off. "Wouldn't it mean getting married first?"

"Not necessarily, but you'd be happier if we were, wouldn't you?" She grinned. "We could make it a double wedding with Richard and Vanessa!"

For a moment Karl was tempted by the idea, then he thought better of it. "No. I wouldn't want to steal their thunder by having the prettier bride." As he looked into her eyes, again he felt that kick of excitement deep inside of him. He glanced around to check there were no eavesdroppers. They seemed safe enough. "It's too important a day to share and I'd want to get married here in Germany. Then we can drag the British over here for once."

"You realise you haven't actually proposed to me yet?" Silke rebuked him. "You just sort of mentioned marriage in passing."

"If you're so keen on this equality lark, you can jolly well ask me to marry you!" he told her firmly, struggling and failing to keep a straight face.

Silke burst into a fit of giggles. "All right," she spluttered. "But not here!" Controlling her laughter she added: "I'll do it properly. Soon."

"I'll hold you to that promise. Once Ilse's sorted."

Their hands touched briefly over the table and they both smiled before withdrawing them to their own sides of the table and their drinks.

"Don't take too long shaking off Ilse," Silke pleaded. "This is hard."

"I know. We've got this dinner with the Münzels tomorrow. It's going to be hell. Then the following week we'd talked about going up to see the twins. They're the big problem. I don't want to find myself cut off from them."

"Of course you don't," she said earnestly. "Family commitment is the most important thing there is, speaking as someone who hasn't got any, that is." She drained her paper cup. "Well, how about another spin around the ice, now you've got the hang of it."

*

Paul was horrified by Richard's revelation.

"But she's Margit's friend, isn't she? Which makes her about the same age as Bina!"

"A little older," Sarah told him, seeing his dismay. The news had certainly cast a cloud over the birthday celebrations.

"Oh yeah? She's still half his age. It's disgusting."

216

"Why?" Richard asked patiently. "Or is it more the fact that he's seeing someone other than Mum now? Are you expecting him to stay faithful to her memory?"

Paul was silent a moment as he gave this serious thought. "No," he said finally. "And I wasn't disgusted by the thought of him seeing Ilse again. But this Silke could be his daughter!"

"But she isn't," Sarah pointed out, torn between the need to make Paul accept his father's choice and her own jealousy. "She's actually rather nice and jolly. You'll love her when you meet her, I'm sure."

Vanessa was keeping well out of this family dispute. She ate her steak steadily, observing Paul's anger and Sarah's discomfort. She caught Richard's eye and smiled her support for his father.

Paul however was not to be persuaded. "It's awfully sudden, isn't it? They weren't seeing each other when you were there three weeks ago, were they?" he asked Sarah.

"No, they weren't. At least I don't think they were. Silke arrived at Ilse's house with one of the hospital anaesthetists as her partner. They seemed to be considered a couple," she added, not daring to mention that Silke had lost Mick to Audrey. She hoped Silke had not snatched at Karl on the rebound. Perhaps Karl had been taken in by the attentions of such a young woman.

"We could always give Bina a ring and ask her to suss out what's going on," Paul suggested.

"But we already know what's going on," Richard told him in exasperation. "Dad has found a really nice girlfriend, who Aunty Sarah has met and likes too. If it makes him happy, then I'm all for it!"

"Hear! Hear!" Sarah applauded him.

Paul grunted, knowing he was outnumbered. He was still going to write to Bina and see what she had to say.

*

Sophie left Berlin for the long drive home with no further information about Gustav and Siegfried, but with an enormous bouquet of flowers delivered to Markus and Sonja's flat that morning. The flowers had been sent to her by Udo Kopleck, the contact Kurt had put her in touch with, who had turned out to be one of Berlin's most highly respected city developers. His links with the construction industry had immediately warmed her to him, a gentle reminder of Siegfried's former livelihood. The meeting, scheduled for a brief ten minutes in his lunch break, had turned into a protracted lunch followed by an evening at the theatre.

Udo knew all about Gustav, herself and Siegfried, demonstrating just how high up in the neo-Nazi hierarchy he was, but if he had known anything at all about any secret plans of Gustav's, he was not telling her. What he had told her was how beautiful she was, how much she was still respected by them, and that her current task of rearing the new generation of the Master Race was of supreme importance. He had given her his card and strict instructions to visit Berlin again soon.

*

Ernst Winter hurried home from his new job as a delivery driver for a florist's and found his writing pad. The name on the expensive bouquet on his delivery list that morning to an apartment in the residential district of Charlottenburg had been achingly familiar, but he had thought nothing more about it until he spotted the identifying letters SO on the licence plates of the Mercedes parked nearby. There could only be one Sophie Driesler living in Soest, and that had to be the daughter-in-law of his old wartime comrade, Karl Driesler, with whom he had only recently got back in touch. Karl wrote regularly and kept him up to date about the goings on in his family. Ernst knew that Sophie was widowed now, and was intrigued to find out who could be sending her the best flowers in the shop. When he returned to the shop and checked the name on the account in the order book, he was shocked.

Since Ernst's reunion with Karl, he had found a new mission in his strange and secretive life: hunting out neo-Nazis, who were a threat to his old friend. His mission posed a conflict of interests for him, however, as on the one hand he longed for the comradeship and sense of purpose the Nazis had created, yet on the other hand they had destroyed the Germany he had loved and threatened the safety of the only friend he had.

It was not just Karl's safety he was concerned about but his own too. One day his Soviet paymasters would demand their pound of flesh from him, and he hoped he could get by with simply supplying them with names and addresses of neo-Nazis in Berlin. To that end he had recently begun to infiltrate the neo-Nazi system, finding it relatively easy to persuade them of his undying loyalty. They were vain, all too ready to lap up his praises, and he had found doors opening to him. One of those doors bore the name of Udo Kopleck.

Ernst thought Karl should be warned.

*

After their skating session, Karl and Silke had a few drinks in a bar then Silke offered Karl a lift home.

"I won't come in," she said before he could ask her, as they pulled up outside. "I need to get back and catch up with a few things. That's my trouble. I lead such a hectic life!"

Karl felt disappointed but said nothing to dissuade her. "Enjoy your swimming and archery."

"I will. And you enjoy your dinner tomorrow night. I'm sure it won't be hell, but the whole weekend without seeing you will be hell for me. I tell you what. Why don't you join me for archery? Mick's not coming."

Her offer was too tempting to refuse. "I'd like that."

"Right, then. Meet me at one o'clock at the woods where we went before. The rest of the club will be there."

"Great. Till one o'clock tomorrow." In the darkness of the car, her hair haloed by the streetlight outside, Silke seemed like a goddess, real but unreal. His hand reached out to touch her face, as if to prove her existence to his doubting self. "I can't believe how happy I feel," he said, leaning across the seat towards her. "I've really enjoyed this evening."

"So have I," she breathed.

Their lips touched, their mouths melting into each other's. Karl felt that sense of total unity with her that not even making love to Ilse had achieved. There was no comparison, none whatsoever. His lips moved on, brushing against her cheek then her ear. "I love you,

219

Silke," he whispered. "I love you so much. You mean everything to me now."

"I know," she whispered back. "I want you forever, Karl. Don't keep me waiting too long. Please."

"I won't," he promised. He kissed her, making it last as long as he could, not wanting the perfect evening to end and the time come when he had to enter his empty house alone. Come it did, however, and as he watched her rear lights disappear into the darkness, he felt a powerful sense of loss.

Saturday brought no respite from his aching emptiness. He mooched about the house, hand-washing his underwear, cleaning the bathroom then driving into town to stock up on provisions. After a quick bite to eat he set off for the woods, knowing he would arrive too early for archery but unable to stay a moment longer in the house alone.

Silke had beaten him there.

"We're the first," she grinned. "Keen, aren't we?"

"Definitely," he said, snatching a kiss before anyone else turned up. "I dreamt about you last night," he told her, his eyes shining with pleasure.

"Did you? And what was I doing?"

"Swimming. In the sea. Then you came out of the water all wet, like Ursula Andress in that James Bond film and -" A car was coming up the lane towards them. Karl smiled. "I'll tell you the rest some other time, but it had to do with a tent on the beach."

"That must mean you want children," Silke commented slyly. "A tent on the beach is where we're going to bring them up, isn't it?" she laughed, waving at the car's four occupants.

Silke introduced him to Michael, Dominik, Egon and Luise, then to the other members who arrived in dribs and drabs and began unloading their equipment ready for the afternoon's shoot. Michael and Dominik set off round the course to pin up the paper target faces while the others chatted, traded insults and generally made ready. Silke had a spare bow and a quiver with half a dozen arrows for Karl, and soon they were splitting into groups of four to shoot the course. Michael and Dominik made up the other half of Karl and Silke's group, and Karl quickly discovered that Dominik, a plumber by trade, was highly competitive, whereas Michael, a retired teacher, was more easy-going and patient with their new member. It took the pressure off Karl somewhat, especially when Silke had some poor shots. They made allowances for him as a novice, letting him to stand closer for the longer distance targets, but his previous skill with a rifle stood him in good stead, and his score by the end of the afternoon was a creditable one hundred and fifty-eight compared with Silke's two hundred and thirty-four, Dominik's two hundred and fifty-two and Michael's two ninety.

"Well done, Karl," Michael congratulated him. "Not bad for a beginner. We'll have to make you stand back with us next time or you'll soon be beating us."

"Hardly," Karl laughed, pleased nevertheless at his score. "That big bear was a stinker of a shot with all those trees to get past. I was damn lucky with that ricochet not to lose my arrow. The deer was nice though. It looked almost real, standing in that glade. The trouble is we've nothing to show for our shoot. Nothing for the table, I mean."

"No, but that's the joy of the sport. We can shoot as much as we like and nobody's going to complain." Michael told him. "Are you coming next week? You seem to be enjoying it."

"Not next week. Other commitments, I'm afraid, but hopefully the week after."

"Good, we'll see you then," Michael said with a handshake of farewell. He turned to Silke. "Mick not coming any more?"

"No, he's off to Hong Kong shortly."

"That's a shame. We'll miss him. Friendly chap, for a Britisher." He shook her hand.

"He's Irish," Silke reminded Michael.

"So he is. That explains it. Well, see you all next time."

The others all made their departures too, leaving Karl and Silke alone by the wood. It was beginning to drizzle gently but they did not notice, wrapped up as they were in their hats and jackets.

"They're a friendly bunch, aren't they?" he commented, not wanting to leave.

"Yes. I like them. Dominik's a bit of a pain sometimes when he gets over-competitive, but Michael's a dear. He must have been a lovely teacher." She looked up at him then picked off the twig that had attached itself to his jacket collar and held up her mouth to be kissed.

"You make an excellent teacher," Karl said after he had satisfied her demand. "You're very good with people."

"And so are you, except you don't realise it." She looked at her watch. "Well, I'd better leave you to get spruced up before your evening with Ilse. I suggest you give your hands a good wash before you go. You seem to have been rather intimate with a certain mossy bank."

Karl looked down at his filthy hands then reached for hers. "You can't talk, but you're right. I'd better be off."

"Good luck."

"Thanks."

*

A huge yawn engulfed Sabina as she returned to the apartment after her Saturday morning stint in the travel agent's. She had been out singing again last night and had found it difficult waking up early to go to work. She found Wolf tinkering with the new sound system's amplifier on the kitchen table, soldering iron in hand and the smell of hot flux pervading the air.

"Delicious!" she commented, taking off her coat and giving him a peck on the cheek. "Is that what we're having for lunch?"

"Sorry. Got carried away. I didn't notice the time," Wolf said, concentrating on his soldering. "I'll tidy up in a minute." He suddenly remembered the telephone messages he had to deliver. "Thorsten asked if you'd give him a ring about tonight. Something about changing the song you're ending with."

"Oh, right. If that agent's going to be there, we've probably got to end with something more traditional."

"Probably. And Paul phoned."

"Paul? That's unusual."

"Yes. He said he was going to write but couldn't wait that long for your reply. Could you phone him straight away?"

"Nothing's wrong, is it?" Sabina asked, worried now.

"Nothing that urgent, if he was going to write to start with.

Teenage problems, I expect. Wants some sisterly advice."

"Oh. I see. I'll go and ring him, then."

Paul must have been waiting for her call as he picked up the phone almost straight away. "Bina? Is that you?"

"Yes. What is it, Pauli?"

"What's all this about Dad and that woman he works with?"

Sabina was flummoxed by his question. "Silke? What about her?"

"Hasn't he told you?"

"Told me what?" Bina asked, concerned by Paul's anguished tone of voice.

"That he's going to marry her."

"What!" Bina cried loudly. "Who on earth told you that? It's ridiculous!"

"Dad told Richard yesterday."

Sabina found herself momentarily speechless. "Sorry, Paul, but I can't believe … Are you sure?"

"You don't know anything about it then?"

"Not a thing. Last time I spoke to him he was taking Ilse to Medebach for the weekend. He must have been joking, Paul."

"No. Richard was positive he was serious. Said he sounded really happy."

Sabina did not know what to say. "Honestly, Paul, there must be some kind of a misunderstanding. There's no way he'd want to marry Silke. She's going out with a chap called Mick for a start, plus she's only a few years older than me!"

"That's what Aunty Sarah said, but she and Richard both seem to think he would marry her."

Sabina thought for a moment. "I'd better look into this. I'll get back to you, Pauli. Everything all right otherwise?"

"Yes, fine, same as ever. Oh, except I've decided to go to college after all. Arboriculture."

"Good for you! Sounds up your street. Well, have fun with lambing. Take care. Lots of love to everyone."

Sabina slowly returned to the kitchen, mulling over what Paul had said.

Wolf was waiting expectantly. "Did I overhear something about your dad wanting to marry Silke?"

"Yes, it's crazy, isn't it? For one thing, he's going out with Ilse and for another, what on earth would he see in that drug-taking hippie?"

"Not any more, she isn't. Besides, he does spend every day with her. He must know if he likes her by now."

"You don't sound surprised."

Wolf shrugged. "She's nice. Lovely even. Charming, fun, quite pretty, clever and what's more she's -"

"Don't tell me you fancy her too!"

"Well, I wouldn't go so far as to say that, but I can see what he sees in her, if what you say is true."

"I see," she responded huffily.

Wolf smiled. "You're jealous, that's what it is. Honestly, Bina, I wouldn't want anyone else but you, and as for your dad, he's old enough to make up his own mind whether it's Ilse or Silke he wants. Personally, I hope it is Silke, much as I like Ilse."

"Well I don't like Ilse, but I'd rather he married her than some young floozy who'd never understand all his troubles and everything!"

"You don't know that, Liebling," Wolf soothed, seeing she was getting herself upset. "Stop fretting and forget about it for the moment. Go and ring Thorsten and discuss songs with him. That'll take your mind off it."

"I don't want to take my mind off it. I need to know. Paul needs to know." She made her decision. "I'm going to give Daddy a ring."

Wolf watched her go out to the hall and return a minute later.

"No reply."

"Good. Now go and ring Thorsten, there's a good girl, and leave your father be."

What a catch! Wolf thought, as he watched Sabina go out again. Well done, Karl! Wolf would back Silke to the hilt when it came to any arguments with Sabina, but it made things very awkward with Ilse now. Trust Karl to make life difficult for himself.

SEVENTEEN

The conversation around the Münzels' elegant dinner table bored Karl. A dozen people sat around it, with at least two conversations on the go at any one time, if not three, and yet he could not contribute to any of them to any significant degree. To his left was politics, to his right literature and opposite him it was economics and finance. Ilse was caught up in the literature conversation and did not seem to notice his silence. Corinna Münzel caught his eye once from the far end of the table and smiled but everybody else was intent on making his or her opinion heard.

He watched the other guests as he picked at his guinea fowl. They were all successful business people, several known to Ilse from her earlier days in Iserlohn. Apparently he had even met one couple at Siegfried's twenty-first birthday party five years ago, but he did not remember them. They recognised him, however, and feigned delight at Ilse's taking up with him, although he could tell they disapproved of her leaving Paul. As talk to his left finally turned to travel and holidays, Karl paid attention again in the hope that he could join in.

"We love Venice," an elaborately made-up lady, introduced as a beauty consultant, was saying, "don't we, Felix? We go there every spring before it gets too hot."

"We've just discovered Delphi," her neighbour, a balding man of sizeable proportions announced. "Again, it's best seen in the spring with all the flowers in bloom and the air so crisp and clear. There's a fabulous peace to the place, despite all the tourists wandering around, and the smell is heavenly!"

Corinna did her best to drag Karl into the conversation. "Do you know the Mediterranean at all, Karl? Can you recommend anywhere?"

"No, I've never been – at least to the sea. I was in Yugoslavia for a time in the war, but inland, in the mountains."

"You should go back and visit," a woman opposite him said. "We visited Dubrovnik last year. What an enchanting city! I bought some paintings done by a local artist, and he's captured the feel of the place beautifully."

The conversation steamrollered on without him again, nobody listening to what the others had to say, all intent on impressing the assembled company with the extent of their travels. Ilse seemed to be in her element, joining in with advice on what to take on trips abroad.

Karl's thoughts resumed their own wanderings. The bird carcass on his plate reminded him of the frame of a tent: the tent on a beach he and Silke would have to inhabit, with just a bottle of wine and some bread, cheese and fruit to keep them going while the fish took the bait on the line. Silke seemed to appreciate the simple things in life. Of all the places mentioned by the other guests, he thought Delphi sounded most up her street: the smell of olive groves and warm thyme, the scent of wild freesias growing amongst the backdrop of mountain peaks. But anywhere with Silke would be fun, even the middle of London on a foggy day, he thought wistfully.

It was not until he was driving Ilse back to her apartment well after midnight that Karl had the chance to speak to her.

"Well, I felt a bit out of things there," he said. "I must be too much of a peasant for the likes of them. All I can talk about is the price of a ton of cider apples or how to fell a tree."

"That's rubbish, Karl, and you know it. You're very talented in many spheres, but they tend to be practical and physical rather than intellectual."

"I notice you had no trouble in that department," he commented. "You were in your element." This is it, he thought to himself. Here goes. "We don't actually have all that much in common, do we?"

She turned in her seat to look at him. "What do you mean by that?"

"Just what I said. Apart from Siegfried and the twins, we only have a few shared memories from the war. Since then I've changed completely but I don't think you understand that, even now. You still think of me as that young man from long ago and I'm not, Ilse. Really I'm not. You mustn't delude yourself and nor must I. I'm not Karl Driesler, aged twenty-two, nor am I like Paul. I think you and he were well suited, despite his philandering."

"Meaning you think we're not suited?" Ilse asked bluntly.

226

Karl pulled in to the side of the road and stopped the car. He turned sideways on to face her, knowing she deserved total honesty now, or as total as he was prepared to give. "I really tried last weekend, Ilse. I hoped we could rekindle our love, but I felt nothing. You and I, we're so different now, have led totally different lives since the war. We've grown apart and I can't turn back the years, even if you can. I know it seemed right to try, especially for the twins' sakes, but I don't think it will ever work. I'm sorry, especially after you left Paul and everything for me."

He realised she was crying, silent tears running down her powdered cheeks, and he reached for her hand. "We're good friends, the best, and I want it to stay that way, to see you, visit the twins together, whatever. I like you very much, but I don't love you."

"But I love you," she whimpered through her tears. "Please, Karl, give us more time. I realise it must still be too soon for you after … I don't blame you, honestly. I did feel you were finding things difficult between us. We can be friends, as you say, and I won't expect anything more of you, I promise."

He squeezed her hand gently. "I want more than that, Ilse. I want the freedom to find love again, and I can't while you still think I'm yours. I'm not." He brought her hand up to his mouth and kissed it gently, feeling it shudder with her stifled sobs. "I have great respect for you and I love you as a good and trusted friend. You will always hold a special place in my heart, but I need to move on now."

"You've found someone else," Ilse gulped. "Haven't you?"

"Yes," Karl admitted softly. "And I know that I love her. I wasn't looking elsewhere. I thought I had you, but it just happened. I'm sorry, Schatz."

Ilse swallowed hard, withdrew her hand from his and rummaged in her bag for a handkerchief to wipe her eyes and blow her nose. When she was ready and more composed she faced him again, her eyes still bright with tears. "In the past I've sometimes got a bit hysterical in times of crisis. Perhaps I'm finally older and wiser, perhaps I'm even finally less self-centred than I was. I know you didn't ask me to leave Paul and come chasing you the moment you were free. I appreciate the way you've tried to love me again, and I can hear that you truly love her, whoever she is." She took a deep, shuddering breath. "I'm going to be very noble, very sensible and totally unlike my normal self, because I love you so much, Karl. I want you to be happy, and if we can still be good friends, I'll learn to live with seeing you with your new love, just as I had to learn to live with seeing you with Katherine. I've done it before and I'll do it again for your sake. I'll be jealous, and you and she will both know it, but we can live with that. I'd rather still be a friend than lose you completely."

Karl was staggered by her unexpected generosity. He had anticipated a scene, acrimony, anything but this calm acceptance. He leaned across and hugged her close.

"Thank you. Thank you so much. We're still Oma and Opa for the twins. We mustn't forget that."

She drew back and smiled weakly up at him. "No. We mustn't forget who we are."

She wiped a tear from her eye. "Perhaps you could drive me home now so I can have a jolly good cry."

"Of course."

Not another word was said until she stepped out of the car outside the apartment block. "Goodnight, Karl. See you soon, I hope."

"Soon," he agreed. "Perhaps we can go and see the twins next weekend. We haven't been since before Christmas." He saw her nod. "Goodnight, Ilse."

He watched her let herself into the apartment building then drove off back to his house. Somehow it did not seem so empty any more.

*

Sophie was in the middle of bathing the twins when she heard the telephone ringing. She could have ignored it, but decided to risk leaving them alone briefly to answer it. She could always ring whoever it was back in a few minutes. She left the bathroom door open and hurried into her bedroom, where she had had an extension phone installed shortly after Siegfried's death.

"Hello?"

"Hello, Sophie. Udo here. How are you?"

Sophie could hear the twins chuckling in the bath and decided a quick chat with Udo was possible. "I'm fine. Bathing the twins so I can't speak for long. Thank you for the lovely flowers. I was going to ring you this evening but you've beaten me to it."

"Well, I'll be out later. I wish you could be with me. I really enjoyed our trip to the theatre together."

"So did I. It was so nice to get out again, especially with such a charming companion." Sophie wondered if she was laying it on a bit thick, but Udo seemed pleased.

"You know, you could always leave your children with their grandparents again and come to Berlin. Perhaps we could do more next time."

She clearly heard the innuendo in his voice, but she also heard a shriek from the bathroom. "I'd love to, but right now I must dash and see if the twins are all right. I've left them alone in the bath. I'll phone you again some time. Sorry. 'Bye." Slamming down the phone she ran into the bathroom to find Friedrich hitting Freia with a wet flannel. With a sigh of relief she sank down onto the wet floor by the bath and dried Freia's face. Much as she loved them, she found looking after the twins on her own extremely hard work. It left her no time for relationships and most men ran a mile a soon as they heard she had two children. But not Udo.

She smiled as she hauled the twins out of the bath and wrapped them in towels, remembering Udo's parting kiss on her hand; very formal, very proper, until his lips lingered a fraction too long. He was certainly interested in her and the flowers had proved it, but she had not asked whether he was married and she had no intention of becoming a long-distance mistress for him. Udo was an attractive proposition. She guessed he was about thirty-three, mid-brown wavy hair, not especially good-looking but certainly not ugly. He dressed with flair, and appeared to have the means to support her and the twins. That was her prime consideration now, she realised. She had become used to a certain lifestyle with Siegfried, and even though there had been a period of belt-tightening when Paul and Ilse had fled the country and Siegfried had taken over the business, he had managed to set Zopf Construction back on track. She received a dividend on Siegfried's share of the firm now, as well as the interest from his life insurance, but with two growing children to consider, she knew her life would not be as comfortable as if he had still been alive.

Dressing first Freia then Friedrich in nappy and pyjamas, she remembered the exhaustion on her mother's face when she had arrived there late yesterday evening. The twins were fast asleep in bed by then and she had spent a few welcome minutes chatting with her parents, glad to stay overnight after her long drive from Berlin. She could not ask her parents to have them again too soon, but she did so want to see Udo again. Perhaps she could ask Ilse to come up for a long weekend? The twins knew her a bit now. It would be even better if Karl came too, as they were happy with him and it might be a chance for Ilse and Karl to spend some time together. Karl's presence brought back instant reminders of Siegfried, and she wanted to encourage his duties as grandfather.

She smiled at the prospect. Siegfried had wanted Karl involved with the twins; she had seen that at the christening, the way he had held on to Friedrich at first, refusing to pass him to anyone but Karl, almost symbolically handing him over. As she replayed the scene in her memory, seeing the solemnity with which Siegfried handed Friedrich to Karl, she could have sworn he knew he was about to die!

The thought wormed its way deeper into her mind, working its insidious way down until it gripped her heart, clenching it tightly within its coils. He had left everything so well ordered, his family financially secure. She had thought that was just his natural thoroughness, but now she felt suspicious.

With the twins finally tucked up in bed, teddies clutched to their chests, Friedrich's thumb in his mouth, she made her way downstairs to the living room and found the photo album of that last fateful day they had enjoyed together. She leafed through it slowly, examining Siegfried's face in each photograph, studying it to find a trace of explanation for what was to happen later that day. Perhaps there was a trace of strain, she thought, in the later photographs, but equally it could be her imagination. Nevertheless, she began to assess what Siegfried and Gustav's deaths had achieved. Gustav had been openly questioning Siegfried's loyalty to the party and was a threat to them both as well as to Karl and Wolf. Now he was gone, talk of retribution for Josef Garisch's killing had almost died down. So had Siegfried tried to kill Gustav and it had all gone horribly wrong? Or had Siegfried intended to kill himself along with Gustav? Her first thoughts on the matter led her inevitably to that conclusion, but she could not understand why. Gustav killed, possibly, but suicide?

She shook her head in confusion, wishing there was someone she could discuss this with, but she could not risk raising doubts about Siegfried's loyalty again. What had given him such doubts? Who had given him such doubts? The answer came as she flicked through the photographs once more and found one of Siegfried deep in conversation with his father. Karl was the person Siegfried had suddenly learnt to trust! It had started with his trial, but Karl was ultimately responsible for Siegfried's death!

Sophie went to bed that night thinking about Siegfried, dwelling on his single-mindedness, his total commitment to National Socialism and his final warming to his long-lost father that had changed his commitment so radically. He could not reconcile his old life with his new. He had a conflict of interests that had proved unbearable. Rather than betray her faith in him, he had chosen to die for his new cause and rid her of the threat of Gustav. He had been very brave and she loved him for it. If he had felt so strongly that Gustav was in the wrong as to kill him, then perhaps she needed to think about it too; to question her own beliefs just as Wolf and Ilse seemed to have done. If he had not died, she knew she would never have felt like this, her own convictions far too strong to be persuaded otherwise. Siegfried had known that. She would have argued with him, dubbed him a traitor, fought and eventually fallen out with him. He had been right. It was better this way. She loved him still.

When her mother-in-law phoned the next day suggesting a visit the following weekend, Sophie immediately asked: "Is Karl coming too?"

"Yes, of course."

"Good. You must come and stay for the whole weekend some time, both of you. Then the twins can really get to know you."

"That sounds lovely," Ilse agreed. "But you've only got one spare room."

"Oh, I can doss down on the floor of the twins' room, if necessary," Sophie told her, before adding saucily, "but I rather thought you both might like to make use of the master bedroom."

Ilse's voice nearly cracked but she managed to keep it steady as she replied: "Not just yet, I think. Karl's still not got over Katherine."

"Oh, too bad. Well, just give me a nod when the time comes!"

"I will," Ilse replied quietly. "When the time comes."

*

Karl woke to the sound of a church bell tolling solemnly in the distance. He stretched luxuriously, having nothing better to do than to enjoy a rare lie in. He had spent a restless night reliving his conversation with Ilse, arguing his case for Silke. Again and again he had thought about the twenty-three year age difference between Silke and himself. How *could* it work? But again and again he remembered that all-consuming love he felt for her. It had been like that with Katherine. They had worked together for some months, quietly getting to know each other before they had realised they loved each other. So it was with Silke now. Love had simmered away, unnoticed, deep inside only to burst out unexpectedly and explosively at Ilse and Margit's party when he had first felt that jolt inside while chatting to Silke. If he denied his love for her, he would regret it for the rest of his life. Equally, he might also regret it if she left him in a few years, when his age became more of a problem for her. He had to make a decision, and, since a crystal ball was not available and he had no time for palm readers or astrologers, he chose to love her. He believed it would work and he could not bear to forfeit a life with her for the sake of Ilse.

Lying back on his pillow in the clear light of day, he reassessed his decision, knowing in his heart it was the right one but feeling duty-bound to give Ilse's case every last consideration. He knew who he wanted lying beside him right now; the space was Silke-shaped. Nothing and nobody could persuade him otherwise, and now he had told Ilse how he felt, the way to Silke was clear. He would phone her shortly to tell her.

Throwing back the bedclothes, he headed for the bathroom with a smile on his face. Looking in the mirror as he lathered his face, he could not help noticing the change to his whole demeanour. Ten years seemed to have been wiped from him. He had seen the same effect on Ilse when she had been kicked out by her violent first husband and then found refuge and happiness with Paul Zopf. The transformation in her had been astonishing and he was beginning to see it in himself now.

He was halfway through shaving when he thought he heard the telephone ringing downstairs. Grabbing a towel for his face he ran downstairs to answer it, wondering whether it was Silke or Ilse, or even some crisis at the hospital.

It turned out to be Sabina. She was in high spirits. "Hello, Daddy! Guess what! An agent signed us up yesterday after seeing our performance. He's been looking for a folk group to form part of a new TV show touring round Germany, doing the songs, sights and dishes of the different regions. He's convinced we're perfect for the songs part of it and we'll be meeting the producers next week sometime to see if they agree. Isn't that great? You'll have a TV star for a daughter!"

"Whoa! Steady on!" Karl laughed, as excited for her as she was. "What's Wolf got to say about all this? Won't it mean you're away a lot? And what about your job at the travel agent's?"

"Oh, he can see it's what I want, and it might even give him a lead into a technical job with the TV station. You never know! He's going to enquire about it now that he's got his electrical engineering qualifications." She paused long enough to take breath. "Actually, the real reason I'm ringing is to see if we can come down to visit you today. I tried to phone you yesterday afternoon but you were out. We both fancy a bit of fresh air, and we haven't seen you for a while. We can have a bit of a walk then take you out somewhere for lunch. Is that OK?"

"Of course it's OK," Karl replied happily. "No doubt you can tell me more about this group of yours and this TV show." For a fleeting moment he wondered whether to suggest bringing Silke but decided against it. She would probably be busy today being entertained by her mother's matchmaking friends, as often seemed to be the case on a Sunday.

"You can ask Ilse along if you like," Sabina added casually, trawling for information.

"I was out for dinner with her last night, actually," he told her. "But -"

"Oh well, it's our turn to enjoy your company, then" Sabina interrupted, relieved that all this nonsense about Silke was just that: nonsense.

Karl decided Sabina was not in a listening frame of mind, and would save his news until they arrived. "When do you expect to get here?" he asked instead.

"What time is it now? Half past nine – let's say eleven o'clock."

"Fine. I'll look forward to seeing you both. Safe driving."

Karl went back up to the bathroom to finish shaving, got dressed in a pair of navy corduroy trousers and blue checked shirt. Walking with Sabina and Wolf did not mean promenading in Sunday-best clothes, as many did in the woods around Iserlohn. Today though Silke would be dolled up in a dress, probably, fending off the local eligible bachelors. Time to phone her and find out.

She answered on the third ring, expecting his call. "Hello, Karl. I'm on tenterhooks to hear how it went. Tell me!"

"All clear. Ilse was amazingly accepting of the situation. I told her I loved someone else and that she and I would remain very good friends and grandparents together. I didn't mention you by name. I thought it was enough for her to deal with -losing me - let alone to someone so young."

"That still bothers you, doesn't it?"

"Well, I did lie awake quite a lot of last night thinking about it and-"

"Don't, Karl. There's no need, I assure you. Believe me!"

How could he not believe her when she said it like that? "I do. I decided last night and again this morning that it would work. And even if I have to work until I'm seventy, it'll be worth it. After all, my father still helps out at the sawmill and he's seventy-three."

"Whatever, but I keep telling you, a tent on the beach will do!"

"I know," he laughed. "I was thinking about it at the dinner party last night, imagining you and me together with a bottle of wine on a deserted beach backed by olive trees -"

"Or palm trees," she pointed out.

"I thought it had to be somewhere affordable," he objected. "Some tiny Greek island, or Cyprus you wanted, wasn't it? I know that's not tiny," he added before she could correct him.

"You're right. Olive trees it is." There was a pause as they both found themselves together on their imaginary beach.

"So, what are your plans today?" Karl asked, tearing his thoughts away from the idyllic scene. "Is it off to a social gathering at one of your mother's friends as usual?"

"No, not today. I'm going for a farewell meal with Mick. He phoned last night and suggested it."

"Where? I'm only asking because Bina and Wolf are coming down today and we were planning on eating out. Should we avoid you or join you?"

Silke chuckled. "It would be fun if you accidentally joined us, wouldn't it? Mick wouldn't mind, honestly. You know it's not like that between us. He hates eating in the Mess and we're just company for each other. The more company the merrier, eh?"

"Great. And it will give Bina and Wolf the chance to meet you again. They don't know about us yet, and I think it will be a bit of a shock for Bina. She's a bit protective of me, has been ever since she was about twelve, and especially now since ... Well, you know how it is with daughters." He instantly realised his mistake. "No, of course you don't. I'm sorry."

"That's OK. But I can see what you mean. Bina won't like it, I don't think. I'm not exactly her idea of a stepmother, am I?"

"And you won't be until you propose to me," he reminded her. "But she'll have too much on her mind today to worry about us, I think. She'll be telling you her big news."

"Ah. You obviously know what it is, but I won't ask you, so it will be a genuine surprise when she tells me. But we can't leave her in the dark long. You said Richard knows already."

"Yes, you're right. Better I tell her, than she hears on the grapevine."

"Exactly. Well, we'll see you accidentally at about one at the Waldhaus, shall we?"

"The Waldhaus it is. 'Bye Foxy."

"Foxy?"

"You. You're very cunning."

"Am I? Well, 'bye then, Bear."

"Bear?"

"Big and strong, but soft with it. And it reminds me of that card you sent me: the teddy who asked me to be his Valentine."

Karl laughed. "I thought that was you, with your big brown eyes."

"It's both of us, then. We're one and the same."

Karl liked that thought. As he set about having some breakfast and tidying up before Bina and Wolf's arrival, he found himself humming 'Teddy Bears' Picnic' to himself.

*

The Waldhaus was already quite full when Karl led Bina and Wolf in through the door. They were already familiar with the place having eaten there after their joint archery session shortly after Christmas. Karl had telephoned before eleven to book a table, mentioning he would like it, if possible, near the table for two booked for O'Reilly. As the waitress led them to their table he saw Silke and Mick already seated close by. Silke had cleverly sat with her back to the door so that it would be Mick who spotted their arrival. Mick did just as they had predicted.

"Jesus and Mary! Look who it isn't," he boomed jovially in English. "Our fellow archers."

Silke had turned round by now and smiled in welcome. "Hi there. Nice to see you again, Bina, Wolf," she said, nodding to the pair while trying to ignore catching Karl's eye and giving the game away by grinning.

"Hello," Sabina replied, vaguely disconcerted by Silke's presence after what Paul had told her. He must be wrong, she decided. Silke was still with Mick.

Mick stood up to shake hands with them all, forcing the waitress to hover close by before she could seat them and hand them their menus. Mick had other ideas. "Come and join us. I'm sure we can push these tables together. We can make a party of it. A farewell party – the first of many!"

Karl was already asking the waitress if they could move the tables as Sabina asked Mick: "When are you off to Hong Kong?"

"In three weeks, but I've got so many leaving dos to attend I thought I'd better start early. Darling Silke's always game for a free meal anyway, aren't you?" he said, patting her on the head.

Karl frowned. So much for insisting on paying her way, he thought. But Mick could afford it and he couldn't. She was right to be so charitable towards him.

It took a few moments to get the tables sorted but soon they were

236

all seated together and studying their menus. Karl had made sure Sabina sat next to Silke so they could chat easily, while he sat next to Mick on the opposite side of the table facing Sabina and Wolf. It meant he could easily see Silke without being too close to her.

As before, Mick gallantly offered to buy drinks for them all, but Wolf insisted they would pay. "We're celebrating the start of Bina's new career, and possibly mine," he told Silke and Mick.

This was the big news, Silke realised, and knew she must milk it to the full to make Sabina happy. "What new career? Come on, tell us!"

Karl smiled. Despite her youth, Silke really had a way of understanding and getting the best out of people. How anyone could fail to like her was beyond him.

Delighted to oblige Silke's request, Sabina launched into the details of the Leuchleute's big break. They were well into their first course as she concluded: "So our agent advised we should concentrate on German folk music rather than pop. Once we've cracked the local market then, if we're lucky, we can go bigger."

"Well, I wish you all the very best of luck," Silke said. "It all sounds tremendously exciting! I'd love to come and hear you some time."

"You must come up to our next performance. Daddy too," Sabina said, fixing him with an accusatory look. "He hasn't heard us yet, shame on him!"

By the end of the meal, Silke and Sabina were chatting away like old friends, discussing endangered species and the atrocities of the fur trade, while Mick, Wolf and Karl were into a technical appraisal of longbows versus recurve bows.

"I've recently acquired a copy of 'The Archer's Craft' by A E Hodkin," Mick told them eagerly. "You might want to try to get hold of a copy, if you get really keen," he said to Karl. "It's a veritable bible on the subject, and it's inspired me to have a go at making my own equipment. It'll give me something to do in Hong Kong, when I'm stuck in my room all alone," he joked.

"You alone? Never," Silke butted in, having overheard his remark. "Any party going and you'll be there, whether it's in the Officers' Mess, the nurses' block or the nearest opium den."

"My reputation goes before me, I think," he laughed. "I've heard they're already shipping in crates of Bushmills' whiskey, ready for my arrival." Ever the congenial host, he looked around the table. "Everyone for coffee?"

There were nods all round but Karl, wanting the pleasure of Silke's company for as long as possible, intervened. "Why don't you come back to my place for coffee? We can have some schnapps too," he added for Mick's benefit.

"Now you're talking. Is that all right, Silke?"

"Yes, of course," she said with a smile. "I've never been in my boss's house. Now I can be nosy and find out whether he's as tidy at home as he is at work."

"He is," Sabina laughed, relieved to hear Silke had never been to her father's house. "Unless you're being sarcastic and mean he's messy at work."

"No, he's quite tidy. He even washes his own coffee mug out sometimes!"

They all left the Waldhaus together, Karl noticing that, as usual, Silke had driven Mick. She really was thoughtful in that respect, saving him the long return trip to her house, wherever it was.

Once inside, Sabina and Wolf made coffee while Karl poured out schnapps for those who wanted it. Silke declined, as did Sabina, so it was just the men who worked their way gently through the bottle as the afternoon wore on. At four, Sabina went out and made tea, finding some biscuits in her father's kitchen cupboard. A burst of laughter reached her ears from the living room and she smiled. It was good to hear him so happy again.

By six the party was in full swing, with Mick singing his most lachrymose Irish ballads while Sabina and Silke countered with the most sentimental German folk songs they knew. There were one or two false starts and much giggling, but they got it together in the end. Karl did a performance of 'Westfalenlied', a song he had once performed at Donald and Gertie Murdoch's Hogmanay party in 1946 whilst still a prisoner of war and longing for his, as yet, unknown release date. He had choked up on it then, and now, surrounded by friend, family and the woman he wanted to marry, he felt his throat constricting again. Must be the schnapps, he thought, clearing his throat in between verses and trying not to look at Silke.

At seven they all raided the cupboards again for something to eat, finding some rye bread, cheese and cold meats to sustain them. Karl wondered what he would eat for breakfast next morning after seeing his larder emptied.

Silke too looked concerned. "I'll bring you in something at work," she told him quietly as everyone filled their plates and returned to the living room while Karl went down to the cellar to bring up some bottles of beer.

At ten, after everyone had helped clear everything away in the kitchen, Wolf and Sabina set off back to Dortmund. Mick showed no signs of wanting to leave until Silke confronted him in his chair half an hour later.

"Well, Lt. Col. O'Reilly. Shall I drive you back to the Mess? I expect Karl wants to see the back of us."

"Oh, if you have to," Mick muttered, heaving himself out of his chair and swaying gently on his feet. Silke led him out to the hall and helped him on with his coat before bundling him into her car. She turned to Karl who had followed them out to the pavement.

"Thanks for a super evening, Karl. Bina and I got on really well."

"Good. I'm really glad. See you tomorrow." He wanted to kiss her goodbye, but smiled instead, aware of Mick's bleary eyes on them from inside the car.

"Are you coming dancing with me tomorrow evening?" Silke suddenly asked him as she sat down in the driver's seat. "All those single ladies would be thrilled if you did."

Karl grinned. "I'm really not that good, but I'll come. It'll be something different."

"Rather you than me," Mick growled, having understood the word 'dancing'. "She's been trying to get me to go, but I refused," he told Karl. "Good luck, mate. You'll be like a lamb amongst the wolves."

"No, he won't, Mick," Silke laughed. "Karl can look after himself, can't you, Karl?"

"I hope so," he replied, blowing her a kiss once he was out of Mick's vision.

EIGHTEEN

In view of the parlous state of his larder, Karl went food shopping at lunchtime. When he returned home to put it and his usual Monday morning bag of laundered shirts away, he found a letter from Ernst Winter lying on his doormat. Pressed for time, he left the letter lying on the kitchen table. It was not until he sat down to eat his evening meal, prior to Silke picking him up at seven to take him to the dancing session, that he finally opened the letter.

He and Ernst wrote to each other about once every two months or when they had any particular news. Ernst had apparently started a new job and Karl's interest was aroused when he read of Ernst's floral delivery to Sophie in Berlin.

> *I tell you, Karl, I was shocked when I checked up who had sent them. I only did it because I thought you might be interested to know if she was seeing somebody here, but I'm glad I did so I can warn you about him.*
>
> *Udo Kopleck is one of the top dogs in the neo-Nazi network in Berlin. I came across his name recently while sniffing around their ranks. I won't say too much about why I'm investigating them, except that it's useful ammunition for me, should I ever need it. Your daughter-in-law ought to know who she's getting involved with, if she doesn't already. He is a dangerous man, powerful and influential. Be warned!*

Damn her! Karl swore to himself. Of course Sophie would know who he was. Hadn't she worked for them in Berlin before coming to Dortmund and meeting Siegfried? What was as worrying, however, was Ernst poking his nose in. Ernst was a vulnerable and lonely man who craved the comradeship he had found during the war. He could be susceptible to coming back under the spell of National Socialism while still being a supposedly sleeping agent for the Soviets.

Whatever way, he was playing with fire, while Sophie seemed bent on rekindling her contacts in Berlin. There was no way Karl wanted to see her moving back there into those circles with the twins, and nor would Ilse.

He did not have time to dwell on matters, however, as he hurriedly washed up, had a shave and hunted in his meagre wardrobe for suitable dancing clothes. Pushing aside his dinner jacket and the ancient Harris Tweed jacket that had been an old friend in England but had not seen the light of day since coming to Germany, he put on a clean shirt and tie with his work suit. His lack of clothing was becoming a problem, having worn the same jacket and trousers to nearly all the social functions he had been attending since coming to Iserlohn. Much of his money had gone on meals and entertainment recently, but he would have to cut back just when he was wanting to go out more with Silke.

She arrived promptly at seven, waiting outside in her car until he saw her through the kitchen window and hurried out to meet her. Despite the darkness, he noticed Virginia Mitchell walking past and she gave him a wave. Now everybody would know he was going out with Silke.

As they drove to the local community hall where the class was held, Silke chatted about the people he would meet and what to expect from them. She found his responses offhand, so asked him suddenly: "Do you mind coming? I hope I haven't forced you into it. You just seem a bit quiet."

"Do I? Sorry." He thought he had better explain. "I was reading a letter earlier from an old friend in Berlin. It had some rather unsettling news in it."

"Oh, I'm sorry. Do you want to talk about it?"

"It's … er … a bit complicated. Family stuff." He remembered then that she was going to be family some time. She ought to know what she was getting herself into. "You know my daughter-in-law, Sophie, the one in Soest with the twins, my grandchildren?"

"Yes, of course. You've often spoken about them."

"Well, she and my son, Siegfried, were involved with the neo-Nazis."

To spare him explanations she said: "Yes, I read all about it in the papers."

241

So she knew of his trial. That made things easier. "Good. Well, it appears from my friend Ernst that Sophie's got an admirer in Berlin whose political affiliations are rather worrying, to say the least."

"Oh dear. You'd rather hoped she'd left all that behind, hadn't you?"

"Yes, I had. But it seems she's been seeking out her old friends."

"Is there anything you can do?"

"I doubt it. She's very strong willed, is Sophie. She'll probably be encouraged by her parents too."

"Is it a question of finances, do you think?"

"Not entirely. She's young, wants some fun and companionship. You can't blame her, it's just typical of her to look to the neo-Nazis to supply it."

"Yes, but do you think if she met a nice young man nearer home she'd fall for him, regardless of his politics?"

"Who knows? Look at us! We're not exactly the ideal match, are we!"

"Oh, but I think we are," Silke said vehemently. "Here we are," she declared pulling up in the car park of a large, modern hall on the outskirts of town. "I told Herr and Frau Schmalhorst I was bringing my boss to swell the ranks of men and they were thrilled."

"Just as long as I get to dance with you once in a while," Karl pleaded.

"We'll have to see whether the other ladies will let you," Silke grinned. "Come on. Let's put the cat among the pigeons!"

Karl saw what she meant the instant they walked through the double doors of the hall. A large-bosomed lady with grey hair and wearing a silver-grey dress fastened her beady eyes on Karl and came strutting forward to greet Silke.

"Good evening, Fräulein Sommer! Is this your boss? My word, we are in luck!" She turned to Karl and held out her hand. "Welcome to our dance group, Herr ...?"

"Driesler," Karl introduced himself. "Fräulein Sommer told me you were short of men."

"We are indeed, as you can see," she replied waving an arm at the assembled company. Of the two dozen, six were men, although the general age range was greater than Silke had led him to expect. She clapped her hands loudly. "May I have your attention please, ladies and gentlemen. I'd like to introduce Herr Driesler, whom Fräulein Sommer has kindly brought along this evening. I'm sure you'll all make him most welcome." There was a smattering of polite applause then she turned back to Karl. "I'm Inge Schmalhorst," she cooed at him. "My husband, Edgar, is just over there, by the lady in pink, and we're here to set the ball rolling, instruct where necessary and sort out disputes over partners. There are plenty of those," she added with a hefty wink before asking: "Have you done much dancing, Herr Driesler?"

"Just the normal stuff. I don't know any of the fancier ballroom steps."

"We'll soon get you confident in no time, I'm sure. You probably want to start off with Fräulein Sommer, since you know each other. We always begin with a gentle waltz to get everybody warmed up and moving. Excuse me now while I make sure everybody's got a partner."

With that, she left them to hustle the group into order. Silke grinned at Karl. "Isn't she wonderful?"

"I see what you mean about pigeons. Look, there are two more over there! It's just like that Joyce Grenfell song." He nodded across the hall to where two mature ladies faced each other, bosom to bosom.

"Who?" Silke asked.

"Joyce Grenfell. She's famous in England for her comic songs, and she's done one about this very situation - a dance with not enough men. It's rather sad actually."

"I can imagine. Now you know why I brought you, to bring some sparkle to these ladies' evening."

"So you don't want to dance with me?"

"Not all the time, no," Silke replied honestly. "Can I suggest you ask Frau Wittke, over there in the dark blue, first? She's been lacking in confidence ever since her husband died five years ago. It'll give her such a boost to be asked to dance by a handsome young man."

Karl was astonished by Silke's perception of himself as a young man. It showed just how well she had put herself into Frau Wittke's shoes. "You obviously like older people," he commented.

"Yes. Maybe because I missed out on grandparents. I enjoy my Thursday evenings at the retirement home. Older people are so interesting – when they can remember what they're talking about," she had to add sadly. "There are a few like that there."

Her words chilled him, as he pictured himself in that condition with her having to look after him, but he had no time to reflect as Edgar Schmalhorst placed the first record on the portable record player in the corner of the hall and they all set off in a gentle waltz.

In the Officers' Mess it had been too crowded to do much more than negotiate the bodies, but here there was plenty of room to sail around the floor and enjoy the full extent of their partnership.

"Next is a foxtrot," Inge Schmalhorst boomed across the hall. "Same partners, and here we go!"

" I'm not quite so good at this one," Silke muttered, placing her left hand firmly on Karl's upper arm as if afraid she would lose him.

"Nor am I," he whispered in her ear. Sure enough, halfway round the hall he caught the perceptive eye of Frau Schmalhorst, who was leading a frightened-looking young woman of about twenty. Karl knew he was in for it when the dance ended and she approached rapidly while the assembly changed partners under the control of her husband.

"Herr Driesler, let me assess what you can do before I let you loose on my flock. We'll try a military two-step, I think, Edgar," she instructed her husband.

They waited while Edgar found the right track then scuttled to his new partner. As the music started Karl found himself moving swiftly around the floor, unsure whether he was leading or not. If not, Inge Schmalhorst was an expert teacher, instructing almost by telepathy, it seemed.

"Not bad," she told him as they came to a halt. "Perhaps you would like to dance with one of our ladies now."

"Silke suggested Frau Wittke," Karl told her.

She nodded. "A good choice. And I must look after young Veronika over there. Her parents want her competent in time for her twenty-first birthday, but it's proving a struggle!" she confided with another of her strange winks.

As he walked over to where little Frau Wittke stood, Karl noticed Silke being collared by one of the men, the youngest at about thirty.

He wondered who exactly young Veronika was supposed to be dancing with at her twenty-first birthday party, if no young men her age were learning how to dance. Perhaps her parents had found one of their mature friends to take her on as his wife. She certainly didn't seem confident enough to form a relationship by herself.

Karl approached the diminutive lady, seemingly in her early seventies, who Silke had pointed out earlier. "May I have the honour, Frau Wittke?" he asked her with a stiff bow, towering over her.

Frau Wittke's face lit up. "I'd be delighted, Herr Driesler."

As they danced they shared pleasantries, neither having to concentrate too hard on the dance steps. Frau Wittke was nimble-footed and Karl found it a joy dancing with her. She too seemed to have found it a pleasing experience.

"Thank you, Herr Driesler. Silke is a dear for bringing you. It'll make such a difference to our Monday nights having you here!"

Karl glowed. "I'm glad to be of service. Silke does love helping people."

"Just like her poor mother," Frau Wittke said. "Such a sad loss. Did you know her?"

"No, I never had the pleasure."

"You should have. She was a wonderful lady." She saw Silke approaching them and smiled her appreciation.

"Was that good, Frau Wittke?" Silke asked warmly.

"Lovely, dear. You must bring Herr Driesler round for coffee and cakes one Sunday and I can show him off to my friends. They will be jealous!" she crowed, patting Karl's arm fondly. "Oh, that is …" she added, suddenly flustered, "… I don't know if you are married, Herr Driesler."

"Widower," he told her without hesitation.

"Ah," she smiled and gave Silke a long look. "Then you must come. Both of you."

"You made a big hit with her," Silke congratulated him after Frau Wittke had been claimed by a new partner for the next dance. Karl and Silke stayed together, indicating to Frau Schmalhorst that they wanted this dance for themselves.

"She was telling me about your mother," Karl said, starting them off on a polka.

"Was she?" Silke tried not to sound anxious.

"Said how wonderful she was. I can imagine. You must be very like her."

Silke smiled with relief. "I try to be. She would have liked you. In fact, don't think me daft, but I know she approves of you."

"How come?"

Silke looked up at him and grinned. "You will think me bonkers, but the first day you came to work, I got home to find her photo had fallen over."

"So?" He guided her past a pair who had come to a temporary halt in the middle of the dance floor.

"It always falls over when she wants to approve of something," Silke told him. "Like when I started working at the retirement home. She used to say there was a photo of my father that fell over when she was trying to decide about something important. If it fell over, she went ahead with whatever it was, and it always worked out for the best, so she said."

Karl almost stopped dancing but just managed to keep in step. "Did you ever see it happen? Surely anything could have knocked it over: a door slamming, a lorry driving past perhaps, or even an earthquake!"

"I said you'd think I was daft. No, I never saw my father's picture fall over, but I suppose my mother's could have been knocked over by Maus, my cat."

Karl laughed. "A cat called Maus?"

"Yes. Why not? He's grey and white, and when he was a kitten my mother said he looked like a mouse, he was so small. Now he's a lumping great thing but great company. You'll like him."

"When do I get to meet him?"

"Soon. Very soon," she promised. "In fact," she decided suddenly, "are you doing anything this coming weekend?"

"I'm going with Ilse on Sunday up to see the twins. We haven't been since before Christmas. I'm free on Saturday, though."

"No, best make it the following weekend. Any good? Come for a meal on the Saturday – that's the … er … seventh of March and we'll see how things go, shall we?"

She meant stay overnight, Karl thought eagerly, but said nothing except: "You'll have to let me know where you live first."

"I'll draw you a map. It's difficult to find and I don't want you getting lost!"

As the dance ended Silke squeezed Karl's hand, knowing what she had just offered. Two whole weeks to prepare herself! Could she wait that long?

*

The music agent, Peter Drewermann had arranged to meet Sabina, Thorsten and Jörg over lunch on Tuesday in a spacious modern restaurant on the outskirts of Dortmund. Dressed in a beige, English cut suit he extended a warm handshake to all three of them, indicating they should sit at the table he had reserved near the bar.

"I wanted a few words with you before the TV people get here," he explained as the waiter brought glasses of wine for them all, "just to go over what we agreed. If all goes well today, you'll be launching on a new career to tap into the home market, concentrating on traditional music for the time being. What's planned is a series of ten programmes each featuring a different region. You'll be sent there to film on location and record the soundtrack in the studio. You'll be provided with costumes and the songs you'll be singing. Any questions?"

Sabina had an important one. "When is this scheduled for? I have to hand in my notice for my current job at some point."

"Once contracts are signed they reckon on starting in mid-May and filming over the summer. You must be available the whole of that period. Any other questions?"

Jörg had a few about the musical content of the series but all three were quite happy by the time the series' producer arrived with his assistant, the meal ordered and contracts discussed further.

At the end of the meal, as Sabina put her signature on the contract, she just hoped she was doing the right thing. By the end of the afternoon, however, she had handed in her notice at work. If things didn't work out she could always find another job, especially now she had experience in the travel industry.

When she got home that evening she eagerly shared all the details with Wolf. He too had had a productive day making enquiries into a technical career in television.

"I managed to speak to someone at the studios who was very helpful and sounded encouraging. He even asked me if I wanted to visit and look around, chat to the engineers and so on, see what I think. Sounds like they're in need of new recruits."

"That's wonderful! I'm sure you're just what they're looking for," Sabina told him with a hug. "Do you mind if I phone Daddy before we eat and tell him?"

"Go ahead. Catch him before he goes out somewhere. He never seems to be in these days!"

To her relief, her father was in and she gleefully told him all the details of her new career. "We're starting off on the island of Sylt, working our way south down towards the Rhine and Black Forest to Bavaria, then back up the east side, through the Harz Mountains, ending up in Berlin. It's going to be fantastic seeing the whole country like that!"

"You'll see more of it than I have," Karl exclaimed, happy for her. "I'll have to let my friend Ernst Winter know you'll be in Berlin. He'd love to meet you."

"You ought to come to Berlin too, Daddy, while we're there. Wouldn't Ernst love to see you again?"

"That would be great if I could fit it in. Taking the time off work is the problem, of course, especially if Richard and Vanessa fix a date for this year."

"Surely you could manage a weekend?"

"I expect so," he laughed, "although my weekends seem to get pretty full these days. This weekend Ilse and I are visiting the twins, next weekend I'm having dinner with Silke -"

"Silke?" Sabina exclaimed in undisguised horror, remembering what Paul had told her. "What, dinner as in … *dinner*?"

"Yes," Karl said slowly, measuring her response. "Ilse and I have decided we're just good friends and fellow grandparents, whereas Silke and I really get on -"

"But she's half your age, Daddy!" Sabina interrupted him forcefully.

"I know that, Sabina," he said calmly, having anticipated her response. "But we love each other-"

"So Paul was right," Sabina barged in. "He said you'd told Richard you'd found someone to share your life with. How come I haven't heard or seen a thing about this? Is it because you knew I would disapprove?"

Karl heard her mounting anger and was saddened by her response. "It wasn't a secret from you, Treasure. I just had to sort things out with Ilse first before Silke and I could-"

"What if she dumps you in a few years time, Daddy? What if she leaves you just when you need her most, when it's too late to find someone else? I wouldn't want that to happen to you!"

"It's never too late. Opa could find someone now, if he really wanted to, I'm sure."

"Yes, but that's different. Silke's bound to want children, isn't she? I mean, how could ..." She broke off, embarrassed by such talk to her father.

"Ye-e-s?" Karl teased her. "Do you mean how could she do that with an old man like me?"

"No!" Sabina retorted, her cheeks flaming in embarrassment now. "That wasn't what I meant at all! I know Margit's always fancied you, so Silke obviously can too, but what I meant was, wouldn't you have problems financing children when you're getting on a bit?"

Karl sighed. "Yes, that is the biggest worry, but it mustn't stop us."

Sabina heard the doubt in his voice. "That's Silke, talking, isn't it? Would you really want more children, Daddy? You've had four. Isn't that enough?"

"Silke hasn't any family of her own, Treasure. Having children is very important to her. Besides, I'm enjoying seeing the twins. It might be fun to have children nearly the same age they could play with."

Sabina thought about that for a moment. "But your children would be younger than your grandchildren! That's absurd!"

It was the wrong word to use. Karl felt slighted. "Well, it's my life, Sabina. I never criticised Wolf as your choice of partner, despite ... certain incidents, and look how well things turned out for you. You enjoy your life, and I'll enjoy mine."

Rarely had she heard him sound so frosty, but she could not accept Silke as a sensible choice for him. "I'll do that. 'Bye." She put the phone down and immediately wished she hadn't. Her hand hovered over it to dial again, but his angry voice lingered in her ears. She returned to the kitchen.

"Oh dear," she murmured to Wolf, her throat tightening with emotion.

He saw the tears in her eyes, had overheard her side of the conversation. "Your dad and Silke?" he asked.

"Yes. It's stupid. What is he thinking of at his age?"

"Love, I expect."

*

A car drew up outside and Sophie looked out of the living room window. It was a blue VW Beetle. Karl's.

"Opa Karl and Oma Ilse are here!" she called out to Friedrich and Freia, who were running around in circles chasing a wind-up train.

"Opa!" Freia shrieked in delight.

"Opa!" Friedrich echoed, rushing to the front door and reaching up to try to open it. Sophie followed him and flung wide the door.

Karl caught hold of his grandson as he hurtled towards him and held him up high in the air above his head. It was Friedrich's turn to shriek now, chuckling with glee as Karl helicoptered him safely down to the ground.

"Me! Me!" Freia squealed, forcing Karl to repeat the process.

Ilse waited her turn to be greeted, but Karl seemed to be the focus of their attention. Instead she went to kiss Sophie on the cheek.

"You're looking well," Ilse commented, handing her a bunch of spring flowers. "That break in Berlin obviously did you a power of good."

"Yes, it did. I can't wait to go back. It was so good to have a social life and be myself again," Sophie said, leading everybody inside. "Friedrich! Stop shouting like that. You'll deafen us all!" She turned back to Karl and Ilse, helping her mother-in-law off with her coat. "They're so excited to see you. It's been too long since your last visit."

"I know. It's very naughty of us," Ilse said humbly. "We must try to come more often." She noticed Karl bent almost double, as he was dragged by the twins into the living room. "Perhaps for a weekend," she added quietly.

Sophie's eyes sparkled. "That would be lovely. You know," she added while she had the chance to speak alone with Ilse, "I was hoping to ask you both if you wouldn't mind coming some time to baby-sit for a weekend. Give me a chance for a bit more freedom. I can't keep asking my parents, they've done so much already and the twins are pretty exhausting. Karl's so good at playing with them."

Ilse trembled inside. "I'll put it to Karl, but I'm sure we could oblige for you."

"That would be wonderful," Sophie said fervently. "Now, let me get you both a drink of something, then we'll take the twins out for a walk to the duck pond to get rid of some of their energy before we eat. Coffee?"

Unaware of the plots hatching in the hall, Karl allowed Friedrich and Freia to show him their railway set. Friedrich kept kicking the train off the tracks, much to his sister's annoyance. Karl remembered his conversation earlier in the week with Sabina about the twins being older than their possible aunts or uncles. It didn't seem absurd at all. They would all be more like cousins, that was all. He smiled at the thought. Vanessa and Richard, Bina and Wolf, eventually Paul and whoever. There would be a whole tribe of children appearing over the years. His and Silke's would fit in along with the rest of them. "Coffee, Karl," Sophie said, handing him a cup.

"Thank you," he replied, coming out of his reverie. "Friedrich's quite sure he's the boss, isn't he?"

"Don't tell me!" Sophie groaned. "If someone offered me a nanny right now, I'd worship them forever. Still," she added, "you seem to work wonders with him. Perhaps he just needs a man about the house."

"Anyone in mind?" Karl asked, seeing his chance.

Sophie looked coy. "Oh, maybe. It's very early days yet, though. And he lives in Berlin, which is a problem."

"Yes, it would be," Karl agreed. "Can't you find anyone closer to hand? It would make life so much easier for you."

"Yes, but the trouble is I never get out to meet anybody. I had to go all the way to Berlin just to have time to myself."

"Then perhaps you should go away but somewhere closer next time. Pamper yourself at a spa and find some nice young businessman to provide you with a nanny."

Sophie laughed. "You make it sound so easy, Karl! The only ones who'd want me would be the divorced ones to help look after their own brats when they come to visit."

"Don't underestimate yourself. There's plenty would want a beautiful and intelligent woman like you. But don't go getting mixed up in politics again, Sophie. For the twins' sakes," he warned.

She looked hard at him and he returned her look. Unnerved by his apparently telepathic powers, Sophie looked around for Ilse as a diversion. She was just coming back from the toilet and was oblivious to the atmosphere in the living room.

"Where's that coffee?" Ilse asked breezily.

"Here," Sophie said, handing her a cup from the tray on the coffee table. "Karl was just suggesting I should go off and pamper myself at a spa and find myself a new husband at the same time."

"Why not!" Ilse said. "Karl and I would look after the twins for you, wouldn't we, Karl?" she said, fixing him with a firm look.

Karl realised it would be very awkward to refuse, having made the suggestion to Sophie. "Yes, of course. You tell us when and we'll come." He saw Ilse's smile of victory and cursed inwardly. So she wasn't taking no for an answer. The sooner things became official between himself and Silke, the better.

NINETEEN

The atmosphere in the office became increasingly charged as the week wore on. At the dancing class on Monday, Frau Wittke had invited them both to her home three Sundays hence, recognising them as a couple, but this coming weekend would be the important one for them. Karl thought Silke seemed nervous during the week, but he put it down to possible anxiety about the onerous duty he had bestowed upon her in jest of formally proposing marriage. He had no idea how she would set about it, but was quite prepared to help her out and take over the duty, if necessary. Besides, he needed to present her with an engagement ring at some point, but he decided they would have to choose one later, when he had saved up a bit of money.

On Friday afternoon, when he got back from the usual administrative meeting, Silke handed him the map she had promised. "That's where I live. It'll take you about fifteen minutes to drive there. I'll tie a red balloon to the front door, so you'll know you've got the right house. Oh," she added, as if it were an afterthought, "I thought we might dress up a bit, make it extra special, if you could wear your dinner jacket."

"Well, that lets me off the hook of trying to decide what to wear," Karl said appreciatively. "I'll look forward to seeing what outfit you come up with."

Silke gave a nervous grin. "Yes. I hope you like it. I've bought one especially."

"Really? I'm honoured." Glancing back at the door to check nobody had crept into the office, Karl risked a quick kiss of her hand. Up until then he had stuck rigidly to their policy of keeping their relationship out of the office, but the temptation for even the slightest physical contact had proved overwhelming. "And what have you got for Maus to wear tomorrow?" he asked, deliberately breaking the seriousness of the moment.

"Some flea powder, probably - no, I'm joking!" She grew serious again. "I'm going to take my box of chocolates home tonight. I'm hoping I won't need them again after tomorrow, nor will you. We'll have each other."

Again he heard the offer she made, and her eyes confirmed what she meant. They stood a few moments in silence, lost in each other before Karl had to break the spell.

"Work," he sighed. "Let's get to it."

"Slave-driver!" she hissed, blowing him a kiss as she returned to her desk.

As they were tidying their desks at the end of the day, Silke reminded him: "Don't forget, mine's the house with the red balloon tied to the door. Just so that you know it's the right one."

"I won't forget," he promised. "Don't you forget to put it there. I don't want to go knocking on the wrong door and be greeted by an ogre instead of Snow White."

"I think you're mixing up your fairy stories, but never mind. Maus can be Puss in Boots, I'll be Cinderella, I think, rather than Snow White. I don't want to be poisoned by my wicked stepmother, thank you, and you'll be … who do you want to be?"

"The king in Rumpelstiltskin," Karl said, remembering Sarah's choice of fairy story. "I'll make you spin all my straw into gold, since you say I'm such a slave-driver!"

"Very well. You're the king. I'd better make sure I prepare a feast fit for one tomorrow."

"Don't go to too much trouble though," Karl pleaded. "I quite like things simple."

"I know," she reassured him. "That's what I love about you." She straightened the collar of his coat as he put it on. "Except I want you in your dinner jacket just this once. Special occasion. Next time you can wear jeans."

"I don't have any. Dinner jacket it is." He took a last look around the office then switched off the light. "See you tomorrow at seven-thirty."

*

He had chosen as big a bouquet of flowers as he could afford, but it still looked on the mean side for such an important occasion as this.

Silke obviously wanted this to be as grand an evening as possible, and he had thought about buying a bottle of champagne but decided against it, choosing the much cheaper but, in his opinion, almost as good Sekt instead. The money would be better spent on a ring.

Removing the Sekt from the bucket of cold water he had put it in to chill, Karl wrapped it in paper. Then he checked his new haircut in the hall mirror, straightened his bow tie, picked up the bouquet and his keys and headed out to his car in which he had already stowed a small overnight bag, in the assumption he had read Silke correctly.

The sky was clear, with the stars twinkling more brightly as he set off away from the streetlights of Iserlohn up into the wooded hills beyond. He had Silke's map on the seat next to him and he needed to refer to it a couple of times, turning down residential roads that became more and more sparsely populated as the houses grew bigger and the trees more dense. He thought he recognised one road junction as leading down to Paul and Ilse's old house, but his map led him left instead of right. Finally he came to the end of the road where Silke's house was marked as the last one. She had written on it that there was a large gateway into the property and Karl had expected a farm so far out of town, but this gateway was grand, the pillars topped by two stone bears facing each other, each with a paw raised in greeting.

Karl hesitated. Was this the place? From the little he could make out through the gateway and surrounding vegetation, it looked like a house even bigger than Paul and Ilse's. Perhaps Silke's mother had worked there and, out of kindness, the family had allowed Silke to stay on in a small flat somewhere. No doubt that was why she had told him about the red balloon, to make sure he went to the right door. He had better not park in the middle of the drive but tucked out of the way somewhere.

The turn of the century mansion had a mews block to the rear of it, now partly converted to garaging, with additional space beside it to park, although there were no other cars in sight. Leaving his car there with his overnight bag still in it, and clutching the flowers and bottle of Sekt, he stood and looked for the red balloon. The side of the house where he stood had no sign of doorways or balloons to guide him. All the lights seemed to be on at the front. He stepped out of the shadows and walked further up the drive, round to the main entrance, which

255

looked out over the view ahead, through the surrounding woodland to the distant lights of Iserlohn beyond. The house had three stories, the upper walls tiled in elaborately patterned grey slates like the roof, the lower walls painted in a wash of yellow ochre with green window frames and shutters. As he rounded the corner to the front, Karl saw a flight of stone steps leading up to the imposing front door, illuminated by a large wrought iron lantern hanging overhead. Attached to the doorknocker was a fluttering red balloon.

Karl hesitated again, but the balloon finally convinced him to climb the steps up to the front door. Shifting the bottle into the same hand as the flowers, Karl grasped the knocker and rapped on the door, sending the balloon bobbing about. He noticed the smiley face drawn in felt pen on it and it made him smile too. This was the right door.

Almost immediately the door opened revealing a man a little older than himself, dressed in the stiff collar and suit of a servant.

"Good evening, Herr Driesler," the man said politely, standing aside for Karl to enter. "Fräulein Sommer is expecting you. Please come this way."

Karl realised the smile had frozen on his face. He warmed it up again. "Thank you." Following the man across the marble-floored entrance hall to a door on the left, Karl had to make a rapid readjustment of his perceptions of Silke. He took stock of his surroundings, spotting a huge Chinese porcelain urn on a pedestal in a niche on the bend of the broad staircase, while vast painted canvases on the walls leading up to the first floor depicted families long gone. If this was all hers, she was clearly very rich. As he was shown into the room where Silke was waiting, he was almost overwhelmed by its opulence. Ignoring the plush red walls and gold paintwork, however, Karl concentrated on the woman he had come to woo.

She was almost unrecognisable as the vibrantly clad office assistant or muddy trousered archer he knew. Here stood Helen of Troy, Aphrodite, Cleopatra and the Queen of Sheba all rolled into one, her white evening gown draped succulently about her, her dark brown hair piled up on her head, small tendrils curling past her ears in the Classical Greek style. Around her throat was a necklace of diamonds and pearls, a matching bracelet adorned her left wrist while sparkling teardrops hung from her earlobes.

"Welcome to my house, Karl," she greeted him, stepping forwards to accept the flowers he still held.

Karl shook his head in astonishment. He handed her the flowers and Sekt, realising how inadequate they seemed now. "You look ..."

"Like a million dollars?" she laughed, enjoying his bewilderment. "So do you, Karl. You look gorgeous. Let Willi open a bottle for us, then you can relax and take all of this in. I know it must be rather a surprise for you."

She handed the bottle to the manservant, who stood patiently waiting nearby, asking him: "Could you ask Rosa to put these in a vase for me, please, Willi? I don't want to risk staining this dress with pollen!"

Karl noted the informal and friendly way she spoke, more like to a friend than a servant. As Willi went out with the flowers and bottle to deal with them, Silke gestured to Karl to sit down on the gold velvet sofa.

"It's very difficult not to play the part when you're dressed like this," she said with a smile, carefully arranging her long gown as she sat next to him. "It's why I asked you to wear evening dress. I didn't want you feeling out of place in these surroundings the first time you came. They are a bit intimidating, I know."

"That's very thoughtful of you," he said. "Can I kiss you now that Willi's out of the way?"

"Of course!" She leaned forwards and their lips met, but the kiss was more formal than intimate. She guessed he was still overawed by the situation he found himself in. "Don't mind Willi. He knows why you're here. Willi and his wife, Rosa, are like family to me. Rosa's worked for us since just before the war and Willi joined us after he was released. He was a prisoner in England too, you know? You'll have much in common to chat about, I expect."

Suddenly Willi was a potential friend rather than a servant, and Karl recognised Silke's skill at handling people.

"Talk of the devil," Silke said, seeing Willi entering bearing a silver tray on which stood two bubbling champagne glasses. "I was just saying to Karl that you were a POW too. Ah, and here comes Rosa with the flowers. I know she's dying to meet you, Karl."

Karl saw a beaming, broad-shouldered woman entering the room.

She placed the crystal vase containing the bouquet he had brought on a small table by the window then approached the sofa.

Karl looked at her and understood. "My shirts!" he declared. "It's you who's been washing and ironing them, isn't it, Rosa?"

"Yes, Herr Driesler," she beamed, her whole face registering her full approval of the man Silke had finally brought home.

"Thank you very much," he said. "You make an excellent job of them."

"My pleasure, sir." She turned to Silke. "If I may be excused, I have the dinner to attend to."

"Go on," Silke laughed, "and stop making out it's all your own work! I helped too – a bit."

"Yes, you peeled the prawns and toasted the almonds. Apart from that ..." Rosa chuckled and scuttled out of the room, followed more sedately by Willi, who carefully closed the door behind him.

"Aren't they lovely?" Silke said, raising her glass.

Karl nodded and raised his glass likewise in preparation for a toast. He could have felt shattered by her bombshell, but she had succeeded in making him feel totally at home. "To the most wonderful, kind, considerate, beautiful, scheming and conniving girl in the world!" he said, chinking her glass then taking a sip. He instantly knew it was not the bottle he had brought. This was vintage champagne.

Silke allowed him his drink, then returned the toast. "To the most noble, accomplished, handsome, heroic man in the world!"

"Heroic?" he queried. "Definitely not! And I'm not quite sure what you mean by 'noble.'"

"Ohhhh, dignified, chivalrous, honest, reliable, all and any of those," she told him. "And I'm sure I can add to the list, but the champagne will have gone flat before I finish."

Embarrassed by her flattery Karl glanced around the lavishly decorated room. "This is the tent on the beach, I presume," he said pointedly. "The home for our numerous children. You weren't being very honest there, were you? But I can understand why."

"Go on, tell me why."

"You wanted to be sure I loved you, not your money."

Silke nodded. "Partly that," she agreed, "but also so that *you* would be sure you loved me not my money. I think it would have been a big problem for you if you had known just how wealthy I was."

"And how wealthy is that?"

She gestured around her. "This is just the tip of the iceberg."

"I see." He took another sip of the champagne that had probably cost the equivalent of a week's wages, if not more. He had no idea about such things. "You're right. I would have found it very difficult. At least this way I'm sure that it's you I love and I'm eternally grateful to you for allowing me that knowledge."

"Thank my mother. When she was dying, she made me promise not to allow my wealth to come between me and the right husband. It's why I got the job at the hospital, to be among people who didn't know who I was."

"But you could have lived elsewhere among strangers and had a fantastic life."

"I did go abroad – California – and blew my mind but then found it again, thanks to Tom. He knew what I really wanted was familiar surroundings and a husband and family of my own to look after. He told me to get a mundane job and live a simple life, then the right man would come along. I would know him when I wanted to share things with him. He was right. The first thing I shared with you was Rosa. The second thing was my love of archery. The next was my chocolates."

"But you shared archery with Mick too."

She shrugged. "Not the same. I never saw him as husband material, whereas you were, from the moment I first saw you."

"Love at first sight, you mean?"

"Lust at first sight, which is important, don't you think? But love was there when I offered you my chocolates. To me they represented my mother, so I was sharing my love for her with you. The chocolates you gave me with the Valentine's Day card confirmed we were meant for each other. You said they were for sharing, and from then on I was convinced you were the one. But you were with Ilse. It was only after that skiing weekend with her that I knew you were having doubts about her. I made my move, and now here we are and I've been honest with you at last." She set her glass down on a table and edged closer to him, reaching to hold his hands in hers. She looked up into his steel grey eyes. "I'm asking if you are willing to take me and all this on for the rest of your life. Will you marry me, Karl?"

He looked away a moment and her heart fluttered in alarm before his eyes met hers again. Now they looked troubled but his hands had not left hers. Instead his now enveloped hers as he spoke. "You just spoke about honesty, so before I reply I must be fully honest with you, no matter how hard it is for me. I love you, darling Silke, and right now there is nothing I'd like more than to marry you and have children together, even without all this." His eyes roamed around the room then returned to hers. "But you need to know that along with my list of attributes should have come 'mental instability' – hardly an attribute!"

"But that was all covered in the newspaper reports of your trial, Karl," she objected. "After what happened to you at Dachau, I'm not surprised you had problems coping. It was the war and then seeing that man again who had done such awful things to you. No wonder you snapped."

"You think I did it?" he asked slowly

"Didn't you?" she asked in all seriousness.

Karl knew she wanted to be told the truth. "In all honesty, I don't know. Sometimes I think I did kill him, other times I'm sure it was the dog jumping on me that made the gun fire. The judges decided not to convict me. I respect their judgement." It had all become too serious suddenly. "You've certainly done your homework on me," he said lightly.

"Yes, but you can't blame me, can you? I went and looked it all up the other week, after Ilse's party. I understand your problem over drugs now," she said gently. "I'll do my utmost to keep you out of harm's way." Again he looked away and she knew there was more he needed to tell her. "Well?" she prompted.

He gave a deep sigh as he unburdened himself further. "I'm still not over my time at Dachau, if indeed that is the cause of it, although I tend to think it is. It's left me prone to bouts of depression, nightmares and also … I don't know … hallucinations, maybe, at times of stress. It happened when Siegfried died. Katherine had to seek help for me from my old friend Robert Murdoch. He's a trained psychiatrist. Katherine was always on the lookout for strange behaviour from me, and now it will be up to you to do the same. At the first sign of trouble you would need to contact Robert. Does that sound too frightening for you?"

Silke understood now why his eyes looked troubled. By way of answer, she leant forward and kissed them, first the left then the right then she kissed his mouth. When she looked again his eyes were calm.

"Darling Silke," he asked her now, "if you are willing to take me and all this on for the rest of your life, will you marry me?"

"Yes, Karl, I want to marry you." She removed her right hand from his and raised it, like the bear on the pillars of the gateway, he noticed. He raised his own hand, placing his palm against hers to seal the promise of their undying love.

"I'm afraid I don't have a ring to give you yet," Karl said. "But perhaps in a month or two I might -"

"I don't need gold or diamonds," she replied. "Make me one out of silver foil and I'll happily wear it for you."

"And that would make me look mean. No, I insist. I bought Katherine's wedding ring from the little I earned as a POW. At least allow me to do the same for you and include an engagement ring this time."

"She never had one?"

"No. I was going to buy her a diamond ring for our Silver Wedding but ..." He stopped himself. Silke didn't want to hear about Katherine.

"Let's have dinner, shall we?" Silke suggested, rising to her feet. "We'll bring our glasses through as we don't seem to have drunk much champagne yet."

She led him across the room through another door, which led into a dining room. A large, highly polished table was set with silverware, candelabra and flowers at one end, while beyond stood Willi and Rosa, waiting to serve them. Silke sat Karl at the head of the table, seating herself adjacent to him so the candles and flowers did not come between them. She nodded to Willi to top up their glasses of champagne while Rosa stepped forward and placed a dish of avocado and prawns in front of each of them.

"I learnt to love avocados while I was in California," Silke told Karl. "Simple but truly delicious."

"I've never had one before," he said, "but I'm sure I'll love them too."

She picked up her spoon to attack her avocado and watched as he sampled his first mouthful.

"Mmm," he approved. "That's really nice."

"I'm addicted to them," she said with a prawn slipping from the corner of her mouth. "So expect plenty more of them!"

The avocados were followed by trout in an almond and cream sauce. With the champagne finished, Willi poured out a light and fruity wine from a vineyard in the Mosel valley then left the room discreetly.

"The trout are from a local fishery," Silke said as she cut through the crispy baked skin covered in the toasted almonds she had helped prepare. "You can go along and catch your own. Have you ever done any fishing?"

"Not seriously. Tiddlers and such-like with the children. I've always fancied having a go. It rather went with my image of the tent on a beach," he told her, with a smile.

"Catching our own supper and cooking it over an open fire," she said, warming to the subject. "Bliss!" After another mouthful she went on: "I think I'll hand in my notice soon. I don't need to work there any more and it will give me more freedom to do what I want now, planning things."

"Such as?"

"Our wedding, our honeymoon."

Karl grinned suddenly, but his grin faded almost immediately. "I was about to suggest you consulted Sabina over travel arrangements, but that might not be such a good idea just yet."

"Oh?"

"She's not happy about us. It's the age thing," he explained, delicately. "She doesn't want me to find myself alone in ten years' time."

Silke reached for his hand. "You won't, I promise. Unless you outlive me. My mother died relatively young of cancer. Perhaps I will too. Who knows? We love each other and that is the most important thing. Sabina's a lovely girl, and I can understand her concerns for you, but we must convince her this is the right thing for us. We must make her see how happy you are."

She took another forkful of trout but found a bone in her mouth. Delicately fishing it out, she smiled. "If we'd been eating this on the beach, I'd have simply spat that out onto the sand. Our surroundings dictate our behaviour. You aren't really happy working in an office, are you, Karl? You're very much an outdoors person but you've worked extremely hard all your life. Now you can enjoy life: fishing, skiing, walking in the mountains, sailing. You can do whatever you want. Surely Bina will realise what a good life you will have from now on?"

"She will argue that money can't buy happiness, but once she's experienced a taste of what you describe for herself, she might change her tune," Karl said with a knowing grin. "You said you wanted to be part of a large family, and my large family will certainly want to enjoy what you can offer. Is that part of the deal?"

"Of course! Absolutely! What's the point of owning a villa in the South of France or a ski chalet in Switzerland, if you've nobody to go on holiday with? I can just picture us all there - children, grandchildren. We'd have a ball. It would be such fun. And Sarah and Audrey could come too. We'd have to find them a nice man each, as I'm not sharing our bed with them. I draw the line there!"

Karl chuckled over his trout. "I must say, your attitude to sex is refreshingly honest. I presume we have California to thank for that."

"Yes, and while we're on the subject, you are staying the night, aren't you? I didn't want to presume too much, in case my fabulously rich lifestyle spoilt everything. But it hasn't, has it?"

"No, it hasn't, for the simple reason that you're so laid back about it all. And yes, I am staying the night, if Willi and Rosa have no objections."

Silke almost blushed. "Rosa's smitten by you already, even before she met you face to face. I caught her changing the sheets on my bed this morning before I'd asked her to!"

"I see. So she'll be bringing us an early morning cup of coffee, will she, just to see if it was worth her while?"

"No. It's Sunday and they have the day off. They won't come near the house." Silke looked serious. "I wanted this to be like a trial-run wedding for us. Here I am, dressed in white, inappropriately," she added with an apologetic roll of the eyes, "and we've promised to love each other through thick and thin. Tonight I will give myself to you as your slave, to do with as you will. If you don't like what I have to offer, you can still back out."

Karl looked lovingly at her. "I can't get used to your honest way of speaking. But the same has to go for you. If you find you don't like my threadbare and battle-scarred body, you'll still have time to find a -" He broke off as Silke dissolved into helpless giggles. "What's so funny?"

"You!" she choked. "I just pictured you as an old teddy with one eye and an ear falling off. I could never throw away a much-loved teddy. The more threadbare, the more he's loved."

"If only that were true," Karl said in all seriousness. "My scars are from hatred not love."

"Then I shall love them and make them worth bearing," she replied, completely sober again.

His hand reached for hers. "What did I do to deserve you?"

"We reap what we sow," she told him simply.

"You believe in God?"

"No, not as such. But I learnt from my mother that courtesy and consideration are all that is needed to make the world run smoothly - plague, famine and whirlwind excepted, of course. Consideration for others, consideration for the planet – it covers how I like to live my life. The little control I have over my wealth, I try to make it work for the good of others where I can. My financial advisers sometimes manage to make a return on my crazier schemes, but not often. But the big money I leave in their very capable hands and they keep providing me with enough to throw away on idealism. It keeps my conscience quiet."

"So what's your current project?"

"Just at the moment, you! And I'm willing to throw away as much money as it takes to buy Bina's approval, but I know she won't be fooled by money."

"It will help, though," Karl said, understanding his daughter well.

"Good. Now eat up, because I know Rosa's waiting to bring us our dessert and then get herself off to bed." She pushed back her chair and went over to the wall, pressing a button to ring for Rosa. When Rosa appeared with dishes of cherry tart and whipped cream and a pot of coffee, Silke told her: "Thank you, Rosa. We can look after ourselves now, if you and Willi want to finish for the evening."

"Very good, Fräulein Sommer. Enjoy the rest of your meal," Rosa beamed, noting with satisfaction that all was well between the sweethearts.

As she was disappearing through the door, Silke said, loudly enough for her to hear: "Rosa's trying to impress you. Normally she just calls me Silke. As I said, we're just like family here. But there's one member you haven't met yet, have you?"

"Do you mean the venerable Maus?" Karl asked tucking in to his dessert.

"I do. And I'm glad you appreciate his importance to me. Tonight however, you are more important. Normally I leave my bedroom ajar so he can come in and sleep on my bed if he wants, but tonight he won't be allowed in."

"So he'll scratch and meow at the door until you let him in, I bet," Karl pointed out.

"Well, if he does, you won't mind him coming in, will you?"

"It depends on what we're doing at the time."

That decided her. "Perhaps I'd better shut him in the kitchen tonight."

They took their time over coffee, spinning out the evening, making it last as long as possible, knowing they had the whole night ahead but by eleven o'clock they could not wait any longer.

"Let's take these dishes down to the kitchen then I can make sure Maus is shut in or outside for the night," Silke suggested. She carried the dessert bowls and glasses, Karl took the coffee pot, cups and saucers and together they retreated downstairs to the basement kitchen, where all was now clean and tidy. Sure enough, Maus lay curled up on a fluff-covered cushion on a kitchen chair, opening one eye sleepily at their arrival. He got up and stretched then moved to a door leading to the outside of the house.

"I'll put him out. Then there won't be any problem," Silke decided. She picked him up, kissed him and brought him over to be introduced to Karl, who gave him a quick stroke between the ears before Silke ditched him outside.

"So," she said, bolting the door and turning to Karl, grey fur clinging to her white dress, "time for bed."

TWENTY

At the end of the interminably long play Sarah left Worcester's Swan Theatre still in doubt as to what had happened. "Any the wiser?" she asked Audrey as they headed towards the car park.

"None whatsoever. In fact, I'm so confused I need a drink to unscramble my brains. What a way to spend a Saturday night!"

"Is that a cry of desperation I hear?" Sarah asked. "Because if it is, we're in need of help, the pair of us. I don't know, suddenly I'm beginning to feel more and more cheesed off with life."

"Don't tell me you wish you'd never given up your job in London!" Audrey cried in disbelief.

"No, on the contrary. I wish I'd left sooner. What have I got to show for my life? Nothing! At least you've got your children." She knew Audrey would not be impressed by that argument but it was true. "Here we are, dare I say it, two still reasonably attractive women in our early forties, yet unable to find male companions of any worth who stick around. Is this going to be it for the rest of our lives?"

"Oh dear, this sounds bad. What's brought this on so suddenly?" Audrey unlocked her car and they both got in. "You'd better tell me all. You're obviously brooding about something."

"Yes, you're right," Sarah replied. "I am."

Once safely out of the city and on the road to Hereford, Audrey looked across at her oldest friend. "Right. Spill the beans. What's bothering you?"

Sarah looked disconsolately back at her. "It's really stupid, Audrey. I'm such an idiot and I should have known it would happen."

"Come on, Sarah! I'm not a mind reader. Tell me!"

"I've only fallen in love with Karl, haven't I? How stupid could I be? And not only that," she added, resentment creeping into her voice now, "he's gone and fallen in love with that young assistant of his who's half his age."

"Silke, you mean?" Audrey asked in disbelief.

"Yes, damn her! Why do men do that? Why can't they grow old gracefully like we have to?"

"How do you know about this?" Audrey could see that Sarah was devastated.

"Karl told Richard the other week when he phoned on his birthday. Paul was upset too, so I tried to justify Karl's behaviour for Paul's sake, but the more I've thought about it, the more I realise how damned jealous I am! I just want to run away to the end of the earth where I'll never have to see Karl with her. Ilse I could understand, even though I don't think she's right for him, but someone so young!"

"She's not *that* young," Audrey objected. "It's not like she's only nineteen. She's mature enough to make a good wife for him."

"Oh don't say that!" Sarah wailed.

"You really are smitten, aren't you?" Audrey sympathised. "So Karl's breaking two hearts in one go – Ilse's and yours. Quite an achievement!"

Sarah paused a moment, digesting Audrey's remark. "I hadn't thought about Ilse being dumped. She's going to be even more devastated than I am. At least she had some hope of marrying him."

"Which you never had, you mean?"

"Absolutely none whatsoever."

"So why is losing him such a big deal? I've got no hope of marrying Mick, and precious little chance of seeing him again either, if I'm realistic. But I'm not plunged into the depths of despair. You'll find someone, Sarah, trust me. Maybe he'll be second best to Karl, but beggars can't be choosers, and at our age we're beggars."

How depressing those words sounded to Sarah. "Saturday night," she mused morbidly. "I wonder what Karl and Silke are up to right now."

"Oh don't," Audrey groaned, rolling her eyes in her own despair. "I can't bear it either!" They looked at each other and suddenly both burst into giggles.

"That's better," Audrey said eventually smothering her laughter. "We can only laugh about it and share our secret sorrow together. From now on we must redouble our efforts to meet the right kind of man."

"Which is?"

Audrey shrugged. "Your guess is as good as mine. Until then, we have each other."

Sarah nodded. "And our dreams."

*

Ilse sat on her own in the empty apartment. All three of her daughters were out with their boyfriends, leaving her with nobody to speak to. Since Karl had told her he was seeing someone else, she had felt like she was in freefall. She had given up her reasonably happy marriage to have him back, but it was all for nothing. She had never felt so foolish in her entire life. This was the second time he had let her down. No, she was being unfair. Both times it had been her own stupid fault. She had thrown him away the first time and now he did not want her back. What was she to do now? Go crawling back to Paul in Uruguay? No. She couldn't. She hated it there, so far away from everyone.

Ever since Margit had told her what Silke's friend, Mick, had let slip about Karl sleeping with Audrey, Ilse had known who her rival was, but at least Audrey was now far away in England. Her only option, she decided, was to quietly keep her sights on Karl, with her best chance being the following weekend when they were both baby-sitting for Sophie.

*

Wolf listened to the telephone conversation in the hall, not liking what he heard. Sabina seldom called Lane Head Farm because of the expense, but she clearly needed moral support from Paul in her campaign against Karl's new relationship with Silke.

"You seem to be on a mission now to break them up," Wolf observed upon her return to the kitchen. It was Saturday evening and they were both due to leave shortly for her next performance with Leuchtleute. "What right have you and Paul to meddle in his love life?"

"Every right. We don't want to see him hurt or making a fool of himself."

"You think he is?"

Sabina looked at him candidly. "Yes. I do. A man of his age going out with someone so young! He'll be a laughing stock."

"Why? I think most men would be extremely jealous."

"I'm not talking about men."

"Oh, I see now! It's more a question of Silke taking over from you as his favourite young woman, isn't it?"

"No!"

"It is, Bina, and you damn well know it!"

"There's no need to shout at me."

"There is when you're being so silly."

"Silly? Me?"

"Yes, you. You're the one who's looking foolish and I suggest you leave him be, and allow him to find some happiness again. He deserves it."

They had never argued like this before, but Sabina felt too strongly to give in. "He deserves someone who understands everything he's been through. How can *she* do that? And he'll be too proud to tell her his problems and something will happen and he'll … he'll …" Her imagined outcome caused her to burst into tears and flee to the bathroom.

Wolf heard her sobbing in there and tried to go in to comfort her, but she had locked the door.

"Bina, let me in. Come on, Liebling. It's all right. This is silly arguing like this."

"You don't understand what I feel for him," she sobbed through the door. "Your father wasn't like him."

"That's beside the point," he retorted, trying to quell his anger. "I *do* understand how you feel, but I just happen to think she's right for him. Perfect even. You've got to give them a chance."

He heard a loud sniff from behind the door.

"That's what Richard says," Sabina muttered.

"Well then, shouldn't we do that? At least give Silke a chance to make your father happy. She will. I know she will."

After a moment's pause he heard the bolt on the door slide back and Sabina appeared, her face streaked with tears. "You think I'm being very stupid, don't you?" she said, hugging him hard as a plea for forgiveness.

"Over-protective possibly, but understandable and I love you for it," he told her tenderly, kissing the top of her head.

Sabina began to cry again, but this time with relief that their argument was over. "I'll try to accept her," she promised. "I know I like her really."

"There you are then. Look on her as a new big sister not as a stepmother. It'll be fun."

Sabina did not feel convinced, but for the sake of peace with Wolf she nodded. "I'll have to patch things up with Daddy first."

"That will be easy. He loves you dearly." He kissed her on the mouth. "As I do." Wiping away her tears with his hand, he smiled. "Now go and wash your face!"

*

It was the third time that week that Udo had phoned Sophie from Berlin, first wanting to know when she would be arriving next weekend, then whether she wanted to eat at a particular restaurant, and now, could she not stay longer than a weekend?

"No," Sophie told him firmly. "I'm relying on my in-laws to baby-sit and they both work. They have to be back for Monday."

"Well, what about your mother, or your sister even? Can't she take over on Sunday night?" he demanded.

Sophie was sorely tempted but his pestering was beginning to annoy her. He obviously had no understanding of the problems of childcare. "Why can't you come here for a long weekend?" she suggested. "Then you could meet the twins."

There was a longer silence than she would have liked before he replied. "Maybe. But I have a very busy schedule right now."

Sophie made no comment. What he said was undoubtedly true, but that pause had been revealing. "Well, I'll phone you later in the week, perhaps on Wednesday," she said, wanting to indicate her displeasure by ending the conversation.

"Wednesday's no good. I'm out. I'll ring you some time. Take care of yourself, my Beauty."

"Yes. Goodbye, Udo." Sophie put the phone down. Suddenly a trip to a spa seemed a more attractive prospect. Right now she had another lonely Saturday night to get through. Her parents had gone out, her sister was never in on a Saturday. Who could she call to come round to keep her company?

*

Karl woke to find Silke's warm body nestled into his. A tremendous feeling of peace and joy washed over him, confirming what he had known the night before. He loved Silke with all his heart and mind. When he had made love to her the connection was there, the meeting of souls, just as he had felt it nearly thirty years ago with Ilse then later with Katherine.

He moved his hand up from where it lay on her right hip to her left shoulder and gently turned her to face him.

"Good morning, Cinderella" he said, kissing her lips.

"Good morning, Your Majesty," she murmured with an appreciative smile before stretching her entire body luxuriously for a full five seconds then suddenly rolling on top of him. Pinning him down, she lay gazing into his adoring eyes, soaking up the glorious sensation of his long firm body beneath hers. He was irresistible. Slowly she sat up astride him and ran her eyes over his chest and abdomen, now seeing what she had felt last night. Her fingertips lightly brushed the scar on the lower left side of his torso and he flinched at her touch.

"Does that hurt?" she asked anxiously.

"No, it tickles."

"Oh." She picked up his right arm and brought his scarred forearm and hand to her lips, kissing his old injuries, aware of their history, only trying to nullify the hatred that caused them with her love.

"I felt your back last night. It's covered in scars," she commented.

"And I've one on my right leg," he informed her. "But you can leave all those for later. Right now I've got other things on my mind."

Silke grinned and began to move on him, enjoying watching his pleasure until her own matched his. When she finally rolled off him, she realised that for the first time in her life she felt happy to be carrying a part of a man still inside her. Laying her head on his chest and looking up at him, she said: "I love you, Karl. Don't ever leave me."

He saw raw pain in her eyes, the pain of losing both her parents, and the difference in their ages flashed through his mind once again. "One day I'll have to, but not for many, many years, I hope." He hugged her to him, feeling her wrap herself around him in her anxiety not to let him go. "And you'll have our children to love you then."

Silke burst into tears. "I'm so h-happy!" she wept.

Karl kissed the tears from her cheeks. "And so am I, my beautiful Queen of Sheba."

They lay quietly together for a while as Silke stifled her tears then she drew back. "I need the bathroom then I'll go and make us some coffee and let poor Maus in. He's probably scratched the back door down by now!"

She wrapped herself in a warm towelling robe and pottered out. When she returned, followed by a loudly purring Maus, Karl was sitting up in bed with the pillows behind him. Maus promptly leapt onto the bed and investigated the stranger in it, still purring.

"He doesn't seem to mind me being here," Karl said, stroking the cat as it settled down beside him. "Is he used to strange men in your bed?"

"No. I've never brought anyone home before. Not even Mick!" she added with a hand over her heart.

"It's all right. I believe you. I could tell from Willi and Rosa's attitude that I was a novelty."

"Honestly, Karl, what I got up to in California was not the real me. It was the time, the place and my need to forget my grief."

"Don't worry. I understand. More than you know." As she got into bed beside him and sipped at her coffee, he thought about how much of his life she should be told. At first he had wanted her to stay ignorant of his wartime experiences, but now he knew she was aware of some facts from the newspaper reports of his trial. She ought to know it all.

"I was thinking," he said slowly, his fingers gently rubbing Maus on the stomach, "that perhaps I would invite my old friend Robert and his wife Alice over to stay."

In the context of his previous statement, Silke could guess the reasoning behind his suggestion. "You want him to tell me all about you?" she asked.

272

Astonished by her perceptiveness, Karl nodded. "I just don't think I can tell you myself. I never managed it with Katherine - Robert told her everything - and I only gave the barest of details to my children when they were still quite young. I had to pre-empt Siegfried," he hurriedly went on to explain. "He was going to dish the dirt to them and I needed to do it myself. Paul was too young to understand, Richard just thought it made a good gory story but Sabina was really upset by it. That's why she's so protective of me now. I hope you'll understand that."

"Of course. But how did Siegfried know?"

"Ilse told him, and she knew from her husband, Paul. My parents had contacted him to try to help me. As you may have read in the papers, he was in the SS, had influence in high places and managed to track me down eventually. I'd probably be long dead if it weren't for his intervention."

Silke grimaced. "It's going to make grim listening, by the sound of it, but you're right. I do need to know more than what little was in the papers. And I think you'll feel happier for my knowing. Tell Robert and Alice they must visit any time they can. They can stay here."

"Or with me."

"Whichever you like, but there's more than enough room here. And I'm so looking forward to having friends and family to stay here at last."

"Here it is, then," Karl agreed. "I just have to invite them now. It'll be good to see him again – and not be needing him professionally."

"I hope you won't ever have to again."

"So do I, but it's good to know he's there if I do."

His remark touched her deeply. She knew she could never leave him or the consequences for him might be terrible. Not that she could see herself ever wanting to leave him. "I'll always be here for you," she promised him. "Whatever happens."

She took another sip of coffee and studied his profile, his sharp features still reasonably firm, his cheekbones still well defined. "Gosh, I hope I look as good as you do when I'm your age," she sighed. "I suppose it's all that fresh air and hard work that's kept you in trim."

"And it's hereditary. My father's just the same." He studied her rather round face, her brown eyes, compact nose and broad mouth. "Are you like your mother?"

"I'll show you her photo and you can see for yourself. It's over there on my dressing table." She nodded towards the window then gasped. "It's done it again! The photo's fallen over!"

Karl followed her gaze. Sure enough, he could see a silver photo frame lying face down on Silke's dressing table. "We weren't that energetic last night, were we?"

In demonstration, Silke got out of bed, stood the frame upright again then jumped up and down firmly several times. The frame did not even move. "No," she marvelled, picking up the frame and bringing it back to bed with her.

"And Maus wasn't in here," Karl commented, "unless it was already knocked over before we came in here last night."

"It wasn't," Silke told him assuredly. "When I sat there to let down my hair I noticed it was definitely upright."

"But you could have knocked it over after that."

She handed him the photo frame. "Ask her yourself."

Karl looked at the black and white, head and shoulders portrait of a woman in her mid thirties, her dark hair rolled and styled in the fashion of the nineteen fifties. He was reminded of Leonardo da Vinci's 'Mona Lisa', the face in peaceful repose but with the trace of a smile. It was a loving face, a caring face and he felt he knew the woman to whom it belonged. "She's lovely," he said. "I can see why Frau Wittke called her a wonderful lady. She looks very kind."

"She was. But what did she say?"

Karl was taken aback by her question, but he knew what the answer was. "She said she knocked it over to show she approves of me."

"Good. I told you she did. So when shall we get married? Easter's a bit too soon. Perhaps Whitsun? It won't be too hot in the Mediterranean for our honeymoon then. Or would you prefer the summer? That might be better I suppose. It gives us longer to organise everything."

"You really are in a hurry, aren't you?" Karl said, handing her back the photo of her mother.

"Yes. I can't see any point in delaying things for the sake of it. I want to live again, to enjoy life to the full, to see you enjoying life instead of slaving away in that dreary office, doing a job you're good at but you don't really like. And most of all, I want to start a family, one to be proud of, one you can enjoy and see grow up."

Now he understood her haste. "How about the end of May?" he suggested, before remembering that the thirtieth had been Katherine's birthday. "That gives us three months, just about, to plan it."

"Perfect. Let me look in my diary." She went back to the dressing table, stood the photo back in its place then rummaged in her handbag for her diary. "Here we are. Saturday the thirtieth. How's that?"

Was that good or bad? Karl hesitated, felt Silke's impatience for an answer as she snuggled up beside him again, and explained his dilemma. "That was Katherine's birthday. My family might not like the idea of me getting married again on that day."

"Or else it can show them that Katherine is not forgotten, that she is a welcome part of my life and that I respect the love you still have for her. We'll celebrate her day along with ours."

Put like that, how could he say no? He spoke through the lump in his throat. "She and I got married on my birthday, and now you and I will be married on hers."

"Continuity of love. Your family will understand, Karl."

"I hope so."

TWENTY ONE

Frau Wittke was intrigued by the subtle change she detected in her new friends' relationship. She had guessed Silke had brought her boss along to the dancing sessions as more than just an extra male, which was why she had wanted to invite them both to her house one Sunday in case Silke needed some help finding excuses to be with Karl. But help was clearly not needed. Tonight she saw an extra sparkle in their eyes and a lightness of step they were both barely hiding. Whatever had happened since the previous week was significant and she felt glad. Karl and Silke were both such lovely, caring people that they deserved each other, she thought fondly.

When Karl asked her for the second dance, Frau Wittke eagerly accepted. "You and Silke seem very happy tonight," she commented, surprising herself by her unaccustomed boldness.

"We are," Karl told her proudly, steering her down the length of the hall, deciding to reveal all. "We hope to get married in May." He felt her hand grip his in excitement.

"Really? Oh, many congratulations, Herr Driesler. I'm so pleased for you both. May is such a lovely month too." At that moment Silke passed by with her dancing partner and Frau Wittke threw her a warm smile.

"Nobody else knows yet," Karl told her. "But I don't suppose we'll manage to keep it a secret for long."

"Not once people see her ring," Frau Wittke warned.

Karl looked embarrassed. "I haven't actually bought her one yet. I need to save up a bit first."

Frau Wittke was aware that Karl was not a wealthy man. "She won't want you to buy her anything flashy, you know," she advised him.

"I know." Suddenly he felt it was all right to reveal his straitened circumstances to Frau Wittke. She wouldn't judge him adversely and it would explain any delay about buying a ring. "Even so, I might have to get a small loan or buy it in instalments. I haven't managed to put any money by yet since starting work here."

Frau Wittke frowned. "Have you been to Silke's house yet?" she asked him cautiously.

Karl understood. "Yes. I know now that she's wealthy, but that's not the point, is it? I'm supposed to give her a ring."

She nodded but could not help smiling constantly throughout the remainder of the dance.

When Karl was driving Silke home later, he told her that Frau Wittke knew of their wedding plans.

"She'll be thrilled for us," Silke said happily. "It'll give her something to look forward to. We must invite her, Karl. I don't think she has much family of her own. But first we must think about where we want to get married."

"You're the bride," he told her. "It should be your choice. And since you'll probably be paying for it all, I'll leave the budget up to you too. Whatever you want, but we'd better get a move on."

"Right. It'll have to be somewhere pretty big, the number of people we're going to want to invite between us. Since I've got no family, I'll have to invite all my friends. It may be that the church in the village here is too small, but we'll see. You just make sure all your family can get over here for that date and then we can organise the rest." She paused as she considered her next question carefully. "What about Ilse and her family? Should we invite them too?"

Karl bit his lip. "I'm not sure. I'll see how things go at the weekend. I told you we're baby-sitting for Sophie?" He saw her nod. "It would be nice to have them all there. They were Siegfried's family, after all."

"I must say I'm surprised Ilse's taken it so well. She doesn't strike me as the sort of person who would let you slip through her fingers so easily."

"She isn't. I was as surprised as you are by her reaction. But she doesn't know it's you yet. Whether that'll make it better or worse, I don't know. And I've yet to get Bina and Paul on your side."

"I know. I'm sorry I'm such a problem for you, Karl. All I wanted was to have a lovely large family and I seem to be driving you all apart."

"I'm sure they'll come around to the idea. Bina likes you a lot, as I've said already, and Paul will probably develop a crush on you once he meets you," he added with a knowing grin. "It's just a matter of time."

"Which we don't have if we're getting married in May."

Karl slapped the steering wheel with his hand. "I've just remembered. Bina's supposed to be starting her TV career in May. I hope she'll be available then."

"Hopefully they won't be working on a Saturday. I know! How about hiring them as part of the entertainment for our wedding reception?"

Karl had to smile. "I can see your mind is starting to work overtime planning this. We can certainly ask Bina and her friends." He pulled in through the bear gateway and drew up outside the front steps. "Do I get invited in?" he asked boldly.

"Of course!" She pecked him on the cheek. "And I might even persuade you to stay the night. Who knows?"

"Who knows?" he agreed.

*

Sabina put down the phone again. It was the sixth time she had tried to contact her father since the weekend and he was still not in. She was beginning to get worried.

She confided her fears to Wolf as she undressed for bed. "Do you think he's all right? Perhaps he's had an accident?"

"We'd have heard something," he reassured her. "Just remember he's got a new girlfriend. He'll be seeing her."

"Sleeping with her, you mean," Sabina said with a shudder of revulsion.

"Oh for goodness sake, Bina! Stop being so prudish. He's a man not a saint. You promised you'd try to accept the situation."

"It's not that easy. I just don't like the idea of him having somebody else so soon."

"You just find it embarrassing, that's all. Hurry up and get into bed," he told her briskly, "and I'll soon put him out of your mind."

Sabina sat on the bed and bent over to take off her tights. She remembered the stocking she had found under her father's bed during Aunty Sarah and Audrey's stay. She never had got to the bottom of that, but it was possible now it might have been Silke's ...

or Ilse's … or Audrey's. Or surely not Aunty Sarah's? She gave a chuckle. "I'm beginning to see Daddy in rather a different light these days," she said, waving her tights round her head before flinging them with gay abandon across the bedroom. "Now I know where I get my sex drive from!" So saying, she stripped off her knickers, sent them flying then hurled herself into Wolf's waiting arms.

*

At work the following day, Karl found his thoughts drifting to the weekend and Sophie's trip to Berlin. While walking back to the office from a meeting with the Officers' Mess manager, he thought about Ernst Winter's letter. He was really worried that Sophie was becoming embroiled with a neo-Nazi again, and wondered whether he should ask Ernst to keep an eye on her to see if she met up with this Udo Kopleck character. What he would do about it if Sophie was seeing him, Karl did not know, but the information might be useful.

In his lunch break he returned home to get some food down himself and write a quick letter to Ernst. Silke was going into town to make a start on the wedding preparations and Karl knew he must contact all the members of his family tonight to inform them of the wedding date. It would come as a shock to his Medebach family, who had no inkling about his feelings for Silke. He had not been in touch with them recently, and, as far as they were concerned, he was still seeing Ilse after their skiing weekend together. Darling Silke took up too much of his time these days, he thought with a satisfied smile. Then he thought about Sabina and their last conversation. He must phone her first, he decided.

Sabina beat him to it, calling in her lunch hour in yet another attempt at contacting him.

"At last, Daddy! You're never in these days!" she remonstrated with him the moment he picked up the receiver.

"Sorry, Beauty. How are you and Wolf?"

"Fine. Look, I just wanted to say I'm sorry about what I said last time we spoke. I realise I was being selfish and well over-protective, I guess. Silke's a really nice person and I hope you'll be very happy together."

"Thank you. You don't know how glad I am to hear you say that, Beauty, particularly as we've decided not to wait very long to get married. No, she's not pregnant!" he added hastily with a laugh. "But she wants to be."

"I don't think I need to know that, Daddy, but never mind." Sabina was pleased to hear him use her new pet name again. It meant they had repaired the rift between them. She could concentrate on details now. "So, when's the wedding?"

Karl paused, remembering the significance of the date again. "It's Mummy's birthday," he told her. "It would be nice to commemorate her on the same day," he said before adding pointedly: "That was as much Silke's idea as mine."

Sabina was silent as she digested the information and, to her surprise, found herself warming to the idea. "That's nice," she said truthfully.

Karl breathed a sigh of relief. "Are you free then? I know you start touring about that time, don't you? We were rather hoping Leuchtleute could perform at the reception."

Sabina was stunned but also pleased. Her father and Silke had certainly not lost time in planning their wedding. "Well, I'll have to find out. If we can, I'd be delighted. Where are you planning on getting married? Silke's not got any family, has she?"

"No, but she has plenty of friends here in Iserlohn." He realised his daughter had no idea about Silke's wealth as yet. "You and Wolf must come over soon and meet her properly now that we're engaged. I'm busy this weekend baby-sitting with Ilse, and the following -"

"Ilse? Is that wise, Daddy?"

"We want to stay friends. Baby-sitting seems a good way of doing it."

"And what does Silke feel about that? Is it for the whole weekend?"

She did not need to be more explicit. He understood her concerns well enough. "Yes. But Silke's fine about it. She knows exactly how things stand between us."

"Well, I hope for your sake that Ilse does. It sounds awfully risky to me!"

"Don't worry, Beauty. I think I can look after myself."

"Let's hope so," Sabina said fervently. "Oh, by the way, does everyone at Lane Head know yet?"

"No. I'm ringing them tonight."

Over the years protecting her father had become second nature to Sabina. "You know Paul's not very happy about Silke?" she warned him. "And I don't think Aunty Sarah is either. She phoned me last night to ask me about you two. Somehow she seems a bit on the … over-interested side."

"What do you mean?"

"I don't know exactly; jealous, perhaps. She and Audrey are having trouble finding available men, I think."

"She told you that?" he asked in astonishment.

"Aunty Sarah and I have always found it easy to talk to each other, " Sabina said smugly. "She was the first person I asked about coming over to live here with the Zopfs that summer."

"Ah." For a moment Karl was transported back what seemed a lifetime ago now, to the time before all the recent trouble started, when life with Katherine had been so straightforward and simple. Quickly he despatched such thoughts from his mind before they could take a hold on his mood. "So Sarah and Audrey are finding themselves at a loose end are they? I'll have to ask Silke if she knows any eligible men we can invite to the wedding for them."

"Mature ones, please, Daddy! It's bad enough you going for someone much younger." She was able to tease him about it now, she realised. No matter what he did, she loved him too much to bear grudges. "Would you really invite Audrey?"

"Yes. Why not? I told her she was an honorary member of our family now, and I meant it."

"That's very generous of you, considering her husband …" She quickly curtailed that line of thought.

"You can't blame her for what her husband did," Karl said emphatically.

"I know. Sorry." She decided she had said enough. "Well, I must get back to work. I can't wait to tell Wolf the news!"

"You seem quite excited about it."

Sabina laughed. "Do you know? I think I am!"

After they had said their goodbyes, Karl returned to the office.

Unusually for her, Silke was not back yet but she hurried in a few minutes later and blew him a kiss.

"Oh this is exciting!" she beamed at him. "Word will be round town in no time after all my visits today. We're going to have to announce this formally, you know?"

"Yes, I know." Karl told her about Sabina's phone call and she hugged him in relief. As she did so Major Pascoe waltzed into the office.

"So the rumours are true!" he grinned. "I wondered why your resignation had appeared so suddenly, Silke. And Lt. Col. O'Reilly's devastated by your treachery even before he's left these shores!"

"Is he?" Silke asked in horror.

John Pascoe gave a hearty chuckle. "No. Pleased for you both, more like. Said he could see the way the wind was blowing from the start." He winked. "Don't tell him I said that, though."

"So how many people know about us?" Karl asked.

"Just about everybody, I should think. You can't do much around here without the word getting about!"

Virginia Mitchell had seen him going out holding flowers, Karl remembered, but it could have been any social call, such as dinner with the Münzels. True the bouquet was bigger than was normal on such occasions, and his neighbours might have noticed that his car was not parked outside the house at night. But how did they know it was Silke he was seeing? With a flash of inspiration he worked it out. The ice rink!

John Pascoe shook his hand and kissed Silke on the cheek. "Well, let's hope we can find a replacement here for Silke."

"Then you'll be looking for one for me shortly after," Karl told him.

The major was shocked. "Really? But why? You've made such a good job of running things in the short time you've been here. You can't leave us so soon."

Karl did not want to have to explain about his future wife's riches. "We want to see the world a bit after we're married – in May," he added to save on further speculation.

"Oh." John Pascoe could not argue with that. It just seemed a bit Bohemian for a fifty-year-old man to want to do, even one with such a young bride! "As long as you give us plenty of notice for a handover period," he said resignedly, "bearing in mind you're both leaving." He looked at the pair of them, saw the glow of love shining about them both and could not begrudge Karl his decision. "Well, I'll go and leave you two love-birds alone and let everyone know the rumours are true!"

Once he was gone they returned to their desks. As she sat down, Silke let out a gleeful squeak. "Isn't this fun? Who do you think we should invite from the hospital? There's so many!"

Karl swivelled his chair round to speak to her. "We'll sit down and make a list tonight, that is if you're not going out with Margit and the rest to the bar. Tuesday's friends night, isn't it?"

Silke's face dropped. "Yes, but I'd rather be with you. I tell you what. Why don't you come with me, then we can tell them all about our wedding plans? Margit will hear, and she'll tell Ilse! How's that?"

Karl frowned. "I rather think I ought to tell Ilse myself."

"But then it sounds like you're asking her permission, which you're not!" Silke objected.

"I think she deserves the courtesy of me telling her," Karl maintained. "I'll give her a call before we go out. Then at least it won't be such a shock for poor Margit either."

"Oh yes. I know how much she'd like to be in my position." She gazed longingly at him. "How many women love you, Karl? It must be hundreds!"

"Don't talk daft!" he protested. "They don't know me for the rotter I really am. You can expect me to beat you severely every Friday night when I get home drunk."

"I don't mind," Silke laughed, "as long as I get to beat you back!"

"Fair dos. That's settled then. Every Friday night we battle it out together."

"Maus can be the referee."

"He's biased in your favour. No referee. Now if you don't mind, Fräulein Sommer, I have work to do." So saying, he swivelled his chair back to face his desk.

"Sorry, Boss," Silke murmured, stifling another giggle.

*

283

At seven o'clock Karl bit the bullet and got through to Ilse's number. Roslinde answered, expecting it to be her boyfriend, but presently Ilse came to the phone.

"Karl?" She sounded frosty, uncertain why he was calling her.

"Hello, Ilse. How are you?"

"Miserable," she replied shortly. "I can't understand why you had to go and find somebody else after all we've done together. I thought we were having such a good time the other weekend."

"I know. As I said, I'm truly sorry, but there's nothing I can do about it."

"So why are you ringing?"

He paused and took a deep breath. "I thought I ought to tell you who she is before you hear it from someone else."

"Oh? That's nice of you." Her voice was heavy with sarcasm and Karl realised just how upset she was. "Who is it then? Is it that English tart, Audrey?"

"No, it's ..." His hesitation proved how difficult this would be for her. "I'm going to marry Silke."

There was a moment's silence then the phone went dead in his hand.

*

Ilse returned to the living room in a state of shock. She had barely comprehended what Karl had just told her, that he was going to marry Silke! Edeltraud walked in wrapped in a towel and with her hair rolled up in another.

"Do you know where my new jeans are, Mutti?" she asked, rubbing her hair dry with the towel.

"No," Ilse replied, automatically lighting a cigarette to steady her nerves.

"I thought they'd been washed, but I can't find them," Edeltraud whined.

"Roslinde's probably borrowed them."

"If she has, I'll kill the cow!" Edeltraud stormed, hurrying off to her sister's room to hunt for the missing jeans.

Ilse sat and stared at the wall, suddenly yearning for the peace and tranquillity of the flat in Montevideo where she and Paul had enjoyed so many evenings together on the balcony, watching the ships sailing up the River Plate estuary on their way to Buenos Aires. Paul often strayed but he always came back to her. And now Karl had been led astray, blinded by the wealth and youth of some rich baby doll looking for a daddy. It couldn't possibly be love! She would try her hardest at the weekend to persuade him of his folly and win him back. He would come to his senses soon enough.

Stubbing out her cigarette, she returned to the hall, picked up the phone and dialled his number.

"I'm sorry about that, Karl," she said as soon as she heard his voice. "You caught me rather by surprise there. It was very rude of me to put the phone down on you like that."

"That's all right, Ilse. I understand."

"I just wanted to make sure everything was still on for baby-sitting at the weekend."

"Yes, of course. I'll pick you up on Friday evening as we agreed."

"Good. That's all right then. See you then."

After finishing her phone call, Ilse knocked on Margit's bedroom door. "Can I come in?"

"Yes. I'm just doing my make-up," Margit replied.

Ilse entered the untidy room and sat on her daughter's bed, which was strewn with outfits tried on then discarded. "Bruno ought to see the palaver you go through on his behalf. I presume he'll be there this evening?"

"Yes, and the usual crowd." Margit pursed her lips to apply her lipstick.

"Silke too?"

"Mmm." Rolling her lips together, Margit inspected them in the mirror and was satisfied with their appearance. "I presume so. She hasn't said she's not going."

"I wonder if Karl will be with her."

"Karl? Why Karl?"

"Because apparently they're going to get married, or so he just informed me."

"What!" Margit spun round on her dressing table stool. "You're joking!"

"No, I'm not."

"But how dare she steal him off you like that!" She put down her lipstick with a crash. "She was going out with Mick too. What's she up to?"

"I don't know, but I want it stopped. You know her better than I do, Margit. You must talk to her and warn her that I'm not so easily shoved out of the way."

Margit looked hard at her mother, her loyalties suddenly in question. "You don't mean you'd resort to Siegfried's methods, do you, Mutti?"

Ilse held her gaze. "What do you think?"

Margit saw the steel in her mother's blue eyes. "I think you would. Karl means that much to you, doesn't he?"

"Yes, he does. I didn't come all this way to be pipped at the post by some spoilt little bitch."

Margit was devastated. "Silke's not like that, Mutti! She and I are good friends. I can't go telling her who she can or can't fall in love with!"

Ilse had expected more support from her daughter, but without Margit's co-operation things could be a lot harder. Ilse did not want Karl forewarned of any problems. "Sorry. Of course you can't. I'm being very silly, aren't I? It was just a bit of a shock, that's all. You just congratulate them on their engagement and forget I ever said anything. I'll just have to get over him, won't I?"

Margit understood her mother's feelings well enough. "Yes, Mutti, you will. I'm sorry it's turned out this way for you, but if Karl doesn't love you, then there's not a lot you can do."

"No. There isn't."

*

"Next time I visit the twins I'll take you," Karl promised Silke as they left the office on Friday afternoon.

"I'll hold you to that! I can't wait to meet them - and Sophie, my future stepdaughter-in-law. What a mouthful!" Silke openly kissed him farewell in the car park, not caring who saw them now. "Take care and have a good weekend, but watch out for underhand tactics from Ilse, please, Karl."

"I will. But just looking after the twins will probably take all our time and energy. I'll come back to work on Monday absolutely shattered."

"It can't be any worse than spending a night with me," she murmured, clutching his coat collar to draw his head down to hers for another kiss.

"Perhaps not," he agreed with a soft smile. "I'll have to get into training for our honeymoon."

"I can help you with that." She opened her car door, then had another thought. "Did you write to your friend in Berlin?"

"Yes. I don't quite know what I expect Ernst to do, but it would be useful to know what Sophie's up to."

"If anything," Silke said as she sat behind the driving wheel. "There's only so far you can meddle in peoples' lives. If she's determined to see this guy, she will, whatever you say."

"I know. Anyway, have a nice weekend and give my apologies to the archers for not making it this week."

He watched her drive off then headed home to get ready for the weekend in Soest. He had packed a weekend bag that morning, so it was just a case of getting changed out of his work suit into his casual jacket and corduroy trousers ready for crawling around on the floor playing trains with the twins.

Ilse was ready and waiting in her flat for his ring on the door. She appeared on the street clutching a surprisingly compact weekend bag. Karl loaded it into the car for her and then they set off towards Soest in the evening traffic. Sophie had asked them to get there as early as possible after work. She herself had left for Berlin in the morning, leaving her mother looking after the twins until their arrival.

"I hope the weather stays dry this weekend," Karl began the conversation neutrally, "so we're not stuck indoors all the time with the pair of them."

"I heard the forecast just before you came," Ilse replied, her voice equally neutral. It should be sunny." Then she smiled. "We're all going to have such a lovely time together!"

TWENTY TWO

Berlin greeted Sophie with its brash noise and neon lights, glowing islands of life amidst the darkness of the remaining bombsites. The border crossing had been as tedious as ever, the East German Border Guards as terse and uncompromising as only they could be. Still, she was here now, and Markus and Sonja Fiebrantz had been delighted to receive her again as a guest so soon after her previous stay. They were fully aware of her real reasons for returning to Berlin, so had invited Udo to dinner, along with Kristof Kemphausen and a few others. They had felt it might be a good idea to allow Sophie more time to get to know him amongst company, in case she had any doubts about spending the entire weekend with him.

It was a sensible precaution, Sophie decided, as she scarcely knew Udo. It was partly at her parents' insistence that she would be staying with Markus and Sonja, but she had to admit she had not had the same instant rapport with Udo as she had had with Siegfried. Her parents had warned her that Udo, like Siegfried, was used to getting what he wanted, and that might not necessarily be in her best interests now that she had a family to consider. Sophie had taken their warning on board. Since Siegfried's death she had learnt to respect their advice.

Pulling up outside the apartment in the Charlottenburg district, Sophie parked next to a florists' delivery van. Sonja must have ordered flowers for the table or perhaps Udo had sent her another bouquet? Maybe not. The driver seemed to be reading a newspaper, she noticed, as she rang the doorbell to the apartment, clutching the bouquet she had bought for her hostess.

Sophie was soon relaxing over drinks with her two friends awaiting the arrival of the other guests. A brief glance at her watch told her Karl and Ilse should be in Soest by now. She had made up separate beds for them but she felt sure one would not be used. Smiling at the thought, she noticed Markus showing Udo into the room, and stood up to greet him.

Udo approached her and kissed her hand formally. "My dear Sophie. So good of you to return to our fair city. How was your journey?"

Whether it was her parents' warnings or her own impatience with him earlier that week for his persistent calls, she suddenly found his manner somewhat pompous. "Tedious," she told him. "I wouldn't like to do it too often."

"Come and join us here!" he commanded. "That would solve the problem, wouldn't it?"

"Indeed it would," she replied, finding the idea less appealing than on her previous visit. She had originally come to Berlin to find out about Siegfried and Gustav, and when nothing had been forthcoming, she had been flattered by Udo's unexpected attentions. Would she really want to give up her cosy home in Soest to start again here?

"We could find plenty for Sophie to do here, couldn't we, Markus?" Udo remarked confidently.

"I'm sure we could," Markus agreed with genuine warmth.

Sophie glanced aside out of the apartment window, uncertain as to how she felt about a move. Through the net curtains she noticed the lights of the florist's van heading away up the road. Heading home, she thought. Is this all my time here will be: a coffee break away from the twins? We'll see, she decided, suddenly determined to make the most of her temporary freedom.

*

Ernst Winter returned exhausted to his solitary flat in a back street near the Radio Museum, also in the Charlottenburg district. He poured himself a beer and settled down to write his report to Karl. Having called in sick to the florist's for the day, he had spent the whole of Saturday morning loitering outside the apartment building where Sophie was staying. Finally at midday his patience was rewarded when Udo Kopleck drew up in his flashy Mercedes to collect her.

Making a dash for his own battered old Fiat, Ernst bravely kept pace with them through the Berlin traffic, out to the south-western boundaries of the city and the castle and parkland of Grunewald. They were obviously seeking peace, quiet and cultural enlightenment rather than city-life. Ernst was surprised at their choice, but decided it was probably Kopleck's rather than Sophie's. As a Berliner he would want to escape the everyday hustle and bustle that Sophie probably craved. It made his job harder in some respects, keeping out of their sight, but simpler in that it would not be so easy to lose them. He watched then strolling through the park together, always a respectful distance apart, then paid up his entrance fee to tour round the *Jagdschloss* itself, feigning a keen interest in the recently restored architecture and picture galleries. He smiled as he saw Sophie's stifled yawn and rubbing of her stiff back and painful legs as Kopleck rhapsodised over yet another painting by Lucas Cranach the elder or younger. Surely he was aware of her serious injuries after the car crash?

By the end of the afternoon Ernst rated Kopleck's chances of capturing Sophie's heart as zero. Nevertheless he followed them back to the heartland of West Berlin as they found somewhere to eat, prior to attending a theatre show. Kopleck had not even given Sophie the chance to get changed first, and his lack of perception at her discomfort astonished even Ernst.

Selfish bastard, he thought to himself, as Sophie hobbled stiffly to the car after the show and was driven back to the Fiebertz's apartment shortly before midnight. She had clearly had quite enough of the company of Herr Udo Kopleck.

*

Ilse looked down on the two little heads poking out from under the covers of their cots. Friedrich, as usual, was sucking his thumb, while Freia clutched hold of a comforter blanket. They had both gone to sleep without a murmur, exhausted by her and Karl's efforts that day to keep them entertained. There had been a long walk to the duck pond in the morning then, after lunch and a nap, chasing games in the garden, a messy cake-making session, an even messier bath-time and a long and animated story before bed. The latter had been Karl's task while Ilse had begun preparations for their own dinner. So far they had acted as perfect grandparents, but now she had Karl to herself.

Creeping out of their bedroom, Ilse went into Sophie's room, temporarily hers, to freshen herself up for the evening ahead. She changed out of her cotton blouse and slacks, still bearing Friedrich's cake-mixture handprint on the left buttock, and into the dress she had carefully selected for that evening. It was dark blue and figure hugging, but not enough to reveal the few unsightly bulges she was only too well aware of. Not that Silke's figure was exactly sylph-like – sturdy and compact more like. I had a better figure at her age, Ilse thought proudly, then remembered her slimness was the result of poverty and deprivation rather than intent. Silke had never known hard times, Ilse thought bitterly.

On her return downstairs she found Karl sitting in the living room, engrossed in reading a novel he had found in his room. It was a translation of Alexander Solzhenitsyn's 'One Day in the Life of Ivan Denisovich'.

"Isn't that a bit too close to home for you to read?" Ilse asked anxiously, seeing Karl's grim expression. "I suppose you were a kind of political prisoner too."

"All the more interesting to read and compare my fate with his," Karl replied, his eyes never leaving the page.

Ilse stood looking down at him for a few seconds longer, but he seemed oblivious to her presence so she went out to the kitchen to check on the chicken casserole she had prepared. Was this his way of showing his lack of interest in her? She was certainly not going to let him get away with sitting with his nose stuck in that book all evening! She put the potatoes on to boil then went to pour them both a drink from the bottle of wine she had brought in her weekend bag.

"Here you are," she said, placing the glass of white wine at his side. "*Prost!*"

To her intense relief, Karl closed the book and picked up his glass to join her in the toast.

"What can we do to entertain them tomorrow?" Ilse asked quickly to establish a conversation.

"I promised Freia we would visit the little zoo. She wants to see the camels and bear there."

"Oh? Is it far away?"

"No, I don't think so, but we should be able to make a day of it.

Sophie left a leaflet about it in my room – obviously as a hint! She must have been intending to take the twins there and was waiting until they were old enough to appreciate it a bit, which they are now, I think. The book we were reading just now had lots of animals in it and we had fun making all the right noises."

"Sounds like the zoo it is," Ilse agreed. "I just hope it doesn't smell too much. I've been to these places before and the animals are stuck in tiny cages that stink to high heaven. I feel so sorry for them. A bit like your Ivan Denisovich, I suppose!"

"Hmm," Karl grunted. Suddenly the zoo did not seem such an attractive proposition. Smelly cages, tormented animals. His thoughts raced on, sparked by the book he had been reading until, unbidden, the image of the tiny, sometimes terrifyingly dark room he had inhabited for several weeks at Dachau flashed before his eyes. It had been a living nightmare in there, suffering the traumas of first drug dependency then the horrors of total withdrawal as his captors used his body for their experiments.

Ilse noticed his distress. "What's wrong, Karl? You've turned quite green all of a sudden."

He swallowed hard, trying to control his shallow breathing and concentrate on sending himself off into the vision of calm that Robert had first helped him find for moments such as this. He needed to shut off completely to achieve it but Ilse was not aware of that. When she saw his eyes close she shook him, beginning to panic.

"Karl! What's happening? Are you all right?"

"Leave me alone!" he hissed, shrugging her hand off his shoulder, as the nightmare images tightened their grip on his mind.

"What's happening?" she persisted, grasping his hands to try to steady him and stop him pushing her away.

They were coming for him again; there would be hours and hours of torment ahead. He tried to fight them off, attempting to wield some control over his life, if only by showing resistance. His fist made contact with one of them and the hands left him alone.

Nothing happened – only blackness. He waited, gradually realising his eyes were closed and that the chair beneath him was not hard and restraining but soft and upholstered. He could hear the sound of sobbing. Slowly Karl opened his eyes.

Ahead of him stood Ilse, her left hand clutching her cheek, tears streaming down her face in pain and shock. She was the one who was sobbing, but when she saw him look at her she moved back a pace, fear in her eyes.

Karl raised his palms towards her in a gesture of reassurance. "It's all right, Ilse," he murmured reassuringly. "Don't worry. I'm all right now. I won't hurt you, I promise."

He rose out of his chair to try to comfort her, but again she stepped backwards. Now he noticed the glass of wine spilt on the floor and the trickle of blood between Ilse's fingers.

"You're bleeding," he said as calmly as he could, his own anxieties taking second place to hers for the moment. "Let me take a look."

She said nothing but after a few seconds of indecision, she gave a small nod, apparently reassured now that he was fully in control of himself. There was a box of tissues on a table by the wall, ready for accidental mess from the twins, and Karl pulled out several then went up to Ilse. This time she bravely stood her ground, letting him remove her hand from her cheek. Her upper lip had split slightly and he mopped the blood up as carefully as he could, then steered her towards the sofa to sit down.

"Are you all right now?" he asked, sitting beside her and holding her still trembling hand.

"Yes," she managed to say through her swelling lip. "A bit shaken, that's all." She paused as though it were an effort to ask. "How about you?"

He smiled feebly. "Likewise. I'm so sorry I hurt you. I've never done that before. Well, not for a long, long while. It's rather caught me by surprise, I'm afraid. Worrying."

"Yes," she agreed. "Very worrying." She looked closely at him, feeling bolder now. "What happened to you, Karl?"

"Do you mean just then?"

She nodded.

"I was back in Dachau, like it was real. I've had hallucinations before, but nobody's ever got in the way or I've realised what was happening in time. When Siegfried died it got bad and I had to go and see my friend Robert – you know, the psychiatrist."

Again she nodded. "You never hit Katherine?"

"No," he said quickly. "I wasn't usually with her when these episodes happened, or if I was, she knew how to deal with me and let me sort it out in my head. I'm sorry you didn't know that."

"And does Silke know?"

Her question caught Karl by surprise. "Silke?" He stopped to consider what he had told her. "Well, she knows something about the problems I've had, but I couldn't have foreseen this."

"Well, you'd better make sure she does know everything before she marries you." She took a deep breath before announcing her decision. "She's welcome to you, Karl. I don't think I could live with the worry of you. Katherine may have been strong enough to cope with your … problems, but I had enough of this with Erich," she said, indicating her bruised cheek and lip. She meant her first husband, Erich Röbel, the father of her children. "Much as I love you, I don't think I'd ever feel totally safe with you again."

Karl lowered his eyes, condemned by her judgement of him as mentally unstable. His euphoria of the last few weeks had been shattered and now the all too familiar depression was sinking in.

"It's all the fault of that book," he said finally, nodding towards the fallen copy of Solzhenitsyn. "It was stupid of me to start reading it."

"It was a timely warning, more like," Ilse told him, beginning to feel sorry for him now that she had stopped shaking. "Come on. Let's get that spilt wine mopped up and pour some more, then we can eat."

Karl looked at her. There was a gulf between them now, one he had sought but not like this. She no longer desired him. He stood up slowly, tired suddenly by emotional stress as well as the day's exertions. "I'll get a cloth."

"And I'll serve out dinner."

A few minutes later, as they entered the dining room carrying their plates of food, glasses of wine and cutlery, both noticed the large framed photograph of Siegfried on the sideboard. He smiled up at them, lifting their spirits temporarily as they remembered happier times, but as they sat down to eat their meal together they grew subdued and withdrawn. Ilse found herself wondering what Paul was up to in Montevideo, while Karl was struggling with his thoughts as he tackled his food.

The silence would have persisted had not Ilse become aware of

Karl's growing depression. She sought a means of showing her sympathy. "I think I understand now how much you must have hated National Socialism," she began slowly. "Before it was just words to me. Now I've seen for myself what they did to you."

"To me and millions of others," he pointed out.

She let that pass without comment. "Paul's still committed to them. Sophie too."

"I know. The man she's seeing in Berlin right now is one."

"How do you know that?"

"A friend of mine there happened to tell me," he explained, not wanting to give the impression he had been spying on her.

"That clearly worries you, though."

"I'd like to see her bringing up my grandchildren away from their influence."

Ilse thought of the two little cherubs asleep upstairs and found herself agreeing with him. They must be kept safe from the evils of the world. "So would I."

"Really?"

"Yes. Really. She's not seen for herself the harm they do."

"And you have?"

"I have now."

"You just chose not to believe it before."

She shrugged, admitting he was right.

"So what should we do about Sophie?" he asked her.

"Find someone more suitable. I did it once, I can do it again. Or perhaps Silke knows some wealthy young man she could fall for."

"Does he have to be wealthy?"

Ilse nodded. "Sophie has standards she expects to be met."

"I would have thought love was as important."

Ilse looked askance at him across the dining table. "And didn't Silke's wealth influence you?"

"No!" Karl was able to state categorically. "I had no idea she was rich when I fell in love with her." Ilse clearly disbelieved him. "But what about you and Paul? Didn't his wealth buy your love?"

She smiled at his swift counter-attack. "Possibly. But I learnt to love him for himself soon enough."

"And by that wistfulness I can hear in your voice, you love him still." She was staring at her plate, he noticed, unable to meet his eyes now that he had hit the nail on the head. "You should never have left him, Ilse."

"You don't need to tell me that!" she burst out, shoving her chair back with a crash. "I can see that all too clearly now!" With tears in her eyes she fled to the kitchen where she flung herself on a chair and began to sob.

Hearing her crying, Karl followed her out and put an arm round her shoulders to comfort her. He felt her tension ease then she turned to him, burying her face in his chest until her last sobs gradually subsided.

"Go back to him, Ilse," he advised.

"I can't." Her voice was muffled against his chest. "Not to Uruguay. It's too far away."

"Then persuade him to come back here and face the music."

"That's asking too much of him, Karl."

"And wasn't he asking too much of you?"

She looked up at him then sat back on her chair, making an effort to pull herself together. Karl handed her one of the tissues he had put in his pocket, so she could wipe her eyes, which were bleeding mascara. "No," she said, accepting the tissue. "It was my duty to be by his side. I deserted him, so why should he come back and face imprisonment for my sake?"

"At least make the suggestion to him."

"No, I can't possibly ask him to do that," she said with utter finality, her blue eyes shining with tears and newly found determination to pull herself through this crisis.

Karl nodded slowly, seeing where this was leading. "So you'll have to find somebody else for you as well as for Sophie."

She braved a smile. "It could be fun trying!"

"That's the spirit!" he said giving her an encouraging hug. "You and I, we'll always be friends, but not lovers again. Too much has happened since nineteen forty-three. The clock won't turn back."

"No," she agreed. "I guess it won't." She raised her hand gently to his face, caressing his firm jaw. "You're a good friend, Karl. I hope Silke looks after you well."

Carefully he removed her hand from his face but held onto it for a few moments longer. "So many people have been good to me over the years. It's my turn to repay them, if I can."

"With Silke's money?"

Put like that it sounded brash. Karl sought a more delicate representation of the truth. "She wanted a family; now she's got one."

"Lucky old Silke," Ilse said, but without a trace of bitterness now.

Karl smiled at her welcome response. "And so have you, Ilse. Make the most of them."

Right on cue, one of the twins began to cry. Ilse grinned. "Come on, Opa. Let's both go up and sort her out."

"Her? It's Friedrich."

"Rubbish! It's Freia."

They both cocked an ear.

"Now it's both of them," Ilse groaned. "One each."

*

"Insufferable, arrogant, conceited, self-centred pig!" Sophie raged at Udo. "You nearly got me run over just then!" They were standing on the central reservation of the Kurfürstendamm after a dash across the road in front of a tourist bus, which was suddenly overtaken by a speeding taxi. "Why couldn't we cross at the lights?"

"We were fine," he protested, surprised more than angered by her outburst.

"You may have been, but I wasn't," she retorted angrily. "The whole weekend you've managed to forget I'm not very good on my legs, even when I keep reminding you! I'm really stiff after yesterday and I'm finding it hard work keeping up with you, but you don't seem to notice. I've had enough. I'm going back to Markus and Sonja's. You can forget about keeping in touch!"

She would have liked to have stormed off to the nearest bus stop, but her legs really were painful this morning and a careful hobble was all she could manage. Udo made a brief show of following her, but a determined shove from her changed his mind. He was not about to be pushed around and made a fool of in public.

"Suit yourself," he hissed. "Go home to Mutti and your precious babies. That's all you're good for!" With that, he abandoned her to her fate and strode off in the opposite direction without a backwards glance.

Sophie stood and watched his retreating figure amongst the Sunday morning strollers. Good riddance! She took a deep breath and exhaled sharply, blasting Udo out of her life, before taking stock of her situation. The spring sunshine was filtering through the bare branches of the trees and the air was warming up after the long winter. Now she was out, it seemed a shame to waste the rest of the morning. She spotted a nearby café and was lucky to find a seat inside in a patch of warm sunshine. Already she was beginning to feel happier but she ordered a coffee and a piece of cake to complete the process.

"Do you mind if I sit here?" a voice asked politely.

She looked up and saw a middle-aged man, smartly but inexpensively dressed in a suit and tie, pointing to the chair opposite her. The café was filling up quickly, so she smiled politely.

"No, please do."

"It's a lovely day," the man said pleasantly as he made himself comfortable, "but too cold yet to sit outside."

She heard from his accent he was not from Berlin. Further west she decided: North German Plain, similar to her own accent.

"Are you local or visiting?" he asked her after he had ordered his coffee from the waiter bringing Sophie hers.

"Visiting," she replied. "I live near Soest, near -"

"Soest? That's a nice town. Famous green stone churches if I remember rightly."

Sophie nodded. "Yes. I was married in one of them."

"Your husband's not with you here?" the man asked casually.

"No." Her recent bad experience with Udo made her seek out some friendly conversation. "He died eighteen months ago. This is a kind of break for me, away from our children."

"Oh, I'm very sorry, Frau …?"

"Driesler," she replied readily. The man seemed nice enough, not flashy in any way, but sympathetic.

"Driesler!" he gasped in amazement. "Would you be Sophie, by any chance?"

Sophie's jaw dropped. "Yes, but how on earth do you know that?"

"I've known your father-in-law, Karl, since the war. He often writes about you and the twins – Friedrich and Freia, aren't they?" He held out his hand. "I'm Ernst Winter. You've probably not heard of me, but I met Karl's wife and family in Hereford. I was so sad to hear about Katherine's death. A wicked waste, wicked! Such a lovely woman she was."

Sophie shook him by the hand, thinking now that he looked a bit familiar. Perhaps she had seen a photo of him somewhere. Reassured, she relaxed and took a forkful of walnut cake.

"Do you live here, Herr Winter?" she asked him.

"Yes. I've been hoping Karl might come to visit me now he's living here in Germany again."

"Or you could visit him? I'm sure he'd love to see you."

Ernst grinned. "Two bachelors out on the town together. Wouldn't that be fun!"

"You're not married then?"

"Briefly, some years ago. It didn't work out."

They chatted amicably over their coffees until Sophie declared she had to be getting back to prepare for her long drive home. As she stood up to leave she stumbled slightly on her stiff legs and Ernst hastily offered her his arm.

"May I accompany you to the bus stop? You look as though you could do with someone to lean on."

Sophie realised he must know all about her accident. "That's very kind of you, thank you, Herr Winter. But I don't want to be a nuisance."

"Oh, it's no trouble. No trouble at all. You can tell me all about your dear little children."

They strolled gently along the broad pavement, Ernst taking great care not to walk too fast, until they reached a bus stop. As a bus approached and Sophie removed her arm from his in preparation for leaving him, Ernst said innocently: "This is my number. Will you be all right now?"

"But it's mine too! How strange!"

He helped her on board and soon after sitting down she found herself saying: "You must stop off and meet my friends, Markus and Sonja, as proof of this amazing coincidence." Privately she thought they might be useful contacts for him. He had been telling her about his catalogue of odd jobs in Berlin, all quite menial considering how reasonably intelligent he seemed.

"They won't mind?" he asked carefully.

"No. They love meeting new people. Markus is in the art business. He owns a gallery just off the Ku'damm - 'Fresco'. Have you seen it?"

Ernst shook his head despite being familiar with the place from his floral deliveries – the one job he had not mentioned to Sophie in case she had made the connection with him.

They did not have far to ride on the bus. Ernst gallantly helped her off it and Sophie smiled at the joy of having a man, even one as old as Ernst, being attentive to her again. Udo had failed miserably in that respect, apart from his flowers and phone calls. She had felt like some attractive accessory for him to use and discard when necessary. He had not been interested in her, only her looks, she realised. Unlike Siegfried. He had truly loved her and she missed him terribly.

Ernst noticed the tears in her eyes as she tried to insert her borrowed key into the apartment door.

"What's wrong? Are you in pain?"

She smiled at him, wiping away the tears. "No. Just thinking about Siegfried and how much I miss him still." She managed to insert the key and entered the apartment calling out to her friends to announce her arrival.

Ernst was promptly invited to stay for lunch, and afterwards Sophie dropped him off at his modest flat in a drab modern block overlooking the railway line, before setting off back to Soest. Again there was the long wait at the East German border while papers were checked and her car searched for fugitives from the East.

She arrived home exhausted but curious as to how Karl and Ilse had fared. She entered the hall and was greeted by the sight of Ilse's split and swollen lip and bruised cheek.

"Whatever happened?" Sophie asked in dismay, noticing Karl had not ventured out to greet her.

Ilse's fingers went up to her mouth as if to hide her blemish. "Oh, it's nothing. Friedrich was on my lap and he suddenly threw back his head and clouted me. He wasn't hurt," she added hastily to reassure Sophie.

"Oh, poor you! He's done that before with me," Sophie smiled her apology and began to take off her coat. "Were they all right otherwise?"

"Yes, fine. We took them to the zoo today but Freia's so excited that you're coming back that she won't settle down. Karl's got her in the living room so she doesn't keep Friedrich awake."

Sophie smiled at the thought of being needed by her daughter and headed for the living room, where she found Karl sitting with Freia in his arms, the zoo animal book open in front of them. Freia leapt up when she saw her mother, nearly hitting Karl in the face just as her brother had done with Ilse.

"I should be paying you both danger money," she laughed as she scooped up Freia and gave her a big hug. Suddenly she remembered about Ernst Winter. "You'll never guess who I met in Berlin," she said, looking specifically at Karl.

"Who?"

"Ernst Winter. He sent you his best wishes and asked when you would be visiting him." Strangely enough, she got the impression Karl had guessed who it was.

"Really? Well I never! Where did he crop up?"

Sophie told them about her Sunday morning on the Ku'damm, while Freia clung to her and looked to be slowly nodding off at last. "I'll go and put her down then come and have a quick chat with you before you go. I expect you're anxious to be away before it gets too late."

"I'm in no particular rush," Ilse said. "Are you, Karl?"

"Not especially, but I expect Sophie's tired after her long drive." Karl did actually want to get back so he could write a letter to Robert, telling him what had happened today, but he sensed Ilse wanted to grill Sophie about her unsuccessful trip to Berlin. It was time to let Sophie in on his news too.

Once Sophie was back downstairs she and Ilse disappeared off into the kitchen together to make a light snack for them all. Karl could hear their murmured conversation emanating from the kitchen and when they appeared with a tray of sandwiches and cups of coffee he saw immediately that Sophie had been told about Silke. She handed him his cup of coffee with a saucy look in her eye.

"Well, Karl, you are a dark horse, keeping this Silke girl a secret from us like that! So the twins are going to have yet another Oma to contend with. How will Silke cope with that at her age?"

He smiled at her forthright comment. "She'll call herself an aunty, I expect. Ilse's the real Oma."

"And you've left her high and dry, I gather?" Sophie stated, but not maliciously. Ilse had obviously convinced her of their continuing friendship, if not romance.

"Yes. She refuses to consider going back to Paul, don't you, Ilse?" he asked bringing her into the conversation.

"Well ..." Ilse shrugged her inability to do anything else. Uruguay was out of the question, not Paul.

Sophie spotted the hesitation, as did Karl. She caught his eye and an unspoken message passed between them. They had to try to get Paul back, even if it meant imprisonment again for him. Ilse needed him.

TWENTY THREE

The office felt oppressive, the freshness of the spring air barred by the windowpane. Karl stood up from his desk and opened the window, but still he felt caged in. For the first time since starting work there he yearned for the freedom of the farm: checking on the rabbit-proof fencing and progress of the tree nursery, pruning the orchards, coppicing the woodland. Even rounding up the stupid sheep with Molly or retrieving stray lambs would be better than sitting here surrounded by paperwork. He missed the outdoor life. Perhaps that was why his pent-up energies had resulted in him punching Ilse. At least she had forgiven him for it, even pecked him on the cheek in farewell as he dropped her off last night. Now he had Silke to deal with. She had sensed his mood and needed an explanation.

"Do you fancy a walk up the hill?" he asked, turning from the window as she cleared her desk ready for lunch.

"Sure," she readily agreed. "Food can wait. You need to talk, I can see."

They had barely negotiated the first turn in the path up the hill before she asked: "Why are you so gloomy today?"

It was going to be difficult to explain and he began slowly. "I was going to phone you last night but it was rather late by the time we got back and I needed to write a letter to Robert."

"To *Robert*?" she asked with foreboding. "Does this have anything to do with Ilse's split lip, by any chance?" The how-on-earth-did-you-know-that? look that shot briefly across his face confirmed her fears. "Margit phoned me last night. She was really worried when Ilse told her Friedrich had done it accidentally, when it was blatantly obvious that she was lying. The only possible explanation was that you had hit her, which was why she phoned me, to warn me about you. Of course, she might well have been trying to scare me off, leaving the path clear for her mother again, but I could hear she was telling the truth and your reaction just then confirmed it." Drawing breath, she asked him outright: "So why did you hit her, Karl?"

He noticed no hint of accusation in her voice; even so he initially avoided giving a direct answer to her question. "That's why I wrote to Robert. I told him about us and our plans, and that either he has to come over here or we must visit him in Edinburgh before we can think any further about getting married." Only then did he look her squarely in the eye. "I didn't hit her on purpose, Silke. I promise, and she accepted that. That's why she told the white lie: to protect me."

"So what did happen?" she asked calmly, reaching for his hand as they walked up the hill.

Reassured by her hand he elaborated a bit more. "You remember that incident at Ilse's when Sarah and Audrey were here? You noticed Bina helping me out?" She nodded. "It was something like then, but much worse. Ilse didn't know how to handle the situation and it resulted in her getting hurt. I want you to meet Robert, get to know all about me and what to do with me when I crack up."

"I see. And you can't tell me yourself?"

He stopped and held her to him, resting his cheek on her head in the way he found so comforting. "Robert will do it so much better. I find remembering too painful still and it can trigger off events like Saturday night's. The last thing I want is to hurt you, Schatz."

She stepped back out of his embrace to speak to him. "I'm looking forward to meeting Robert. He sounds a great guy."

Her up-beat tone heartened him further. She was so supportive. Surely she would handle things better than Ilse had done. "He is. And you'll love Alice, his wife, too. The only thing is," he hesitated as he summoned courage, "I wasn't sure how much leave he has or whether he has other commitments for Easter. I said if time was a real issue and it took too long to drive, we would pay for his and the family's flights over here. He had to understand how urgent this was. I hope you don't mind my spending your money already."

She shrugged. "Not for such a worthy cause. If it means you feel happier about trusting yourself to my care, then that's fine."

"It is that, isn't it?" he commented unhappily. "I need a carer. I can't live on my own. Everyone recognises it. That's why they all allowed me to leave England, my sons and the farm so I could flee home to be looked after. Now, they don't object too strongly that I'm marrying again so soon. They know I need someone by me. I can't be alone."

She saw where this was leading him. "Don't be silly, Karl! There'll be far more times when you're caring for me. Just think how well you cared for Katherine and all your family all those years. You did a splendid job, and now you're going to do another. Stop fretting about yourself and plan what you're going to do with your new freedom. The sooner you get out from that office the better, I think. You were like a caged bear in there this morning."

He smiled at the simile. "That's exactly how I was feeling. My heart lies in the forests, like a bear's."

"Well then, we'll set you up with a workshop in the woods, and you can turn out as many carvings, toys, statues as you like and I'll set up a gallery to display and sell them. I can even put some of my own paintings in too. Even if neither of us sells anything, it doesn't matter; we'll be happy. But I know it will be successful, and in time coach loads of tourists and art collectors will come flocking to buy work by the famous Drieslers."

"Oink, oink!" Karl laughed.

"What?"

"That was a pig flying by, but it sounds a wonderful idea. My idea of heaven."

"And mine," she laughed with him. She gave him a hug and felt him relax within her arms. She was learning how to handle him, but a talk with Robert would be most welcome.

As they headed back down the hill to the bar down by the Seilersee for a snack, Karl summoned the courage to mention something that had occurred to him the night before. "Do you mind putting off the wedding until a bit later in the summer? I don't think May is such a good time after all, what with Paul's end of term exams. And I really want you to know exactly what you're taking on with me, so no decisions until you've spoken with Robert. It's not as if we're tied to a particular time, is it?"

Silke thought about all the plans she had set in motion so far but realised the sense in his suggestion. "As long as you're not having cold feet, then of course I don't mind. But don't you dare let Robert change your mind for you, if they come over."

Karl laughed out loud. "Never!" To confirm his intentions he asked: "Am I coming back to your place after dancing tonight?"

"Of course! I told Maus this morning he should expect to be shut outside again tonight. He told me he didn't mind."

"That's all right then. As long as Maus is happy."

The office felt far less oppressive that afternoon and later on in the evening Karl had a spring in his step as he waltzed around the floor with Frau Wittke.

"Don't forget you're both coming over on Sunday afternoon," she told him over the music. "Three o'clock prompt! Silke knows where I live."

"We're both looking forward to it," Karl promised her. "But please don't go to too much trouble."

Frau Wittke almost skipped a step in her excitement. "You don't understand how much I'm looking forward to having a few friends round again. Since my Hubert died I've rather kept myself to myself, as Silke must have told you. Now I'm beginning to feel more alive again, thanks to everyone here, but especially you and Silke."

"Us? What have we done?"

"Given me an interest in someone other than myself again. I've come out of my shell at last and I feel so much better for it. So you see, I have reason to celebrate along with you both."

Karl smiled and gave her a gentle twirl. She was a dear, another kind soul. He seemed surrounded by them these days.

On the way back to Silke's he thought about how Willi and Rosa had accepted his place so readily in the household. Maus too.

"Silke," he said as he saw the bear gates looming ahead.

"Mmm?" she asked dreamily, her mind on the pleasures to come.

"I love you so much."

"I know," she replied. "I love you too."

*

"Here, have a read of this." Robert pushed across Karl's letter to his wife, Alice, as they were sitting in the living room of their Edinburgh town house, drinking coffee after their evening meal. Douglas and Stewart, their sons, were both out at football practice, so they could talk freely about Karl.

Alice donned her glasses and gave the letter her full attention. "Blimey!" she gasped after the first paragraph.

"Read on," Robert told her. "It gets worse." He watched the expression on her face grow increasingly more concerned as she read down the page. "See what I mean? Even Ilse's abandoned him now, and not just because of this Silke girl."

"But surely that's what he wants, isn't it?" Alice objected.

"He thinks he does at the moment, but think about it, dear. She's only ... what, nearly twenty-six? Sabina's almost that age. It's typical of a man of his years to fall for a much younger woman, but the chances of it lasting are remote. Her parents won't want -"

"She hasn't got any," Alice interrupted. "He says that half way down the page."

Robert was annoyed with himself for missing that, especially bearing in mind his profession. "Where?"

"Here." She handed him back the letter. "Where he says she's looking for a family as she hasn't got one."

"That doesn't necessarily mean her parents are dead. Even if it does, it probably means she wants a father-figure in her life and I don't like the sound of that."

"Well then, it looks like we'll be booking ourselves a trip to Germany for Easter, " Alice decided. "The boys will like that. This Silke obviously has room to put us all up."

"It's lucky I've got some leave left."

"That's hardly surprising, Robert Murdoch! And who's the one who never takes enough leave? We need a break, all of us. Douglas could do with getting away from his schoolbooks before the exams and it'll be a good opportunity for him to practice his German. Besides, I'm intrigued by this Silke. Karl seems really smitten with her, doesn't he?"

"He certainly does. But there's no way I'm having him pay for all of us," he added firmly. "He couldn't possibly afford it. No, you get on and find out some ferry details tomorrow and I'll book a week's leave and try to get a locum in. At least if we drive down we won't be totally dependent on him." Robert was familiar with the area from his visits during Karl's incarceration and trial, but then he had been with

Katherine as well as Sabina, who spoke fluent German. He would have to hope everyone spoke English or get Douglas to practice his schoolboy German. "What if Silke doesn't speak any English?" he wondered aloud. "How am I supposed to talk to her in German? I only know words like '*Schadenfreude*' and '*Angst*'. "

"Of course she speaks English," Alice pointed out, taking the letter back off him. "Listen." She read out another section of Karl's letter. "'*I would like you to tell her all about my past, sparing nothing, not even the bits you spared Katherine.*' She's going to have to be pretty fluent in English for you to do that, and Karl jolly well knows it. Besides, she works in the British hospital with him, doesn't she? She'd have to speak English."

Robert smiled in defeat. "It just goes to show how much I need a holiday, doesn't it? Watch out, Germany. The Murdochs are coming!"

Later that evening Robert called Sarah in Hereford. After preliminary enquiries as to each other's health were over, Robert came to the point. "Karl's invited us over for Easter to meet Silke. I presume you know all about how things stand between them?"

"Yes," Sarah told him. "They want to get married."

"And what are your views on that?" he probed.

Sarah laughed. "Isn't that your job, Robbie, to make your own assessments? You don't need my biased opinion."

"Which is?"

Sarah found herself hesitating. "I'm not sure. She's lovely, but she's too young."

"Apart from the age thing, you have no objections, then?" he persisted.

Again Sarah hesitated then came right out with it. "Quite frankly, I'm jealous. Really jealous, Robbie. Isn't it silly? I can't get him out of my head now. I should have left Audrey to get on with … things rather than get involved myself. I thought I could be dispassionate about it, but I was wrong."

"He seems to have that effect on women, unfortunately. I'm surprised Audrey's left him alone, but then she never was one for settling for one man, was she?"

"No. But I think I probably always wanted him, and foolishly married Perry as a distraction from him. I know I wanted him that time he and Gustav stayed with us in London back in the fifties. I was a bit of a wild thing then, as you probably gathered!"

Robert ignored that path. "Does this Silke strike you as a bit of a wild thing too? Is she young and trendy or old-fashioned and motherly?"

Sarah found herself stumped as to what to reply. "A bit of both," she eventually replied, "depending on who she's with."

"So you're not sure which is the real Silke?"

Again Sarah was stumped. "You think she's a bit of a chameleon, taking on the character of the people she's with?"

"It sounds like it, but most people are to some extent. They don't like to stand out from the crowd. But what I'm after is, do you think she's genuine in her love for Karl or is he just a means of finding a ready-made family?"

"I really couldn't say, Robbie, I'm afraid. I never saw them together as a couple. She was with Mick, another older man, when we were there."

Robert felt troubled by this latest revelation. "We're going to be staying with her, apparently, so I don't want to fall out with her, but the more I hear, the less I like the sound of things."

Sarah decided not to try to influence him any more. "Well, you must make up your own mind about her. Just try not to hurt Karl in the process." She realised, too late, that she had left him with a negative opinion.

*

They had spent Saturday afternoon making love while outside it poured with rain. In the early evening they went to the ice rink, returning to Silke's again for a meal cooked by them both in the huge kitchen. They had asked Willi and Rosa to join them, wanting the couple to get to know Karl better and soon, after a few glasses of best Rhine wine, Willi was reminiscing with Karl about his life as a prisoner of war in England. Silke slipped out to answer a phone call from Michael from her archery club. He was calling to say that the shoot had been called off for the next day as the weather forecast was so bad, and Silke had to remind him they would be missing it because of attending Frau Wittke's coffee afternoon.

"Ah, yes of course," Michael said. "I'd forgotten. Have fun, then. See you next week."

Retiring to bed later that evening, Silke cuddled up close to Karl. "I suspect Frau Wittke's invited more than just a few friends round tomorrow afternoon. She was like a cat on hot bricks on Monday."

"Yes, I noticed," Karl murmured sleepily. "She really likes you, you know?"

"And she adores you!" Silke told him proudly, kissing him on the nose before turning off the light. At her feet Maus purred loudly for a few minutes, having been granted dispensation to join them for once. Soon he too was asleep.

Karl woke first, saw daylight outside and turned to look at his watch. It was just after seven. At the end of the bed Maus was twitching in some feline dream, while by his side Silke was snoring very gently, her snub nose buried in the pillow. He lay and watched her, marvelling at how quickly he had come to love her. Life without her now seemed impossible, as it had first with Ilse, then with Katherine. How lucky he was to have found love not simply once, but three times. Perhaps it was something in his makeup that made love come easily? Poor Ernst had never found love. Not that he had been granted much opportunity to do so until recently. A visit to him in West Berlin was urgently called for, and of course he must visit them here.

As he let Silke sleep on, Karl began to speculate on what life would be like living here as her husband. He had inherited first Katherine's lifestyle and now he would be inheriting Silke's, if he allowed it. Was that what he wanted though: a life of luxury with no aims or goals? No. It was a pointless existence. She was right about the woodwork and painting gallery. He could teach would-be wood-carvers, run courses, give demonstrations amongst the prison community even. Scrap that idea. They would not be allowed the sharp knives and tools required. But he wanted to do something for the men inside whose lives were so empty. His cellmate, Auer, had complained bitterly of the boredom, and he knew for himself just how long a day could be. Perhaps he should write to Auer more often, visit him occasionally. Auer had always been interested in sharing Karl's news from home.

He saw Silke begin to stir. She kicked against Maus who woke up, stretched out his front legs then padded up Silke's back to sit on her shoulder, purring loudly for his breakfast.

"Oh, you noisy cat," Silke murmured, her eyes still closed. "Shh. You'll wake Karl."

"Karl's already awake," he said, leaning over to kiss her but was nuzzled and head-butted by Maus in the process.

"Come on then, you pest!" Silke laughed. "Let's get us all some breakfast." She shook Maus off her shoulder, kissed Karl then got out of bed and reached for her dressing gown. She pointed to the bedroom door. Hanging there was a new, dark blue towelling robe. "I bought that for you, Karl. You can come down now too, although I can assure you, Rosa won't be in the house. They never are on a Sunday."

Karl felt awkward accepting her largesse, but he would just have to get used to it. It made him more determined than ever to buy her an engagement ring as soon as possible, even if it meant borrowing some money from Papa or Rudi.

They spent the morning pleasantly enough looking through old photo albums of her family, while outside the rain lashed down, battering the daffodils in the lawn. Karl knew it was important for Silke to show him what little family she did have and he listened attentively to the names of distant relatives, long since dead. There were photos of her great-grandparents looking suitably stiff in their formal Victorian clothing, photos of cars and servants and garden parties between the wars, when Silke's grandparents' cunning had saved the family wealth from the worst ravages of the Great Depression and hyperinflation. Then he saw the photos of her parents, young and in love, as the Nazis rose to power. On joining the army, her father had rapidly risen up the ranks, and had been a major at the time of his death in November nineteen forty-four, when Silke was only three months old. Then at last came the photos of Silke and her mother, few at first, then more as life settled back to normal. Colour photos appeared of holidays in their villa in the South of France, skiing in Switzerland, teenage parties with local boys and girls of well-to-do families, including Margit. There were several of Silke with one lad in particular, then the photos where her mother began to look ill, the parties ceased and no more photos were taken, except one of her mother looking very frail, holding a familiar furry friend on her lap.

"She loved Maus," Silke said with a lump in her throat. "He spent hours with her at the end while she just stroked him and he purred to her. He helped her a lot, I think. That's partly why I'm so besotted with him now. He's such a strong link to her."

"What happened to Maus while you were in America?" Karl asked.

"Willi and Rosa looked after him. I was just so freaked out by her death I had to get away and go mad for a bit. You see, I do understand you, Karl. I know what it's like to lose control. I know my experiences must be nothing compared with yours, and I'm not really looking forward to Robert telling me all about what happened to you, bearing in mind what I know already. But it's clearly important that I do know, otherwise I'll be raiding the freezer every so often for frozen pea bags to put over my black eyes."

"Silke, I'd never mean to hurt you, you know that."

"Of course," she smiled. "But if you do, I'm a tough little bear."

"I wish I could promise it will never happen, but after last weekend I don't think I can do that. Doesn't it make you anxious for our children?"

"Not in the slightest, because I intend to be as competent at looking after you as Katherine was, and nothing like that will ever happen, I promise." She closed the photo album and stood up, holding out her hand to him. "Come and see my art studio up in the attic. You can be as critical as you like, I won't mind, but perhaps we can choose one to give to Frau Wittke as a little gift for her party today."

Again he marvelled at her thoughtfulness. She seemed to love caring for people, and they, in turn, cared for her.

As he stood in the light, well-equipped studio, gazing round at her finished and unfinished watercolours, oil paintings and charcoal drawings, he was drawn in even further to her world. "Why didn't you show me these before? They're really good!"

He picked up a canvas depicting a forested hillside with soaring clouds above. Her style was unmistakeably modern, the trees streaks and splashes of colour, the clouds bold explosions of paint. It spoke of Nature's might and he liked it immensely.

"May I have this one?" he asked, seeing her pleasure at his choice.

"With all my love," she said with a kiss. "Now we've got to find one for Frau Wittke. Something a bit more traditional maybe."

Rummaging around behind a pile of stacked canvases she produced a watercolour still life of some fruit and flowers, pretty rather than dramatic.

"Perfect," Karl told her. "How long have you been painting?"

"Seriously, since I came back from the States, but I've liked painting all my life. Tom told me it would help me expel my demons and calm me down, which it did. Most of these I've started off at my evening classes then finished later. The charcoal life drawings I did there. It would be nice to do some of you."

He realised 'life' drawings meant nudes, but he felt flattered that she should find him a suitable subject. "Will you put in all the scars or only some?" he asked, flicking through some of her other efforts and noting her flair for capturing the essence of the human figure in a few spare lines.

"None. I will draw you as I see you – perfect."

"There is always a flaw, and you must put one in," he told her firmly. "Otherwise I won't let you draw me."

"That's a promise, then? Next time it rains all weekend we can come up here and I'll draw you. Or," she added mischievously, "come the better weather, you can get an all-over tan in the garden."

"That sounds more like it," he agreed, "as long as the artist gets one too."

"Well, on that basis, I'll have to insist that you have a go at drawing me."

"You're on!"

After spending a few more minutes looking at her artwork and finding a suitable frame for the still life for Frau Wittke, they returned downstairs, past the formal family portraits, to prepare themselves some lunch, which they ate in the kitchen. Silke wrapped her painting in some gift paper and then disappeared to get changed into a dress suitable for afternoon coffee. Karl was wearing his suit and a red and gold striped tie that Sabina had given him in one of her less flamboyant moods, otherwise it might have been purple and green Paisley. The mood he was in today, he could have worn one like that, he decided. Silke made him feel so young and carefree. It was wonderful.

As they set off in Karl's car for Frau Wittke's, the rain was beginning to ease off a little. Huge puddles covered the roads and Karl took care not to park beside one when they eventually arrived at the tidy house standing in its own grounds that Silke had directed him to. It stood in a road of other moderately large houses, a prosperous area judging by the number of cars around, Karl thought.

A shaft of sunlight broke through the ragged clouds as they walked up the front path to her door. Silke rang the doorbell and a few moments later Frau Wittke opened it to them, her smile as radiant as the sunshine.

"Welcome, my dears! Do come in. And look, you've brought the sun with you."

As they stepped into her hallway, Silke and Karl saw the big banner suspended from the upstairs landing, which read *'Congratulations to Silke and Karl!'*. Then they heard a champagne cork pop and a cheer go up as the hall filled with people who had been hiding in various rooms on either side of the hall.

Silke was stunned as she began to recognise the family friends, dancing group members and even her archery club. There must have been fifty or more people there at least.

"Frau Wittke!" she exclaimed, her hand over her mouth in sheer delight. "However did you manage to get this lot together?"

"Subterfuge and deception," Frau Wittke said, giggling like a schoolgirl at the success of her scheming.

Michael from archery approached bearing a tray with brimming champagne glasses and handed them out to the guests of honour. Karl and Silke each took one and raised their glasses to the assembled crowd then to each other before taking a sip.

"We're all so happy for you," Frau Wittke declared to everyone once the hubbub had died down a bit. "We've been waiting for years for our lovely Silke to make her choice, and I think we could all see at once when she had. She couldn't have made a more perfect choice, if I'm allowed to say so," she said with twinkling eyes to Karl, "and I hope you don't mind, both of you, that I couldn't wait until your wedding to wish you both a long and happy life together."

Silke had tears in her eyes when she kissed Frau Wittke's powdered cheeks. This was her family, all these people who had turned out in the pouring rain to come and show their love for her and Karl. "Thank you so much, everybody, especially you, Frau Wittke."

"Gretel, please, Silke. We surely know each other well enough by now." As much to give Silke a chance to compose herself as doing her duty as hostess she asked: "How's that champagne flowing? Has everybody got one now? Then here's to Silke and Karl. *Zum Wohl!*"

The party settled down into full swing as Silke took Karl around all the guests to introduce him to those he had not met. Several were ladies of his own age, whose sons had been passed over by Silke as suitors, but they seemed to bear him no grudge and many invitations to forthcoming social events were offered.

"You see just how big a wedding we're going to have to have," Silke whispered to Karl after they had paused to take on board some of the cake and coffee laid out on a large sideboard and dining table. "Perhaps it's just as well we're giving ourselves more time to organise it."

He was about to agree when Gretel Wittke took him by the elbow. "May I have a quiet word with you, Karl? If you'll excuse us a moment, Silke, dear?"

She led Karl out to the hall and into a small study looking out over the side of the house. Closing the door she opened the flap of the large bureau that stood against the far wall and removed a blue plush ring box.

"Now, I don't want to be an interfering old biddy, Karl, but I do know you need to give Silke a ring. I also know that you want to buy her one yourself, but here is a perfectly good ring going to waste that I'd dearly love to give you for her. If it's not to your taste then never mind, but it would give me such a thrill if I knew it was being put to good use instead of sitting locked away in a safe somewhere. And, I may be wrong, but I think Silke would rather re-use something than waste your money. She's into that kind of thing, isn't she?"

Karl took the little box off her and gently opened it. Sitting on a layer of blue velvet was a gold ring set with a large sapphire surrounded by diamonds. He could never have afforded to buy such

315

a lavish ring and Silke would know it. But what Gretel said was true. Silke frowned on wasting money, so why not give her a ring offered from two sources of love? He looked at Gretel and smiled his appreciation. "It's beautiful. Thank you." He stooped to kiss her on the cheek and, to his surprise, she blushed.

"I'm so glad you like it. It was my husband's grandmother's, then his mother's, so you see, it has a history of being passed on. It's going to a good home now."

"It certainly is," Karl agreed. "But, if you don't mind, I'd like to give it to her in private. I will tell her where it's from, though," he promised.

Gretel patted him on the hand. "I quite understand. Now, we'd better get back to the party, before they think I've kidnapped you."

Karl slipped the box into his inside jacket pocket, not daring to guess the value of what he was carrying. He saw Silke's look of enquiry as he rejoined her, but he only smiled and put his finger to his lips to gesture a secret. He would wait until after Robert's visit, when Silke was fully cognisant of what she was taking on, before giving it to her.

TWENTY FOUR

Udo had not telephoned. The more Sophie thought about him, the more relieved she was that she had not become embroiled with him. Siegfried's children deserved a better stepfather than he could ever have been. But it was not just her own relationships that concerned her. Ilse's revelations at the weekend that she and Karl were going nowhere had come as a surprise. Less of a surprise was that Ilse still seemed to love Paul, and the only stumbling block now to their relationship was his exile to Uruguay.

In the peace and quiet of the evening she wrote Paul a long letter. The next day the weather was bright and she decided it would be good to escape the house for a bit and take the twins into Soest to post it at the main post office. Loading them both into the car, she drove the short distance into Soest and parked near the town walls. A battle ensued to get Friedrich sitting in the double pushchair as he wanted to push his sister himself. Sophie let him as far as the nearby duck pond, by which time he had had enough and allowed himself to be strapped in too. Sophie headed into the centre of the old town, with its narrow cobbled streets and picturesque houses. Stepping out into the market square she could never forget her marriage procession, walking so proudly at Siegfried's side from the church of St Petri, down Rathausstraße and on towards the hotel *Im Wilden Mann* in the market square. The day had been so perfect, Siegfried so handsome and she felt the tears welling once again in her eyes. How could she ever find anybody to match him?

As she handed her letter in at the post office counter to be weighed, Sophie thought about Paul and whether he was missing Ilse. Definitely, she decided, but did he have what it would take to return to West Germany and a possible prison sentence? Her parents had got off lightly, considering their neo-Nazi involvement, but would Paul be so lucky? As she watched the letter disappear into the collecting sack on its way to Uruguay she sent her urgent wishes with it that

Paul would take heed and choose to return. Zopf Construction would welcome its former managing director back with open arms, prison record or no. Paul had made it what it was during the boom years since the war. He deserved to benefit from its continuing success, secured by Siegfried's noble efforts after Paul took flight. The current management team was coping well enough without Siegfried, but Paul's dynamism would ensure the company would continue to reap dividends. Her own finances depended on it.

On leaving the post office, she took the twins to a shoe shop. They were both growing fast, beginning to lose their baby faces and developing the features that distinguished them as hers and Siegfried's children. Already old ladies would stop to congratulate her on what a beautiful pair they were, and she knew that as teenagers they would both break many hearts, but she suspected that, to keep him in order, Friedrich would need a strong man about the place.

As they were leaving the shoe shop, new shoes proudly adorning their feet, the twins spotted a man walking towards them.

"Papa!" Freia shrieked, pointing a chubby hand at the man.

Sophie's heart skipped a beat as she followed her daughter's gesture to a tall blond man in his late twenties. To her dismay the man heard but he grinned broadly at them as he walked past. Freia's head turned like an owl's to keep the man who looked like her daddy in view and she reached out her hand to try to grab hold of him. Sophie too could not help feeling deeply disappointed as she watched him disappearing amongst the shoppers. She had turned the pushchair so that Freia's neck was not straining and for a moment she just stood there, wistfully watching the spot where he had been swallowed up by the crowd. Suddenly she saw him again as he crossed the road, his head turned to watch for traffic. He saw them all watching him, smiled then continued on his way.

It was as if Siegfried's ghost had walked by, reassured them he was all right then moved on to another place. But Sophie didn't want him in another place; she wanted him here with her and the twins.

Freia began to cry. "Papa!" she wailed, both arms reaching out to the distant figure. "Papa!"

"It wasn't Papa," Sophie said crouching down to reassure her daughter. "Just a man who looked like him."

But Freia was convinced her special daddy was across the road and leaving them. She howled her disappointment and Sophie found herself promising an ice cream to try to distract her anguished daughter. Friedrich looked scornfully at his sister's continued tears, deciding to make his own demands at the mention of ice cream. His shouts and her tears brought more than a few glances in their direction as Sophie hurried to the ice cream parlour up the street.

Ordering herself a coffee, Sophie struggled to sit the twins in the high chairs provided. Friedrich was boisterous as usual and unwilling to be strapped in, bending his legs so they caught on the tray of the chair.

"Sit down if you want your ice cream!" she snapped at him. Suddenly he sat, gazing over her shoulder and then Freia screeched excitedly.

"Papa!"

Sophie turned to find the stranger standing beside her. "Oh!" she gasped, startled once again by his resemblance to Siegfried.

The young man looked embarrassed. "I'm sorry to be the cause of so much bother," he began, nodding at Freia's excitement, "but I wanted to find out who my apparent double is. I'm from Kiel, not around here. The name's Ortmann, by the way. Anders Ortmann." He held out his hand formally and Sophie shook it, feeling a spark of familiarity at the touch of him.

"Sophie Driesler, Friedrich and Freia," she responded. "We're pleased to meet you."

"I can see that," he said with a smile at Freia, who beamed back at him, squirming in her seat to get closer. "I must look extraordinarily like your husband. Your daughter thinks I am him!"

"She remembers him only from photos," Sophie explained. "He died last year. But you do look very like Siegfried," she added, seeing his instant discomfort at her revelation. "I believe his mother came from Hamburg originally – not so far from Kiel. Perhaps there is a family connection." She saw his eyes relax again and the desire to keep him there with them overwhelmed her. "Would you care to join us for a coffee, Herr Ortmann? Perhaps we can discover if you are a long-lost relative."

He looked at his watch, obviously debating whether to accept her offer before giving in with a shrug. "Why not? I've just about got time. It's not every day I get called 'Papa'!" he laughed.

On hearing the word 'Papa', Freia felt compelled to join the conversation. "New shoes!" she told him proudly, rotating her feet as she sat in the highchair.

"Are they?" the man replied. "They're very smart. Did you choose the colour?"

"Yes. Red!"

"Brown!" Friedrich intervened, not to be outdone in the colour-naming game. Then he pointed at the man's shoes. "Brown."

"Yes, they are, and they could do with a bit of a polish, I'm afraid," he laughed. His smiling grey eyes turned to Sophie. "They must be quite a handful for you."

"Sometimes," she admitted. "My parents live nearby and can help out quite often, fortunately."

"That is fortunate."

Freia's excited voice broke through to them. "Papa! Papa!"

Sophie hurriedly intervened. "Look, Freia, here comes your ice-cream. Now try not to make too much mess," she warned them both. As the twins eagerly attacked their ices, she smiled in embarrassment at Anders. "Sorry about that. I'll have to explain to them you're not their father, but it might be difficult. They both seem to have taken to you so readily."

As I have, she added to herself.

It soon transpired that Sophie did not know enough about Ilse's family to find a connection with Anders. They tried Karl's side too, since Siegfried had looked as much like his father as his mother, but to no avail. It would need Ilse's presence to progress further and Sophie found herself asking for Anders' address and telephone number as they drained their coffee cups, so she could contact him once she had spoken to Ilse.

He fished in his jacket and pulled out his wallet and a scrap of paper to write on then waved to the waitress to settle the bill for them all.

"Oh, but I invited you to coffee," Sophie objected immediately, noticing his wallet was as worn as his shoes.

"But I caused all the trouble," Anders insisted, handing a note to the waitress. He glanced at his watch and got to his feet. "Please get in touch if you find out any more about your husband's family, Frau Driesler. Nice to meet you." He shook her hand politely then turned to the twins. "I must go now. Perhaps I'll see you again soon. Goodbye."

As he waved to them all, Freia waved back, his half-promise enough for her to let him go without making a fuss.

*

"Thank God for that!" Paul exclaimed when Sabina phoned to tell him the wedding was postponed till later in the summer. "I couldn't have gone, otherwise. Did you have to remind him about my exams or did he remember himself?"

"He said it suddenly occurred to him. He's a bit out of touch with what's going on over with you lot and it wasn't until he started thinking about getting you over that he realised."

"I wish I could meet this Silke before the wedding," Paul told her. "It seems awfully weird going to your Dad's wedding when you've never even met the woman who's going to be your new stepmother." Paul could not hide the distaste in his voice.

"She's actually very nice," Sabina reassured him, "but, as you just said, it's weird to think of her as our stepmother. How's Aunty Sarah adjusting to the idea?"

"Not so well. She's gone into a bit of a decline, I think. She said Robert had called her to ask about Silke. Apparently Dad's asked him and his family over at Easter to meet Silke. Why didn't he ask us?"

Sabina could hear he was extremely hurt by this apparent thoughtlessness on the part of their father. Being the youngest, Paul had never understood his father's problems as well as she and Richard had, which was why his trial, imprisonment and the events surrounding their mother's death had hit Paul hardest. He had simply not been able to understand why his hero was in such trouble.

"It's difficult for Daddy, if he's having to work, to entertain you. Robert and Alice can do their own thing and pay for their own amusements. Daddy's not got a lot of spare cash yet, Paul."

"I've got savings. I could pay for my own trip."

"Don't be daft. He wouldn't want you to use those. Look," she suggested, sensing his keen sense of abandonment, "if you're really bothered, Wolf and I could get you a ticket and pick you up from the airport. You can stay with us or at Opa's, then I'm sure you'll get to see Daddy and Silke too."

"Would you really?"

Sabina's heart went out to her younger brother. "Of course, Pauli, if Richard's happy to be left alone with the farm."

"Oh, Vanessa's always here, with one or other of her brothers. Richard seems to be more a Turner than a Driesler these days."

"I'm relieved to hear it. Well, I'll get on to finding a flight for you. Where would you rather stay, with us or with Opa?"

Without hesitation Paul replied: "Opa. Then I can help out in the sawmill. There's not a lot to do in Dortmund, is there?"

"There speaks a true country boy," Sabina laughed at him. "We'll all meet up somewhere with Robert and Alice too, no doubt. I hope Richard doesn't mind missing out."

"He won't. There's a Young Farmers' Club concert he's in then, I think, anyway. He wouldn't want to miss that."

Sabina pictured her other brother establishing himself at the heart of the farming community with all the self-confidence of his rightful place that, she now realised, their father had never felt.

"Good. Well, I'd better not run up any more of a phone bill. I'll be in touch about flights soon. Love to you all."

Sabina could make good use of her last few weeks working at the travel agent's to find Paul a flight. She had wondered whether her father and Silke wanted a discount honeymoon package, but they had not mentioned anything yet. Presumably the date was still uncertain. When she spoke to her Aunt Anna in Medebach about Paul staying for Easter, she discovered that they too knew very little as yet about Silke.

"I don't mind admitting to you, Bina," Anna told her in confidence, "that Papa has huge reservations about her suitability and age. We've not met her yet and it all seems so sudden. I don't like to suggest it, but ..." The topic was too indelicate for her to continue, but Sabina knew where she was headed.

"No, there's nothing like that, Tante Anna. Quite the opposite I think. They're in a hurry to get married so that she can get pregnant, as far as I can make out."

"Oh." Her aunt sounded flustered by such talk of her elder brother. "I see. Well, we'd love to have Pauli here to stay. I just hope he gets the chance to see his father. We certainly don't see much of him these days."

"No, neither do I," Sabina commented. "And I can never get him on the telephone. He's always out. I'm beginning to think I'm going to have to ask him for Silke's home number, just so that I can keep in touch with him."

"Well if you do find out what it is, let us know. I can never get hold of him either."

Oh Daddy, you are being a naughty boy, Sabina thought to herself as she hung up the phone. All these people wondering what you're up to! I don't know! She realised she was grinning at his antics. He was happy, and that was the main thing. She just hoped it would last.

*

Silke found herself accosted by Margit as she was hurrying round the shops during Thursday lunchtime. She was trying to find a shirt to go with the jeans she had just bought for Karl ready for archery on Sunday. His lack of suitable clothes was proving troublesome; they were either too smart or threadbare and stained with creosote. He did not know she was buying him jeans but she longed to see his long legs clad in that most sexy of materials. She was hunting for a brushed cotton, checked shirt to go with the jeans when Margit pounced.

"How can you stick with him after what he did to my mother?"

Silke turned from the rack of shirts to be confronted by her friend. "Oh, it's you, Margit," she said pleasantly, ignoring Margit's outburst. "Hello. Long time no see."

"No, and it can stay that way," Margit retorted in an unexpectedly angry voice. "How dare you steal him right out from under her very nose!"

Maintaining her calm, Silke put back the shirt she had been holding. "What's brought this on, Margit? You seemed to accept the situation before. Even on Sunday night when you phoned me to tell me … what happened, you were fine. So why are you suddenly angry with me? I'm sorry your mother's missed out, but really, neither of us intended to fall in love. It just happened. I didn't deliberately take him from Ilse."

"But they were as good as engaged! And you knew that!" Margit hissed.

Other customers were beginning to look at them, but Silke ignored them. "No they weren't. Ilse may have thought so, but Karl was struggling with their relationship. He would never have looked in my direction if he'd been happy with her." She remembered what Karl had told her about the weekend. "But your mother's glad to be rid of him now, isn't she?" Suddenly Margit looked uncomfortable. "Isn't she?" Silke repeated.

"Yes, sort of," Margit reluctantly admitted.

"So it's you that wants him, not your mother," Silke guessed.

Margit gave her a scornful glare. "I didn't say that!"

"But it's true, isn't it?" Silke asked, gently placing her hand on Margit's arm. "You've always fancied him but now I've got him."

Margit wanted to brush off Silke's hand, but found herself unable to. She knew she was being unreasonable. "Yes," she admitted with a deep sigh of defeat. "I've always known I would never get him, so I can't complain really, can I?" She acknowledged her moment of intense jealousy at the sight of Silke buying clothes for Karl and allowed herself a smile. "Actually, I think I'm finally in love with dear old Bruno, so I don't even know why I'm so upset. It was the thought of not seeing him again, I suppose."

"Who, Karl? Of course you'll see him again. We're friends, aren't we? And soon we'll be related somehow, through Karl's grandchildren. Of course we'll keep in touch!"

"You'll invite us to the wedding?"

"Of course, if you'd like to come, that is," Silke added with a degree of uncertainty.

Margit considered the idea. "Yes. Yes, I think I would. I don't know about my mother, though."

"Perhaps it's best if we leave the decision up to her."

"Probably. When is the wedding, anyway?"

Silke hesitated. "Not sure yet. In the summer hopefully."

"But that's not far off!" Margit protested. "These things take a lot of planning."

"I know, and I've made a start, but Karl's just got a few things he's got to sort out first."

"Like what?"

Like my commitment to his mental health, Silke could have said but did not. "Oh, just ... things." She picked up the shirt she had been looking at when Margit arrived. "Anyway, I must press on. Give your mother my warmest wishes and I hope her lip is much better."

Margit gave her a hug. "I'm sorry for what I said earlier. You deserve Karl. I just hope he doesn't ... well ... prove too much for you."

"He won't. I know what I'm taking on. At least," she cautioned herself, "I will know once I've met his friend, Robert."

"The psychiatrist," Margit nodded knowingly. "Well, 'good luck' is all I can say, and don't forget the wedding invitation! I'm going to start hunting for an outfit right now!"

Silke watched her heading off into the lunchtime crowds then happily resumed selecting a shirt. She would allow nothing to get in the way of her marriage to Karl, no matter what anybody said, Robert included.

*

When Sabina finally caught up with her father at home on Saturday afternoon she rebuked him sternly for abandoning his family.

"We none of us can ever get hold of you, Daddy!" she told him firmly down the telephone line. "Paul was quite distraught to know that you'd invited Robert and his family but not him for Easter, and Tante Anna said that they had not even met Silke yet! You're going to have to get everyone together at Easter, you realise," she badgered him, trying not to picture his hurt expression. "Paul's coming over, by the way, and will be staying in Medebach." She dropped this last piece of information in quite casually, to make him realise just how much he had estranged himself recently from his family.

325

"Oh dear. Something tells me I'm not the world's best Dad at the moment," he replied sombrely. "But it's all been happening so quickly – too quickly probably. And I've had rather a lot to think about. I'm sorry you all feel abandoned, especially Pauli. I'll phone home and speak to him, apologise for not thinking about him. And I'll give you all Silke's number so you can contact me if I'm not at home."

"Which seems to be most nights," Sabina said pointedly, then instantly regretted her cheekiness. "I'm glad you're so happy, Daddy," she relented. "And everyone else will be too, once they've met Silke, I'm sure."

So there was still dissent in the family about his decision, Karl realised. Love had made him blind to everybody else. "Silke and I will organise a big family get-together at Easter," he told her. "You make sure you and Wolf can get down to Iserlohn, and I'll get Opa and everyone to come up from Medebach. What with Robert, Alice, Douglas and Stewart as well, it's going to be quite a party."

"It's going to be a bit of a squash in your house!" Sabina commented.

"Yes, it would be. So we'll hold it at Silke's. I'll send you all instructions on how to find it. It's a bit out of the way."

She must have access to a big barn or something they could all fit in, Sabina decided. But at least that way we'll get to find out more about Silke, nosing around her home. She was reminded of something else she had wanted to ask him. "Daddy," she ventured anxiously, "was there a particular reason you invited Robert over?"

She heard him draw breath slowly. "Yes. He's coming to tell Silke my history. She needs to know exactly what she's got to deal with."

"Good," Sabina said, relieved that it was nothing more serious. "She does need to know."

*

Prompted by Sabina's call, Karl spent the rest of Saturday afternoon communicating with people. By the time he got around to writing a letter to Ernst, thanking him for his help with Sophie, and one to Auer in prison, it was getting late and he had yet to do any housework. Not that he was around much these days to make the house dirty. He was wondering how much longer he would be living there, when the telephone rang. It was the Duty Officer telling him there was a problem with the electricity supply in the maternity ward. Hurrying over to his office, he consulted his list of electricians and called one out, arranging to meet him at the hospital main entrance. As he stood there by the German eagle aloft on its stone pillar he wondered how long this was going to take to sort out. He and Silke had been invited to dinner by one of the guests at Gretel Wittke's last Sunday, and Silke was supposed to be picking him up in an hour's time. He had not seen her all day and he was missing her sunny presence at his side.

The electrician turned up promptly, fortunately, and had soon informed Karl that it was a case of overloaded wiring. The old Field Artillery Barracks was simply not designed to cope with modern electrical demands. He assured Karl he would sort things out for the moment, and, after a word with the ward sister updating her on the situation, Karl felt able to leave the electrician to it and hurried home.

Silke was waiting in her car outside his house.

"I'm sorry, Schatz," he said, kissing her through the open window to the strains of Grieg's 'Anitra's Dance' emanating from her car radio. "Duty called. Come in while I tidy myself up."

Silke got out, clutching the carrier bag of clothing she had bought earlier that day. "Here," she said, presenting it to him once the front door closed behind them. "I hope you like them."

Karl peered into the bag, saw the jeans and checked shirt and thought: Is she trying to turn me into her friend Tom? Nevertheless, he thanked her and promised to wear them to archery. Silke followed him upstairs and sat on his bed while he disappeared into the bathroom to have a shave. With his face covered in lather, Karl could only listen in astonishment as Silke suddenly said from his bedroom: "Karl, I've been thinking. Do you mind if we get married on May 30th after all? It's just that everything seems to be snowballing out of control and suddenly I just want a nice quiet wedding, just us and Willi and Rosa as witnesses. We can have lots of different receptions for our various friends and relatives at different places and different times. Do you mind?"

Karl wandered in from the bathroom, razor in hand. "Of course I don't mind. I was beginning to think the same, actually, but I thought you wanted a big wedding."

She smiled fondly at the sight of him. "There are just too many people and it's all getting impossibly large. We'd never be able to speak to all our guests, and wouldn't it be so much nicer if we held a reception in Medebach and one in England for your friends and family there? Save them coming all this way. It would spin the celebrations out over the summer and we'd have one long party."

Karl's soap-covered jaw dropped. "That's a brilliant idea! Separate wedding celebrations in Iserlohn, Medebach and Penchurch. You're a genius, Schatz." He blew her a kiss in lieu of a proper one. "What made you think of that?"

"I met Margit while shopping, invited her and the rest of her family, then began totting up just how many people had to be invited. Besides," she added, blushing prettily, "I didn't want to delay the wedding. I've got my heart set on that beach in June."

"So have I."

"Just one thing, Karl."

"Yes?"

"Now you know all about me and my money ..."

"Yes?"

"Actually the beach is our private beach at our villa in the South of France. I've already told the agents who run the place to have it vacant and ready for us then."

"We can still find a tent somewhere though, can't we?" he asked hopefully. "I'd be awfully disappointed not to spend a night under canvas after all our talk about it."

"Of course!" she laughed. "As many nights as you like."

TWENTY FIVE

Weary after their long journey from Edinburgh, Robert pulled up outside Karl's house and hoped for the umpteenth time that he would like Silke. Her ousting of Katherine's place in Karl's heart still struck him as uncommonly swift. No wonder Karl's family had their misgivings about her.

Robert opened the door of the heavily loaded Rover just as Karl opened his front door. Close behind Karl stood a dark-haired young woman, clad fashionably but decorously in a white peasant-style blouse and a long, deep purple skirt. Robert ignored her briefly as he greeted his old friend.

"Karl!"

"Robert!"

They both hugged and slapped each other's backs like long-lost brothers. "It's good to see you again!" Karl exclaimed, breaking off from their embrace. He turned and drew Silke to the fore, standing slightly behind her with his hands resting lightly on her shoulders. "And here's the person you've come to meet. May I present Silke, my fiancée."

Silke stepped forwards and was able to look both Robert and Alice directly in the face, the same height as them both. "Welcome all of you." She kissed them both on the cheek before smiling at the two teenage boys, who, she knew, would not appreciate being kissed. "Karl has told me so much about you that I feel I know you already." Her American/German accent surprised them all as she continued: "I hope your journey was not too exhausting."

Alice had noticed Karl's look of pride when presenting her and understood the depth of their love for each other, but she still felt disconcerted by Silke's obvious youth. Robert too was suffering similar reservations about the age gap as well as seeing Karl with someone other than Katherine, but both allowed politeness to overrule their thoughts and responded to her question.

"It was very interesting," Alice told her, "especially for Douglas and Stewart. We've not been abroad before, except for Robert of course, so we've spent the time pointing out all the different things we've seen. Quite an education!"

"Travel does broaden the mind," Silke agreed as she led everyone into the house.

Alice noticed how it was Silke who took on the role of hostess, rather than Karl as host, even though it was Karl's house. She was competent and secure in her role, pointing out toilets and quickly establishing preferred refreshments while Karl and Robert were already deep in conversation about the health of Robert's parents, Donald and Gertie Murdoch, and Karl's own family. Alice followed Silke out to the kitchen to see if she could help with anything while the boys mooched around in the lounge on their best behaviour but longing to stretch their legs.

"Is your house nearby?" Alice asked Silke, pouring milk into cups for tea.

"No, about fifteen or twenty minutes' drive away. There's more room there than here, and Douglas and Stewart can play football or tennis or whatever. More private too," she added confiding in Alice, whom she perceived as a broad-minded woman. "I don't stay here with Karl. It would not be the done thing!" She said this in exactly the right tone of voice for Alice to chuckle.

"No, I can understand that," she smiled, realising what fun Silke must be for Karl after all the hardships and heartache of the past two years. He needed her youth. Silke had brought life where before had been only death. "I'm so glad you're happy together. Karl's been such a worry for Robert over the years. I think he'll feel relieved to find him in such capable hands."

"That's why we asked you over," Silke pointed out as she poured tea for them all. "To make sure I am capable. Robert needs to tell me how to look after him. I know what a good job Katherine made of it and I want to do just as well."

Alice was pleased to hear her reference to Katherine. There seemed to be no jealousy towards Karl's first wife. "I'm sure you will, Silke. But even Katherine had trouble sometimes. If you ever need Robert's help or advice, call us immediately. Please."

"I will," Silke said, laying her hand on Alice's arm to emphasise her intention. "Now, we'd better take this tea in to the troops!"

As they all gathered in the dining room later to eat the meal of sausage and mashed potato Karl and Silke had prepared, Robert and Alice relaxed, enjoying Silke's enthusiastic conversation, which ranged from field archery, the delights of Edinburgh, which she had once visited with her mother, to environmental concerns.

"I wonder why we didn't go straight to her house," Robert said as they set off once more in the car, this time following closely behind Karl's VW Beetle but with a map as well, should they become separated.

"It was probably easier to find Karl's house," Alice suggested, "judging by this map she's given us. I've really warmed to her already. She's nice, isn't she, boys? Very down to earth."

"Yes," they chorused enthusiastically.

"Pretty too," Douglas added, his sixteen-year-old hormones fired up.

Robert grinned. He would have described her more as charming rather than pretty, but since his own wife had never been famous for her looks, he knew how important character was in establishing relationships that would work. Silke had character aplenty.

When the VW ahead of them drove through a large pillared gateway adorned by two bears, the Murdoch family fell strangely silent. Ahead of them stood a large and stately house, lights ablaze to welcome the visitors.

"Crikey!" Douglas gasped in awe. "Is this it?"

"Look at that garden," Stewart piped up. "It goes on forever!"

Robert peered through the darkness as the influence of the house lights filtered down lawns and shrubberies with no sign of an end. Reserving judgement for the time being, he parked next to Karl's car and they all got out onto the neat gravel drive and began unloading their luggage.

Silke saw their perplexity and grinned but said nothing as she led them all up the grand stone steps to the front door, through which Willi and Rosa were coming to assist them.

"We'll show you your rooms first then we can all finally relax over a glass of wine. Boys," Silke said, turning to Douglas and Stewart, "there's a room near the kitchen where you can play table tennis, darts, table football and a few other things. Use them if you want, or you can explore the house, watch TV or sit with us. Just make yourselves at home."

Karl smiled at Robert, seeing his friend's incredulity at what Silke had to offer. Robert raised his eyebrows to show he was impressed, but inside he still reserved judgement on the young woman who was about to take on the burden of caring for Karl.

The next day, over breakfast in the large dining room, Karl told his visitors about the large cave complex nearby, the *Dechenhöhle*. "Silke tells me they're pretty impressive so I thought we might pay them a visit, especially since the weather is a bit grey. Would you like that?" he asked with his eyes on the boys.

"Yes, please," Stewart replied enthusiastically. He still could not get over the size of Karl's girlfriend's house, nor the fact that Douglas had discovered that Karl and Silke shared a bedroom, even though they weren't yet married.

"That sounds a good idea," Alice agreed.

"But you and I, Robert, can stay and have a chat," Silke murmured quietly. "That is, if you don't mind missing the caves."

"I don't mind at all," he smiled. He had warmed even more to Silke yesterday as the wine and conversation had flowed until late in the evening. She had a mature head on her shoulders, and, to his immense relief, her wealth was not an issue. The fact that she had more money than she knew what to do with, but was still careful with it, had surprised and intrigued him. It had transpired that what she spent, she spent wisely but often indulged in supporting good causes. Karl and his family seemed to be her current good cause. Robert just hoped it would not prove a whim on her part. He caught Karl's eye and saw his friend's anxiety at Robert's task for the morning.

"Don't spare her anything," Karl muttered to him later, as Alice and the boys got into the VW ready for the excursion.

"I just hope I remember everything," Robert replied. "It's quite a while since I had to tell it all to Katherine."

"I'm sure you'll be fine. Just tell it to her, warts and all, and don't gloss over anything."

"I won't," Robert promised. "I'll tell it to her straight."

As he wandered later through the ornate natural grottos of the *Dechenhöhle*, Karl's mind also wandered to muse on what Silke was feeling right now. As he peered into the still waters of the pool in the Nymphs' Grotto, he saw his worried face staring back up at him. Would her opinion of him change? Could she accept what he had done all those years ago or would she find it impossible to connect him with what she was hearing? The latter seemed most likely, he thought, to one of her generation. It was too long ago: mere history to her, but so real still to himself. Yet she had to understand how deeply affected by it all he still was, despite first Dr Goldberg's and then Robert's ministrations.

It was only recently he had realised how supremely fortunate he was to have been treated by Dr Goldberg in the summer of nineteen forty-seven. Dr Goldberg had been at the forefront with his care of 'shell-shocked' soldiers, quickly being offered a research post by a prestigious American University. Karl had been one of the comparatively few POWs treated by Dr Goldberg before his work was recognised and lauded. He shuddered to think what might have happened to him in another doctor's hands.

"Cold?" Alice asked, seeing him shiver.

"A bit," he lied. "And you?"

"Not warm," she admitted. "I'll be glad to have a cup of coffee in the restaurant when we get out of here." She cast her eye around for her sons and saw them laughing at the garden gnomes sitting by the pool, guardians of the water nymphs after whom the grotto was named. They were enjoying themselves, as was she. Which was more than could probably be said for Silke right now. It was such a shame Karl's past still weighed so heavily on him. She linked her arm through Karl's to offer warmth. "Let's go and find that coffee!"

Karl found himself driving slowly back to Silke's house after their morning out, but as he parked the car on the drive he saw her and Robert strolling in the garden, examining the shrubs in a border, and knew their talk was over. Silke turned and waved gaily at the returning troop and hurried across the manicured lawn to greet them.

"Was it good?" she asked the boys, giving Karl a gentle hug to reaffirm her love for him.

"Fantastic!" Stewart gushed. "We had chocolate and pistachio ice cream afterwards!"

"And I bet you are starving now," she commented, catching Alice's eye with a grin. "Lunch is ready."

"Wipe your feet!" Alice called after her sons as they sped up the front steps of the grand house. She and Robert followed after them, wanting to give Karl and Silke space.

Alone on the drive Karl looked down into Silke's eyes. They were as warm and loving as ever but he could see the horror of it all had touched her. "All right?" he asked her.

"Yes. I'm glad I know. Robert said he told me everything. Absolutely everything." Including something you don't know yourself, Silke thought, remembering Robert's strict instructions never to reveal what she knew to Karl unless it ever seemed to become a problem. His most terrible memory of being made to kill a child while kept hooked on drugs at Dachau had been wiped clean, first by himself and then again by Dr Goldberg, although the psychiatrist had kept a note of it in the records Robert was privy to. It was one memory too much for Karl to live with. "I understand your terror of drugs now," she added calmly. "You're not to blame, but I do know you blame yourself and you will for eternity."

He nodded but her gaze was too penetrating for him to hold and he looked away to the distant skeletons of the trees. "No more mention of it, please. If you think you can handle me, after everything Robert's told you, then we can get on with our lives."

"Too right we can!" Silke grinned, although inside she still felt sick with shock at what he had done and had had done to him. The thought of eating lunch made her feel even worse but she had to behave normally, for his sake. "Let's join the others and eat."

Karl was not fooled by her apparent cheerfulness but at least she understood just how terrible it had been. She needed to feel horrified and he watched as she picked at the food on her plate, their eyes meeting every so often in silent communication while the Murdoch boys told their father all about the stalactites and stalagmites in the Palm and Organ Grottos.

"Silke was telling me that Paul is coming over for Easter too," Robert finally managed to say to Karl as the boys' attention was drawn by the pineapple cheesecake that Rosa had just brought in.

"Yes. None of my family has met Silke yet, apart from Bina and

Wolf. Oh and Sarah, of course. We've never both managed to get away from work at the same time before but now she's quitting work, they've moved someone from another hospital to cover her job for the time being. So we're all invited over to Medebach for Easter Sunday. Silke finds it's best to meet people away from here first time around, you see."

"I can understand that," Robert agreed. "That's why you had us arrive at your house first to meet her, wasn't it?" He paused then added: "So they don't know you're marrying an heiress?"

"No, because I'm not. I'm marrying Silke, not her money. It's important people understand that."

"Absolutely!" Robert noticed Silke listening in and added: "You couldn't have found a nicer bride, Karl. We didn't just chat about your past this morning." He turned to her. "Did we, Silke?"

"No. Robert interrogated me about my intentions towards you, Karl. It looks like I passed his test."

"With flying colours," Robert confirmed.

"He means 'very well'," Karl explained the idiom to Silke. "Now we just have to get my family's seal of approval."

*

Sabina, Wolf and Paul arrived at Haus Fichtenblick on Easter Sunday to find Karl and Robert's cars already parked outside. Paul had stayed his first two nights in his sister's apartment but was now itching to see his father and grandfather and be let loose in the sawmill. His desire to meet his future stepmother was not so urgent.

It took him some time to spot the new face amongst all the people gathered at the doorway to greet them, and when he did he was surprised. Everybody had said how young she was, but to him she looked quite old. She was hanging back, he noticed, not forcing herself on him as he was swept up into the family. Douglas and Stewart were like cousins to him, while his real cousins, Uwe, Monika and Lothar, were all at home for the holiday. Cousins Andrea and Martin arrived shortly afterwards with his Uncle Rudi and Aunt Adele. It truly was a gathering of the clan and made a nice change from being swamped by Vanessa's family. He suddenly felt how Silke must be feeling and he gave her a more sympathetic glance. She smiled cheerfully at him and he smiled back. She was all right, he decided abruptly. She'd do as a companion for his father but there was no comparison between her and his mother. Silke would never take her place.

Later, as the family overflowed out into the small garden, Paul found Silke had finally sought him out. She stood by him as he demolished a plate of sandwiches. "There's certainly a lot of you Drieslers," she commented, stroking one of the household cats she was holding in her arms. "I hope I can remember everyone's names."

He noticed she spoke to him as an equal rather than a child. "Who's that?" he tested her, pointing to the lanky young man practicing his English on Douglas and Stewart.

"Lothar," Silke said confidently.

"Well done," Paul said. "And who is Onkel Rudi married to?"

Silke was momentarily stumped. "I know," she said, as Paul was about to help her out. "Adele. It's a good thing your father went over all their names with me before we came." She touched him on the arm gently, sensing his diminishing but residual distrust of her. "I do love him, you know. And I will look after him."

"Bina says you want to have children as soon as possible," Paul said boldly, giving voice to his biggest grievance.

"Yes," Silke replied. "But they won't ever come between your father and his older children. And I promise I won't try to be a mother to you," she smiled. "I'm not old enough, am I?"

"No, but it'll be strange for me not to be the youngest any more."

He was beginning to accept the situation, Silke realised with relief. Karl's children were proving remarkably amenable to having her as a stepmother, considering their initial reservations. Their innate sense and tolerance shone through. Could she produce such robust offspring for Karl as Katherine had done?

"Tell me about your ambitions, Paul. From what Karl says, you and I seem to have a lot in common. You want to study forestry, am I right?"

"Yes and not just temperate forests. I think the world could make far better use of its forestry resources. Who knows what's lurking out there that could be really useful? And when they do decide a tree is useful, we must make sure the resources are managed properly and not harvested to extinction. I've recently joined the World Wildlife Fund," he went on eagerly. "'Saving the Panda' as Richard likes to joke. But they do far more than just look after animals."

"Good for you! And have you decided where you want to study?"

"I'm still looking around, but I'm thinking of applying to the University of Bristol. They have a good Department of Agriculture and Horticulture. Aunty Sarah studied there – at Bristol. I'll have to discuss it with Dad though. I'm not sure Richard can manage without me on the farm. If he has to hire someone and pay for my maintenance it might not be possible. Aunty Sarah said it was a struggle for her father to see her through university. I've saved up some money from my garden furniture business, and I'll obviously try to earn as much during the vacations as I can but …" His voice tailed off and he shrugged.

"You really want to go, don't you?" Silke commented. "There'll be a way, I promise. Such important dreams of feeding the world and saving the planet must come true."

Paul realised she shared his dreams and grinned. "Are you a member?"

"Of what?"

"The WWF."

"No, but I'd like to be. You must send me the details and I'll join."

Karl was watching the conversation from the kitchen door, pleased at the rapport the pair had struck up. Beside him stood Robert, beer in hand.

"She has a gift for making people open up," Robert commented, taking a swig of his beer. "She got me talking about my experiences with the Japs the other day when you were at the caves."

"Oh?" Karl studied his friend's face. "Do you still have problems from those days too?"

"Occasionally," Robert replied nonchalantly. "But I'm coming across more and more ex-servicemen who are realising they have a problem; ordinary men who still have nightmares and can't talk about their experiences. We're not alone, you and I, and the problem's going to get bigger the more wars we have. Vietnam's going to produce a big harvest for the Yanks."

337

"Dr Goldberg will be busy then. Do you still hear from him?"

"I met him at a conference in London a couple of years ago. Did I tell you?"

"No! How is he?"

"Very prosperous and highly respected. Sent you his best wishes by the way. That was very remiss of me not to pass them on, but I think you were in a spot of bother at the time and I didn't get to see you."

Karl smiled at the phrase 'a spot of bother'. The British were such masters of understatement, yet it kept things nicely in perspective. Life was so good now with Silke, especially now he was sure all his family liked her. Everything was going right at last.

Robert saw his friend's smile and followed the direction of his eyes. "She's a rare gem, Karl. You seem to have the knack of finding them. Best of luck, mate, but I don't think you'll need it."

"Oh, you always need luck on your side," Karl told him. "You can never take anything for granted. Silke desperately wants children. What if she can't have them?"

"Don't talk rubbish!" Robert scoffed, then immediately poured some of his beer onto the ground. "A libation to the goddess of fertility, in case I've offended her," he explained.

Karl hurriedly poured some of his beer on the ground too.

"She'll have twins now!" Robert laughed.

"Good," Karl smiled.

TWENTY SIX

Silke eased herself down onto the garden seat under the fruit-burdened pear tree at Lane Head Farm. It was her fourth visit here in the two years they had been married, and still she marvelled at the beauty and tranquillity of the place, seemingly so far removed from all the sordid troubles of the world. The recent terrorist attacks by the Baader-Meinhoff gang were a worrying development, and what with a bomb yesterday in Montreal, plane hijackings, the Northern Ireland situation and the continuing war in Vietnam, Silke wondered what kind of a world this new baby, busily stirring inside her, would be entering. But if anyone could protect it from the world's horrors, its father would. She felt so safe in his presence, apart from during the occasional nightmares he had warned her to expect. Then he frightened her with the fierceness of his terror. The world really had not changed, she decided sadly. Still, the ongoing Munich Olympics showed the world could get together in peaceful gathering when it wanted to.

She spotted Vanessa picking her way carefully up the garden path, carrying a tray laden with glasses and a large jug of lemonade, ice cubes chinking merrily. Vanessa carefully set the tray down on the garden table, one of Paul and Richard's earliest creations, and poured out drinks for them both.

"Here you are," Vanessa said, handing her a glass. "It's surprisingly hot today, isn't it?"

"Not as hot as the South of France, I assure you!" Silke laughed. "When are you and Richard going to get away for a holiday down there with us? Everyone else has been except you two."

"Oh, you know what these farmers are like. There's always something cropping up!" Vanessa sat down on the seat beside her. "But it would be nice. Perhaps next year, and who knows what the result might be!"

Silke looked squarely at her. "Getting broody, are you?"

Vanessa blushed. "I suppose we must make a start sometime, even if it's just to catch up with you and Karl. Where is he, by the way?"

"He took Sandi down by the river for a paddle. He said there's a little pool in the shallows that's safe enough for her. I couldn't face the walk down there, let alone back up, and it's given me the chance to have a little doze."

"I don't blame you. Have you got any names for the new baby in mind yet?"

Silke gave the contented smile of a woman for whom life was panning out exactly as she had planned. "Tobias, after my father, or Klara, after my mother."

"Where did the name Sandi come from then?" Vanessa asked, thinking it must be from Karl's side, although it didn't sound very German.

"The beach where she was ... made!"

Vanessa spluttered with laughter. "Really? Whose idea was that?"

"Mine. Karl's letting me choose all the names - says he's had his turn at it. My father's mother was Italian, Alessandra, which is how I justified choosing the name, but of course we always shorten it to Sandi. Maybe when she's older she'll want to call herself Alessandra." Silke sipped her lemonade then rested her glass on her belly and gazed out across the garden and sheep-dotted meadows towards the distant escarpment of Hay Bluff. The farm would need an heir and she felt like helping Richard and Vanessa along. "You and Richard should have a holiday there too and follow our example."

"But we couldn't choose the name Sandi," Vanessa said with a chuckle. "If we used the same theme, it would have to be Frances or Frank, something like that. Or something totally different." She sighed and caught herself eyeing Silke's bump with a touch of envy. "You've got me thinking now."

Silke smiled happily. Her new family would enlarge in leaps and bounds; the family she had always longed for. "I'd be very surprised if Sophie and Anders didn't decide to produce soon," she speculated. "It's a year since their wedding and I can see the signs in Sophie. I'm glad you managed to come over for that, by the way."

"We felt we had to, but I'm glad we did. Karl was pretty insistent on the Drieslers attending en masse. He's desperate not to lose his links with the twins, although Anders seems a good sort. Being a teacher, he understands the importance of family ties. Poor Ilse's still a problem though, isn't she? She couldn't really have expected her Paul to leave Uruguay."

"Sophie tells me she did her best to persuade him but he's settled where he is now and that's that. Ilse's just got to try to forget about him and Karl and look elsewhere. She'll find someone one of these days, once she takes her blinkers off." Silke's glass jumped and nearly spilt its contents over her embroidered cheesecloth smock as her belly moved beneath it. "It's telling me to drink up. What time did you say Sarah and Audrey are expected?"

Vanessa looked at her watch. It was ten past three. "At three but they were going for a ride first. I expect they rode further than they thought." Vanessa caught sight of Karl making his way up across the farmyard with his toddler daughter sat upon his bare shoulders, wrapped in a towel. Vanessa waved to them and they both waved back. "I never thought we'd hear the end of their holiday in your villa," she continued on the theme of Sarah and Audrey. "The poor things don't seem to have much fun these days. They're both still stuck in boring secretarial jobs. Sarah was determined at one time to go off and do something worthy but she never gets around to it. 'Stuck in a rut' describes them both perfectly."

"She likes it too much here to want to leave," Silke explained. "Herefordshire is her home. I felt the same about Iserlohn when I was in California." She smiled fondly at her husband and daughter who had just joined them in the garden.

Karl deposited Sandi in a controlled nose-dive down on the lawn then grabbed the towel she threw off as she made a dash for the swing hanging from a limb of the tall pear tree. "No peace for the wicked!" he groaned, hurrying to lift her up onto the wooden seat.

"It's all right, Karl. I'll push her. You come and sit down," Vanessa offered, making way for him on the garden seat.

"Phew! I'd forgotten how steep that hill was," he said to Silke, wiping beads of sweat off his forehead and chest with Sandi's damp towel as he sat down beside her in the fraying, bleached denim shorts he had worn all summer.

"Now you know why I didn't want to join you!" she laughed.

"Here, have a drink." She poured him a glass of lemonade from the jug on the table in front of them. "We'd better fill this up before Sarah and Audrey arrive."

"I think I can hear a car now," Vanessa said, peering over the hedge down the lane. "Yes, it's Sarah's Mini."

There was the usual commotion as the new visitors arrived and were introduced to an excited Sandi, who could not remember having seen them before. Eventually Sandi was settled down on a rug with a beaker of lemonade and a biscuit, and the adults could chat in peace.

"Gosh, you're looking well, both of you," Sarah commented to Karl and Silke, while trying to keep her eyes off the sun-bleached hairs on Karl's long, golden brown thighs. "In fact you're looking younger than ever, Karl. The decadent lifestyle obviously suits you!" she teased him.

"I'd hardly call keeping an eighteen-month-old toddler amused 'decadent', but we have had a good summer, I must admit. Sophie, Anders and the twins kept us on our toes for three weeks in Antibes. Friedrich must have shown us every lizard in the South of France. Anders is doing a great job as stepfather. They're both turning out to be super children."

Sarah could see the pride in his eyes. "So is Sandi. She's going to be bilingual, by the sound of things," she commented to Silke, on hearing the little girl using English to Vanessa, who was offering her another drink.

"Yes," Silke replied. "We both thought it would be best. It worked for Sabina and the boys. Karl always speaks to her in English and I always speak to her in German. Naturally she favours German, since we live there, but she's happy to use both and seems to know which is the appropriate language."

"How useful for her," Audrey marvelled. "I wish someone had taught me French when I was that age. We had the devil of a job getting by on holiday. Do you manage all right?"

"I got lots of practice when I was younger," she explained modestly. "Karl's starting to pick up a few words and phrases now, but he's very lazy and mostly leaves the talking to me."

"I'm not lazy!" he protested. "I'm working quite hard on my French. I just don't seem to have much to show yet for all my efforts. Too many other distractions around, I think. Not like when I learnt

342

English." He was reminded of Katherine's patient corrections to his mistakes and Sarah saw what he was thinking.

"Do you know what Audrey told me when we were out riding!" she said quickly. "Apparently Andrew is selling Froxley Grange!"

"Is he?" Karl asked Audrey in amazement. "Why?" He thought he could guess the reason and Audrey proved him right.

"It's partly the fault of the last Labour Government," she told him, "taxes and such-like, and partly his own lack of interest in the place since I left him. It needed modernising all the time I was there but he's really let it go to rack and ruin recently. He's seldom there these days – daren't show his face around here any more after what happened to Katherine. Besides, the repairs cost too much," she went on, anxious not to upset Karl at the mention of Katherine's death, "and neither Alan nor Angela wants to be lumbered with the upkeep of the place. They've got their own lives now and can't be bothered with an old and crumbling inheritance."

"I wonder what will happen to the place," Karl mused as a very oily Richard and Paul finally joined them in the garden to gulp down some lemonade prior to continuing their overhaul of the tractor.

Audrey nodded a greeting to the pair before speculating: "Who knows whether anyone will even want to buy it? It's a bit out of the way, and whoever buys it is going to have to spend an awful lot on renovating the place."

"I know what I'd do with it," Sarah said instantly. "I'd turn it into a training centre where women can be taught how to compete with men in the labour market. I'm sick of being refused jobs just because I'm a woman."

Karl, Richard and Paul all grinned in recognition of Sarah's long-standing grievance since she quit her good job in the planning department of the Greater London Council.

"I'd turn it into an environmental research centre," Paul said, joining in the fun, "combined with a field studies centre for schools or colleges, like the one I went to last year in Shropshire. After all, it's got all that farmland, gardens, greenhouses and outbuildings going to waste otherwise. The stables could be turned into dormitories, while the house would be used for classrooms, dining area and teachers' accommodation."

Silke could see everyone was warming to the theme. "If you could have it, Audrey, and money was no object, what would you do with it?" she prompted the next person in line.

Her answer took them all by surprise. "I've been speculating about that ever since I first heard Froxley Grange was on the market. After what happened to my son, Alex, I would turn it into a refuge for reforming drug addicts. Somewhere they could go to sort out their lives, to find security and a purpose in life, learn different skills then go on to lead fulfilled lives. I would call it the Alex Kellett Centre," she concluded, seeing their understanding nods before realising that Silke was possibly ignorant of her son's tragic history. "Alex died of a heroin overdose when he was still at school," she explained to Silke. "His father ignored his needs at the time. It would be fitting to use Andrew's property to try to right the wrongs he did."

Silke remembered now Sabina telling her about Audrey's son, Alex, at Ilse's apartment that fateful February of nineteen seventy. "That's very ... worthy." The word Vanessa had used earlier that afternoon in connection with Sarah seemed appropriate and it set one part of her mind racing. With the other part she asked: "And you Richard? Your suggestion?"

"Tourism," he declared succinctly, determined to outshine his brother's suggestion. "It could be a family hotel offering, let's say, fishing or riding holidays and other outdoor activities for the urban dweller. We're having to turn away bed and breakfasters these days as we're fully booked much of the time. It would help the local employment situation and economy - Aunty Sarah and Audrey could be the hotel managers. That would keep them busy!"

"You sound like a representative from the Herefordshire Tourist Board," Karl grinned.

"Or the president of the Herefordshire Young Farmers' Club!" Vanessa added, giving her husband a playful punch on the arm. "But I think that's a good idea. That would be my suggestion too."

"And you, Karl?" Silke asked him, last but not least.

He guessed what was going on in Silke's mind and knew his contribution would be important. He caught Audrey's eye and his face was serious as he spoke. "Bearing in mind my own experience of the horrors of drug addiction, I'd go with Audrey's suggestion. I think it's fitting that what Alex should have inherited should bear his name and for such a worthy cause: sorting out young people's ruined lives."

Silke nodded in agreement and faced Audrey. "I feel the same. It could be set up as a charity once the building was ready. You and Sarah could be the managers, Audrey, though you'd need professionally trained assistants and maybe a few volunteers there to care for and occupy the residents. Hopefully there'd be a steady throughput of young people."

"It would need a lot of money to run a place like that," Sarah pointed out. "We'd have to think of all manner of ways of fund-raising – and not for trifling amounts either. It would be worth it, though," she added fervently, caught up like everyone else now in the dream. "And we'd show 'em what we can do!"

Everybody was in no doubt she was referring to all the men who had refused her a job.

Silke looked at Karl and raised her eyebrows interrogatively. He smiled and nodded, glowing with satisfaction at the thought of taking over his arch-enemy's property.

"Let's buy it, then," Silke said decisively. "I'll ask my financiers to organise a thorough survey and a bid for Froxley Grange. The worse the state of repair it's in, the less we need to offer your ex-husband for it, Audrey."

"You're joking, aren't you?" Audrey asked in disbelief. Despite experiencing the delights of Silke's villa, she was not aware of the full extent of her wealth.

"No, I'm serious. It seems to fit the bill for most of your suggestions. Paul can have a part to play too, maybe get some of the youngsters interested in environmental issues or horticultural pursuits and he could do his research there too. There's room enough and he could have volunteers to help with the dirty work. Sarah could develop the feminist inclinations of any young women there, and help them achieve their ..."

"Potential," Karl finished for her. "Obviously there is a lot of research and planning to be done. We'll need professional guidance from the start in terms of building regulations, legal issues and planning approval just for starters."

"Absolutely," Silke agreed. "This must be done properly. If you want to, that is?" she asked, looking at first Audrey then Sarah.

The pair only needed to exchange one glance. "You bet!" they chorused.

"Just one thing, though," Audrey added cautiously. "I don't want Andrew to know that either Karl or I have anything to do with this. He wouldn't sell to us. He'd refuse."

Silke nodded. "It can all go through an independent agency. He won't know exactly who the buyer is until it's too late."

Audrey seemed satisfied then one more thing occurred to her. "I'd like Katherine to be remembered too, but I'm not sure how. Any suggestions?"

There was a brief pause then they all started speaking at once.

Shades of Grey by Caron Harrison

In October 1946 who is truly free?

Katherine Carter believes she is. With all her life spent on her father's Herefordshire farm, her future seems mapped out – until she meets Karl.

Karl Driesler has little freedom. His future is bleak. Still a prisoner of war eighteen months after Germany's surrender, he suffers from nightmares and his fiancée has just married another man.

Robert Murdoch, the village doctor's son, also suffers from nightmares. A former prisoner of the Japanese, he finds freedom unexpectedly hard to cope with – until he meets Karl.

These three find their growing bonds of friendship and love tested to the full as Karl's dark secret is revealed by Katherine's jilted fiancé. Katherine withdraws her love, shattering Karl's hopes of a future with her. Suffering a mental breakdown , he is helpless as his British friends rally round to assist, while his rival for Katherine's love does his utmost to break him entirely.

Divided Loyalties by Caron Harrison

The horrors of war are receding for former prisoner of war, Karl Driesler, now happily married and living with Katherine on their Herefordshire farm. But a new war is about to begin.

Ilse Brünninghaus has taught her illegitimate son, Siegfried, to hate his father, Karl, as a traitor to Nazism. But when she is forced by her brutal husband to find a new home for Siegfried, she has only Karl to whom she can turn. As Ilse hands over her son to her former lover, she realises she still loves Karl, and Siegfried is her access to him.

All too soon Karl discovers the extent of his son's hatred, as Siegfried's aggression leads to an increasingly bloody chain of events. But love can prove an equally disruptive force.

Eclipse of the Son by Caron Harrison

In the summer of 1968 a wedding reunites Karl and Katherine Driesler's entire family in Herefordshire, but there is a spectre at the feast in the form of Karl's illegitimate son, Siegfried. His boyhood friend and neo-Nazi, Gustav Halstrup, forces him into a lethal game of bluff involving everyone he knows. Only Siegfried knows the truth of his actions, which have devastating consequences.

Into the maelstrom step Andrew Kellett and Ilse Zopf, Katherine and Karl's former partners, as well as Gustav's lover, Christian Bracht. Each plays a part in the tragedies that unfurl.